WHERE THE WIND BLOWS
The Halls of Faith

BOOK 3 OF WHERE THE WIND BLOWS SERIES

by Dorothy Gable

The wind blows where it wishes, and you hear its sound,
but you do not know where it comes from or where it goes.
So it is with everyone who is born of the Spirit.

– John 3:8
English Standard Version

DEDICATION

THIS SERIES IS dedicated to faithful believers; may we continue, resting in the power of God.

Therefore, since we are surrounded by so great a cloud of witnesses, let us also lay aside every weight, and sin which clings so closely, and let us run with endurance the race that is set before us,
                                        – Hebrews 12:1

Chapter 1

Tom repositioned the pack on his shoulder, pausing by a corner café. They had better lattes than the Hebrew Centre. Digging into his pocket, he felt some euros, and stepped in.

With coffee in hand, Tom joined the press of people on their way to work or school, or whatever else directed their day. He strolled, turning to the broad walkway along the River Liffey. Gulls, pigeons, and flocks of birds he could not name darted or swooped, glided past and continued on like the undulating waves. Tom leaned against a wrought-iron railing, watching the river's steady current push flotsam in swirls and eddies by a parked boat.

He sighed, remembering last summer's late evening kayaking adventure down the river with Catherine. Scents of moss-covered rocks, weathered wood, and dampness had surrounded him, mingling with the dark on the water's surface. The light craft cut through the river silently. She led the two crafts downstream as whiffs of salted air rose up on the wings of a slight breeze.

"It's harder going back. Ready?" She paddled close to a stone pier and grasped an upright. "Don't want to get so close to the mouth that we'd be swept out to sea."

Tom brought his kayak close beside hers. The current seemed non-existent unless he charted the progress of a bunch of twigs and leaves floating by. "You're the native guide." Their eyes met.

Her smile shining in the dim light of a streetlamp, she began to sing a Celtic hymn, the melody rising and falling with the slight currents.

Tom knew better than to join in. "Beautiful," he said when she glanced his way.

"It's your turn."

"*The heavens declare the glory of God, and the sky above proclaims his handiwork. Day to day pours out speech, and night to night reveals knowledge.*"[1]

"You cannot even see the stars with the lights of Dublin. Don't you know a verse about a river?"

"'*Whoever believes in me, as the Scripture has said, "Out of his heart will flow rivers of living water."*'"[2]

She tossed her head, ready to tease him further.

"The lights of your love pierce the very light canopy and dark of night. The glory of the heavens cannot be hid from us, even in the darkest depths of the earth."

He drew close and clasped her hand. They heard couples walk by, talking lightly. Music flowed into the streets when pub doors opened. The traffic lighter, tap-tap of tires on the cobbled sections, sounded periodically. "The city breathes, never truly sleeping." His eyes glanced up to see lights in many apartments. "How do we reach the people here?"

"One family at a time." Catherine watched him look back at her. Her heart beat faster, but she held back her desire to be joined now.

Reluctant to return—he to the shelter, her to a small flat. "It is hard to wait, but if God wills, nothing can stop it," he said.

"Yes, Lord willing, but I can put in my request." A light laugh broke forth, and together they turned to paddle upstream.

Tom pulled against the deceptively slow current.

He shook his head, blinking in the rising sunlight. They had to wait. Despite his growing longing to marry Catherine, he knew. Dropping his head, he begged the Lord again for the two of them to have a future together. Ending with an acceptance of God's will, Tom stepped away from the river and headed for Trinity College.

He had no appointments until after lunch—no Bible studies at Cloverhill Prison or counseling at Cary House. Arriving early at the center would give him time to dig into Isaiah 49. He set his face. As he walked, he rehearsed the Hebrew alphabet along with the curling letters, jots and tittles Ron had taught him.

Tom placed his pack on his favorite table in their small library, pulled out his Hebrew interlinear and the slim computer his father had given him. Even though he could use online lexicons, he strode to a nearby case and pulled out his two favorites. He preferred real books with heft and weight and printed pages. Writing down the results on paper brought ideas to light.

Chaim, the director, headed Tom's way when he saw him at the third table. "A man after my own heart. But digital references do aid the search."

"Pointers." He sat back. As expected, the large man sat in a nearby short-backed padded chair.

"Are you well? Your case? Is it going well?"

"Solicitor Boyle smiles more. Myra tells me we have enough affidavits and video testimony for a case. Whether it is enough, God only knows."

"Have you thought about what you will do, after…" Chaim held back a smile. Everyone knew Tom and Catherine were engaged.

"First, become an official volunteer at Cary House. Try to raise up churches in outlying towns and villages to sponsor refugees."

"How is that proposal going? Catherine told me you presented the program to the International Protection Office (IPO). Was it two days ago?"

Tom shook his head. "Yesterday. I didn't think it went well, but…" He glanced over. "I don't do well with those sorts of meetings. Presenting a plan to a board."

"Questions? Resistance?"

"That's a mild way of saying it."

"Direct Provision has made some progress helping to settle asylum seekers outside of Dublin."

"But they need support. The success rate could be higher if…" He met Chaim's eyes, but in his mind, he only saw the North Platte Review Board.

"Ask Ron. He is very skilled in presenting a plan to a resistant board." Chaim's chuckle shook his belly. He leaned forward. "Tell him I approve the use of his time to assist this cause." Chuckling again, he added, "Makes the Centre look good, and Cary House is one of our charities."

"Thank you. He's not just a Hebrew scholar, but…" Tom stopped and looked away. "He's a great teacher. Hebrew's starting to make sense." He tried to match Chaim's usually jocular mood, but he caught the man's look.

"I thought I heard my name," Ron said, entering from the far door.

"Your boss is volunteering you again." Tom laughed. "Seriously, I need help with the outreach program."

"Didn't go well?"

Chaim observed the two. "I'm surprised, Tom. You work so well with the refugees."

"That's the problem—I act like a refugee."

The tall director pulled out a chair for Ron. "What you experienced left its mark." He nodded. "Ron, how did you escape?"

Tom watched Ron's eyes widen, and as they exchanged glances, Tom jumped in. "I'm glad many believers and fellowships fly under the radar. The Task Force doesn't have the resources to go after all the Christians—not yet."

"How did you come to their attention?"

"Through my uncle." Tom explained how his uncle had seeded copies of the Bible throughout the United States. "I didn't find out what he had done until I was in prison. The agents followed me to every prison I was in and then to my church in Kansas. I finally admitted the only way I could survive in my own country was to live homeless, wandering from place to place."

Ron added, "I had heard enough to know when my university told us we had to cooperate that I had to find…" Ron stopped, exchanging glances with Tom. "Helping at this center was a gift from God." He smiled at Chaim. "And I have the opportunity to experience Hebrew as a living language."

Chaim nodded as he rose. "Well, things to do." He smiled his broad, caring smile. On his way out, he overheard Tom's first question and wondered again about Ron as he listened to the answer.

Tom and Ron met with Catherine after the day's Bible studies at Cary House to make plans. Ron agreed to help present the initiative to support refugees settling in outlying areas. If they could find local churches willing to adopt asylum seekers and set up regular visits to make sure all was well, perhaps more would thrive in smaller municipalities.

Assessing the situation, laying out the plans for the next attempt to convince the directors at IPO, Ron said, "Maybe Catherine and I should go in."

Tom nodded. "I was going to suggest that." He rubbed his hands together. "I choked, and I know I will the next time."

Catherine looked at them both. "But I thought having you there, letting them know what it feels like from a refugee's point of view…"

"I think we've already established that part of the plan," he interrupted. "Now…" he leaned toward her, "*you* have to convince them you can run it."

Catherine opened her mouth to object.

Tom reached for her hand. "This is the right call. Get it going and I'll help, but Ron's executive experience and confidence will push it forward. If they table it, wait and try again later."

Tom walked Ron out to the bus stop.

"You're not afraid? I mean, you're the one engaged to her."

"I trust you both. And Ron, promise me, if anything happens, help her move on with her life."

"Tom, get a grip. You're going to win. It'll work out." He hugged the man, now a close Christian friend.

"This world is the shadowland, just a whisper of the spiritual world to come. The goodness, the joy, the gifts of this world are a hint of what awaits us. That I have the chance to experience true love for Catherine, even if never consummated, is still a gift from God. Nothing, on this side, is forever. All things in this life will come to an end." Tom patted Ron's shoulder, seeing the bus round the corner blocks away. "And don't forget what I said."

Ron nodded and watched Tom turn back to Cary House.

A week later Tom opened the latest letter from Bruce. Glancing at it quickly, seeing Wallie's name mentioned, he folded it to look at later.

It wasn't until the next morning at the Hebrew Centre that Tom gathered the courage to read Bruce's letter. The last few had mentioned Wallie was in hospice. Perhaps this one would echo the good news the most recent letter had—that Wallie's cancer was in remission. But his heart quivered. Taking a sip of coffee, he swallowed and read:

Dear Friend,

Wallie is in heaven. I am sorry to have to tell you, after a brief recovery, he weakened quickly. Thankfully, he did not suffer and is now at peace. At a memorial service in Hannibal, many came to express how much he had meant to them. Several testified that they believe because of his witness.

Tom crumpled up the letter. One part of him was thrilled for Wallie;

he was in the best place, but his heart was torn. He did not feel ready to let go—not yet.

Ron joined him at the table. "Had a phone call I couldn't ignore. What was that?" He nodded at the paper in Tom's hands. Tom reached over and put it on the table in front of him. Spreading it out, he read. "Wallie—your friend from prison? Did he believe in Christ?" Seeing Tom's nod, he was about to try to reassure him, but Tom turned a tearful face to him.

"I saw a vision." Clearing his throat, he tried again. "When I was dying in Rosemont, I'd lost all hope of life. I couldn't eat. I couldn't sleep. In torment, I cried out, and He showed me heaven. Wallie was there." Tom looked at Ron. "Heavenly time is so different from ours, but I sensed that shortly after Wallie died, I would join him there." He shook his head. "I don't know how, but *they* will kill me."

"We can hope it's twenty years from now?"

Tom nodded.

Wiping his eyes, Ron grasped Tom's hand and nodded.

CHAPTER 2

J OE LYLE, A Secret Service Agent in the Cyber Division, watched the modern glass and steel terminal of the Dublin Airport grow in the airplane's small window. Yesterday he had driven to the JFK Airport in New York, boarded a flight to Heathrow Airport near London and a cybersecurity convention. Arriving in the morning, Joe passed through customs and doubled back to the Aer Lingus ticket counter to book passage to Dublin.

He prayed the short notice would give him the time he needed. Clasping his small soft case, knowing the files it contained, he set his face and reviewed the script he would say to the customs agent.

Waiting his turn, he rose, helped an elderly woman retrieve her bag from an upper bin, let her pass and turned toward the exit.

Seeing the on-screen details of the man's recent arrival at Heathrow, the agent lifted a brow. "Reason for your visit?"

"Meeting a long-lost cousin and seeing the sites." Joe leaned forward and lowered his voice. "Arrived early for a convention to see Dublin." That comment brought a smile to the agent's face, and he stamped the passport.

The way memorized to Solicitor Boyle's office, he prayed again and entered the offices of Murphy, Walsh and O'Brien on the third floor. A young man in a dull blue-plaid blazer with the British fit of wider lapels and stiff chest sat at the front desk.

"How may I help you?" the receptionist asked with just a hint of an Irish brogue mixed with British English.

Joe smiled slightly, shifted his weight and said as authoritatively as possible. "I am here for a deposition." He glanced at his watch. "With Solicitor Boyle."

"Is she expecting you?"

"No, this is a delicate matter that could not be set up beforehand. One of her associates may take the affidavits and certify the evidence." Joe stepped forward and lowered his voice. "I could only get away for a short time." Seeing the blank look on the man's face, he added, with a little more edge to his voice. "I have evidence for an asylum claim. Please direct me to Solicitor Boyle's offices."

The receptionist began to ask for the refugee's name but seeing the American's tightened gaze, he rose. "I will see who is at desk." He turned when Joe followed, but decided not to insist the man stay in the foyer.

A matronly woman with a broad chest and sturdy legs turned when they entered the suite of offices on the north side.

Joe stepped past and extended a hand. "Special Agent Joe Lyle with the US Secret Service. I have evidence and wish to make an affidavit on behalf of Tom Hutton."

"Oh, the Hutton case. Nancy Hayes, pleased to make your acquaintance." Nancy nodded at the receptionist.

Hearing the door close behind him and the receptionist's footfalls die away, Joe relaxed slightly. "I couldn't make an appointment for fear I would be intercepted. Where can we set up?" He hefted his small computer case and rolled his carryon to the side.

"Yes, I understand. This way please." She led him to a conference room. "Ms. Boyle is in court, but Ms. Myra Moore has been assisting with the affidavits."

Joe nodded, drawing his computer from the case along with several USB drives formatted for the region. He waited, praying for the right words, knowing his torturous path with the Task Force was meant to lead here.

A young woman entered the room. Her dark eyes met his; a broad smile revealed perfect teeth. "Joe Lyle? Is that correct? I'm Myra Moore. Let's start with your identification." She stepped through the process.

"Do you have a video recorder?" Joe asked.

"Yes." She returned momentarily with a camera perched on a tripod. As Joe inserted a drive, he gave a brief description to set the place, time and location. They worked through half of the evidence. Miss Moore glanced at her watch.

"I'm sorry I couldn't give notice. We must finish tonight. If you need to call in someone else?"

"No, Mr. Lyle, what you have brought might assure Mr. Hutton's claim will be accepted. Shall we?"

Joe nodded. "You can call me Joe, Myra, if that's all right."

"Of course. It's not every day I have the opportunity to take an affidavit from an American Secret Service Agent." Her light laughter filled the room.

Joe smiled, inserted the next drive, and their faces hardened again as another video of torture ran its course.

Solicitor Boyle entered, exchanged greetings with her assistant and acknowledged Joe with a brief nod. "Let us know when we can meet tomorrow."

"I have commitments through Saturday and fly back to London Sunday afternoon."

Helen pursed her lips. "Set up something for Sunday, Myra. At the airport?" She smiled when Joe agreed.

Myra said, "I'll send you the details." After Ms. Boyle left, she asked, "Long day?"

"Flew last night to Heathrow, arriving early this morning and then hopped a plane to Dublin. Meeting a cousin tonight at O'Shea's. I think I'll be able to make it."

"On holiday?"

"Something like that. Taking in the sights. He has a castle he wants to show me—from the family, I gather." He leveled his gaze at the camera.

"Yes, time's a wasting." Myra started the recording, adding the front matter details. She stepped out of sight of the camera and asked, "How did you come to be a part of the Task Force, Agent Lyle?"

Joe faced the camera and began. "I started with the Secret Service right out of college, but when I was unable to transfer to investigations, I accepted a position with the Task Force in their education and outreach division. My first unit, for the most part, was composed of DHS, Department of Homeland Security; HHS, Health and Human Services; and FBI, Federal Bureau of Investigations agents. I enjoyed the variety of assignments. After that I transferred to the Investigations Division." He paused, taking a breath. "Unlike those who were arrested with copies of illegal classics, the methods and sentencing for those with illegal Bibles were very harsh.

"At first, I enjoyed the weapons, tactics and assault sessions that surpassed my earlier training, but I was clueless to the use of force in the field. We assumed we would be pursuing career criminals also engaged in other criminal activities such as extortion, weapons, drugs and human trafficking. The unit had agents from ATF, Bureau of Alcohol, Tobacco, Firearms and Explosives, as well as DEA, Drug Enforcement Administration. I realized there might be a problem when the rules of engagement included shoot-to-kill orders. We were told these protocols came down from the White House. Some operations were conducted legally without excessive force. However, too many included torture, kidnapping and murder."

"Please provide examples, Agent Lyle."

"Two weeks after Tom Hutton's arrest, I was ordered to bring supplies and pick up reports at a farm in Southern Ohio. This was the first time I realized some suspects had not been booked and charged with a crime shortly after their arrest. I entered a large barn with a trapdoor in a back room. The stairs led to a functional prison. Three prisoners were there, and I was told to stand guard while the operators did their work. I will never forget the screams. A week later they booked Tom, altering his arrest date.

"I managed to transfer to another unit tasked with developing their own prisons led by Will Masters. At first protocols and procedures implemented federal standards. However, when Masters was named Northeast Director, the new management turned the prisons into re-education and death camps, again with the understanding the President and his Chief of Staff endorsed the measures." Joe described the chain-link cages, education sessions, and reporting requirements for released inmates. "I didn't last too long in the parole unit—that wasn't the official name, but what we called it. We traveled to the homes of released inmates, collecting leads for those resistant to the new laws. Unless they submitted ten names a month, they were returned to prison." He shook his head and breathed.

"I witnessed executions shortly thereafter. They are detailed in the video evidence I submitted. I thought I had finally found a place where I could be proud of my work when I was transferred to the Internal Investigations Division. I had no idea this unit was dedicated to developing false charges against resistant wardens, judges, senators and some of the top agents in the Task Force. By that time, I had become a Christian. As I grew more and more concerned about the mission and methods of the Task Force, I deliberately underperformed and was allowed to transfer to the Secret Service."

Joe stopped. Left unsaid were the cases he had purposely mismanaged to hide evidence, and his recording, hiding, and spiriting away evidence that deserved to see the light of day.

Myra ended the session with a few questions and stopped the recording. "Do you have anything else?"

"No."

"That must have been difficult."

He met her gaze, not trying too hard to hide the pain. "It was...it was devastating, terrifying, and if I had not found the Lord, I would have become cynical, almost suicidal."

"But you never joined them."

"I saw how joining them hardened the ones who did. They are on my prayer list. The Lord could still rescue them. Myra, I took this risk for Tom and for all the others who can no longer speak for themselves. If he is sent back, he will be tortured and executed. They're desperate to uncover the identities of those who helped him flee the country. They intend to destroy the church in America, and the destruction won't stop at America's borders."

Joe replaced his computer in the case, taking one last look at the evidence. He asked, "Do you have a secure vault for these drives?"

"Yes."

"I'll stand guard while you put them away." He followed her to the end of the hall and took up position. Even without a firearm, he could give her enough time if someone were to come in. Joe shook his head, trying not to descend into paranoia. *Will they be watching me?* Certainly, but he had paid for the overnight bus and ferry ride that would have landed him at Dublin the next morning. He had made the date with his cousin through secure email—they shouldn't have been able to trace that. The only weakness to his plan was the scanning of his passport by Dublin customs earlier that afternoon. He prayed he would be on his way before they could send an asset to intercept him and discover that he had stopped by the solicitors.

Myra returned with the time for his meeting with Ms. Boyle at the airport before his Sunday flight.

"Thank you. That will be fine." Joe tipped his head, grasped his case and turned. She walked him to the first door. "Myra, if you would allow me, I'd like to walk you to your car."

"The busses are running. I should be fine."

"Let me walk you out." He smiled. "You could point out some of your favorite landmarks."

Her broad smile lifted his mood, and he waited for her to gather her purse and lightweight coat. "It seems Ireland is never really too hot or too cold."

"But it does get damp," Myra added.

They walked together down the street around the corner and to the first bus stop. Few people were about. Graffiti marred some of the brickwork of mostly closed businesses. "I'll wait with you…" He glanced her way. "After all, it was my fault you were kept late." However, it did appear to him that staying late was not that uncommon for her.

Myra smiled, eyeing him, but not willing to ask if he was always this jumpy. "O'Shea's is west just south of the Liffey." She smiled, her dimples showing. "You should walk the Quay. Go left until you reach the Temple Bar area. Anglesea Street will be on your left."

"Is this a good time of year to watch the Liffey?"

Laughing, she said, "Watch paint dry or the pot boil for tea?" She shook her head. "It's going to be a nice evening. Just right and with the lights of the city coming on earlier, you can feel the life of Dublin."

"I will." Joe's eyes roved the area, but nothing suspicious caught his gaze. When her bus slid to a stop a short time later, he said, "Thank you, Myra, for taking the time." He paused, but his inner tension increased with the darkening of the day.

"Drop by, if you make another visit."

"If it works out, definitely." He almost added, *if the Lord wills*.

He turned north toward the Liffey, assuming the Quay roadway, broad and well-traveled would have some pedestrians. Perhaps if this was the middle of summer, that might have been true. He hoped the Temple Bar area would be livelier. He missed his chance to go down Westmoreland but hated retracing his steps. Prices Lane, the next street heading south, was barely wide enough for small cars, but was lit. Hurrying, he plunged in. Posters graced some of the solid walls, what windows showed were barred and closed. He increased his pace, breaking his stride only momentarily to note where the cameras were.

A figure in a long trench coat with a pulled-down flat Irish cap approached far down the lane, shuffling his feet and nearly falling against a wall. Sounds from the Quay lessened. Joe hugged the opposite side as the person passed, head buried deep in the raised collar.

Just as Joe approached a recessed entrance, he thought he heard the man coming up behind him. He began to turn, but a gloved hand grasped his shoulder. Joe swung his right arm back as he stepped aside. He turned his head. The blood chilled in his veins when he recognized his attacker.

"Joe the snitch!" Trainer growled, recovered quickly and pushed him into the recessed doorway.

Focusing on the right hand, Joe did not see Trainer bring up a K-bar knife with his left. Joe felt the pressure against his lower ribs, a burning pain shoot up his side, and the blood pounded in his throat. He gasped for breath, unable to speak.

"You filthy maggot. What you gonna do? Tell 'em? You're too late. We're onto you, and everyone will know this is the last one that's going to get away." Trainer twisted the blade and watched Lyle open and close his mouth.

Joe tried not to hide his joy, knowing that Trainer didn't appear to know the evidence had already been delivered. His computer held only conference files. *This is why God sent me to the Task Force. This is how I will be able to make amends.* His eyes looked upward as he collapsed.

Trainer shoved the body into the doorway, rifled through Joe's pockets, and tucked the computer case under his dirty trench coat. He made his way down to the lower walkway by the docks, tossed the carry-on into the river and shuffled off. It would look like a robbery by a homeless man.

CHAPTER 3

DETECTIVE ANDREW KELLY the made his way to Prices Lane and ducked under the yellow crime-scene tape. Sean, a Garda patrol officer Andrew knew, nodded in his direction. An unhappy civilian, probably a nearby pub owner, stopped talking when he saw him. Gathering a breath, Andrew scanned for any signs the crime scene unit had been by and reminded himself to be polite.

He extended his hand. "Detective Kelly, did you see the incident?"

"No, but we need this cleared soon." The man waved his hand toward the Quay. Traffic had died down as it was past the evening rush hour, but some strolled along the wide street by the Liffey.

"He looks like an American tourist, Detective," Sean observed.

"Any witnesses?"

"None that I can find, except for the CCTV." He flicked his head to the sparse cameras pointing toward either end of the short lane.

"I'll pull the feeds." He nodded to the businessman and made his way to the body crumpled in a recessed doorway. "They left the shoes," he remarked.

"Sir?"

Andrew shrugged his shoulders, pulled out his mobile to check on the arrival of the forensics team. *Shouldn't be long.* It had been a quiet night for a change, and the morgue was almost around the corner.

"They'll be here shortly. The coroner's due in any moment. We'll make every effort to clear the scene as soon as possible," Andrew told the worried pub owner. He glanced at Sean. "Did you take a statement?"

Andrew perused the notes entered in the officer's notepad. He pulled out his own, just in case. Turning to the civilian, he listened to the sparse details—walking over for a smoke he had found the body; no, hadn't touched anything; saw no one else. The man rambled a little, but for the most part had little to tell.

Andrew's ears perked up when the pub owner offered to let him see what their cameras had recorded. He tapped Sean. "I'll be back. Text me when the techs arrive." They smiled. This wasn't the first time they had met after a mugging or murder. If it was a drifter, it could be hard to solve, but the department took seriously a murder in a popular tourist district such as Temple Bar.

He continued to debate whether this was simply a botched mugging, but the blurry images of the trench-coated man dealing death in minutes and departing moments later seemed to rule out a typical robbery and crime of opportunity. The bloke walked away with the carry-on trailing behind him and disappeared by the Quay. *Something's off,* Andrew decided. *The John Doe still has his top-of-the-line shoes on.* "We have the time frame. Can you send it over—make it an hour before and two hours after?"

"That would be in the future, Detective."

"Oh." He paused. T*his case is fresh.* He checked his messages, saw the text and excused himself.

The two-person forensics team—a middle-aged man and a young woman—nodded in greeting and continued toward their objective. He stepped back to let them work. No watch, not these days, but no mobile, wallet or ID. "That's it?"

"Looks that way."

Andrew tipped his head, trying not to get in the way. "Cause of death?"

"Well…" the man smiled.

"I don't need the official." Sometimes grainy CCTV feeds could obscure important details.

"One knife wound."

Andrew pursed his brows. "Where's the blood?" The amount of blood pooling on the concrete seemed minimal.

The tech shrugged, not about to venture from his area of expertise. "Take that up with the coroner."

Andrew requested the rest of the video feeds for the evening and waited.

The coroner arrived, and the detective let him do the initial screening. "Recent?"

He nodded, looking at the liver temp.

"Two hours ago?" Andrew asked.

"Have the time of death?"

"By the CCTV." Andrew gathered a breath. "Shouldn't there be more blood?"

"Not with this wound. The rest will be in the body cavities."

Andrew knew better than to ask more than cursory questions. Those might be answered with the official report and walk-through by the medical examiner at the morgue. "Seems more than your typical knifing for this district." Kicking himself he had not framed it as a question, he waited, uncertain if this coroner would answer in anything more than monosyllables.

The man rose and gestured for the crew to bring the stretcher. He surveyed the young detective. "Possibly, but we'll know more with autopsy."

"Thanks, I'll look for it." He had no choice but to ask. They always did. From here, the crime looked like a hit instead of a robbery, but then he would know more after viewing the video feeds.

Andrew watched the tech team continue their search for evidence and trace after the body had been removed. While waiting he had quickly perused the larger area but saw nothing of interest. The team worked quickly and were soon on their way.

Back at the station house, Andrew worked the CCTV feeds, tracing the John Doe's path back to a bus stop. Looked like he was seeing a friend off. He would follow up on that lead later. Next, he eventually found the feed from the river's edge and watched the suspect dispose of the luggage and nimbly step back to the Quay.

Tracking back to the bus stop, he expanded his search. Yes, trench-coat man appeared walking swiftly up Westmoreland before turning left on Fleet Street. The suspect paused at times, tapping his ear, as if receiving instructions in an earpiece. Andrew ran through the movements. It appeared as if someone with access to the feeds directed the suspect so he could intercept the John Doe. Andrew sat back. The short lane was the perfect spot for a hit.

Puzzled, Andrew hoped an identification would help answer some of his questions. *Was he visiting? If he is a local, hence the girl at the bus stop. But why was he dressed like an American?* However, he was clearly not dressed as a tourist—or not how most tourists dressed. He glanced at the time, wondering how long it would take for the prints to come back. Before he could backtrack the victim's steps, a red-flagged notification appeared in the case file dashboard.

The prints matched a registry with an international London convention—*Agent* Joe Lyle. Andrew sucked in his breath—*of the United States Secret Service.* The photo in the passport matched the victim. Running the name through their system flagged the time he cleared customs at the Dublin Airport. Should he contact the Special Detective Unit (SDU) immediately? He hated to hand it over before he had more to tell. In time, the SDU or even the Irish Military Intelligence (G2) would stick their noses in this one, but he'd see how far he could get. Perhaps he could backtrack the mysterious man in a worn Irish flat cap.

While he was in the system, he read the man's bio, noting the Task Force he had been a part of, but that notation didn't tell him anything.

He tried to track Joe's movements before the bus stop, but they stopped at a large building on the Quay—home to a few penthouse flats, a coffee shop on the northwest corner and the offices of Murphy, Walsh and O'Brien. "What were you up to, Agent Lyle?" Andrew muttered to himself.

The detective captured the best image he could find from the videos, uploaded it to the daily briefing logs to alert the uniforms. A glance at the time explained his mental fog—long evening shift. He checked the other five active cases he was pursuing with his partner. Verifying there was nothing he could accomplish at this hour early Saturday morning, he shut down his computer and headed to his small house north of the city. The coroner's report wouldn't land in the case file until Monday at the earliest. Thankfully, he was on days next week.

CHAPTER 4

MONDAY MORNING STELLA Hutton returned to Dublin to assess the evidence collected for Tom's case. She knew in her heart it would have been enough if Tom had been from another country, but the bar was set high for a safe country of origin and an ally of Ireland.

Solicitor Boyle and Myra Moore described the evidence Joe Lyle had brought the Friday before.

"I'm sorry I missed him, but I couldn't get away until this week." She gauged the lawyers' faces, but they revealed little—as expected with professionals. "Is this enough?"

"Yes, with the rest."

"And a date?"

They both shook their heads. "While the backlog has eased, there are still too many claimants for timely hearings. We'll keep you apprised of forthcoming dates."

Stella noticed the two exchanging looks. "Is there something you haven't told me?"

"Mr. Lyle missed his flight back to London. We were to have met there Sunday afternoon." She hesitated to voice her fears.

"Why was he going to London?"

Myra explained his reason. "He did stress that he was taking a risk, but since he's no longer with the Task Force, I didn't envision he'd have any problems."

"Technically, if the Task Force had completed the protocols for security classification, he could be jailed for leaking agency documents and operations. Some would consider him a traitor."

She paused. "I need to see his evidence."

"It's not pretty," Myra hedged.

Stella surveyed the young lawyer. "I'm sure you have seen worse with other claimants."

"Some." Myra turned to her laptop, activated the projector, starting with the videos.

"Please pause it," Stella said when she recognized the man partially stripped and shivering, beaten and chained to a chair. She gazed into the dull eyes of a broken man. "Alex Hutton, my brother-in-law." Turning to wipe her eyes, she shook her head. "Now I understand why he died in Leavenworth three years later."

With empathy in her voice, Helen said, "I see your family has clearly suffered under the hands of this agency."

"Yes." Stella searched their faces. "As I know Tom has stated, his case is not simply about him or our family. It is for all whose lives have been destroyed..." Seeing the understanding in their eyes, she added, "Tom can't see these."

It was a rough afternoon. Stella called the Hebrew Centre, but Tom was already at Cary House. She arrived in time to watch Tom and Catherine lead the afternoon children's program. *They work so well together.* Her spirits lifted with the happy songs, smiling faces, and laughing children.

She didn't object when Catherine invited them for supper in her small flat.

"Everything okay, Mom?" Tom asked from the front seat of Catherine's car. "Do I need to stop by the offices?"

"No, they have enough now." Seeing Tom's doubtful look, she added, "New evidence arrived." Tiredness froze the words forming in her mind. Shutting out the images, she continued, "The lawyers are assembling the binder for the Tribunal."

Tom's smile broadened when he glanced at Catherine, busily navigating narrow streets crowded with busses, bicyclists and pedestrians.

"That means we're just waiting for the date."

"That's great, Tom." Catherine smiled. "It will be a relief when this is over."

Stella refrained from correcting her future daughter-in-law. Tom's asylum was only one step. How the United States would react—that she could only commit to prayer.

Catherine's stew was luscious. "You're a good cook, my dear," Stella said in a voice soft with affection.

"Mom, you look tired. Should we drop you at your flat?"

"Yes, can't hide it like I used to. Well, you two have plans?"

"It's too chilly to kayak the Liffey, but the trees are beautiful at the gardens. If I could find an escort…" She glanced at Tom.

"Kayak the Liffey?"

"At midnight in the summer," Tom said, exchanging laughs with Catherine.

"Aww, to be young again." Stella leaned forward to hug her son. "Don't forget to live and take advantage of your energy."

"Hasten the day, Mom, for Christ. Just like my sweetheart."

Stella picked up some items from a convenience shop along with the day's issue of *The Irish Times*. After a long shower to wash away the travel, she relaxed with her herbal tea and began to go through the daily. Her eyes focused on a headline for a small article on the local page— "American Slain in the Temple Bar District." The body was discovered Friday evening. Despite the headline identifying the victim as an American, few facts were included as it was still under investigation, and the victim's name not yet been released. "Of course," Stella voiced, "family notification. The police must know something since they identified him as an American."

She lifted the apartment phone but changed her mind. *It will have to wait until the morning.*

CHAPTER 5

S TELLA ARRIVED AT Helen's suite early Tuesday. She smiled at Nancy and tapped on the doorframe to Myra's small office. "How are you, Myra? Have a moment?" Seeing the nod, she sat on the chair across from the desk.

"Did you see the notice in yesterday's paper about the murder of an American not far from here?"

"What? No." She glanced at the files on her left. "I skim the headlines online." She leaned forward. "Have they released the name?"

"It wasn't in the article." Stella added, "Could you call the Pearse Street station and check—just to make sure it's not Joe Lyle?" She raised her brow. "He did miss his Sunday flight."

"Sure," Myra agreed as she turned to her computer, found the number and dialed.

Stella sat back, letting the exchange go forward.

"Yes," Myra said after being on hold, "Detective Kelly? This is Myra Moore of Murphy, Walsh and O'Brien. We wondered if you have made an identification of the man slain on Prices Lane Friday evening?" She paused. "Who do we think it is?" She looked at Stella. Seeing a nod, she said, "Joe Lyle, a US Secret Service Agent."

She covered the handset and said quietly, "He wants to know why he was here."

"Tell him."

"Yes, Detective Kelly, he was here for a deposition in an asylum case. He brought video evidence." She furrowed her brow. "It's not public information. I will set up." She clicked to Helen's calendar. "I will set up an appointment with Ms. Boyle, the lead solicitor."

Myra's hand hovered over the phone after her call with Detective Andrew Kelly.

Stella rose. "Is she in?"

"Yes." Myra and Stella headed to Helen's corner office.

"Helen?" Seeing her nod, they entered. "Agent Lyle was murdered Friday evening." Myra tucked her hand to her side to keep it from shaking. "Probably shortly after I took the bus home. He wanted to walk me to the stop and waited until I was safely on my way." She began to shake her head.

"Myra," Stella said with quiet empathy, "There was no way you could have known."

Myra relayed the few details they knew. "Could you see Detective Kelly this morning?"

"Have Nancy clear my schedule. Also, have Tom brought to the penthouse suite by the back way. Is Lucas on today?"

"I saw him this morning. I'll see to it."

Stella stepped aside.

Helen said, "While we don't know if Joe just happened to be in the wrong place at the wrong time, it might have been an orchestrated hit. We'll see what we can discover from the detective." She pursed her lips. "There will be repercussions if the Task Force was behind this hit."

"Agreed. The murder of Joe Lyle would be a violation of Irish sovereignty," Stella said.

"An activity only rogue states engage in." Helen paused. "However, for Tom's sake, we need to try to keep the IPO from sending him back to Mountjoy."

"Protective custody?"

"Mrs. Hutton, protective custody is strict solitary confinement, and Tom didn't do well the last time he was there." Helen surveyed Stella. "I'll have Nancy take you up to the suite."

"If I may, I'd like to sit in on the meeting with the detective. I can join him after that."

Helen nodded. "Do you know where Tom is right now?"

"Check with Cary House. He's good about telling them where he's going. He keeps himself busy."

"So I've heard."

Helen, Stella, and Myra met with Detective Kelly in a first-floor conference room. Helen pushed to receive an update on the investigation before answering questions concerning Joe's deposition.

"Detective Kelly, does Agent Lyle's death appear to be a random event, a failed mugging?"

Andrew looked at the three women across the table. He pursed his brow. "Miss Moore? Were you with Joe Friday night at a bus stop?"

Myra nodded. "I was."

He pulled out his mobile and swiped to a CCTV image of the killer walking up Westmoreland. "Do you remember seeing this man?"

She recognized the area—not far from her bus stop. Myra forced her hand to remain steady. She shook her head. "No, but I was talking with Joe. He looked about but didn't seem alarmed at anything." She handed back the mobile. "So, he was targeted?"

"The matter is still under investigation."

"Detective Kelly, unless you are forthcoming with further details, this office cannot divulge anything about Agent Lyle's visit to this office on Friday." Solicitor Boyle raised her brow and looked pointedly at the young detective.

Andrew ran through his options, but his desire to push past any hesitancy due to legal ramifications overcame his reluctance. "While the suspect made every effort to make it look like this was a murder in the commission of a mugging, it appears to have been a calculated attack." He hesitated to name what he suspected. The lack of conversation, and lethal efficiency of the kill pointed to an assassination by an asset with a team.

"That's all?"

"At this point, we have not identified the assailant, but the G2 has been notified of the incident. Ms. Moore stated he came to make an affidavit for an asylum claim. Who is the claimant?"

"Tom Hutton."

Andrew nodded. *So, the incident was related to that refugee from the States.*

Myra, with a nod from Helen, slid a notepad over with Agent Trainer's photo. "Tom identified this Task Force Agent as one who had tortured him in the States."

Andrew leaned forward. "He's in Dublin?"

"He was. That was taken by Irish intelligence a while ago."

Myra's mobile vibrated, and she peeked at the text. Tom was in the upper suite. She showed it to Helen.

The front desk receptionist tapped on the door and peeked in. "Ms. Boyle, some officers are here about the Hutton case."

Andrew moved down his side of the table when four officers entered the room—he only recognized one from the SDU, the special detective unit of the Irish police force. The third one looked like G2—military intelligence.

Helen rose. "Officer Stanley, I see we meet again." They shook hands. "Shall we?" Myra made the introductions.

Miles Stanley, the IPO officer in charge of Tom's case, asked, "Where is Mr. Hutton?"

Helen scanned the room before speaking. "He's in this building. Is he to be detained?"

Officer Stanley equivocated. "That remains to be seen."

The SDU detective stated, "An agent of the United States was killed on Irish soil." He looked at Solicitor Boyle, "And it appears to be related to the Tom Hutton case. He was in your offices that evening?"

"Yes, my associate, Miss Moore took his deposition and logged his video evidence."

IPO Officer Stanley leaned over and whispered to the SDU detective. Seeing the nod, he looked at Boyle. "We will need to see Mr. Hutton."

Everyone waited, glancing about the room or consulting their mobiles.

Lucas tapped on the door, opened it and stepped aside for Tom to enter the room.

Stella watched her son's face go white when he saw the officers sitting on the near side of the large conference table. He took the seat at the head of the table, closest to the door.

The officers pulled out their voice recorders or mobile phones. Stanley opened the session. "Tom Hutton, refugee from the United States fleeing religious persecution." The IPO officer introduced the three officers he knew, pausing with the Garda detective.

"Detective Andrew Kelly, Pearse Street station, first on scene for the murder of Agent Joe Lyle." He observed Tom had not reacted to the name. "Mr. Hutton, had you known Agent Joe Lyle?"

"I don't think so, but I often don't know the names of all the agents who have…" Tom shot a questioning look at his mother. He relaxed a little upon seeing her calm demeanor.

Myra slid her notepad with a photo of Joe from Friday night.

"Oh, he was at the house the night they arrested me." Nodding at his mother, he added, "But I never knew his name. I think I briefly saw him at Rosemont, but he didn't participate in any of the killings. He seemed to be one of the good guys."

"Good guys?" the G2 officer asked.

"Not all the agents stepped over the line; however, some were definitely…" He hesitated to call them evil. "…not treating suspects in any civilized way." He glanced at the lawyers. "Was he the one who brought evidence Friday? Is he…?"

Tom looked at the image Andrew showed him. Forcing himself to breathe, he noticed there was no bullet hole in the forehead. "How?"

"One knife wound, Friday evening, three blocks from here."

Stella's pulse quickened. She had not realized how close this was.

Tom tried to smile. "It'll be okay, Mom. The Devil had to ask permission of God before he could hurt Job. God has allowed this." He didn't know the young man. Had no idea if he had been saved, but he prayed, nonetheless.

They stared at the officers. Stanley glanced at the detective. "Have you ID'd the assailant?"

"Not yet, but I located him on the CCTV feeds on Westmoreland tracking Agent Lyle." Andrew hesitated. He had so many questions. *Was this hit sanctioned by their government? Why would they take this risk? How many US operatives are roaming our streets?*

Officer Stanley fixed his gaze on Tom, who met and matched it. "I ask you again, Mr. Hutton. How many other people from your program are in Dublin?"

"As I told you before…" Tom's eyes roved the line of officers. "the Task Force will be forwarded any information I divulge that you enter into your systems." He looked directly at the man he suspected to be British Intelligence. "Also, anything sent to Britain as well as what is known by Irish intelligence."

"You also face serious charges for entering the country with false identification. We can arrest you right now and proceed with your trial, damaging your chances with the Tribunal."

Tom faced him. "I will not answer that question—no matter how you try to scare me." He stopped at bragging not even death could force him to talk. Fear rose up, but he fought it down. Memories of the Mountjoy solitary wing choked his throat, but he refused to blink.

"That's enough, officers. If that is the extent of your questions, this meeting is over," Helen Boyle stated succinctly.

The G2 officer shot a look at Stanley. "I apologize, Ms. Boyle." He looked back at Tom. "What evidence do you have that the organization pursuing you would be privy to confidential intelligence? And it has yet to be determined that they are responsible for the death of Agent Lyle."

"Because the Task Force has the support of the current administration, up to and including the President. The agency has assets in the American intelligence community."

"With no proof yet submitted to establish that…" Stanley said.

"We do now," Myra blurted out. She stopped, seeing Helen's sharp look.

"Please continue, Ms. Moore."

Solicitor Boyle interjected. "I'd like to confer with my clients."

Tom interrupted. "I agree to let them see the evidence Joe brought. They have a right to know." He added, "For the sake of the people of Ireland, I'm sorry I brought them to your shores, but I saw no other way to bring their activities into the light of day."

"What Mr. Hutton is referring to," Ms. Boyle added, "is that the past pattern and actions of this group is clear, seeing they have hounded him wherever he went—even to Dublin."

Stella glanced at Tom. "You should not see this."

"Mom," Tom said, "it's okay. I need to know the extent of the evidence. I choose to stay."

With a nod from her boss, Myra brought in a computer and connected it to the projector. "I'll begin with Joe's summation, and then we can step through the various files. He has authenticated time and place of each incident as well as identified those involved."

Tom's heart raced. He forced himself not to smile broadly when Joe repeatedly mentioned the administration's support for the actions and methods of the Task Force. He stopped breathing when he recognized his uncle Al, but he knew he had to see this through. For the most part, the faces of the officers were neutral. He thought he saw some glimmer of sympathy from the younger detective.

While Ms. Boyle allowed them to view Joe's statements and videos, she would not release copies. "These will be part of the package delivered to the Tribunal at his hearing, along with many other pieces making the case for religious persecution in the United States. Please keep us apprised of the developments of the investigation into Agent Lyle's death. Is there anything else?"

After exchanging glances, Officer Stanley asked Tom, "Do you at this time request protective custody?"

"No, thank you," Tom stated, relieved they had given him the option.

Miles rose with the others. "You will be hearing from us about your hearing date, probably sooner. I'd make the case ready," he said to Ms. Boyle.

She answered only with a tight smile.

After the officers and detective were shown out, Tom asked, "Does this help us?"

Helen smiled. "I think they'll move up the case and grant your asylum. Please understand, if they confirm that a Task Force operative executed a witness in Ireland, there will be severe consequences for your country." She added, "You cannot talk to the media about any of this—not about Lyle, his evidence, or his death. I will keep up the pressure to have the document charges dropped, but we have to tread carefully and not cause problems." Looking at Tom, she asked, "You don't worry they'll kill you?"

He considered what to say. "While I believe God is in control and they will not be able to harm me unless He allows it, I think I should stay in Cary House. When I leave, I'll go with some sort of escort. My days of roaming the streets of Dublin are over—for now."

Helen smiled. "That sounds like a good idea." She waited for Stella's response who nodded in her direction. "Well then, we have a secure apartment on the top floor, accessible only through our secure basement car park. It will be available if you need some privacy."

She rose, and Myra collected the computer. Stella looked at Tom. "We'll stay for a moment. Will be up shortly."

"Join us for elevenses?" Myra asked.

"Thank you. It's that late?" Stella sat back.

Tom nodded. Elevenses—a light snack and tea usually served around eleven o'clock—had become a habit he looked forward to with Catherine. "Mom, text Catherine. Let her know..."

"She'll understand. After lunch?"

"No, I'd like to be back for lunch. Let's not keep Myra waiting."

Tom knew his mother was exhausted as she let him lead her to the elevator.

She said, "I wanted to protect you, but..."

"I needed to see." He chanced a smile. "This evidence strengthens my case."

"Considerably."

They waved at Nancy and passed through the back offices and a cozy kitchen-dining area tucked between conference rooms and offices. Myra had the tea and coffee ready with Irish soda bread and fresh jam. "Welcome, my ma sent along her homemade blueberry jam. The berries were good this year."

Stella poured her tea. Tom added cream and sugar to his coffee this time.

"Indulging, are we now?" Myra teased. She paused and reached over to squeeze his hand. "Were those some of the blokes who interrogated you in Mountjoy?"

Tom nodded. "And Cloverhill. Mountjoy's still hard for me to visit."

Myra looked at them both. "I have a question, if it's not too forward, about your faith?" Seeing their nods, she asked, "What did you mean, Tom, when you said God was allowing all of this?" She paused, her eyes tearing. Gratefully accepting a tissue from Stella, she dabbed her eyes. "Joe was a proper gentleman. He escorted me to the vault and the bus stop. Didn't leave the stop until he saw it safely away." She looked at both of them. "How could God have allowed this to happen to someone like him?"

Tom nodded. "It's so hard to understand why God would allow this to happen to someone like Joe. He sounds like he was a caring person. That he took the risk," Tom shook his head. The man must have been a believer. "It was a shock to see what they did to Uncle Al. I remembered their fortieth anniversary photo. He was so full of life, a true leader."

Stella brought up the picture on her phone. "Larry, his son, sent it to me at the funeral."

Myra admired the handsome couple.

"Aunt Sallie was a wonderful person."

"Where is she now?"

"In heaven. The Task Force shot her when they assaulted the farm and arrested Uncle Al." Tom nodded. "I spent a long time in solitary, accepting that God allowed my imprisonment and the destruction of Uncle Al's family. But then God showed me that I hadn't looked far enough. Alex and Sallie are together in heaven forever—never again to know fear or anger or sorrow or pain. Myra, compared to eternity, this life is so brief. And eternity in heaven with God, Jesus, the Holy Spirit and other believers is worth every heartache."

Stella added, "And when we ask Christ to save us, He helps us through these times."

"Uncle Al considered the cost for defying the laws. He packaged and distributed thousands of Bibles throughout the United States. From the world's point of view, he lost everything, but from God's perspective, he gained everything that really matters. Jesus said in Matthew 16:26, 'For what will it profit a man if he gains the whole world and forfeits his soul? Or what shall a man give in return for his soul?'"

Stella and Tom shared their walk of faith. "Knowing God and trusting He has a plan makes it easier, but it's still hard."

"There's a Sunday evening service at the Hebrew Centre. Would you like to come with me?" Stella asked.

"So, if what you're saying is true, Joe Lyle is in Heaven this very minute?"

"If he believed, he is!" Tom wiped his eye. *Someday it will be my turn.*

She glanced at her watch. "I'll have Lucas drive you to Cary House. Let me set it up."

"Thank you, Myra."

CHAPTER 6

Tom and Stella joined Catherine for lunch at Cary House. She scanned their faces and said hello before she was briefly called away. Finally, back to their table, she asked, "What's the news?"

Tom looked at her, but his brain refused to work.

"Catherine, we'll have to talk in your office or the back suite. There's great news and bad news," Stella said.

With a light smile, Catherine said, "I'm sure the Lord will sort it out. After all, it's His business, and we just have to follow His lead." She reached for Tom's hand. "Should I cancel your afternoon study and the club?"

"No, I should be able to do it, but…" He longed to tell her everything. *Should I?*

Stella and Catherine made small talk about everyday things—the weather, the crowded flights, the latest happenings with the children. Tom listened, saying little.

Catherine walked them past her office and to the back suite. She opened the door and offered more tea.

"I think I've had enough for now," Stella replied, as she headed for the short, padded chair and slipped into its soft embrace.

"You both look exhausted."

"Catherine," Tom held her hand and faced her on the love seat. "An agent came last Friday to make an affidavit with video evidence." He paused, "What we tell you can't be shared with anyone until the investigation is made public, and my case is heard." Seeing her nod, he continued, "The man, Agent Joe Lyle, was murdered Friday night on Prices Lane. I suspect it was someone from the Task Force, but it's not been confirmed."

Stella described the evidence Joe had brought.

Tom watched her process the news.

"He's going to win," Catherine said and leaned forward to hug Tom. "That poor agent and his family. Have they found the killer?"

"No, I have to be careful."

"Will they detain you this time? Protective custody?"

"I declined. I'll stay at Cary House or travel with an escort. We have to let Ron know about this." Tom shook his head. "I'll tell hm."

Stella added, "Ms. Boyle hinted that they might move up the hearing. It might be soon."

"I'd think so. The pressure on the IPO is growing to get your case settled, one way or the other."

"Then there are the false identification charges," Stella added.

Catherine smiled. "I wouldn't worry about those. With other cases, if there's evidence of imminent danger and the charges are linked to their flight, they are often dropped. But that happens only after the hearing. Everything rests on the Tribunal."

Stella sat back, relieved.

Tom looked at the two women he loved deeply. The Lord reminded him of his time in Rosemont and his wish he had been warned of the pit. Maybe he would have been ready to see it if the others had told him. "There's one more thing," he said looking at both of them. Tom shared his heavenly vision and what he feared it might mean. "Ron knows. I've asked him to help you," Tom grasped both of Catherine's hands, about to speak, to unburden his love, hopes and dreams.

She drew him to her and wept on his shoulder. "My love, as you love God, so do I. I agreed to marry you because He means more to you than life. Could I stand in God's way or discourage you from following the path He has chosen for you? May I never, ever." She wiped the tears from her cheeks. Holding his hands, she grasped them tightly. "Let us treasure each day as if it's our last, hoping for a life here and an eternity together."

Tom extended a hand to his mother. Smiling through her tears, she nodded. "We're with you, Son."

Hearing a rap on the door, Tom rose and answered.

Ron stepped through with a bag slung over his shoulders. "Oh, here you are. When I didn't see you in the halls, I feared the worst." He placed the bag on the table. "Your books from the center. Not sure what was up, but…"

Tom gave the update. "Guess my Hebrew classes are on hold," he added.

"Just a change of venue. I come here. What about the prisons?"

"I hate to ask you to take them, but for now, until we know more, going to prison to run Bible studies might not be wise. I'll write Seamus, Clint, Paddy and Link in Cloverhill to let them know I can't meet them in the prison." He added, "Will you pray about it?"

Ron sighed and shook his head, tapping Tom on the arm, "Hand over your lessons—plans and past studies. Any tips?"

"Thanks," Tom sat, thinking through the classes.

CHAPTER 7

W ILL, COLLAPSING INTO bed after a long day in the FBI office at Gillette, Wyoming, scanned the ceiling before he turned out the lights. The FBI databases were a hungry monster, but helped him and Scot, his supervisor, assist local law enforcement, including the State Patrol. His friend Christine Worden, still with the US Secret Service, had sent a cryptic message, but he was too tired to run through the possibilities.

The apartment complex, the back building facing the open prairie, was as still as ever. Now a believer, he slept most nights—the regrets of his time with the Task Force fading away. Turning over, he almost returned to consciousness, but sleep had its way; he descended into its depths.

The team cracked open the door with a copied key. Surveillance from a mini camera planted months ago indicated Will would most likely be so deep in sleep at this hour that he wouldn't hear the sounds of entry or feel a needle's prick. Two fingers on the wrist confirmed he would be out cold for hours.

Two agents methodically removed all traces of hidden bugs and cameras; another walked to the treasure box and extracted the illegal Bible with a gloved hand and slipped it into an evidence bag. The three folded him into a large wheeled suitcase and headed out. The black SUV, the team's entrance and their exit were erased remotely from the complex's recording system. Textbook. They drove without incident to the off-book site—keeping Will under.

Director Chuck Norton watched his team place Will in what resembled a dentist's chair with added restraints. It took a few minutes for the drug to awaken the almost comatose man. Kincaid's contact at the State Department had forwarded the notification to Kincaid and Norton that a former Task Force agent had been killed in Dublin. Norton didn't need further details to know what had happened. He had activated the extraction team that day—before Kincaid had a chance to grab Masters first.

When Norton entered the room, Will turned his head, his eyes working to focus on his former supervisor. The Task Force Southwest Regional Director nodded to an agent to give Will a drink of water. He watched dispassionately as the former undercover operative came to his senses and the reality of his situation.

After sweeping the room and feeling for his position in the restraints, Will tilted his head as far to the side as the head clamp allowed. "Director Norton," he tried to say but heard only a thickened mumble, barely recognizable as speech. He accepted another sip from a water bottle but didn't attempt to speak again.

"Mr. Masters, I assume you've heard the news?" Seeing Will's confusion, he added, "One of your agents—former agent—betrayed us." He leaned into Will's face. "He delivered video evidence of the inner workings of our agency." Norton stepped back. "Of course, he's been dealt with."

"Who?" Will tried to ask.

"Joe Lyle." *Good, get the man conversing. That would make it easier to get him to talk without having to resort to unpleasantries.* "Our mandate required foresight to lay the groundwork for the direction our country needs to take. While you see us as having overstepped, in time, our country will recognize the solution had been forced upon us."

Will tried to hold his gaze and not roll his eyes. *Is the man trying to convince me?*

Norton turned to let Will see a cart loaded with equipment, an electroencephalography (EEG) headset, along with various syringes, vials, and probes. "I hope I don't have to introduce you to our latest innovation. After all, the Oklahoma branch prides itself on humane methods. So…"

Not having the time to work up to it slowly, he ordered, "Tell us the identities of the group that smuggled Hutton out of the country." His voice deepening, he snarled, "I know you infiltrated them, that you helped them, and that you are shielding them."

Norton flicked a remote and the large monitor on the wall came alive with shots of Will's conversation with Texas Ranger Larry Hutton in Amarillo, Texas, almost a year ago.

Will sighed. Despite himself, a tear rolled down his cheek. Something within him whispered, *They know nothing. They have no proof.* Praying for strength, he remembered "*Do not be anxious beforehand what you are to say, but say whatever is given you in that hour, for it is not you who speak, but the Holy Spirit.*"[3] Will prayed, *Shut my mouth, Lord. Protect them.*

With a nod, an agent standing behind Will leaned over to taser him.

Will fought to settle his breathing, twisting against the hard clamps.

"Now, Mr. Masters. I asked you a question, and I want an answer. Who sent Tom to Dublin?"

Will focused on Norton. "I won't tell you because I know that you'll use it to destroy more good people. They are not the enemy. Only the love of Christ can overcome evil and…" He arched back with the tasering; a scream broke past his set jaw.

Norton nodded and left the room. He said quietly to the lead interrogator, "Soften him up but do no lasting harm." Consulting his watch, he added, "I'll be back in the office for some meetings but let me know if there's a breakthrough. I'll drop by later this afternoon."

———⊶⊷———

Scot picked up his cell and called Christine. "Hi, Chris. Will has disappeared."

Chris tried to quiet her gasp. "Signs of violence? Where? When?"

"Last night from his apartment. It's as if he just vanished. Nothing taken that I could see. No forced entry. He usually drops by for Wednesday breakfast and our midweek strategy session." He pondered what else to share over the phone. He knew the apartment complex's video feeds had been tampered with. Will's truck appeared untouched locked in his garage.

"Did you file a missing person report?"

"Yes."

"I'll clear my schedule and come. I'm his POA."

Before she could say anything else, Scot replied, "Alice will be thrilled to see you. Our guest room is always ready."

"Thank you." She ended the call and turned over her phone. She could deliver the news to Butch and Jenny Connors in person. Their house was on the way to Gillette. But first, she had to try to discover why the Task Force had seized Will. Just past nine, with no meetings until after lunch, she reached for her cell phone and searched for Sandy Lyle's number.

The call rang through. Chris prayed she could answer and was not in class at the university. "Hi, Sandy, this is Chris."

"Oh, Chris, hi. Enjoying the day?" Sandy placed her bag on a nearby bench, feeling the cooler fall breezes ruffle her hair. "Aren't you at work?"

"I am. Sandy, I just have a question. Joe's in the UK?"

"Yeah, London for that cybersecurity conference. He was really surprised that they chose him to go."

"Anything the matter? Did he mention any issues about the trip?"

"Well," Sandy held her breath momentarily. "We're pretty close."

Chris nodded. She knew that. They often went to the fellowship gatherings together even though he was more than five years older.

"He was talking about going a few days earlier to visit Mom's Irish cousins. I know he connected with them and had talked about going next spring, but all of a sudden it was set up—like overnight." Sandy paused. "He didn't…He didn't send you any pix of them at O'Shea's? That's where he said they were going to meet up."

"No. I didn't get a chance to talk to him about it. He seemed distracted and a little nervous about the trip." Chris paused, then asked, "When's the last time you talked to him?"

"Wednesday. He drove to New York, flew overnight to Heathrow, and said he'd send a selfie with the cousins at the pub. Not that he would drink beer, but he said those were the best restaurants."

"Of course, so he missed his check-in." Chris rested her head on her hand. Sandy was not an agent. She had to remember that. "I'll check with his supervisor, make sure everything's okay."

"Yeah, like maybe his phone died or… But it's not like him to go silent. He would have messaged me, sent something. They wouldn't have called him in, not from over there?"

"Correct. We'll be in touch."

Chris navigated to her best contact for Joe's division. As one of the training coordinators and on-call presenters, she had three names to choose from. She picked one and prayed the manager would pick up.

After confirming she had the right person and introducing herself, she asked about Joe. The man took a while to answer. It seemed he was looking for something on his computer.

"Aww, there it is…Assistant Deputy Director for Training and Operations Worden? What is your relationship to Agent Lyle?"

"Close friend." Over the past little while, attending the same fellowship, they had become closer.

"Do you know the family?"

"Only his sister. I met his parents one time when they visited her at the university. I just talked with her. She's not heard from him since last Wednesday. His parents live in Waynesboro, Pennsylvania."

"We've been trying to find someone from the agency to make the notification. I assume you're trained in these things?"

Chris' eyes tightened. "Of course. The parents have not been notified?" His answer confirmed her suspicions.

"Can you come to the office? We can go over the incident, that's if…" He hesitated before asking, "Should we send the request through channels?"

"Yes," Chris gave the contact information for her deputy director. "Please send the request with the incident report meeting and location."

Chris set the phone down, shaking her head, but glad for the opportunity to talk with Joe's parents.

Chris made her way to an unmarked office building just north of D.C. While the deputy director had been surprised that they had asked for her by name to do the notification, he sent back the confirmation after hearing her agreement for the assignment. He also approved her time off for the Gillette trip as well. Her mind swirling with the many possible scenarios, she reminded herself to focus on traffic.

The unit supervisor had her close the door to his small, glassed office. Chris listened to the details. The Irish police had attached the video clip of the assault. The supervisor glanced at Chris. "Do you have any idea what this is about? We sent him to London. What was he doing in Dublin?"

"To meet up with distant cousins." Chris reviewed the hit in her mind—something was familiar about it. She met the supervisor's gaze. "They ID the assailant?"

"Not yet." He leaned forward. "If you know something, you need to divulge it now, Christine."

Running through the possibilities, she looked back at him. "Agent Lyle had been with the Task Force."

The man swore and leaned forward. "Hutton? This is connected to Hutton?"

"You asked for my opinion. That's what it is right now. Nothing more." He didn't need to know Will had vanished, and no indictment or charges had been filed against him. *Is the Task Force going around the court system and dealing out justice on their own?*

"Hutton is in Dublin, and word is he'll be deported any day now. Unless, Lyle had incriminating evidence from the Task Force, which would be a serious breach."

Before she could stop herself, she said, "He's beyond your reach now."

The manager glared at her and printed out the incident report. He stepped through the protocols. "Here is your local contact. How soon can you leave?"

It was less than two hours driving time. "Immediately."

The man grunted. "I'll tell them to expect you."

Stopping by her apartment to pack, she was on the road within the hour. In a short time, she would be able to let Sandy know. After giving the notification, she would drive straight to the Connors in Missouri.

"Anything?" Norton asked his assistant when he returned later that day.

"Nothing."

"Not unexpected with this one. How long to get him ready for the headset?"

"Assuming he's resistant…" and seeing the affirmative nod, he said, "Presently we're at a week. His status?"

Norton pursed his lip and surveyed the three operatives, former contractors referred to him by Kincaid from his Marine days. The director had already removed the outright thugs and criminals. The ones left knew he meant business, would not tolerate any criminal activity that benefited them personally, and respected operational parameters—what they were permitted to do for the cause. Always for the cause. If he didn't need Will's information to take down the Texas resistance cells, the man would already be dead.

Lyle was Kincaid's mess. *What had the man been thinking ordering his execution?* Or perhaps Kincaid's agent had gone rogue. Holding back his language, he glanced at the lead interrogator. Senator Roxtson had assured him that if he delivered the resistance cells smuggling pastors out of the country, he could replace Kincaid. Everyone was scrambling with the leaks, and he knew who should get the blame; it would not be him. "By any means necessary, we need the intel on the Texas cells. Nothing else matters."

"Understood."

Norton turned Will's head in the direction of the cart. "That is the latest in EEG headsets. Sensitive enough to detect even the slightest of neural signals and pinpoint their origin. Now," he flicked on the monitor, and Larry Hutton's image appeared. "I know you have the will to resist, but we don't need your cooperation. We show you images of people you most likely met during your time in Texas, and your brain will tell us who you've seen, the ones you talked to, and your newfound friends. Think about it while you're injected with a series of psychotropic drugs that will render you compliant. Enhanced formulas have sped up the timeline; this formulary works within days. Anytime you decide to cooperate, let them know." He leaned in, "We're not concerned about permanent side effects. You should know, this program is still in the experimental stage."

"Director Norton," Will stated, trying to talk as clearly as possible. "It's true; the Bible is true, faith is real, and there is forgiveness for even you and…"

Director Norton rotated his torso, driving his arm into Will's solar plexus. The speed of the attack even stunned the team standing by.

Will struggled to breathe, his stomach emptied, and he began to choke with his head caught in the vise of the clamps.

They released him and pulled him to the floor as he struggled to draw breath. Will leaned against a wall after it was over. He heard a gurney being wheeled in and felt himself being lifted up and strapped in. His eyes met the eyes of one of the men's, but he looked away.

Norton had a final comment. "If you were to survive this—which isn't likely unless you decide to cooperate, you're still going to prison. We found your Bible and have recordings of hate-crime speech. You will *never* be free."

CHAPTER 8

S TELLA MET CHARLES at the airport, and their driver, on loan from the firm, took them directly to Cary House.

Tom wanted to help Catherine cook the meal, but clearly, she was the superior cook. He puttered while setting the table, waiting to hear the double doors open and his parents walk in.

When they arrived, Charles headed straight for his son and hugged him, holding him close for a while. "It took a while to get away, but I'm here." He walked over to Catherine and quickly pecked her on each cheek. "Here for the duration."

"Dinner is ready," she said. "Shall we?"

They found their seats at the small dining table in the visitor's suite and held hands as Charles Hutton offered grace.

"How are you doing, Tom? At least it's not prison."

Tom exchanged glances with his mother. Always the conservative one, they had earlier discussed not to talk of rumors. He had heard from Catherine that the IPO was looking at holding his hearing within the week, but they had heard no news. Ms. Boyle had intimated their binder was ready for the Tribunal.

"Yes, but it's harder than I thought it would be. I really miss going to the cafés. Having Ron bring an espresso is not the same as sipping good coffee with other people. Not that I don't have anyone to talk to here, but…" He laughed.

Catherine squeezed his hand. Unsaid was the hope this was only temporary and for a short time.

"Well, things are heating up back home. People are finally speaking out. Some newspapers are carrying the stories. Tom, you should be glad to hear the Task Force prisons are being closed and the prisoners transferred into federal custody."

"They're not being released?" Catherine asked.

"The law's not been overturned. They were still charged and sentenced."

Tom glanced at his father. "But hadn't some already fulfilled their sentences?"

"A good many and they were released. They've decreased funding for the investigation units."

"What about the black-ops sites?"

"Still selecting a special prosecutor to investigate, and no one's come forward with hard evidence—apart from what has been submitted for your case."

"The truth will come out eventually," Catherine offeredd. "It always does."

"That's right," Tom echoed, reminding himself God is still in control.

"And Joe Lyle's family? Anything happen to them?"

"Well, they are getting media coverage. They're planning a memorial, but his body has yet to be returned."

"Well, dear, how was your flight?"

Not to be deterred, Charles smiled slightly and continued, "I heard the US ambassador had an uncomfortable session with the President of the Republic of Ireland. The US media seems to hint they are looking at sanctioning the States."

"There's pressure from the United Nations as well," Tom added. He smiled at his mother. "All right, it looks like a good week and won't get too cold."

"It never really gets cold in Ireland."

"But never hot," Tom replied. "So, Dad, how's the business?"

"Doing well. People do still buy furniture; keeping up with changing tastes is always a challenge."

Stella smiled when the conversation steered away from Tom's future.

———— ❦ ————

A week later IPO Officer Miles Stanley entered the second-floor conference room at Cary House. His nose twitched at seeing six people at the table. "Ms. Boyle, this was to be a private meeting…"

Charles rose and extended his hand. "Charles Hutton, Tom's father; my wife, Stella Hutton, and my son's fiancée, Catherine." He looked Stanley in the eye. "We have an interest in this matter."

Miles noted Helen Boyle's set face. *She'll back them up.* He sighed, sat, and placed his slim briefcase in his lap. "What is said here today must be kept in the strictest confidence. No media interviews."

Tom smiled. "All inquiries are being directed to the communications department. Only Diane, of the *Times*, has been promised an exclusive after the decision of the Tribunal is made public."

"Make sure it keeps." He glanced at the people at the table.

"I would think, Officer Stanley, our cooperation has been evident. We will maintain strict confidentiality."

"Tom, I'm pleased to tell you that the Tribunal will hold its hearing for your claim next Wednesday at nine o'clock. The hearing will occur in the usual place. Security will be provided." He glanced at the solicitors. "And you will provide security for the trip to the IPO?"

"Of course."

"If possible, a decision will be handed down that afternoon. A private suite will be available for the family to await the decision. You may make arrangements for meals and refreshments. Are you ready?"

"Yes."

"While political pressure has moved up the date, it will have no bearing on the outcome. The Tribunal will take all evidence into consideration, just as in any other case."

"Of course, Officer Stanley," Tom said. "I wouldn't want preferential treatment."

"Seeing we understand each other," Miles leaned forward, "any questions?" Not hearing any, he rose. His nose twitched again when everyone rose as well.

Charles extended his hand. "My wife and I wish to thank your country for providing a safe haven for my son during these troubles." He stopped, seeing the hard look return.

Miles said nothing further. He collected his briefcase, smiled briefly and left.

Charles looked quizzically at the solicitors.

Catherine tried to smile. "They don't like media attention, and they're not happy—not happy at all that I became directly involved with a refugee." She went to Tom's side, "But my choice to become involved was worth it."

Helen added, "They will recover quite nicely once it is over, and your case is won. I have no doubt what the verdict will be. They despise political pressure. That is probably the main reason they're moving up the hearing."

CHAPTER 9

CHRIS FINISHED UP the last task to secure Will's affairs. Having the Esterlys as local contacts helped. She sat down with the couple in their living room. "I'm sure Will would like to continue in your office, Scot, if…"

"We haven't seen an indictment. They can't file charges without bringing him in."

Knowing she could trust them, she said, "There will at least be one illegal Bible charge if not multiple counts for hate-crime speech." The fact the Bible had been taken from the treasure box confirmed Task Force involvement along with long-term surveillance.

Scot and Alice nodded.

"Will was afraid of this. You are probably not on the same level of surveillance as he had been, but your church needs to take steps."

"Did I tell you about Phase Three?" Scot risked bringing it up in front of Alice. "Phase Two took out the church leaders and scholars; Phase Three focuses on removing resistant believers from all levels of law enforcement."

Chris blinked. A chill ran up her spine. "At least they've shut down the prisons."

"Isn't there a prison camp being recommissioned in Maryland?"

"Northern Virginia, but close to the district." Seeing where he was going with this line of questioning, she added. "Yes, if they contact you before me, I'm a member of the Maryland, Virginia, and D.C. Circuit bar. I can be his attorney of record and get his case transferred East."

"When they charge him…" Scot looked at her.

"He will most likely plead guilty and take the punishment. I think…" She leaned forward to squeeze Alice's hand. "I think that's what any of us would do if charged with having a Bible or sharing our faith." The silence hung.

"God will be with us," Alice stated firmly, a slight curve to her lips. "After all, He has overcome the world."

They had met at the house for lunch to make arrangements away from the office. She swept the place for bugs and tried to encourage Scot to repeat the process regularly. Scot headed back to work. The ladies sat, drinking their coffee. "It's going to be a cold week, Chris. Is that sweater warm enough?"

"Yes, thanks. I wasn't thinking of your changeable climate when I drove up. But I'll be home by tomorrow." She was tired, bone-tired—more from the grief of Will's loss than anything else.

"We can store the truck here, if…"

"That would be a good idea." She had weighed the possibilities—if Will had not been rescued within six months, she would return to vacate the apartment and put everything in storage. "I know he'll try to come back if possible." She looked away. *If charged with a felony, his FBI career is over.*

"It's the uncertainty that makes it harder. All the what-ifs."

Chris nodded. "I'll help you with the dishes."

"Don't even think of it. Pack and get on the road. I'll make a meal for you."

"Thanks, anything will do." Chris texted Jennifer Connors that she would be arriving late in the evening.

Settling in at work proved to be easier than reconnecting with her fellowship group. She drove to Delores and Cliff Spencer's house in Annapolis.

"Chris, what a pleasant surprise!" Delores greeted, her voice melodious as always.

"Thank you. I didn't want to call ahead. Is this a good time?" She stepped into the quiet house. "Where is everybody?"

"The twins are at college in Kentucky. The boys have jobs. Cliff's in his downstairs office. Did you eat?" The middle-aged mother of five took in the bags under Chris' eyes and her taut face. "Come on, honey, I'll warm up some sweet buns and hot cocoa."

Chris smiled in spite of herself. "I could use a sandwich. Guess I forgot to grab something on the way. That would be lovely. Thank you." She leaned across the counter, knowing Delores would have shooed her out of the kitchen.

"How are you doing? With Joe gone..." She shook her head and turned to the fridge. Staying busy, serving helped.

Chris told her about Will. "Still missing. I know the Task Force has him. If he's..." She couldn't voice what she feared—as if refusing to speak it could hold back the darkness of death.

Delores met her gaze. "You've already lost two. We are praying for you and Will. You know God will keep him safe—no matter where he is being held."

She knew what Delores meant and was glad she hadn't said it. If she found herself thinking about their killing Will, she automatically prayed for it to be quick. "So, where's church these days?"

"They arrested four more." Delores' lips were tight. "Olson felt we should meet in smaller groups—just for a while." She looked at the sandwich on the plate.

"That's fine. I don't need dressings."

"You'd think they would get the message."

"Delores, the laws are still on the books."

"But they don't have to hunt us down anymore. What is it going to take?"

"It's hard to be patient, hard to keep on going, but we're not the only country struggling with this. Anyway, sounds like a good plan. You have any idea who the informants were?"

She looked at Chris. "We all decided that we will share the saving faith of Christ when He tells us to do so."

"Amen. May I join your group?"

"We wouldn't have you join any other." Delores relayed the details.

She ate her sandwich as she watched Delores make hot cocoa.

They sat in the living room, sipping the hot drink. They tried to chat about everyday things, but every so often it would slide back to Joe or Will or the couple with children who had just been arrested.

Chris tapped on the apartment door and whispered her name. It took a while for Cliff to convince the host she had been invited. She followed them down a dark hall and found a seat in a small office with drawn blinds. Sitting on a folding chair, Chris cradled her phone in her hand, ready to navigate to the Bible.

They sang praise songs acapella so softly that she doubted the group could be heard through the walls. Prayer requests focused on those who had been arrested, the missing—she added Will's name—and prayers for faith to keep holding on. Cliff's devotional from Daniel chapter 3 hit home.

"Let's read that verse again," Cliff said, reciting the words of Daniel's faithful friends. "They trust God will deliver them, but even if He doesn't, they will not renounce their faith or serve other gods. If God had not miraculously rescued them from the fire, He still would have delivered their souls to glory. We know. We believe. We trust— *'the Lord knows how to rescue the godly from trials.*'[4] If we are called upon to make the ultimate sacrifice for the Lord, He will bring us safely to glory."

The following comments and sweet songs swirled past Chris. She wanted to join in, but she could not shake her fears, the certainty, that they would execute Will. More than that, they would never find his body. A gentle touch on her arm broke through.

"Miss Worden," said a young man sitting near her when people began to chat after the final prayer.

Chris focused on him. "Yes?"

"I need to talk with you. Shall we?" he rose and led her down a hall, into a bedroom and shut the door. "Professor Tompkins wants to meet with you."

"You are?"

"Oh, I'm..."

"Sorry, I don't need to know your name. How do you know the professor?"

"Let's say I'm a former student and a family friend. Can you come to his home Thursday at 7 in the evening?"

"Do you know what this is about?"

"He's a...shall we say, he supports the Christians and is in a position to help."

Chris perceived the man didn't feel free to give further details. "Of course." Tompkins had been her favorite law professor and an honest, moral person she respected. She listened to the address and directions. "Is there a number I can call if I'm held up?"

"Probably better if you don't. If you fail to come, he will assume you've declined the opportunity."

"Understood. I should be able to be there." She was rarely called in to work in the evenings.

Chris buzzed the intercom at the gates to Professor Tompkins' property. They swung open, and she drove around to the three-car garage at the back of the house. The young man she had met at the fellowship waved from a side door up a half-flight of stairs. "So glad you could make it," he called to her.

She smiled and followed him into the beautiful house. "Students are invited to his home?"

"They are if they're sons-in-law. This way. He's waiting in the study."

The study was designed with floor-to-ceiling mahogany bookcases, polished wood molding and tall ceilings. A short sofa and wing-backed chairs faced a glowing gas fireplace. A silver-haired gentleman, as spry as she remembered him, rose when they stepped into the room. "Christine, good to see you."

"Professor Tompkins, it's a pleasure." She shook his hand.

"Please, take a seat. Would you like anything?"

"I'm fine." Chris slid into a comfortable-looking winged-back chair. The professor sat on a love seat across from a glass coffee table.

"Well, then," Tompkins glanced her way. "Are you still with the Secret Service?" Seeing her nod, he continued. "Do you lead or manage teams?"

"No, I'm in management, overseeing training, resources. I do consult for the occasional internal affairs case. It's the closest thing to a regular office job I could find in the Service."

"Are you a member of any bar?" He smiled broadly.

Chris nodded. Not really understanding why, she retrieved her credentials from her purse.

He lifted his brow. "In three, I see…D.C. District Circuit Court, and state courts—Maryland and Virginia." He placed them on the table.

She waited.

"Have you fulfilled all the requirements to represent clients in these courts?" Seeing her nod, he asked, "And have you represented anyone, completed an internship or done any pro-bono work?"

"Not yet."

"I might have an opportunity for you."

"I can't accept an unpaid internship at this time."

"Wouldn't think of it." He met her gaze. "Would you be willing to work pro-bono to represent jailed pastors?"

"Of course. Absolutely." Her interest was piqued upon seeing his trademark thin-lipped smile with a slight nod.

"Are you aware of what's been happening recently?"

"The Task Force murdered Agent Joe Lyle and has snatched FBI Special Agent Will Masters without an indictment or charges."

"I'm sorry to hear that. He had a good reputation with the FBI." Tompkins studied her for a moment and asked, "Would you consider Masters to have been the architect for Rosemont?"

Chris maintained a neutral look. "You have to complete the phrase, Professor. Architect for what? If he is the architect for Rosemont the prison camp, I would say, yes. Not even for an instant could he be considered the architect for Rosemont the death camp. He was promoted shortly after he secured the property for the Task Force. Rosemont's transformation into a Level 1 prison camp, fashioned after the federal model, never happened. Will had nothing to do with the creation of that death camp. He hadn't even visited the site after the initial survey trip, until his surprise inspection last year. Don't his actions and Kincaid's response after he saw the pit speak for themselves? Kincaid had him detained, demoted and packed him off to Oklahoma for an undercover operation."

"Well, you know how rumors can be."

Chris shifted, her chest tightening.

The professor cleared his throat. "A Congressional committee was formed to transfer all Task Force inmates to federal prison camps. The process was in the early stages in response to the Rosemont video revelations, but they accelerated the timeline after a Task Force agent assassinated a witness on Irish soil. There's also the matter of identifying the remains in the camps. How involved were you in providing lists of missing citizens?"

"Barely. I merely passed along a copy of a list handed to Masters at a committee hearing. Aren't the missing prisoners either in the three death camps or were executed?"

"Mostly. Genetic typing is being used to identify as many as possible, but there are other places to look. The Task Force has handed over the lists of all active prisoners, and I will say their records are thin and lacking, at best."

"The Task Force was deficient in record-keeping, tracking, monitoring, and supervising their prisoners. Every fact in an inmate's file must be thoroughly checked, particularly dates of arrest, sentencing, and incarceration. Tom Hutton escaped execution because they erroneously entered the date he arrived at Mt. Vernon as his incarceration date. The agents overlooked the fact that he had already served three months in a county jail."

Their eyes met. She wanted to add that Will had told her their incompetence probably allowed some inmates to escape. Rosemont had been one of the worst. However, she suspected the professor was also only telling her what she needed to know and nothing more.

"How did Tom escape?"

Chris met his gaze evenly. "Will ordered his release the day of his inspection."

He shook his head. "No wonder they seized him."

"While they allowed Will to transfer back to the FBI, he assumed they never stopped watching him." She looked at the professor. "I just left Wyoming, as his POA, to settle his affairs. I found proof they had had him under surveillance." She sighed. "What legal help might they need?" She was curious what organization Tompkins represented. *Is it an official government entity?*

"The immediate need is pro-bono legal help for the inmates being transferred from Task Force prisons—verifying the charges, date of entry into their system and negotiating early release, for starters." Tompkins shifted and looked away for a moment. He leaned forward. "They are trying to keep it out of the press, so you cannot repeat this—an FBI team from Philadelphia is spearheading the effort to find and shut down off-book prisons. Efforts are underway to locate other gravesites as well. What do you know about the secret prisons? They have been trying to piece together when and how they originated."

"I first heard of this from Tom Hutton during an interview Masters and I conducted while he was at Hannibal USP in Missouri. He stated he had been held for three weeks and interrogated—calling it torture—before he was brought to the detention center to book and charge him. That was the first summer after the phase-in period. So, I surmise these places have been utilized by Task Force personnel and contractors from the beginning. Are you aware of Major Kincaid's Marine service record?"

The professor nodded.

Chris wanted to bring up the officials prosecuted with false charges and suspicious deaths, but she had to feel this out first.

"I assume you would be highly motivated to help the Task Force detainees."

"Yes."

"Stella Hutton has created a non-profit foundation to help the inmates and discover the truth about those missing."

Her ears perked up. "Tom's mother?"

"Have you met her?"

"No. Charles, Tom's father, was Alex Hutton's brother. Is the Rosemont pit being excavated? How are they making identifications?"

"We are helping with the collection of DNA samples and have secured a contract with a national genetics company to match the remains."

"What about the ashes?"

"Ashes?"

"Will told me the Oklahoma camp used a crematorium. He said they called it the wave of the future—a more humane method."

"A most unfortunate situation. Sources report that Norton issued an order to dispose of ashes with the trash. So, he cremated them!" His lips tightened with this newfound information.

Feeling for the families who might never know if their loved had been killed, she surmised. "Perhaps they kept some kind of records. But we know they died in faith and are safe in heaven; of that we can be certain."

"Considering what I have heard about Kincaid, how did you manage to leave the Task Force unscathed?"

"Ah, I was a woman; he considers us only fit for answering the phone and serving coffee. Once Lyle realized what they were doing, he began to underperform to such a degree they passed him from one unit to the next and eventually allowed him to leave."

"Did you see his statement?"

"No." She shook her head. "I always wondered why Kincaid approved my hiring. He didn't like the fact Will had picked me to lead teams. They were always pulling me away to manage outreach and education."

"Perhaps he had assumed you were Christopher?"

She laughed. "That would be funny and probably why he was so eager to release me."

"Sometimes…" He smiled before continuing, "we can make that work to our advantage."

She nodded, remembering the mock court.

"Well, Miss Worden, I think I can forward a recommendation to the board of directors. Phil, my son-in-law, will contact you with the next steps."

"If so, I request to see copies of incorporation papers, bylaws, mission, strategy, and anything else that state goals, objectives, operational parameters, and funding sources, whatever they are at liberty to provide. I will keep it in the strictest of confidence. May I ask? How is this group related to the Congressional Commission or the federal government?"

"As a consulting agency. We do some of the legwork and are signing on lawyers willing to represent the inmates. The government is making every effort to prove they do not condone such illegal behavior."

"A *loose* private-public partnership?" Chris couldn't resist a sardonic smile. "Trying to keep the UN from going forward with the sanctions?"

"Something like that. A *very loose* partnership."

"Good to hear. We'll need the maneuvering room. The treatment of inmates is merely a subset of the crimes Kincaid's group perpetrated against our people."

For a moment, his face solemn as he stared into the flames of the fireplace, showed the weight of years. "It is a great sorrow that we have come to this—something I never thought I would see in our country."

"But God is able, and if we pursue this, perhaps in time, justice can be restored. I've seen the damage firsthand. I was asked to notify Joe's family." She watched him nod, uncross his legs and place his hands on the arms of the chair. Chris stood, knowing him well. "Thank you for thinking of me, Professor Tompkins. I would be very interested in aiding this group in any way I can."

He shook her hand. "What of your plans, Chris?"

"I'm waiting—waiting for the Lord to show me the next step. I think this might be it." She wanted to ask, almost brought up salvation, but felt perhaps in the future.

"Just a minute." He headed to the copier with her ID cards.

Chris waited by door. She expected to walk out by herself, but Tompkins returned her cards and patted her shoulder in a grandfatherly way. "After you, Chris."

Her hard-soled shoes echoed down the hall, but she caught a whiff of supper. "Just the two of you, now?"

He smiled. "Debbie and Phil are visiting." Pausing in the large foyer under a chandelier hanging from a two-story high vaulted ceiling, Professor Tompkins pulled her into a warm, supportive hug. "I have hopes for the future, knowing people like you."

"More are with us than we know. You, as well, Professor. Thank you."

CHAPTER 10

THE WEDNESDAY MORNING public hearing at the IPO was a blur. His family, close in the front row, held silent vigil. Tom felt the prayers of many. The packed room for the public hearing indicated the media had been watching Cary House. A private hearing would have meant he could not announce the results. Catherine had predicted that once the autos left the car park for the IPO Office, word would spread quickly.

Ron was able to join them for lunch in the private room. Tom listened to the conversation around him, subdued and muted. He could see it in their eyes—even his father's; his mother had told him.

Had it only been six days since Stanley had announced the date at Cary House? It seemed like a long week, or a month, a lifetime. Tom smiled as his mother filled a plate for him and set it in front of him. He pushed the food around. It was lovely, but his appetite had vanished days before. Catherine squeezed his hand, Ron nodded, but all felt the growing tension.

Helen and Myra had joined them at Stella's insistence. After all, they were a team.

Each breath a century, each sentence fell like lead despite the attempts at small talk. By fourteen hundred hours, for they were on a 24-hour day, Tom thanked them for their love, patience, and endurance. The room fell silent.

Everyone jumped when a polite rap sounded on the door. Stanley's aide entered the room and cleared his throat. "The IPO has agreed to present the decision at a press conference convening on the front courtyard. We'll collect you when all is ready."

"This is a good sign," Helen advised. "If your claim had been denied, they would have mailed the decision."

Agent Trainer smiled and assembled the rifle when his local contact sent the text—*Decision soon. Could have used a better choice of words, but the newsroom insider had been right on every other count—the when, the how, and the where.*

One of the main entrances to the IPO Office had a small courtyard tucked away up a short drive—a perfect location for a press conference. A building across the street had a window on the top floor with a sight-line to the event.

Trainer scanned the area again. The Garda seemed absent. He smiled. After Lyle, he had cleared Dublin's border right before Ireland had issued his arrest warrant. For him to return under a different passport was a simple matter, and there was no hint he had been noticed at the airport that morning. The vacant office had been secured months before for this very contingency.

He assembled the rifle, sighted the scope, marking the distance and wind vector himself. He didn't need a spotter. Part of him should have been angry that the incompetent Lyle had managed to elude detection, but the other part was pleased to have a chance to settle the score with Hutton. Now came the wait. Settling back, he lit a cigarette, and perched with the rifle out of view.

Tom's pulse quickened when he stepped out to the courtyard. Three steps up, the roped-off area was ringed by a throng of reporters and spectators. The sound of many voices echoed along the brick and concrete buildings.

Officer Stanley scanned the crowd and nodded to the young woman by his side. "Ms. Lana Murphy, Deputy Secretary of Civil Justice and Equality of the Ministry of Justice and Equality, will make a brief announcement."

The woman, in a trim, dark-blue skirt and blazer, approached a sturdy podium bristling with microphones. "We are gathered here today to affirm our commitment to those fleeing violence and persecution. The Republic of Ireland, remembering well the ones who came to our aid during times of trouble welcome those seeking help and comfort on our shores. We value the friendship of many nations, each respecting the other's sovereignty and values." Her voice strengthened, speaking each word deliberately, "But at times, unique circumstances cause us to acknowledge that certain elements, within those we once considered allies, have forced us to recognize that persecution and violence from wherever it originates should not be tolerated."

She turned to the IPO officer, accepted an envelope, and drew out a single page. "In consultation with the Tribunal, having reviewed all the available evidence, as well as recent events…"

Tom stepped forward, as instructed, watched her turn, and extended his hand.

"The sovereign Republic of Ireland extends to Tom Hutton this Permanent Residency Certificate." She smiled and added, "Tom, you are entitled to protection, and we welcome your contributions to our fair land."

It was his turn. Tom shifted his weight to step closer to the podium. A glint closely followed by an almost inaudible click brought his head around. The muzzle flash and the tinge of a silenced rifle registered an instant before a numbing shock pushed him back and then forward. Falling on his left knee, he glanced at Ron, willing his friend to keep Catherine safe. Tom forced himself to stand. He heard his breath, felt the liquid in his lungs and a rushing sound in his ears. Everything coalesced to a building across the street. The barrel of a rifle cast a pencil-thin shadow against a dirty brick wall above a lighted pub sign.

Nearby plain-clothes officers pulled the minister and the IPO officer into the building. Ron pushed Catherine and Stella toward Charles and the solicitors and into a protected corner. He turned toward Tom, but his friend's eyes were fixed on a distant point. The screams and rush of the crowd, not knowing where to turn to find safety, barely registered.

Before he could reach Tom, Ron watched him fall to the ground from a second shot. Just as Ron moved, a force threw him back. He prayed Charles could keep them safe as he fought encroaching darkness.

A sniper on the adjacent building answered—his shot shattering the window before it passed through Trainer.

Catherine slipped under Charles' outstretched arm. She could see Tom was gone—his soul in Heaven. Hearing Dan's moans, she pulled off her sweater and pressed it against his shoulder. "Help! Help!" she cried.

Plain-clothes officers separated—some to survey and release the crowds, others headed for the side door of the building across the street leading to upper rooms, and four reached the podium.

An officer came up to Catherine. "I'll take over, miss."

Catherine moved down Ron's side and gently held his hand. Charles and Stella stood close, while first responders worked on Tom. She wanted to tell them it was too late, but panic swirled with many voices and shrieking emergency vehicles of an ambulance and a coroner's van along with several Garda emblazoned cars.

Finally, Garda officers cleared a way for an ambulance to back closer to the entrance. Catherine pledged to keep hold of Ron's hand. She accepted Tom was gone. *Lord, please don't take Ron too.*

After a moment's hesitation, they let her stay with Ron. She held his hand and tried to reassure him.

"Tom?" he asked, pushing to stay conscious.

Catherine shook her head. "You saved me," she said, trying to keep from trembling. A shadow crossed his face. "Don't leave," she said. If only she could keep him and never let him go.

The Huttons found her in the surgical waiting area.

"How are you?" she asked.

Charles' face a mask, he cast watery eyes on his wife. Stella squeezed her hand, dabbing her eyes.

Catherine handed them a small box of tissues. "They might be rough," she warned, thinking of the raw feeling around her nose and eyes.

Charles nodded. Stella's shoulders shook. Catherine hugged them both. "Don't know why crying together helps…" She sat up. "But it does." She caught her breath. "I'm glad he warned us."

"You're never ready for this. Never." Charles said. He looked about the half-filled room. "We passed some small conference rooms. I'll ask if they're available."

After a few moments, he escorted them to a small room and shut the door. He fingered Stella's wedding ring while the two women held each other.

In time, they sat back, wiped their faces, and stared.

"We had almost two weeks. Two great weeks."

Stella nodded and reached for Catherine's hand. "And you're part of the family now. You are." She touched the ring. "Keep it. For us."

Charles brought drinks. Stella wanted to stay, but officers came for the Huttons. Later, Catherine listened to the surgeon's report and waited for the escort to his room.

CHAPTER 11

LIGHT PINK AND soft purples spread through wispy clouds. Dan watched the dawn break through the window in his hospital room—a private room, with a guard posted by the door. He shuddered when the door opened. Exhausted, bursts of pain ran up his neck. Every breath sent shock waves through his chest that wrapped around his ribs.

What a wimp. Always avoiding pain—a great trait for an academic. Could I have been as brave as Tom? The image of the man pushing himself up, facing the sniper, keeping him there so the others could get away; he knew that was why Tom hadn't even tried to run.

Wincing with the memory of the force of the bullet, a numbing shock followed by an explosion of pain caused his stomach to turn. The nurse had explained that pain medication could cause nausea, but he knew there was a deeper cause.

A nurse came through the door—the outline of the Garda policeman standing outside his door visible once again. *Are they keeping me safe or guarding me?*

"Mr. Eggers, how are we today?"

He grunted, praying she wouldn't ask if he had slept. *One does not sleep in a hospital.*

Not waiting for an answer, she checked his vitals, entered them into her notepad, checked the IV's and mumbled, "Doctor will be by soon. You seem to be on the road to recovery, young man."

This was Thursday. He wondered what the Huttons were doing,

tried not to think and let the latest dose help him find sleep—light though it would be.

Later, Dan stirred, feeling a soft hand holding his. He recognized Catherine's light perfume before he saw her face.

"Hi," she said, stroking his arm. "They say you're doing very well."

He looked around, but the wall clock was broken. "What time is it?"

"Early. They let me check in on you. We prayed for you and the Huttons. Do you think Joe's family knows?"

"I would assume so." He winced trying to shift. "Can you help me up? Raise the head a little?" Dan's lips felt swollen and cracked.

Catherine raised the bed, helped him sit up halfway and held a mug of room-temperature water for him to sip.

"Thank you." He sat back, trying not to pant from the exertion.

"Try to be still, Ron. It takes a long time to recover from a shoulder injury."

"Oh, you know about these things?" He tried to joke, but the weight of fear and uncertainty refused to yield.

Before she could answer, IPO Officer Stanley and a G2 army intelligence officer entered the room. "We have to talk with you, Mr. Eggers."

Catherine tried to rise, but Dan held onto her hand. "No, Catherine. Please stay. You need to hear this. Officer Stanley, I have to apply for asylum. My real name is Dr. Dan Smith. I'm the…"

"You're the other American, are ya'!"

"I was the second target—not the Huttons or Catherine. I'm sorry I entered under a false passport, but there was no other way."

"Were you ever arrested or charged?"

"No, but I know they were looking for me. I had to flee my home." He looked over when Catherine squeezed his hand. "I'm so sorry I had to lie to you and Chaim—everybody. Tom was right. He did the right thing."

"As long as Miss Walsh is here, we are asking if either of you told the press or anyone else about the hearing date."

"No," Catherine replied firmly. "They were watching. Diane O'Leary of the *Times* did call, but I told her I could say nothing at that time. We didn't want to jeopardize Tom's chances. We all knew that."

"That's correct. Officer Stanley, you told them not to say anything, and they didn't even tell me until lunchtime after the hearing." Dan tried to keep a calm outer manner—holding unsettling emotions at bay.

"I asked him to come to Cary House, and I drove him to the office. He knew nothing until we brought him to the room where we were waiting. You have to understand, the press was watching us night and day. I'm not surprised they came so quickly."

The officers exchanged glances. "Are there any others in Ireland?"

"No."

"In Britain?"

"I only knew of Tom. That's all I needed to know." He looked at Catherine for reassurance. "So, what now?"

"Does your employer know?"

"You are the only ones. May I contact them?" Dan's tension mounted. *Will they handcuff me to the bed railing? Will I be sent directly to Mountjoy?* He remembered Tom's stories about that prison.

"We'll look into the matter." Stanley stared at him, revealing nothing, "Don't leave the vicinity, Dr. Smith. Do you have any identification with you?"

Dan shook his head. "But I'm on the Internet. My positions, my cv, my papers. Would that be sufficient?" His official documents were probably at Taylor's ranch. He had trusted them enough to leave them behind. He tried not to think about the charges he'd be facing when he returned home—if the laws were ever rescinded.

After they left, he stared at the ceiling.

"Dan, Dr. Dan Smith." Catherine reached for him to turn his head toward her. "It's okay. We forgive you. We understand."

"Not everyone's like Tom," Dan replied, his voice catching.

"I'm not surprised. You met him before." A statement, not a question. She said, "I'm glad you're doing this. You have our support."

"What are the Huttons doing? When are they going home?"

"They're waiting for…" Catherine stopped and breathed in.

Dan reached for a small box of tissues and handed it to her. "It takes time for them to release the body." His voice was quiet and steady as he said, "I will be here for you, Catherine." Shaking his head, he added, "If the Lord allows…"

"They'll probably let you into the program, and they like refugees who have a job. Will Chaim let you stay on?"

"I think so. I'd like to see the job through."

Catherine glanced at the clock.

"It's wrong."

"I would hope so. Well," she bent down to plant a quick kiss on his cheek. "On my way to work. But I couldn't wait to tell you they'll be having a memorial for him at Cary House next Saturday. You should be out by then."

"I hope I can be there."

"Plan on it. They want to talk to you about it, but I wanted to give you fair warning and tell you first."

"Can you ask David and Chaim to stop by soon—while it's still easy to visit me?"

"Worrying now, are you? Think they'll send you to the depths of Mountjoy?" Her voice lighter, she laughed and squeezed his hand. "I think the IPO will welcome a chance to poke the Americans in the eye for daring to shoot someone standing right next to Deputy Secretary Murphy. I think you'll find this is the best time to reveal your secret."

Dan nodded. His eyes wanted to close. Fighting the tiredness, he watched her leave the room, the silhouette of the guard visible outside his door.

Catherine dropped by his room later in the day. "Well, what did the doctor say?"

"I'll be going home soon." Dan watched her perch on the edge of the chair. "A lot going on at Cary House?"

"The Huttons have set up their command post," she smiled. "At least that's what I call it. All the arrangements, the plans. Four officers had the gall to accuse them of conspiring with the press to have them flood the press conference."

"Isn't that what a press conference is for? To alert the press? Even with the late notice, the sniper still had time to set up."

"He'd secured the flat over a month ago. That's what the man said." Dan furrowed his brow. "So why do it in broad daylight like that?"

She met his gaze. "I'm glad they were ready. And there's talk of sanctions and a special investigation. That makes your case almost a sure win—especially since they tried to get you too." She leaned forward and kissed his cheek. "I praise God he was a bad sniper."

"I never thought of that. You're right. Maybe he was trying to send a message to scare anyone else thinking of escaping to another country. Anyway, Catherine," he reached for her with his right hand. "I'll be going home tomorrow. I think Chaim will drive me. You go and take care of your people."

She rose, settled her wrap. "Oh, they were thinking of asking you to give the message at Tom's memorial. Odd, you just have one day?"

"It depends on the family. It's different here?"

"A proper wake is followed by the funeral. Anyway, David and Chaim are sitting shiva with them now."

"Will I get to see it?"

"He can bring you around tomorrow, or I can fetch you."

Discharged, Dan waited in a wheelchair by the main exit for Chaim to arrive.

"Traffic, the busses think they own the roads," Chaim said with a broad smile. "So, she says you want to sit shiva. Experienced?"

"Not in the flesh."

"American education these days—can read the prophets in Hebrew but has no real-life experience concerning proper traditions." Chaim stood to his full height with his hands on his hips. "Dr. Smith, I would have never picked that name for you, but we weren't surprised." He eyed the wheelchair. "That's not going, is it?"

"No, protocol." Dan rose, grabbing his bag of personal items. "Where to?" he said as if ready to go, but his first steps were uncertain, and he swayed to the side.

Chaim slipped his arm under Dan's to steady him. "One step at a time. One step at a time. You up for the center?"

"Yes." He really didn't want to face an empty apartment. The wounds were stitched together, and everything seemed to be working, but it took effort to stay awake. Even the slightest movement produced cascading pain.

Stilling his breath, he tried not to move once in the car. Remembering he had to breathe in spite of the pain, he recalled the doctors' threats to put him on oxygen.

Chaim climbed into the driver's side. "You don't want to go home?" Seeing Dan's look, he started the car and put it into gear. "Dr. Dan Smith. I looked you up—definitely over qualified."

"Can I keep my job?" He added, "I deliberately listed only two of my masters on the application to improve my chances. I would hate to have to find another job. Anyway, how did you know?"

"We are glad to have you. Just understand there won't be any raises. Budgets, you know." Chaim laughed. "Your Hebrew was advanced, academically speaking. You still have an atrocious accent."

"I'm working on it."

"Yes, there are improvements. But about your secret—I had already perceived you had met Tom before. We have appreciated your administrative skills, and I am sure the board will ask you to stay for as long as you like."

"I'm glad. Tell me about sitting shiva in Ireland."

Chaim described the blend of Irish and Jewish traditions of sitting with the family open ended, where friends and relatives could come and go.

"I look forward to being a part of it."

Once they arrived, Dan tried not to be the center of attention, but he was glad they made room for him near Stella and Charles.

During a lull in the visitors, soft music playing in the background, Stella and Charles inched their chairs closer to ask him to lead the memorial service. "Do you think you'd be able to speak by next Saturday?"

"I'll make being well a priority."

Talks were underway with the United Kingdom and the United Nations to sanction the United States. The Irish ministers decided to send a message. By the beginning of the next week, a small number of media and officials presented Dan with his Permanent Residency Certificate. The Hebrew Centre let him stay, and everything remained the same—except everything was different.

CHAPTER 12

DIRECTOR NORTON, FOLLOWED by three of his executive staff, entered the abandoned warehouse not far from a small Air Force base near Enid, Oklahoma. Behind several secured doors and thick concrete walls, they entered the hidden complex. "I hope they mean it this time. You certain Masters is ready?"

"That's what they said."

Norton shook his head. "And we had to be here now? You have the files?"

"Ready to go." Leo held the first door and followed the team to a large interrogation room. Masters was sitting in the chair, trying to see who had entered. Leo smiled. "At least he's not comatose like three days ago."

Norton mumbled as he watched the techs fumble with the EEG setup. They didn't have a lot of time. If he thought they were under a microscope after Lyle, it was a nightmare after the Hutton-Trainer debacle. He nodded for his team to set up the laptop and hook into the system. Feeling a large door close and the walls shudder, they exchanged glances.

Seeing without recognition, Will watched a hooded assault team dressed in black shoot everyone, before one of them plunged a needle into his arm. Overwhelming fear rose up just as he descended into blackness.

The third prison stank of mold and mildew. The stench penetrated the heavy bag over his head. He tried not to flinch when rough hands jerked him to his feet. Shuffling to stay upright, he nearly fell when his shins hit hard metal, cutting into flesh, sending sharp tingling pains that threatened to buckle his leg. Hoisted onto a cold chair, his muscles instinctively tightened. Hands shoved him against an upright, and ties secured his arms, accompanied by cursing from two guards.

The hood came off, but he could only see stained concrete wells with large patches of black mold. Will heard the guards pass out of the dimly lit room and a heavy metal door close behind him.

Shifting to find the least painful position, Will tried to calm himself. His head was clearer than it had been for a while—making it harder to ignore his future. He tried to recall the hit that had taken out Norton and his team. He assumed the contractors who had moved him worked for Kincaid.

Warning signs that he had missed or overlooked while working for Kincaid resurfaced. What had Sean called them—black-op contractors, leftover from Kincaid's days running covert operations and secure missions in the Middle East with the CIA? "Everyone goes home, eventually—unless they get you," Sean had stated matter-of-factly. Will had resisted the temptation to try to find out if these types could be responsible for the "accidents" that had eliminated journalists and uncooperative Congressmen.

I keep my eyes on You, Lord, Will reminded himself—the only way to hold the gnawing fear at bay. The panic subsided as long as he focused on Christ. *"He who dwells in the shelter of the Most High will abide in the shadow of the Almighty."*[5] The Holy Spirit brought the verse to Will's remembrance, but he had no clue where it came from.

Sometime later the door opened, and several stepped in. Will looked straight ahead—*will I see what I greatly fear?* He worked at keeping his face neutral when Kincaid and Otis came into view.

Kincaid reached out a gloved hand to grasp Will's chin. "Well, Masters, we meet again," he snarled.

Will forced himself to look Kincaid in the eye.

"Tell me," Kincaid leaned forward, dropping his hand to his side, taking the pose of a general, and stated, "You released Tom Hutton from Rosemont."

"I did."

Kincaid smiled, his thin lips drawing back to reveal yellowed teeth. "When?"

"The day I visited Rosemont. The day I called you. He had served his time—overstayed by more than three weeks."

"Who helped him?"

"I ordered it. I had the authority." He met Kincaid's gaze unblinking. Otis chuckled to his left. He held his breath when Kincaid nodded, and pain exploded up his neck as he heard the taser arcing.

"Who helped him? Who walked him out? Don't tell me he hitch-hiked to Denver!" Kincaid's questions almost rose to a scream—the Marine drill sergeant resurfacing.

Will focused on Christ and Christ alone. Eventually they stopped, and he worked at catching his breath, his heart pounding in his chest.

Slapping his thigh with a glove, Kincaid waved Otis aside. "No matter. Hutton's been dealt with."

Resisting the urge to ask, Will looked forward, his eyes unfocused.

Kincaid leaned in, his breath hot on Will's left cheek, still sensitive after the tasing. "Your little agent, Joe Lyle, the traitor, went to Dublin and handed over evidence detailing our operations. Trainer stopped him." He paced and leaned in. "Tom too."

"Trainer?" the question sounded before he could stop himself.

"The Irish killed him." Kincaid smiled again. "A good soldier. A hero who did his duty." Putting his glove back on, he looked over Will's head. "Keep him. There's a use for him. He doesn't have to be comfortable."

Will heard the chuckle behind him. Pondering what Kincaid meant, he was only slightly encouraged. One part of him had been hoping for a quick execution. After all, Heaven was a far better place.

CHAPTER 13

D AN SETTLED IN his chair behind his desk at the Hebrew Centre, his good hand on the armrest. Willing his computer to turn on didn't seem to work. A month had passed since the hit, and an almost paralyzing lethargy still dogged him. He leaned forward, pressed the button, and waited for the machine to power up.

Physically, he was fine—sort of. Trying to sleep in bed was agony, but he shouldn't be complaining. He was alive, and waves of sorrow rose up.

Chaim tapped on the door frame and sat down in the short, padded chair wedged between the desk and the glassed wall bordering the hall.

Dan flicked his eyes over to his friend. *Chaim must be ready to ship me back home or off to Cary House.*

"A dear friend was murdered. You were shot. You stared death in the face and know they might try again."

"Maybe I'll never be able to go home," he said wearily.

"God's plan for you, they cannot stop it. One day at a time. Breathe, eat, work, follow God, and spread His love—that's how we endure." He tapped the desk. "And work mixed with time is a cure that softens the ground for healing to bring forth faith's blossoms."

"So," Chaim continued, a twinkle in his eye, "you are doing well, considering, but how are things with Catherine?"

Dan shook his head. "Catherine just watched her fiancée die in front of her!" He glanced over. "She seems to be doing better. On the surface at Cary House, it's as if it never happened, but she's working through it, just not…" He shook his head. "Not like me."

"You love her."

That was not a question, but a statement.

"May I ask? I've wondered why you hadn't asked for her hand before Tom arrived."

Dan met his gaze and looked away, tightening his jaw. "I felt like God was throwing up the deception in my face. I couldn't have her marrying *Ron Eggers*. What were we thinking?" He shook his head. "No, it was my decision, and I have to live with the consequences. My goal had always been not to let them get to me—not let them turn me into a lawbreaker, a criminal. I was warned, but the reality didn't hit home until it became a barrier." With a slight smile, he added, "And when Tom arrived and swept her off her feet, well, game over." He held Chaim's gaze. "God's judgment and…" He squeezed his eyes tight.

"She loves you." Seeing Dan's slight head shake, he leaned forward. "You come back to life when you are with her, and her face brightens when she sees you. Think about it. I was there. I saw. As soon as she realized Tom was gone, she went to you. She stayed by you."

Dan sat, immobile, unblinking.

"We are forgiven of all when we take Christ and His Holy Spirit. Would God keep you alive to deny you? Is He vindictive, mean? Would He provide a helpmate only to snatch her away?"

"How do I…" His unfocused eyes mirrored confusion.

"What did Tom ask of you?"

"He wanted me to help her."

"Then ask her how you can help her. And…" Chaim added, "tell her you love her. I think she's waiting. Tom was elixir from Heaven—an intoxicating potion. She loved him and never stopped loving you. I could see the conflict in her every time the three of you were together." It took a moment, but Dan seemed to process and file what he had heard.

Sitting up, he opened his calendar and went over the day, just as they had done every day since he had accepted the position. "I appreciate your patience."

Work helped. He stepped through his days, prayed for the various Bible studies at Cary House, Cloverhill and Mountjoy.

By the end of the week, after the children had flocked to their parents and as the residents began to head to the dining room or separate kitchens, he walked with Catherine to the back suite and slid a frozen pizza into the oven.

How had Tom bonded so quickly with Catherine that she was ready to marry him after only two months? Dan noticed Catherine watching him. Remembering Chaim's advice, he sat by her on a long couch. "How can I help you?"

Catherine shook her head to settle her hair, lifted a hand to run her fingers through the locks on her left side. She extended her hand for his. "I think he knew the time was short. But he talked with me. We talked about everything. Sometimes, it's as if we could have talked all night." Her green eyes studied his face.

Taking her hand, he plunged in and earnestly said, "I love you, Catherine. Since the moment I saw you at my first Sunday evening fellowship. But I was in a strange land, living under an assumed name. It's taken time to put the pieces back together."

Dan breathed and he knew, if ever it was to be, he had to open himself up. "I love you, but I don't know where I'll be. Nothing is certain. I'm practically penniless." He laughed. "Bible college professors aren't paid much above poverty wages."

Furrowing her brow, she shook her head. "Dan, you think that little of me?"

"What?"

"So, you make me wait until you have the proper position and the proper income and the right house and…"

Dan stood up, paced, settling by the oven. "So, you'd risk hitching yourself to my wagon—such as it is?"

"I'd not say it in those terms, but if I was willing to marry Tom, and his future was definitely uncertain, why do you doubt I'd not be willing to marry…" She looked away.

Dan pulled out a few tissues and returned to his seat by her side. He reached out and drew her into an embrace. "I never meant to hurt you." He waited for her tears to slow. Handing over more tissues, he kept one for himself.

"I guess I have to lot to tell you." He found himself stroking her hair to tuck it away from her face. "My family was private…if you know what I mean."

"Reserved." She blew her nose, glancing his way.

"From the time I knew I was to be a Bible professor, I set my sights. It didn't take long for me to know I was a waste trying to teach children or even teens. But in seminary, once I had a taste of Hebrew, I knew I had to learn more. Each layer of Hebrew unlocked more mysteries from the Law and the Prophets. I needed a degree in the ancient cultures since culture shapes a language. Three masters and two doctorates later I thought I was finally ready to publish, and I thought I had found my seminary."

"Then the laws came?"

Dan nodded, describing his years on the run.

The timer sounded indicating the pizza was ready. Dan cut it up. Catherine poured his cold soda in a glass.

"So, how do we do this? Getting acquainted?"

She smiled. "Oh, we discuss the important things—like how many children do you want?"

"That's how it goes?" Dan stopped, looking aside. "I never thought about it." He set his jaw to the side.

Catherine smiled. Her laughter bubbled up. "You really haven't considered it?"

"I didn't even think I'd ever find…" He joined her laughter. "I never thought I'd find anyone who could put up with me. Well, the way I used to be. My studies were everything, and people just got in the way." He said wistfully, "But I have come to understand during these wandering years, that people are what it's all about. We study to understand so we can help others walk with Christ. I had the knowledge, but not the wisdom to know how to live it or teach it. Not dry dusty papers—though there are places and times for them—but fashioning gems from the Word of God about our great God and how He lives in our hearts presented in clear language." He grasped her hands. "And you would walk that path with me?"

"I would. I almost gave up thinking I'd ever find a spiritual man who would be interested in me. Shortly before you arrived, I assumed I'd do my thing at Cary House since all the decent Christian men were already taken. And the others who showed an interest were immature, selfish, uncaring…" Laughing, she added, "…hypocrites who acted like they cared about me, but were hardly interested in church or the Word or even showing consideration to their mothers." She leaned against the counter. "And out of nowhere, two wonderful Christian men I could admire show up. I didn't think you had noticed me."

Dan nodded. "I guess that made it possible for you to…"

"Exactly."

In the brief moment he looked into her eyes, he saw the puzzled hurt. He held her close. "How do we explain the works of God? To bring people together for a short time, only to take them home?"

"I shouldn't be so set back. I've met so many who have lost so much. And there is my cousin who went almost to term and still lost the baby."

"Or those who lose children."

"Or newlyweds, the love of their life."

"So, God, whose thoughts are so much higher than ours…"

"Whose love, plan and purpose are always there…"

Dan breathed as they looked into each other's eyes. "We can only walk the path He sets before us. Catherine, will you marry me—without home, without knowing what tomorrow will bring?" He held her hands tenderly. "I wouldn't want to face the future without you by my side."

Wiping her eyes, she reached into her pocket and pulled out the engagement ring.

"Is that the one?"

She nodded and lifted her face. "Stella Hutton told me to keep it. Charles said it would be something to remember Tom. But…" She held it out to him.

Dan reached for the single, pure diamond—not large, but flawless, dividing the light as he examined it slowly. God's provision—God's provision in the midst of destruction. Plans to bring death creating opportunities for God to build new life. He held it, standing before her and holding her left hand. Reaching forward he said, "Catherine Walsh, will you marry me?"

For an instant her face glowed, but then a shadow crossed it. Pulling back slightly to blow her nose and wipe her eyes, Dan knew.

He turned her palm up, placed the ring in her hand and closed her fingers around it. "I'm sorry. It's too soon. When you're ready, I'll be waiting." Seeing her look of pain, sorrow, puzzlement, tinged with fear, he added, "I'm not going anywhere." It was the wrong thing to say, and her shoulders shook with a torrent of tears.

Dan held her close, letting the storm run its course.

"Should we warm the pizza?"

Catherine laughed, flicked her hair, and plopped down in her chair by the table. "The brave ones eat their pizza cold." She raised a challenging brow.

Dan smiled and picked up his slice.

"But I don't have a box for it." She smiled faintly. "Tom gave me the ring without a box."

———⸎———

The next day Dan walked to Cary House and headed for a short block of storefronts on the way. Hesitating, he entered the middle jewelers, feeling for the euros in his pocket.

"Hello," he said to the gentleman in suit and bow tie, behind the counter. "I have a lady friend who needs a box for her ring. Do you sell ring boxes?"

The man stared at him.

Before he could turn him away, Dan explained, "Her fiancé died, and his parents told her to keep the ring, but he never gave her the box. To keep it safe..."

"You're an American?" The man studied him.

Dan shifted his feet but resisted the urge to bolt.

The door behind the counter opened, and a woman walked through. Her face lit up when she saw him. "Dr. Smith! What a surprise!" She glanced at her husband. "Sal, this is Dr. Smith—the one I told you about. He's going to speak at our church this Sunday."

"Next Sunday, ma'am."

She laughed. "See, he's one of the Americans. You remember, the ones who were..." She stopped.

"Yes, just asking if I could purchase a ring box, but..." He stepped back, trying not to redden.

"Nonsense." She reached under the counter and brought out a gold-trimmed, dark-blue box. She tipped it open to reveal the inner cream silk lining.

"Yes, of course." The man held it out to Dan.

"What do I owe you?"

"Nothing," she said, sending her husband a sharp look.

"Quite right." He tried to smile. "On the house."

Encouraging the man to come to church would have been natural, but he merely said, "Thank you."

"So, that's the US now?"

"We hope and pray, in time, they'll right themselves. Get back to honoring the Constitution and Bill of Rights." But the facts were complicated, and he didn't think they wanted an American civics lesson.

She stepped around the counter and shook his hand. "God is faithful, isn't he, Sal?" She looked back, not letting go of Dan's hand. "God will keep you." Her eyes slid to the box. "May the good Lord bless you and keep you and may He give you and your lass many bonnie lads and lasses."

"Thank you."

"So, what will you be speaking on?" Sal asked.

Dan slid the box into his pocket, straightened up, and said, "That God calls us to forgive those who…" His voice lost its strength. "harm us." Fleeing, he walked purposefully out the door and up the street to lean against a sculptured railing facing the Liffey. Saying a prayer for his enemies, he breathed.

At Cary House, Catherine stared at the box and slid the ring into the narrow pocket. "Just right," she said. Her eyes scanned her office, looking for a proper place. She stared off into the distance, but couldn't think of where it should go in her flat either. Sighing, she handed the box back to Dan. "Keep it for me?"

"It would be an honor."

CHAPTER 14

THEY FED HIM regularly. Everyone wore a hood—a good sign that he just might survive. *But why is Kincaid keeping me alive?* That he didn't have a clue bothered him worse than the acknowledgment that the Task Force obviously was not yet finished with him.

Will's fears of torture never materialized. Some were rough, others yielded to the temptation to cause pain, but they seemed to be on a tight schedule and rarely lingered past seeing to the duties necessary to keep him alive.

After the second move, meals became irregular. Eventually they brought his meals twice a week. He feared the slow process of dying from dehydration when they stopped coming altogether. This underground prison would become his tomb.

Will rolled on his side, trying to keep the shackles from biting more deeply into his ankles. He'd had a good run—leading multi-agency teams, delivering justice, pursuing criminals up and down the Eastern seaboard and through the Plains states. He'd ridden horseback in the Wyoming Rockies and braved blizzards. Good friends had been made, and he had experienced true friendships with the Esterlys and other Christians. *Has it only been two years ago since I met Giles and Alexa and Dan?* Recalling his life, he knew he should have been satisfied, but the desire to live refused to evaporate.

And the Holy Spirit brought comfort, warming his heart with verses and songs and memories of the love of the brethren. Thinking of the lovely Christine warmed his heart with bittersweet regrets they would never be.

Friday afternoon Christine turned her car toward Reston. The director was fine with her leaving earlier on Friday, considering she usually put in over 60 hours a week. Exiting around the halfway point, grabbing a quick meal, and arriving at a nondescript office building on the outskirts of the city had become habit. She pushed open the main door to the suite of offices with "Hutton Foundation" painted in metallic letters on the glass.

"Hello, Trish," she called in greeting. The young paralegal, Trish Hendley, not only manned the front desk, answered the phone, and did the filing, she also was a skilled researcher. "Anything I need to know about?" Chris asked, pulling the mail and notes from her inbox on the back credenza.

"Nothing in there."

Chris perched on the chair near the front desk and opened her notepad. Scrolling through her task list, she asked questions here and there. "Pierce family samples arrived at CGT (the genetic matching firm)?"

"Finally, all three samples loaded just this afternoon. The Wilsons haven't sent theirs in yet."

"Procrastinating?" Chris lifted a questioning eyebrow. Wilson had been arrested and supposedly shipped off to Rosemont, but the pit had been excavated, and the recovered DNA had been logged into CGT's systems, waiting for matches. She knew, in the back of her mind, that some might have escaped. *What would a family do, she pondered, if they were indeed hiding their loved one? Would they risk surrendering him after Rosemont?*

They worked through their lists, and Trish assured her everything she had downloaded from the courts had been uploaded to the files.

"Well, if that's it, I'll be on my way. Little Charlie's having his third birthday at Pizza Palace."

"Sounds like fun. Enjoy," Chris said with a smile.

"For the kids, anyway. My husband wears earplugs. Oh, by the way," Trish added, slipping into her coat. "They set you up to interview Richard Carlson at Purcellville Prison Camp."

"Who? What?" It took her a moment to remember the name of the prison camp where those from the Eastern third of the United States had been sent. She had prepared briefs, written letters on behalf of the inmates, only having to make a few court appearances. Not wanting to create any more bad publicity, the Congressional Committee had the clout to expedite the appeals. "Please remind me again who Richard Carlson is."

"The man they call Pastor Rick—the one who ran hospice at Rosemont."

"Oh…" Chris recalled hearing about him, but she couldn't remember any details. "What about?"

"The team chose Pastor Rick to be the face of the early release legislative effort."

"Right, since Congress passed a law limiting early release for federal offense to no more than 15 percent of the sentence, it would take another bill to overturn it."

"Have you seen it?"

Chris tried not to roll her eyes. "It's in my files, but no, I haven't had a chance to review it. The short version?"

"Since the Task Force prisons failed to meet federal incarceration standards, every year served in any of these prisons counts as two years for determining date of release. It's changing how they count time served."

"All? Including those who cooperated and bypassed the death camps?"

"Well, making it too complicated or specific could create loopholes that could be exploited to limit those who qualify. They felt the simplest, most direct categorization of prisoners would eliminate some of the procedural delay. Anyway, they want him to testify before the committee."

"At Congress in an open meeting?"

"Yes, and…" She paused by the door. "he might be a reluctant witness. I assume they felt your charm would help encourage him to cooperate. The details are in your calendar. I forwarded the documents in an email."

"Have a wonderful weekend." Chris smiled. She reached into her purse. "Almost forgot. Here's his birthday card. Three only comes around once."

"Thanks. Next week."

Chris smiled. The light was on in Marv Stanton's office to the left. It had taken a while for their private investigator to remember he had to be in the office Friday afternoons to go over cases with her.

Chris settled into her office, surveyed her mail and tasks for anything that would need Marv's involvement. In some ways, things were already settling out—the DNA matching was going well, and the glut of inmates ready for release had been sent home. Now only the longer term ones remained.

She stood and headed for Marv's office with her notepad.

"Yo, Chris, getting dark too soon. Too soon. Hear you're on to prep Carlson." His short, clipped sentence hung in the air.

Chris recognized that look. "Okay, what's the problem? Sounds like the perfect witness."

Marv shook his head. "I don't get it—you know, how some react after being in for a long time, and they should be giving the Rosemont group triple for their time there." Seeing her fixed gaze, he explained. "When Olson tried to run a mock hearing, the guy froze. Then he said he didn't want to do it. Didn't want to get special treatment, but they think he's just terrified about getting out."

"Not unheard of. Terry Olson?" She tried not to groan. While the man was a brilliant trial lawyer, he could be curt, abrupt and arrogant with his staff and witnesses. He reserved charm and tact for the judge and jury.

"Hear you on that one. Maybe that's the problem."

"Thanks for the heads up. I'll see if I can allay his fears. Legislative negotiations could drag on or never make it out of committee."

"This is the best time to push this through. The attention might not be there in a few months."

Chris nodded. "Agreed. Anyway, go through your cases." She brought up her list, ready to make notes.

The Hutton Foundation, created by Stella and headquartered in Akron, Ohio, established offices near each of the three prisons housing Task Force inmates, in addition to their D.C. district lobbying office on K Street. Chris stared at the proposed law. *The drafting looks good, but can it pass?* She opened counsel's notes on the mock hearing. Marv had not been exaggerating. Unless something changed, Carlson's testimony could hurt the legislative initiative.

Chris sighed. They hadn't handed her a case, but a mop-up—find a way to convince, coach and prepare a witness for a public hearing. She sat back, remembering the media circus of a contentious hearing, added on to the usual badgering and posturing of the Congressmen. *Should they be asking him to do this?*

Professor Tompkins, who led the team meeting in the suite's large conference room, assigned cases to pro-bono attorneys—experienced attorneys who had represented clients in federal, state, and a few even at the Supreme Court. Not a green, untried member of the bar. She had not felt led to leave the Service for an internship clerking for a judge. She was basically the office manager, making sure the matching initiative ran smoothly. She tried to mute her disappointment at not getting a chance to work a real case by reminding herself she barely had time, along with her sixty-hour-a-week job to manage the projects in this office.

Considering next steps, she was thankful Marv's results for the week hadn't ignited any fires that had to be dealt with immediately. The Hutton Foundation had a bed and breakfast for the wives near Purcellville. Perhaps Mrs. Carlson could help her discover how to engender Pastor Rick's cooperation. She located Irma Carlson's cell number and dialed.

The drive to the Hutton Center at Purcellville took only a half hour since it was past rush hour. She pulled into a large parking lot and looked at what appeared to be a reclaimed hotel. The lobby area had been expanded to include a casual living room, kitchen and dining area. She scanned the groups of women, teens and children sitting in small groups or in the kitchen. A slender, birdlike woman separated from a threesome at a small, square table.

"Miss Worden?"

"Yes, Mrs. Carlson? Where can we talk?"

"In my room." The woman, not quite elderly, but certainly past middle-age, pulled out a swipe card and headed for the doors to the right of the reception counter. "This place gets busy on the weekends."

The room resembled an efficiency apartment with small kitchenette, round table with three chairs and a queen bed. She followed Irma to the table, sinking into the comfortable padded chair. "Looks nice. Do you get a different room each time?"

"This is mine for as long as I need it. Not much sense in driving back and forth. I gave up our house—have a room with my son in Georgia."

"This is home then." Chris glanced at the spare furnishings and walls.

"Tea or coffee?"

"Something without caffeine. Any herbal tea is fine." Accepting hospitality might help put the woman at ease.

Irma set the electric kettle to boil and leaned against the counter. "We have an hour until the Bible study-prayer meeting. You're welcome to stay."

"I'd love to." She noted the time. "Do you mind if we get right into it?"

"It's about the hearing business?" Irma turned to the cupboard, dabbing her eye with a tissue.

"Yes, they've asked me to prepare him for the meeting. Do you think this is a good idea?"

"Do I think he should do it?" Irma studied the strands of light coming in through the closed curtains. "I think the proposed law is the least they could do for us." She looked at the young woman. "Are you a lawyer?"

"I am, though I don't have that much experience. However, I have helped many witnesses prepare for testimony." Resisting the temptation to jump in with explanations and methods for helping a reluctant witness, she reminded herself she was there to listen.

Irma worked at keeping her lower lip from trembling. "It feels like he doesn't want to come home, but I know he's just scared. When in detention and the earlier years in the prison camp, he heard the others complain about probation—the ones sent back because they couldn't keep the insane rules set by the good-time board."

"According to the proposed law, there would be no supervision requirement for this measure. The years added for being at a Task Force prison are to be considered as time served. Rick was in Jessup for four years. Did he transfer directly to Rosemont?"

"Yes, he was one of the first sent there." Irma poured the water into mugs and walked to the table. "Jessup was not that bad. Within a few months they moved him to the prison camp, and I found a way to stay in touch. It took him at least a year to recover from the torture." She looked at Chris. "Had you heard about things like that? I mean, we couldn't talk about it—not back then. Harry, our oldest, wanted me to go to the press, but I was afraid publicity might hurt his chances to transfer out of medium security. What if I had? What if we could have told them what was going on? Would that have stopped Rosemont?"

Chris shook her head. "As soon as they realized their agents had restricted access to inmates in federal prisons, they were set on creating their own. And the press was shut down as well."

"I know that now. But you wonder, just the same. It took me a long time to find out where he had been sent. It was as if he had been swallowed up—no phone, mail or visiting privileges."

"How long was he there?"

"A little over seven years." Irma blew into her tissue and turned her head. "Oh, the tea." She brought over the mugs. "With the proposal, he'd be out in under two years. It might mean he could be released someday and not…." She set the mugs down on the table.

"Irma, do you support Rick testifying?"

"Can I be there by his side?"

"Well, not at the table, but I could arrange for you to be seated nearby, and you would have some time with him in the prep room. Do you have a suit he could wear?"

Laughing, she shook her head. "Not any that would fit him now."

"I can assist you with that. What do you think is the main problem to him testifying?"

"I've tried to understand, pray about it all the time, but it seems as if he's afraid of getting out." Shaking her head, she added, "I know it sounds crazy, but we've lost our home. He certainly can't get a job. Our savings are…." Taking a sip of tea, she looked across the table at Chris. "We trust in God, and I know he knows God will take care of us, but…."

Chris nodded. "This fear is not uncommon. If he understood his testimony would help many other families, would that be enough to help him push through the fears of interrogation?"

"That's probably the major issue. What they did to him…He's great leading a Bible study, praying, or preaching, but he said having to go before a board…it sounded like he had an anxiety attack talking with that lawyer."

Chris nodded. "I'm scheduled to meet with him tomorrow. If I don't think he would be ready, I will recommend they select another…"

"No," Irma grasped Chris' hand. "No, he needs to do this—not just for the others, but for us! I know it's going to be hard for him, but this will help him recover so he can face the ministry God has planned for him after prison."

This was what she needed to hear to get a sense of how hard she could push the man. She asked Irma more questions, looking for hints and insights to help her plan how to encourage Pastor Rick to testify for the Lord's sake and His people.

It seemed in no time at all that Irma reached for her Bible study bag, and they headed to a conference room for the meeting. Chris was not surprised that Irma led the Bible study-prayer session. After, she waited for the room to clear to talk with Irma. "Are these meetings every Friday?"

"Yes, we each take a month or so. It's a fairly flexible schedule."

"Could I attend?"

"Of course!" Wondering at the request, Irma asked, "Are you missing someone?"

Chris knew what she meant. She nodded and shared what had happened to Will.

"Is that the young man who set Tom free? You be sure to tell Rick about him. They pray for all of the ones who have been abducted. Have they found them?"

"The majority of the missing have been matched, but there is still a number that can't be accounted for. Either the family hasn't submitted any sample from a close family member, or the sample doesn't match with any in the database." She studied the woman's face. She did not look surprised, but she shrugged her shoulders.

"We'll keep praying for that group. And for your Will. I keep to myself, mostly, and the family. This ministry to the widows…that's what we call ourselves, has helped. I consider myself to be one of the lucky ones. Poor Alex didn't have his family to help him. That's probably why he died so young."

Chris nodded. Her mind strayed to thoughts of Will, wondering if he were even alive at this point.

"Chris, keep your eyes on Christ. That's how we get through. And I will pray for God to give you wisdom tomorrow. Let him know we'll get some time together."

"Oh, the suit. Do you know his current size?"

Irma nodded. "Medium with a 36 waist, 32 inseams. Thank you for stopping by. Please let me know how it goes. I'll be visiting him tomorrow afternoon."

"Of course. I'll send a text."

"If it would be convenient, may I call?"

"Certainly." Chris walked out, thankful she had Irma's support. *Maybe he will be testifying Wednesday.*

Purcellville Prison Camp, a Level 1 facility that had once held VIP prisoners, had been reopened to hold Task Force offenders. The campus was open with a single chain-link fence. Chris sat in a small room where inmates could meet with their attorneys. Richard Carlson walked in, looking a decade older than his 65 years. She tried not to stare at his left arm, rose and extended her hand, "Christine Worden from the Hutton Foundation. Thank you for seeing me."

He looked past her, nodded, fumbled to pull out a chair and sat, his back rigid, with a thousand-yard stare.

"Pastor Rick," she said. "I met your lovely wife last night. I had a chance to attend her Bible study."

He smiled, relaxing slightly. "The center's been a blessing. Thank you for taking the time. We need all the help we can get."

"Did you have a chance to talk with Assistant Director Will Masters while you were at Rosemont?"

"What? Ah, yes. What is this about?"

Chris drew out a small digital voice recorder. "I would like to hear what Will told you that night he was at Rosemont. Had you seen him there before that day?"

Rick's eyes flicked to the recorder. His face whitened.

"It's not on yet. Mr. Carlson, the thought occurred to me that you might be one of the few who could help us verify Will's involvement at Rosemont. I thought it might be a good idea to record the conversation, just in case."

"What did they do to him?"

She relayed a quick summary, ending with, "He has been missing for weeks."

"Of course. I'll tell you what I know. It's not much." Rick turned to the recorder. "The guard on duty showed him around. It was after the day staff had gone. That was good. He was almost in tears and said repeatedly, 'This is not what Rosemont was supposed to be.' Rosemont was supposed to be a prison camp like this one."

"Did he tell you what he planned to do?"

"Yes, he said he would turn Rosemont into a prison camp with meals, an infirmary, and visitation rights. He apologized and said he would let Director Kincaid know what was going on." He paused. "That never happened, of course. Instead they had us all lined up, after shooting the ones who couldn't walk. We all assumed this was it—the end, but then the head guard came, ordering us back into the rooms. About a month later they trucked us to another camp. I think it was in Oklahoma." He paused before adding "They put us all in the back of a cattle truck and shut the door."

"Any stops? That's what? A twelve-hour drive?"

"It was a long, hot day. We had to carry some of them out. I was shocked to see some medics and medical equipment, though it was minimal. We had a cot, meals, showers with warm water. But several died when they couldn't digest the food. There wasn't any help for that. We still had to make do."

Chris watched his focus sharpen and his shoulders draw back as he sat taller in the chair. His fight was coming back. Chris added the ending statements for the recording, turned it off and put it away. She faced him and looked him in the eye. "Pastor Carlson, are you willing and able to testify at the hearing…"

"I wasn't clear why I would be a help. Isn't it about the numbers?" He paused in thought, then added, "We also need to know what the reporting requirements would be—what we would have to do to stay out of prison."

"You're right—the legislation only changes how time served is calculated. The days spent at a Task Force prison would be counted twice. They are trying to keep it simple. That is why they are not adding in any additional time spent under arrest. Your testimony describing what you experienced and observed firsthand provides the justification for passing this bill. This legislation is in committee. It would have to first be approved by the committee before it could go to the floor for a vote. The Senate would have to approve it as written or pass their own measure."

"I understand, Miss Worden. The bill might not see the light of day."

"That is correct, but your testimony will become permanent public record. This is one of the best ways to have your story heard."

"Not for me, but for all of them."

"Exactly." She smiled. "What changed your mind?"

"Irma. I think I made her cry. The Lord wouldn't let me forget what she had said, and I realized I had to take courage and be willing…" He looked at her, palpable fear in his eyes.

She understood. Being paraded around in public was humiliating. "They will transport you to the building through a secure entrance. Irma will be waiting for you in a private room. She'll bring a change of clothes—a shirt, tie, suit and dress shoes. You'll have some time with her before and after you testify. While they will have an approximate time for your testimony, you might be in the room waiting with Irma for a while." Chris allowed a smile to cross her face when Rick's face brightened.

He laughed lightly. "The Lord also reminded me to get over myself and stand up." He rose and extended his hand. "I would be honored to testify."

"One more thing," Chris said. "Could we?" and gestured for him to sit. "At the Hutton Foundation I have been managing the effort to identify the missing. A number of people have not been matched to any of the remains and were not at any of the prisons. Now, I will take no notes and this will not be recorded, but would there have been periods of time where some might have escaped alive?"

"Most definitely." Rick lifted his left arm. "The first month or so at Rosemont was crazy. We had never, ever considered that our country would create concentration camps. Once we began to realize we were sent there to die with no contact with family, stripped of everything, some became agitated and easily upset. They didn't tell us, at first, about the bonuses."

"Bonuses?"

"Yes, the perimeter fencing is a joke, but they installed several guard towers. The first time they let us out, some tried to slip away and were shot."

"For all to see?"

"Exactly. Then they would take some for trash duties. We were in shock when they returned and described the pit. It wasn't uncommon for a person to get so upset he would yell or strike out. Often, we could talk him down, but sometimes the guards took them away by force, and we would see them in the pit the next day. One day I was trying to help a large man near me, and he started a fight. I was thrown. In the confusion some couldn't get clear and trampled me. My left arm went numb, but with the bruising, it was a while before I realized my forearm was badly broken. Of course, with no medical care, it became infected." He said no more.

Chris nodded. "Thank you for sharing that. What do you think those who escaped would do if we tried to find them?"

"I'd run and not come out of hiding until the laws are rescinded."

"We don't have to do their work for them. We match those we can find. The rest, well, that will take care of itself." She rose. "Thank you for your time."

Pastor Rick reached past to hug her. "I will have them pray for Will." He cradled her hands in his. "God has a plan for him, He can keep him. They can't win against God."

"I try to remind myself. Thank you."

Once back home, Chris emailed Tompkins telling him that Carlson could testify, but she would have to be the one to stand with him at the hearing. The next day she was pleased to see her professor agree to her condition.

CHAPTER 15

CHRIS FUMBLED FOR her cell, trying to accept the call before it went to voice mail. "Hello?"

"Christine Worden? Do you know a William Masters?"

Chris shot up, sitting halfway out of bed, clutching the edge of the blanket. "Yes, I know Will Masters. Who is this?"

"Dr. Leeds, VCU Medical Center, Richmond. Are you by chance a relative?"

"Close friend. Can I see him?"

"You're listed as his emergency contact."

"I'm his POA. How is he?"

"Not good."

"I'll leave right now. Send me the address." She added, "It might take a few hours."

Chris rubbed her eyes, waiting for the doctor's contact info to appear. Joy tinged with fears struggled within her for Will and his future. Trying not to imagine the worst or expect exoneration, she packed her bag and grabbed Will's. Having her take some of Will's clothes and toiletries had been Alice's idea.

Chris found the large medical center and pulled into the first parking ramp near the emergency department, assuming they were most likely to have someone available to direct her to Will. She forced herself to take the time to listen to the instructions. "Go left, second wing, third elevator, fourth floor, ICU."

Chris found the ICU desk, but no one was there. She headed down the hall with the most activity and found a nurses' station. "I'm looking for Will Masters. Dr. Leeds called me."

The nurse looked at her for a moment and said, "Room 7-B, to your left."

Chris walked around the corner, looking for 7-B. Partway down, she slid back the glass door and pushed the privacy curtain aside. A figure lay unmoving with IV's and an oxygen mask, but no ventilator. Will's name was written on the small whiteboard. Chris didn't wait for permission or an invitation, she stepped forward, peeled off her jacket and dropped her purse.

She leaned close to Will's ear and said softly. "Will, I'm here. It's Chris. Come back to me." Blinking away the tears, she lifted his hand and caressed his arm, perching on the edge of the bed.

His eyes were sunken, surrounded by dark shadows and his cheek-bones, outlined by sallow skin, cast shadows along his jawline. She could almost see every bone in his hand and wrist through translucent skin. A moan escaped his lips, and his head turned toward her. "Will," she said again, placing a soft kiss on his cheek. His hand clenched hers. The strength of the grip surprised her. "Yes, I'm here."

Will tried to reach her with his other arm. He peered into her eyes. "Chris?"

"Yes, Will." She bent to kiss him, and he drank in the embrace, wrapping his arm around her shoulder.

"You came. How?" He looked about, confused. "Where am I?"

"VCU Medical Center, Richmond," a voice said behind them. "I'm Dr. Parish, and who are you?"

Will lay back, fighting to focus on the voice. He gripped Chris' hand tightly, his body tensing.

Chris rotated her head to the doctor, not wanting to leave Will's side. "Dr. Leeds called me a few hours ago. I just arrived."

"Family?"

"No..." She struggled to voice an explanation.

Will tried to say, "Yes," but his voice cracked.

Chris reached for a jug on a nearby stand and helped him sip some water.

"She is family to me," he said not taking his eyes off her.

"We'll need some history." Dr. Parish returned with a nurse.

She let Will answer as many questions as he could. Laughing when asked about family history, he replied, "Drug addicts, divorce, betrayal."

"She means medical history!"

"Well, I don't think I'll live long enough for that to matter. Not on any medications, no known diseases, and I'm only allergic to bee stings. Blow up when I'm stung. Quick way to kill me, but bet it hurts..." He coughed spasmodically. For the first time he realized it was hard to breathe, and his chest hurt. "Do you know what happened? How many days?"

"You came in severely dehydrated, unconscious, with some pneumonia. Dr. Leeds will be in later this morning with more information. Now, you need to put your oxygen mask back on."

Chris shifted to step aside for the nurse. "I'm staying, Will. Don't worry." She noticed a U.S. Marshal standing by the glass door. He cupped his hand, indicating for her to approach.

"You are?"

She pulled out her badge and Secret Service ID. "His lawyer and close friend." She ignored the smirk. "Has he been indicted?" The marshal nodded but looked at her coldly. "The charges?"

"Take that up with the agents. I'm not the lawyer."

"FBI?" Relieved to hear no Task Force agents were involved, she answered, "Very well." She turned to go then rotated back toward him. "Where did they find him?"

"West of Gaithersburg, Woodbyran Farm area."

"Why wasn't he brought to the nearest ED?"

"What's a few hours? The agents said he's headed for Purcellville, and they have a contract with this center."

"Life or death for someone in his condition," the doctor said, tight-lipped. He looked at Chris. "May I see you for a moment?"

She followed him to a quiet spot down the hall. "While you seemed to have revived him, he's not out of the woods yet. You need to insist he stays here. I don't think he'd survive jail at this point."

"Agreed. We can request the magistrate appear here. Has this opinion been forwarded to the marshals?"

"I'll check the records. If not, I'll leave a note for Dr. Leeds to file that assessment."

"You handle the Purcellville cases?"

"No, mostly those going through the district court here in Richmond."

———— ❦ ————

Will tracked the nurse's every movement as she recorded his vitals and checked the IV and oxygen flow to enter into a nearby laptop on a wheeled cart. He read the date on the whiteboard—November 10. Will smiled when Chris returned to his side. "Two months?"

"About that. Scot called me the day it happened. Can you tell me about it?"

Will told her everything he could remember. "Why do you think Kincaid told them to keep me alive? How did I get here?"

"The marshal guarding you said the FBI brought you here." She pulled a chair near Will's bed and called Scot. "Yes, Scot. Will is in a Richmond, Virginia, hospital." She glanced about. "The FBI are lead, and he's been indicted. Don't know the charges yet."

Chris handed the cell phone to Will.

"Hey boss, I have to resign, I think. Said they had the goods on me—religious offenses, you know. I'm no longer qualified…"

Scot said, "Don't jump to conclusions. We're just glad you're still alive. They found Norton and his team executed."

"By Kincaid's men. They killed them all and put a needle in my arm, knocked me out. They moved me at least three times. Saw Kincaid, but they didn't do anything. Stopped bringing meals a while ago. Thought I would die there. I'll be charged soon enough. Which prisons are still open?"

"All Task Force prisons have been closed."

Chris said, "Probably brought you here since the nearest prison camp is upstate at Purcellville. Pastor Rick is there."

Will handed the phone to Chris. "He wants to talk with you."

"Okay, text the flight info, and I'll meet you and Alice at Dulles. Can you get a flight into that airport?"

"I'll make it happen."

Chris checked her messages. Her boss had approved her time-off request. She put away the phone to focus on Will.

Two FBI agents followed by the marshal entered the room an hour later. Chris stood and pulled out her credentials. "I'm his POA and his lawyer. You can't take him until the doctor clears him. Where's he going?"

"Charges have been filed in the East Virginia District Circuit. The Magistrate can conduct the initial hearing here if he has not been discharged." The FBI agent studied Will. "Do you request the Magistrate judge for your initial hearing?"

Seeing Chris' nod, Will said, "I do. What charges were brought to the grand jury?"

He shifted his feet, but noting Chris' hard look, he said, "One count HCL literature and five counts HCL speech."

"That's it?" Chris said. "No other charges besides 756 offenses?"

"No, ma'am."

"Then I move to expedite and proceed to sentencing."

Chris asked, "May I have a moment with my client?" She waited for the agents to withdraw, close the glass door and take up residence in front of it. "Will, do you waive, give up, your right to trial, judgment and sentencing before a United States district judge and agree to trial, judgment and sentencing before a United States magistrate judge?"

"I do."

"As soon as possible, I will apply to appear before the Eastern District, Richmond Division, as an attorney. I'll have to locate a notary. But you can proceed with the magistrate whether or not I'm qualified." She pulled out her notepad and navigated to the online form. "Here it is. I'll find a printer, but you can read it."

Chris tapped on the door and nodded at the marshal. "Thank you. I just have to find a way to print the form."

"The magistrate will have an online copy available. He can sign electronically."

"Very well. Who contacts the magistrate?"

"We do," the agents said, then talked briefly with the marshal before walking away.

Even so, Chris found the nurse's station, and they gave her access to a computer. She printed both forms. A notary would be at the bank branch in the main hospital lobby. It would be opening soon.

After Chris left, the marshal stepped in and stared at Will. "Was it worth it?"

"What?"

"Come on. It was your choice. You decided to break the law. Didn't you know?"

Will refused to smile or laugh. *What should I say? The laws violated the spirit of the Constitution and the Bill of Rights?* "Careful, we start legislating speech and thought, and your beliefs might be considered illegal someday." He shifted, holding the mask away from his face. "Seriously, how did you find that prison? Was it underground?"

The marshal stared at him before he nodded. "Yes, we received an anonymous phone tip. Doc says if we'd been a few hours later, you would have been dead. So, did your God make the call?"

Will couldn't resist a smile this time. "I suspect a person called; God can use anyone to speak for Him. Remember Balaam's donkey?"

The marshal's eyes flicked in anger. Swearing, he stepped out and sat on the chair right outside Will's room.

Chris returned with coffees and pastries, and the document ready for Will to sign. She also had her court application notarized and ready to submit. This would place her name in the list of attorneys eligible to represent indigent defendants.

After checking with the nurse, she helped Will sit up a little before handing him a latte and placing the cinnamon roll on his tray.

"Did I do the right thing?"

Surprised he even asked, she nodded. "From what the doctor said, you're still fragile."

Her smile, warm and friendly, brought new life to his soul. Laughing, he shook his head. "And those were his exact words?"

"No, not exactly." She shifted and tried to mimic the young doctor's voice. "He said you were 'not out of the woods and weren't likely to survive jail.' So, I think that answers your question. Assuming you weren't framed, I gather…"

"Guilty as charged." Will sat back, trying to fight the exhaustion. He wiped away a few tears. "After, after…"

"Will, you are forgiven." She caressed his arm. "You didn't see. If you had, you would have bailed a long time ago."

"Well…" His thoughts returned to who had made the call. He told Chris what the agent had told him about the tip.

"I assume it will be a while for the magistrate to appear. Scot and Alice will be arriving mid-morning, so, having just returned from being almost dead, settle in and try to get some sleep. I'll be leaving soon to pick them up at the airport." She leaned over to kiss his cheek, and he turned his head toward hers.

Chris filed her paperwork and headed for Dulles. Parking, she waited for the arrivals. Her mood lifted when Scot and Alice rounded the corner, pulling their carry-ons behind them. "No baggage to claim?"

"Not today. Traveling light." Scot extended his hand.

Alice slid around him and hugged her. "How is he?"

"You'll see." She wended her way through traffic, and they walked across the skywalk to the ICU.

Chris stepped back and let them greet Will who seemed groggy. She hoped that meant he had had some sleep.

Her thoughts shifting, she tuned in when Scot said, "It's official. I am the lead agent for the Gillette Resident Agency. I can hire a staff of five—two agents, two analysts and an administrative assistant." He paused, his smile fading away.

Will tapped his hand. "I'll pray God sends you good agents who want to stay a while. How's Lee doing?"

"Worried about you. Was disappointed he couldn't be here, but we had to catch the first flight out ourselves."

"I'm sure they allow visitors at Purcellville." Will shared the details of the charges. "The magistrate will be coming for a hearing. Doctors won't let me out of here."

"Glad to hear that."

"Ladies," Will said, looking at Chris and Alice, "I need a moment with my friend." He pulled Scot close and began talking to him quietly.

Scot emerged from the room, rubbing the back of his head. "Well, Chris, hate to do this, but I need to borrow your car to get something for Will. It has to be done today."

"Of course. Here are the keys. I'm at…"

"4C, got it." He headed down the hall and turned the corner.

Alice laughed when she saw Chris' look. "Hey, they have their own secrets. We're going to miss Will. I assume this means he's no longer an FBI agent." Her voice lowered. "Sorry, I didn't…"

Chris grasped her hand tightly. "No, it's true. We've already talked about it. Just…" She let Alice lead her to a couple of chairs at the end of the hall.

It took a while, but Chris wiped her face, managed to smile and headed for the ladies' room. She heard Alice say, "I'll go check on Will."

"Where did you disappear to?" Will asked.

Alice sat on the chair near Will. "It's been a long hard two months for all of us." There was so much she wanted to say to the person who had become Scot's close friend, but hesitated. She shifted to another chair when Chris entered and watched them reconnect.

Will kept glancing at the clock on the wall.

"So, what was that errand you sent my husband on?"

"Is he lost?"

"No, that man can find his way across the plains and through the streets of New York City. Very resourceful. Why I said yes."

A short time later the marshal informed them the FBI agents would bring the Magistrate at four that afternoon.

Scot returned before lunch. Again, Chris and Alice were asked to "give them a moment."

"I don't know if I can handle all these backroom deals," Chris said, trying to be lighthearted.

Alice had a suspicion, but she said nothing when Scot opened the door, and the sound of soft music drifted by. He waved Chris in and stood by his wife's side.

Chris, eyes slightly red-rimmed, stared in shock. Will stood by the side of the bed, grasping the handrail. He held a small box in his left hand. Before she could protest and call the nurse, Scot urged her to go in. She tried not to run, but images of Will's collapsing would not leave her mind.

Will shifted the box in his right hand, still gripping the railing, and extended his left. "Christine," he said, voice a little more than a whisper, reedy and thin.

She stepped forward. Her pace increased when he bent his left knee. He reached out his hand to grasp hers. "Christine Worden. For-give me for waiting so long, but now I can tell you. I love you more than life itself." He wanted to say more, so much more, but fearing loss of strength to even speak, he asked, "Will you marry me?"

He tipped his hand. "Take the box, please."

She reached for the box. Inside sat a beautiful woven band of white gold set with three perfect diamonds outlined by a thin heart-shaped ring. "It's beautiful. Yes." She lifted him up and helped him back into bed. "How?" She looked at Scot, who tipped his head in her direction.

"Since you're my POA, I told him to send the bill to you." Will's signature smile matched the dancing light in his eyes.

Laughing so hard she almost fell against the bed, she looked at the three conspirators and slid the ring on her finger. "It fits!"

"This is amazing. I gave the jeweler your dimensions, and he made his best guess."

"God's in this," Alice rejoiced confidently.

"There's another requirement," Scot said. "You have to invite us to the wedding. At Purcellville?"

"Yes," Will said.

Chris shook her head. "Let's see what the Magistrate does. He'll be here this afternoon." She tried to ignore the warning in Will's eyes, but she held to the hope that two months of imprisonment should have some bearing on Will's sentence.

The FBI agents arrived shortly before Magistrate Judge Wallace.

He stepped them through the process and accepted Will's signed waiver. "Representation?"

"I will represent him, your honor." Chris showed him a copy of her application to appear before the court. "I will schedule an appearance as soon as possible."

Judge Wallace nodded and took his place at the foot of the bed. The marshall stood close to Will. The FBI agents occupied the open door. Standing in a side corner, Chris held her breath as the judge read the charges and asked, "Do you wish to make a statement?" upon hearing Will say, "Guilty."

"No, your honor, not at this time."

"Then hearing no remorse or explanation for a federal agent to violate federal law, I sentence you to five years at FPC Purcellville. If it was not for the fact you are unable to travel, I would be sentencing you to Leavenworth." He nodded at the marshal.

The U.S. Marshal pulled up the left bed railing, grabbed Will's arm, and in one swift motion, secured the handcuffs to the bed railing.

Shock pulsed through Will's arm as the cold metal bit into his skin. Memories flashed, and a roaring buzz filled his ears. Struggling to breathe, his heart pounded in his chest.

The monitors sounded as his heart rate accelerated along with three other alarms. The nurse at the station called for the doctor. The male nurse arrived at 7-B just as the heart monitor switched to an even tone, drawing a straight line across the monitor. "Get this thing off the man," he yelled. Quickly, he dropped the head of the bed and started rescue breaths and chest compressions.

Scot pushed past the marshal, removed the cuffs, and slapped them in the officer's hand. "He's not going anywhere, wise guy."

A nurse arrived followed by Dr. Leeds. "Clear the room," he told her. Once in the room, he yelled, "Stop immediately. Didn't you see the no compression order?" Turning to the nurse closest to the door, he ordered, "Get the crash cart." Without looking up, he began to bark orders for epinephrine and succinylcholine. We will have to intubate."

Chris, Alice and Scot stood a short distance away to give the nurses room to work. In shock herself, Chris watched as the Magistrate fled the room with his aide, and the FBI agents rolled their eyes and said to the marshal, "Let us know if he becomes not likely."

The marshal nodded. "I'll let my relief arriving soon know."

It seemed like an eternity, but Will's heart regained its standard rhythm. However, he was unconscious and intubated. Chris watched the doctor place the stethoscope on Will's chest. She heard, "No breathing sounds on this side. Get the tube kit."

Dr. Leeds turned. "Miss, he's back with us, but he has a collapsed lung."

"Were there…were there…Did he have broken ribs?"

"Fractured—why I posted a no compression order."

"It's fine, doctor. They were doing their best." She noticed his look. "Other fractures? Is he likely to survive?"

"I'm guardedly optimistic. What happened?"

"After enduring two months of torture, he was sentenced to five years in prison. I guess he went into shock when they handcuffed him to the bed?"

The doctor nodded. "Will there be any other visitors we might need to know about?"

"Just the U.S. Marshals to guard him. I'll contact their CO's." Seeing his confusion, she explained, "Their commanding officers and let them know that he cannot be moved until you approve the transfer. I am assistant to the deputy director of training and operations for the U.S. Secret Service. That man is Will's former supervisor and head agent for the Gillette, Wyoming, FBI resident agency. Between the two of us, we will make sure everyone is informed and brought up to date."

"While an incident like this can be a shock, if we can stabilize him, he could be on his way sooner than you might think. Like I said, *guardedly optimistic*. His condition is serious, but not grave."

"Thank you." She nodded at Scot and led him to the end of the hall with some padded chairs. They dug out their cell phones and worked their contacts. Chris also set up her appearance at district court to finalize her application.

Alice stood guard near the marshal who avoided everyone's gaze. "You look tired. When's your relief coming?"

"Should be here any minute."

"I assume that was protocol?"

"Yes, ma'am."

"Well, Marshal Dyers," she stated as she looked at him directly. "Will is one of the best agents my husband has ever worked with. We are close friends, but he also believes in Jesus Christ and has been forgiven all his sins. If God had decided that this was Will's time to go to Heaven, I have no doubt that's where he would be. No one knows the day or the hour when God will come for us. That is why we must make ourselves ready, make sure that the Lord Jesus Christ knows our name, so that we do not have to die in our sins."

Alice retrieved Scot and Chris when the nurse let her know they could enter the room. Once everyone was settled, she went in search of something for supper. She returned with sandwiches, fruit and chips. "Hospitals can be hard places to find good meals."

Chris rarely moved past holding Will's hand until he began to stir and look about the room.

"What happened?" he said after they removed the ventilator.

"Your heart stopped, but God didn't let you…" Chris held her lip to keep it from trembling.

"Well, joining the living?" Scot asked.

Will nodded and tried to reach for the mug of water. Alice held it for him. "It must be late. You staying over?"

"I have a place for them. It's Friday, so we can attend a Bible study." Chris had arranged for them to stay at the Hutton Center. She was looking forward to introducing them to Irma.

When it came time, Chris could not leave Will's side. "I'm sorry, but you go. Irma has a room ready for you. I don't feel I can leave him." Her eyes roamed above their heads. "Take my car and come back tomorrow."

"I think that would be a good idea."

"Thank you for coming. For everything."

CHAPTER 16

Sunday evening Dan slipped into the back of the fellowship meeting after the singing and opening prayer. Pastor David, in his usual style, read the passage that would soon be dissected, word by word, mentioning all the points of tense, aspect besides the context. Pausing, his eyes scanned for Catherine's strawberry-red hair. It took him a while. She had it clasped with a band and brought forward over her left shoulder. In the second to last row, three in, not sitting near anyone else, her right shoulder rose and fell as she stroked her hair.

He whispered her name as he drew near. She hated to be surprised and forced to *create a scene*, as she called it, when startled. She turned to him and slid her hand to his. He noticed the slight bags under her eyes; twirling her hair with her left hand now, he felt her shoulder touch his.

"First Corinthians 4?"

She cast a sideways glance. "Shh, 7:17." Following the verse, her eyes on her open Bible, Catherine's hand returned his gentle squeeze.

Daniel reviewed the eight-verse passage in his mind. His eyes settled on *free* and *freedom* in verse 22. He and Thet, a Burmese refugee, had visited three small towns in four days, speaking at six churches. The past six weeks had been a blur.

"Follow the calling God sets before you…" he heard David say and tried to focus on the message.

After the last song, they walked to a nearby café and a small table near the back. "Tea?" he asked. Seeing her nod, he rose. "I'll get us something. Don't want them to kick us out for not being paying customers." Catherine grinned slightly, not even adding a jab or retort.

He cupped the tea mugs in his hand and pulled out a small bag of scones. "Anything happen?"

She shook her head, added just a dribble of cream and double sugars. Her eyes met his. "I've missed you. We hardly have time to talk." Sitting back, she added, "Tell me it was worth it."

After the IPO approved their initiative, a small group of Dublin church leaders had chosen Daniel and Thet to be the face of the project. Going from church to church, they presented the possibilities and advantages of helping refugee families.

"Thet's the charmer."

"I doubt that!" She laughed.

Dan smiled. *It's good to hear her laugh.* "Well, it's hard to tell."

Catherine rolled her eyes. "Well, I remember. That group at Kells promised to take four, and…" She shrugged her shoulders.

"And for the most part, Kildare came through after seeming to have slept through the meetings."

"My grandfather said, 'Fish where the fish are,' meaning we go wherever we can arrange a hearing and focus on the ones who show real interest. And your tour of the far reaches of our fair land?"

"Fair to middling," Dan replied.

"Mocking, are we?"

"Not at all. What Thet said."

She tipped back her head and laughed, shaking her head as she visualized the short Karen refugee trying to sound like a Dubliner.

"So, we take the train to Mullingar Thursday or Friday?" Dan watched her push her tea cup closer, take a sip, look down the hall of the narrow coffee shop and twirl her hair. "Catherine, you have to tell me. What is the matter? I thought we agreed to visit your family—your mother specifically. After all…" He reached for her hand.

She pulled it back, sighed and met his gaze, hoping she hadn't offended him. "All right. Ma didn't like Tom. Not at all. She was quiet during the visit with her thin lips pressed together. He was nervous, but he tried to be friendly." She shook her head. "I had forgotten how she had talked him down to the family. Carol went on for weeks. Every chat involved the 'homeless man' I had brought home."

"Okay, so, take the train?"

"I think I should drive. That way," she flicked her hair behind her shoulder and cradled the still warm mug with her hands. "That way, if I have to…"

"I would finish the meetings, but we have to at least try." He had to ask, "And if she reacts the same?" His resolve weakening, he sat back and began to fumble with his tea cup.

"Dan, no, we will marry. I don't care what they say. It's just me. I'd hate to have us starting off together with too much baggage."

He nodded. They had attempted to begin marriage counseling with Pastor David, but his outreach schedule had made that almost impossible. Stepping through the workbooks together had been non-productive. In the end, he had assured Catherine their love would survive many children or none, poverty or riches, health or disability. Because they loved God and knew the Lord had brought them together, it would work.

"Settled. You drive. I'll try to be…"

"Be yourself." She smiled. "I want them to see the man I married—not the one you think they want to see."

Dan's pulse quickened. His eyes lit up. *Perhaps, sooner rather than later, it will happen.*

After Sunday morning worship, Catherine's Uncle Frank steered Dan to his well-worn truck and followed Catherine's car to Erin Walsh's house. Dan listened to the flow of stories he was growing used to, having stayed with the man each evening.

Every chair, every horizontal surface amenable for sitting was occupied. A baby attempting to crawl, and two toddlers held the center of the room, toys strewn about. Dan paused, trying to take in the sounds and the greetings, fearing he would not remember most of their names. An older, slightly stouter version of Catherine stepped from what he assumed to be the kitchen. She wiped her hands on her apron, navigated the grandchildren and extended her hand. "Welcome, Dr. Smith, Erin Walsh." She seemed to almost giggle. "Finally get to meet Cathy's man."

Dan smiled, nodded his head. Before he could respond, Erin shooed a teen texting on his phone off a prominent stuffed recliner near the fireplace. "Catch your warmth by the heat." He recognized the air of authority as the woman recruited three others to attend to the kitchen.

Frank shook his head, smiled and asked, "Your team doing well?"

"Team?"

"Football, American football. Follow a team? Aren't you all sports crazy?"

"Like football fans here?" He laughed. "Don't really follow any."

The aunties and cousins plied him with questions—mostly harmless. The teen forced to move to a sheltered corner spot by a bookcase asked, "Are all the churches closed?"

"No, just some." The room went quiet while Dan described the last several years back home. "We're praying for the laws to be rescinded."

"Think the ruling class will follow through?"

"A possibility. It's been done before with prohibition when they outlawed alcohol." Dan waited for the room to settle out or move on to another topic.

"What if they never do?"

"Then this is my home. God told the Jews exiled to Babylon to make a home there—to build houses, raise families and work for the peace of the city. And that is what I will do if…"

"But if they do?"

"Then we'd seek the Lord's guidance on where He wants us to go. The next call. Right now, working with the Hebrew Centre and raising up churches to help refugees is what I am supposed to be doing."

The call for dinner rang out. Uncle Frank stood and directed Dan to the head of the table. Erin seated the rest.

Dan smiled when Catherine slipped into the seat to his right. They exchanged smiles but didn't get a chance to talk. Erin began her questions concerning his salvation, his testimony, education and teaching experience.

Toward the end, when Erin was distracted helping her youngest grandson eat his carrots, Dan picked up his plate and cutlery to follow Catherine into the kitchen. They had had little chance to talk during the trip, and there was one last meeting at a church in nearby Delvin Village. "How am I doing?"

Catherine peered out the window. "This is not the welcome Tom received." She took the plate. "Guests don't help do dishes. And don't expect them to raise a finger when they visit."

"Good to know. When do we need to leave?"

"We have a few hours yet." She leaned against the counter. "Ma is thinking of going. How is Thet doing with his hosts?"

"Seems fine. They'll drive him to the community hall."

About to ask the question, he smiled when Erin walked into her kitchen. "Men in the kitchen! A scandal. Scoot and have another sit by the fire before you face the chill of winter."

Dan stepped past the dining table squeezed into the small room and under the archway to the sitting room. Two of the families were collecting coats and their offspring. Erin stepped to see them off. Dan smiled, nodded, and stepped forward for the traditional quick peck on both cheeks from each one—even the teen. Now half-full, the room felt cozier. Frank returned with Dan's bags and set them by the couch.

"Take them back to the guest room. No need to clutter the space." She wished her brother goodbye and surveyed her son, Miles, and daughter-in-law, Sylvia, still lounging on the couch. "Keep the company?"

Dan hated to boot their teen out of the recliner. He took a seat in a short-backed chair.

"Ah, the quiet after the heathens are gone." The father laughed, "We're all born sinners and heathens until the day of decision."

"It's a busy season of life. I remember Christmas Day when everyone came home. Chaos! Do most of the family live close?" He listened to their tales of family holidays and gatherings."

"That's about done for you if things don't right themselves."

"I join a new family." He smiled, feeling at home already.

Catherine washed, as she always did. Erin insisted on making sure everything was right before it returned to the cupboard.

"Your man's a fine one, Cathy."

She tried not to visibly grimace hearing her childhood name. "Ma, why didn't you like Tom?"

"That hobo? Sure, he was a fine Christian, but I couldn't see him supporting you anytime soon."

"Ma, if…" She shook her head, realizing she had to change the subject. "Dan's okay?"

"Yes, love. He'll do good by you. Anyone could see it if they weren't blind. And besides, God told me to stop being a stubborn old woman and give you the blessing. I've always wanted you to put the Lord first in your life. Having to let you go to the wilds of Dublin was hard, but…" She stopped and leaned against the counter.

Catherine slipped an arm around her mother's shoulders—the teacher, faithful wife, diligent mother. "Even if He sends us to the States?"

Erin wiped her eyes, blew her nose and faced her daughter. "Even that. Guess I'd better start saving…"

"Wait here," She stepped aside and headed for the front room.

"Dan, do you have it with you?" Her head swung around, realizing Dan was not in the recliner.

"Yes," he said behind her. Everyone laughed when she nearly jumped. "Ready?"

"I am."

Dan slipped his hand in his front pocket and pulled out a small, padded drawstring pouch.

"Wait." Catherine called, "Ma, can you come here for a moment?"

"What do your folks think about Catherine?"

Dan looked at the couple on the couch. "I haven't dared contact any of my family since I had to go into hiding." Seeing their confused look, he added, "That Task Force goes after the family. If I call anyone from here, the US can tap their phones and all their associates. I will not put them in danger. I wish they could meet you, but my mom had a stroke and Dad takes care of her, so they can't travel anyway." He turned his head to see Catherine standing by her mother.

He extended his hand for Catherine, and she stepped to his side. "I'm so glad I could meet you. It's wonderful you're so close. By American standards, you're almost neighbors." His mind briefly recalled the miles and miles of plains and rolling hills back home. "We've...". He glanced at Catherine, stepped to the side, pulled out the ring and bent his knee. "Catherine, will you be my lifemate, my soulmate, and helpmeet to serve the Lord together? Will you marry me?"

She wiped her eye, reaching for the ring. Dan rose, holding his breath. *Is she ready?* She slipped it on and said, "Yes."

He found himself enveloping her in a hug, though he was too shy to kiss her in front of everyone.

"When?" Sylvia asked.

Catherine smiled. "Well, Ma, thoughts?"

Erin looked at the ring. "It's lovely." She looked at Dan.

"I have to confess. The ring is a gift from the Huttons. It's the one they bought for Catherine."

Miles said, "Well, you have time. Doesn't look like the laws are going to be changed."

"Not that we can see. I have heard they've closed those prisons and have scaled back arresting pastors, but it's still on the books." Dan looked at Catherine. "We'll pray about when to have the ceremony."

They sat for a little bit, discussing the possibilities, letting the family share their ideas.

"You were always one to do your own thing, luv," Erin said to her daughter. "Just give us fair warning to see it happen. I suspect you're going to want it in Dublin."

They smiled. "We'll see where the Lord leads and keep you in the loop," Dan said.

"Loop?"

"He means, we will let you know about arrangements, in a timely manner. Not to worry."

The service at Devlin was sparsely attended, but they were well received. Thet was the center of attention. He rode back with them that night. Dan mulled over the day, still in shock that he was engaged. He would be married, probably sooner rather than later and might even be a father. Reminding himself to trust in the Lord and not worry about future things, he listened to Catherine praise Thet for his message. "It means so much to show that God speaks in many languages—not just Gaelic."

"Or English," Dan added. The spell broken, they talked of the center, the schedules, the cold and demographics of the arrivals changing again.

"Few from Burma. Most go to London," Thet said.

CHAPTER 17

Christine obtained the marriage licenses by the next day. Scheduling a justice of the peace who would officiate in the hospital took a few more days. Scot had to return home, but Alice could stay. She only had to return to the office for a brief time to handle some issues at work.

Butch and Jennie Connors met Alice at the Hutton Center. Butch took in the luggage, waited for Jennie to finish greeting Alice and meet Irma.

"This is Pastor Rick's wife," Alice said, "*The Pastor Rick* from the Rosemont video."

"Oh, now I remember."

"Listen, ladies. Have to run. Meet you at the hospital." He tipped his head to Irma. "Great to meet you. I'm sure we'll have a chance to get acquainted."

"She'll be at the wedding this Tuesday. Just two days away. Remember—ICU, room 7-B."

Irma smiled. "I'm looking forward to it. Well, see you later, young man," she said with a smile.

Jennifer and Alice laughed. They watched Butch walk briskly to the car. "That man always has something going. Ready to go to the hospital?"

Butch found his way to the ICU, headed down the short hall and paused by the glass door for 7-B. Christine sat, reading her Bible. Butch slid the door aside and walked in.

Chris raised her fingers to his lips and walked to him. "Just got him to sleep. I think we're exhausting him."

Butch patted her arm and stepped past. He took in Will's drawn face. The figure on the bed did not resemble the vibrant, active agent he remembered. When Will stirred, he would have stepped forward, but Christine said, "Let him sleep. We can talk in the hall."

Butch asked, "What did they do to him?" He listened tight-lipped to Chris' answer. "Who's the doctor of record?"

"Leeds."

"Okay," he replied then headed for the nurse's station. "Hi, I need to talk with Dr. Leeds."

"And you are?" The nurse looked at him. "The doctor's..."

"There he is, Nancy," the other nurse said with a smile.

Before the nurse could stop him, he approached the doctor. "Dr. Leeds, I'm Butch Connors." He almost said lieutenant with the Bureau of Prisons, but he remembered in time. "Former lieutenant with the BOP. I need to speak with you about Special Agent Masters."

"Who?"

"Masters, 7-B," the helpful nurse added.

"Oh," he looked at Butch.

"Can we?" Connors gestured to a small office off the corridor. "I just had a meeting with the Purcellville warden. How bad is Will?"

"Are you family?"

"Close friend and I have information concerning his facility that you need to hear."

"They brought him in four days ago near death. Not transported in an ambulance but shoved in the back of an SUV. The ER doctor didn't think he'd make it, but they managed to stabilize him. Then his progress stalled. His condition worsened until his friend arrived. What do you have?"

"You need to keep him in the hospital for as long as possible. Prison's hard on the healthy, but for someone in that condition, he's not likely to make it with that warden. Doesn't have a clue about these prisoners. I know because we made the same mistake when they sent them to us at Hannibal. Before Will's abduction, he was leading teams to take down drug smugglers and human traffickers. He's tracked people on snowmobiles, sometimes in a blizzard, and searched for missing hikers on horseback. That man…" Butch tried to keep his emotions in check as he finished, "is the best of the FBI, and he needs some consideration for what he's done to keep the citizens of this country safe from harm." He stepped back. "Wanted you to know that when they ask you to sign off on his transfer."

"What kind of an infirmary do they have?"

"I'm not sure. Didn't get the whole tour. Would your BOP contact have that info?" About to turn away, Butch added, "Don't mention his work with the FBI. If that warden hears of it, he might send him to the super-max. I don't think Will would survive that."

"Wouldn't that be the safest place for him?"

"Physically speaking, but it'd kill his soul. Purcellville is the one prison this side of the Mississippi where he could survive general population. They're all prisoners of faith, serving time for their allegiance to Jesus Christ. They will not harm him. It's the agents and guards I'm concerned about."

"Noted."

"Thanks for hearing me out. I will ask the Lord to give you wisdom."

Dr. Leeds looked sideways at the tall man. After a moment he walked around the desk, turned on the monitor, and found the short video. "This was submitted with his paperwork." He rotated the monitor so Butch could see the video of the team going down a hallway and through a solid door to barred cells.

Butch tried to be objective, but his blood boiled. When the body on the floor did not move, the closest agent kicked Will's side with his boot. Another stepped forward and felt for a pulse. "I don't think Chris needs to see this right now. But can I get a copy?"

"Send an email. Some ribs are fractured or broken. A blow to the wrong place could collapse a lung. Already happened once here." The doctor handed him his business card.

"Does she know?"

"Not sure. He could go either way."

Butch found Christine with Alice and Jennie. "What's up?"

"Making plans," Alice said. "Too bad Scot had to return to Gillette. As head of the newest resident agency, he still has a lot of setup work to do."

"We drove here. Butch, could we drive her home? Scot could show us his resident agency."

"Doable. Hey, need to talk with Chris for a moment."

Jennie nodded. "We have our tasks. Ready, Alice?"

Butch waited until they were on their way to the elevator. "Can he be ready for tomorrow?"

"Hope so. They'll do it in his room."

"Sounds like he has the right doctor. Anyway, Sullivan set up a meet for me with Warden Dailey, Purcellville FPC, this morning. He's the kind who'll ship him out if he learns Will's been in law enforcement. I'm hoping he hasn't looked past the 756 charges."

"Not your favorite warden? Not like Foster?"

"Not even close and definitely not sympathetic to Christians."

"What's Sullivan's price for this access?" Chris asked, the knowing glint in her eye.

"A report. I'd like to meet with some of the inmates." He lifted his brow.

"That can be arranged. You've already met Irma. She'll ask Rick to add you to his visitor list." She sent the text when Butch nodded.

———✎———

The day arrived. Alice and Jennifer helped Chris in the large bathroom across the hall. Butch sat near Will, backing up Dr. Leeds while Will tried to negotiate better terms.

"I need to stand for my wedding."

"Not happening."

Butch added, "He's allowing the ceremony while you have full-blown pneumonia in both lungs. Behave yourself, man. Right now, he's the man."

"You're the good cop and the doctor's the bad cop? Thought I was getting better."

Dr. Leeds crossed his arms. "Not better enough. Those underground prisons harbor dangerous molds and spores. We've seen people come through with strains we don't have medicines for. You're lucky we still have some drugs to work with. Sit up, and be thankful it's happening now. If you want to stand, you'll have to wait until your transfer."

Smiling, Butch said, "And we all know how easy they'd make at an FPC. Clear?"

"Crystal. Thanks, Doc. I do appreciate it, but…"

"This is what you get for waiting so long." Butch couldn't resist the jab.

They turned their heads when they heard voices of people assembling in the hall and the nurses' orders. The justice of the peace was escorted into the room. The doctor made his exit.

Butch surveyed Will's hair. He had been conscripted to make his friend ready with a quick shave and a haircut. It was the best he could do. Butch rose, pushed the chair behind him and straightened his tie, pulling down his sleeves and straightening the cuffs. He smiled when Will winked and sat forward.

Alice emerged in a burgundy dress with black pumps. Jennifer followed in her silver suit. They stepped to the side. Chris stood, beaming, in a long, shimmering cream-pearl gown with a short, jeweled jacket, her hair waved and set with sequined combs that matched the dainty, ivory rose bouquet in her hands.

Two pulled back the curtain and glass door. Fran Shirring stood by the opening, lifted her bow and the strains of the "Wedding March" filled the ICU.

They walked in measured steps, drawing ever closer. The small group of friends held their places by the entrance. U.S. Marshal Doyle lifted a camera.

The justice of the peace stepped from his perch by the short counter in 7-B.

Alice and Jennifer stepped to the side, and Christine reached out to grasp Will's hand.

The sounds of the hymn dying away, Cliff Spencer gave the charge—the blessings of a man and a woman walking together with God.

The justice of the peace stepped through the brief service. Each read their vows, and he announced, "I present to you Mr. and Mrs. William Masters. You may kiss the bride."

They clapped and cheered. The room emblazoned with white and silver balloons, streamers and banner swelled with joy.

Nancy let Alice know the caterer was waiting.

While they were not allowed to come close, they took their turns congratulating the happy couple. The room cleared. Jennifer brought meals for the three in the room. Butch took his and escorted his wife to the group in the waiting room. "I think the nurse is ready to kick us out if we don't let them in for their checks."

Chris sat, holding two plates. She nibbled a little while the nurse went through the standard tasks before smiling slightly and retreating. "Chris," she heard Will say, his voice thin and reedy. Glancing over she saw the darkness under his eyes and heard his labored breathing. She looked at the plate of heavy food. They hadn't thought of what he could eat. "I'll get you some soup and crackers."

Will tried to stop her.

"I'll be right back." She left, delivered the request to Alice and returned, closing the curtains and the door. This was their brief moment. "I'll stay as long as they let me."

Dr. Leeds knocked an hour later.

"Come in, Doctor." Chris caressed Will's hand and turned to face him.

"How are you feeling?" The doctor bent to listen to Will's chest.

"Be honest, Will," Chris said.

"Really can't hide it." Dr. Leeds nodded at the nurse by the counter. "I'll be giving you something to sleep. You need to rest to give yourself time to heal."

"May I stay until he's out?"

The doctor nodded. The nurse lowered the bed a little and pushed the medicine into the IV port.

Chris held Will's hand until he slept. His skin felt hot and papery.

A small group was still in the waiting area. "Thank you, Fran. That was lovely. I didn't know you could play."

She smiled. "He going to make it?"

"That's what I'm praying for."

One by one they talked with Chris and said their goodbyes until only Alice, Jennie and Butch remained.

"Alice, where's my bag?" She accepted the large tote and pulled out her slim laptop. "Butch, I'd like to show you some files I'm working on. Can we talk in that small conference room?" She nodded toward a small room across the hall with a round table and two chairs visible through a narrow window.

She closed the door after they entered. "Tell me if you recognize any of the speakers in this exchange." She played an audio file. When Butch shook his head, she opened a video file for him to see. "And this one?"

"That, along with digital trades, is the evidence used to convict Warden Foster."

Butch laughed. "Seriously? That's not how he talks. And he was the warden. He didn't talk to inmates except maybe on the line, in full view of other officers and residents. They say he made insider trades from comments an inmate told him? You know that's garbage!"

"Why didn't he fight it?"

"Sandra's battle with cancer wasn't going well. She died shortly before he went to Leavenworth. But I think it was the six nonsense investigations against him—an inmate accused him of torture, one fabricated a rape of a female guard, another tried to frame him for embezzlement of commissary accounts. They were crazy accusations he managed to clear because they were internal, and he had the resources to expose the sources. But the SEC charges were a different animal. His lawyer convinced him it was an open-and-shut case. I don't know if the man worked for the Task Force, but he threatened the man with twenty-plus years unless he accepted a deal for three."

"You know the Hutton Foundation is helping jailed believers. The center's a real blessing for the families. The NGO is also working to clear those, like Foster, who were fraudulently prosecuted. Thanks for confirming my suspicions. I'd like to represent him, pro bono, for his appeal. Do you think he'd object to having his case transferred to the D.C. or Richmond courts? That would make it easier for me to attend hearings."

"Have you talked with him? His early release came through. He'd be out soon. It's already done. Why should he bother?"

"But he'd be a convicted felon with extremely limited job prospects and no hope of any career. As his representative with the foundation, I would have access to tools and experts that will be able to discover the true source of the trade orders and where the money came from."

"But wouldn't it be easy to show he never received the funds?"

"The stocks and sales proceeds showed up in his accounts. It was even reported on his tax return."

"Now see here. You and I both know that while we might be able to cite law, quote regulations and administer a large organization, most of us take our tax documents to the accountant, trusting him to report it properly. Shouldn't his financial adviser have caught it?"

"Those investments were through his wife's employer. They barely provided quarterly statements and no personal investment advice."

"Let me talk to him. I'll run down there after I get back. He's set to transition down soon anyway."

"One more thing, Butch. I was thinking of appealing Will's five-year sentence." She waited.

"Not a good idea. It'll cause problems, and the warden might look at his agency record. Five years at Purcellville is the best he's probably going to get. He'd be eligible for up to nine months early release."

"That's not going to fly if they require an apology and remorse with a promise not to reoffend. It burns that Will goes to prison, and Kincaid gets away with sending strike teams to torture and murder!"

"Chris, I know it's hard, but you have to look at the big picture. Will chose to plead guilty. Did he admit he talked to people about Christ?" Seeing the nod, he added, "Leave the vengeance to God. You'll have your day. You both will. In God's eyes, he has done nothing wrong. Maybe, with the elections next year, things will be fixed. But for now, take what you can get. You can visit him regularly. Besides, God can do something with this. Keep the faith." He grasped her hand. "And I'll be praying you can exonerate Foster. He'd be the best choice to head up Purcellville."

CHAPTER 18

CHRIS DROVE IRMA to the Christmas party at Purcellville. It was the Saturday before Christmas, but that didn't matter. "Can't bring a gift though." Chris remembered she had replenished Will's commissary account, and he had recently received Bible study references ordered directly from the publisher.

"Rick always reminds me that visiting is the best present." She dabbed her eye. "Mailed the pictures of the grandkids last week. I hope it's been delivered."

They both shook their heads. It took a while to adjust to being married to a convict.

The pat-downs were slight. The guards wished them a Merry Christmas even though the warden had forbidden holiday decorations. He also adhered to the harsher standards usually restricted to the higher security levels of limiting personal belongings in the dorms. Will had shipped home his extra books to make room for the Bible study aids.

They walked down the familiar hall and opened the doors to the large visiting area. "I'm glad to see so many here," Irma commented.

"Well, the center's full." Chris looked for Will. Thinking he might not have made it to the hall yet, she began to search for an open table. Tiredness soaked through her bones. Sorrow threatened to overtake her. The sounds of family greetings with Christmas songs mocked her. She hadn't even put up her mini Christmas tree or strung any lights around the dining room.

"Chris, Chris," Will called and stepped around several tables to reach her.

"Oh, you're here. I was beginning to fear…" His hug stopped her, and she could hardly wait the week for their monthly visit.

"I have a new podmate. You have to meet him. His family has come to see him." Will led her to a round table surrounded by a large family. "Meet Carlos Rodriguez, his wife Maria, and their children. Carlos?"

Smiling, the short man introduced his four children. "And this is the lovely wife you speak of," he said to Will.

"Did you come far?" Chris asked Maria. "I don't remember seeing you at the center. It has a swimming pool, laundry and a kitchen."

"We drive back after a visit."

"I can send you the details so next time you have a place to stay. It's in town. They should have a brochure in the reception area. Ask for one on your way out." Chris nudged Will. "Let's give them some space."

Will glanced at Carlos who smiled back. "Sure, right." He followed Chris to the refreshment table. The warden couldn't shut down the inmates who staffed the kitchen from baking for the Christmas party.

Chris filled two cups with hot cocoa. Will wrapped cookies and brownies in napkins, and they looked for a place. A lone table in the corner was still free. "What's with your new roommate?"

Will said, "Not a word, but he was in the program, and they sent him to Costa Rica. The in-country contact was a shyster. Carlos practically lived on the streets. He made his way back home, and they hid him. Thankfully, he had destroyed his travel documents before they found him."

"What did they charge him with?"

"Those usual, lovely speech laws. He's a good pastor and a great teacher. Teaching me Greek." They finally sat and looked at one another. Will's eyes lit up with his usual mischievous grin.

"What?"

"What's a fine lady like you doing in a place like this?" He reached over and held her hand. Seeing the shadow cross her face, he said, "I'm sorry. Wrong thing to say."

She tried to hide the tears. Didn't want to say it, but it came out anyway. "I wish you could come home with me and never come back. But..." She wiped the tears, "not to be. Not yet." A day would come. It seemed so long in the future.

"Foster's back with the BOP. Of course, you know that. Connors told me he's negotiating to get his old job back." Will added, "Said you did a superb job overturning his conviction.

"Hannibal?"

"No, Connors has put a bug in his ear for this place. We really need him. This warden gave us some space when I first arrived, but he's pressing to force us to participate with the standard BOP programs—you know like anger management, sex offender programs, and all the rest."

"I thought he approved what you had set up—counseling, reading..."

"Until he looked into what we were really doing—poorly disguised Bible study and doctrine classes. Marriage, family, life skills all from the Word of God. I really think a guard ratted on us, but we're not going there."

"Will, maybe you should cooperate. That way, you'd have some influence. From what I hear, this facility might close if they can't accept enough inmates, right? And there are fewer HCL offenders. There's the occasional one, but more are being released than coming in. What if you could develop the programs to take in those transitioning down, getting short? This group could have a part in shaping the program, embedding Christian principles. This facility is well positioned to help those soon to be released."

"I honestly hadn't thought of it that way." Will smiled. "That's why I love you, Chris."

"Now I'm really offended!" Chris laughed. "You only love me for my brains!"

"No, it's your sparkling personality. I really mean it!"

They turned their heads when three men stood up and shushed the crowd.

"This your thing?" Chris asked in lowered voice.

"Not this time. It's all Pastor Rick, Wren, and Rod. They're the go-to pastors."

Pastor Wren began with praises for God and His constant care. Rod talked about the wonderful gift of God's Son—who came to save the world from sin and despair.

During a call for testimonies, some began to sing praises, hymns and Christmas songs. Without instruments, they sang as one. Chris gripped Will's hand, feeling the joy of the Lord's Holy Spirit, His grace and mercy and love, knowing He would keep her even through this Christmas.

Pastor Rick rose. Before he led the prayer, his eyes scanned the gathering. "Christ said, *If you abide in my word, you are truly my disciples, and you will know the truth, and the truth will set you free.*'

The men listening protested that they were free.

He told them, *So if the Son sets you free, you will be free indeed.*'[6]

"We think we know when we are free, but if we're controlled by sin, we're slaves to that sin—not free at all. Only Christ, through the forgiveness He brought through His blood, can set us free from sin. For we know that if we walk in the Spirit, we will not fulfill the lusts of the flesh, no longer slaves to sin, but free to serve God in truth and righteousness and holiness. This was possible because He was willing to come, be arrested, condemned by His own people. He allowed them to grievously torture and murder Him. All for us. Let us pray."

The prayer flowed from his lips of a thankful, joyful heart. Opening it to others, some stood and gave testimony of the Lord's sustaining grace.

Carlos stood and said, "I want to thank you for encouraging me. Haven't been here very long and I struggled with being marked, feeling I had messed things up. But you have reminded me not to look back but forward, as the apostle Paul said, *'I count everything as loss because of the surpassing worth of knowing Christ Jesus my Lord....But one thing I do: forgetting what lies behind and straining forward to what lies ahead, I press on toward the goal for the prize of the upward call of God in Christ Jesus.'*[7] Please pray for my family, their protection. I thank the Lord for a faithful wife and children, and that I can choose to believe God has a path for me—even if I can't see it right now."

Chris watched Will grip the table, blinking away tears. This was her husband's roommate and her joy rose to Heaven. She almost thought he was going to say something, but others stood. Finally, Pastor Rick raised his hands.

"I'm up," Will said. A resident handed out small bags of what looked like oyster crackers to six residents who circulated through the room, handing out crackers.

Pastor Rick said, "All who have put their faith in Christ are welcome to join this communion service to celebrate our Lord's coming and His ultimate sacrifice. Years ago, at Rosemont after a squad had executed many we knew and loved, a few hours later a kind guard brought crackers—simple crackers like the ones you hold in your hand—and juice." He nodded at the resident in the back who handed small cups to the others and went around putting juice in each one. "I asked Tom Hutton to lead and that guard to pray. We are one in Christ. There is no difference between guard and inmate, man or woman, young or old, and because of the sacrifice He gave, we can love one another, same or different."

Cecil stood, quoting 1 Corinthians 11 from memory and directing the taking of the bread and the cup. Pastor Rick closed in prayer.

Chris watched Will walk back, his face alive, vibrant, and full of joy. "Will," she said when he slipped into the seat, "You're happy!"

"Of course, I have Christ. When I remember to see things clearly, it's easy. Being here, right now and sharing it with you is pure gold."

She looked at him. "Did the Lord tell you something?"

"What? I guess. I mean I pray every day."

"No, did He tell you what He wants you to do, after…you know, when you get out?"

"I want to be a teaching pastor who shepherds his flock and helps them walk with God." Will sat back. That thought had been at the back of his mind. He remembered strands of thoughts blended with hopes and dreams of service far greater than any agency of man could achieve. "This is the answer, Chris, for our country. If we love others as He has loved us, Christ could save our nation. Perhaps this is why He allowed Rosemont. Perhaps, without the Task Force, I wouldn't be here with you, knowing the love, joy and peace of God, and sweet fellowship with other believers. He really does know what He's doing." He held her hand, wishing this night would go on and on and on. "What about you?"

"What about me?"

"Any visions from the Lord? Jeremiah 29:11 leadings?"

Chris thought a moment. "Well, just little things at work and at the center, or the foundation office, but, no, no calling. Not like yours. I'm still waiting." That was the truth. She had prayed about it that morning. "I struggle with working for a government agency, fearing they would someday force me to choose. I can serve both right now. So, I guess if I'm to wait, I make no changes."

"I pray for you every day."

Sounds of chairs being pushed in and people saying goodbye broke through. They watched soft tears with some, others light laughs, but many wistful faces. Chris and Will stared into each other's eyes, held hands and said goodbye, parting for now. "Next week," he said.

"Won't miss it," she replied.

Chris turned and walked to Maria and her children. Carlos was helping the youngest put on his coat. "Maria, follow me, and I'll take you to the Hutton Center. We can register you tonight, and you can make a reservation for your next trip."

"Oh, but…" She looked pleadingly at Carlos.

"I'm sorry, Christine, but we don't have the money."

"I'm sorry I didn't make it clear. There is no charge for families of Purcellville residents. Anyone can leave a donation, but the Hutton Foundation pays for it. I'd like to give you a quick tour." Seeing they wanted to talk about it, she nodded toward the double doors leading to the exit. "I'll wait by the door. No pressure, but we'd like you to see it."

Carlos and Maria met her at the door. "Thank you, Carlos, for teaching Will. He's so excited to learn Greek, especially since his books have arrived."

"It's a pleasure. He learns very quickly. You selected good books."

"I had help. Actually, Will gave me the list." She tilted her head. "Do you have your Greek and Hebrew books?"

"Back at the house."

"Work with your case manager on the procedure for having them accepted as personal items. Each facility has their own rules, but your case manager can tell you how many you can bring in." She added, "When some officers check books, they remove the covers. Just wanted to warn you."

They finished their goodbyes, and Chris and Irma led them out and to the center. Others drove there as well.

As she had hoped, Maria and the children liked the place. Irma found one open room, but she would need a second one. Chris offered hers. Maria accepted. Then Irma invited Chris to spend the night. Now it was her turn to accept hospitality. They found bathing suits for the children and robes for the mothers. Sipping tea, coffee or cocoa, they let the children play in the water before bedtime Bible stories and prayers.

CHAPTER 19

SATURDAY, MARCH 22, AT Miles Walsh's home, Dan buttoned the tan, camel-hair vest. He looked at the dark-blue tie with small, soft-blue dots. He turned his head when Miles walked in.

"You found it! The family bow tie! Promise to tie it on proper."

Dan smiled—for the family and tradition. He lifted his collar and turned to let his soon-to-be brother-in-law form a perfect bow tie. Catherine had also made concessions to family tradition by allowing her mother to refurbish her wedding dress. Of course, they had not allowed him to attend any of the fittings or see his bride for the past few days.

"So, you have survived having to wait months to kiss your bride." Miles patted Dan's shoulder.

He walked to the dresser and surveyed the look. "It will do," he said with muted tone, turning with a broad smile. "Never imagined fair Ireland would require we not only have to appear to register our wedding with the location and officiator selected, but we also had to wait at least three months before we could hold the ceremony."

"Now, now, things are better with age, and they want to make sure you really mean it."

Other restrictions ruled out Cary House and the Hebrew Centre. Discussions with family in Mullingar led to the only reasonable alternative—the Mullingar classic hall (meaning the old townhall that had been converted into a "conference" center), officiated by Pastor O'Malley from their family church.

Miles drove Dan to the hall and to a back room, with dull white paint and one lone bulb in the high ceiling, that was half-filled with folded chairs and tables on racks.

"I see the groom's fitting room has the proper spare essentials."

"The gents make do so our ladies can prepare in style." Miles gestured for Dan to turn full circle. "Just be glad kilts are not in our lineage. Remember, my man, all eyes will be on the lady."

"Quite right." Dan slipped his hand in his pocket to hide a slight quiver.

"All's right here." Miles pulled out the small bag with the rings. "Now for the boutonniere."

Dan walked to the front and waited by Miles, Pastor O'Malley, and Chaim. The ladies had transformed the hall with sprays of white accented by clutches of delicate, blue-tinted lavender flowers. The pianist played Irish hymn arrangements, accompanied by a trio of fiddlers. When all stood, she ended the stanza with an eye to the lead violinist, Catherine's sister. Strains of "Be Thou My Vision" swelled with the ahh of the assembly.

Catherine stood in a light-cream laced bodice. The lace wrapped around the back of her neck. The filigreed pattern continued down the long sleeves reaching to the back of her hands. A light-gold cummerbund outlined her narrow waist. The cream skirt, shining in the light flowed around her and gathered in the back.

Wisps of curled hair framed her smiling face with her long locks, waved and clasped flowing down her left shoulder. Eyes bright, she nodded to Uncle Frank, as they stepped forward with the opening stanza.

Their eyes met as she drew closer. Blushing, she looked down slightly; beaming, he extended his hand as Frank presented the bride. They stood facing each other. Pastor O'Malley spoke. "For such a time as this, God has brought this couple together. For such a time as this, He creates a new family, a new household."

Dan tried to focus on the brief message, but his eyes were only for Catherine. They said their vows and exchanged rings. The pastor led, weaving verses in with the charge to keep the promise to God through the years. Then the announcement. "I present to you, Dr. and Mrs. Daniel Smith. You may kiss the bride."

Cheers went up. Stepping back, not losing their hold of each other's hand, they stepped to the center and up the aisle. Dan beamed again—at his mother in a wheelchair and his father in the second row, seated next to Stella and Charles Hutton.

With music and laughter, Irish stew, biscuits, and cake, the reception chamber across the hall pulsed with life and joy. Catherine's family sat beside her at the long head table and Dan's parents with the Huttons and Chaim on his side.

The various speakers had their say. Dan waited for his turn. Normally, one of his brother's would say something, but that would not be possible. But he had something to say—something God had lain on his heart during the weeks of waiting. After Miles, the elder brother, finished his light-hearted speech, many still wiping their eyes from the laughter, he said with a flourish and a bow, "And the famous Dr. Smith, our very own doctor of Hebrew and the covenants!"

Dan rose with a half-smile. With everyone still laughing, he waited for them to settle. "Thank you for coming to witness one of the happiest days of my life." Not wanting to dissemble, he continued, "The great prophet Jeremiah wrote in 29:11 'For I know the plans I have for you...'" *He could not resist smiling at Catherine.* "declares the LORD, *plans for welfare and not for evil, to give you a future and a hope.'* Many have this famous verse memorized. It is one of the great promises of the Bible, but we have to remember this was first given to a people who had been ripped from their homeland by the Babylonians. In a strange, foreign, hostile land, God told them to have hope. He also told them to build a community, houses, plant, harvest, raise families. He said, *'Build houses and live in them; plant gardens and eat their produce. Take wives and*

have sons and daughter...seek the welfare of the city where I have sent
you into exile and pray to the LORD *on its behalf....*[8]

"Ireland is now my home, and..." He extended his hand to Catherine. She stood by his side. "We will raise a family and seek the peace of your land. I am grateful and thankful for your generosity to welcome strangers fleeing troubles, and for the shelter for as long as the Lord leaves us here." He glanced her way and seeing her nod, he stepped back a little.

"We do not know where our future lies, but wherever God sends us, you will always be in our hearts—a part of us. Thank you for being a part of our special day."

Dan could say and do nothing more but kiss her.

Later, after guests were departing and music lowered, Charles and Chaim found seats near Dan.

"We've been talking," Chaim said.

"Plotting again?" Dan laughed.

"Well," Charles said, "My wonderful Stella has set up a foundation called the Hutton Foundation."

"Of course."

"To help the jailed pastors. She has contacts in Washington, D.C., with lawyers willing to help see justice done. Anyway, I've been thinking of starting my own."

Dan waited. Chaim gestured for the American to continue.

"Faith Hall Foundation—a seminary for the faithful." He added, "For biblical scholarship and pastoral training. It's in its infancy. And Chaim tells me you would be a good candidate for leadership."

"Leadership?"

"President. Would you like that?"

"Well..." Not wanting to be difficult, he furrowed his brow and set his jaw.

"Be honest, Dan. What do you want?" Chaim asked.

"What do I want? For the laws to be rescinded."

"Besides that. Obviously, this isn't going forward until that happens, but pre-planning and having pieces in play will advance the establishment of the institution."

Charles said, "I agree. Would you be interested in having a part of this seminary?"

"Of course, perhaps as chair of an Old Testament studies department. In the beginning, when it's small, I could stand in as academic dean but will want to teach." He leaned forward. "Now that I'm legal, I've been negotiating with nearby universities and Bible colleges for teaching positions. Since the beginning of the year, I have been mentoring my replacements for the refugee outreach program. With Catherine's help managing the IPO side of things, I can find the time to teach."

"And he will be home. Less traveling," Chaim added.

"Yes, that was my initial motivation, but missing the podium and the chance to confuse students with jots and tittles has spurred my motivation." He added, "I would be honored to be a part of your foundation and the restoration of biblical halls of learning. From the ashes of 756, God can rebuild."

Charles extended his hands to Dan and Chaim. "During that brief time with Tom, he shared with me the vision of God rebuilding the church in America—not by copying what went before, but allowing the Lord to lead in reshaping the church for the America of today, not the one enshrined in the last century. To raise up churches that embody John 13:34-35—the Lord's charge to love one another so that the world might know Jesus lives, and He lives in us."

"*Faith Hall,* interesting. What does this name mean to you, Charles?" Dan asked.

"I didn't want to hamper the Lord's leading by bending it toward any group or persuasion. Hebrews 12:1 talks of a *'cloud of witnesses.'*

That's the name of the foundation. The name of the seminary will be decided when it forms." He sat back.

"I have to ask the question." Chaim laid a gentle hand on Dan's shoulder. "Is my friend brave or in denial? What are the risks facing him? Will they send another team here?"

Charles shrugged his shoulders. "Not sure. Hard to read. I'm not a news junkie." He hesitated to affix that label to his wife. Hesitating to ask her, he said, "Don't know."

Dan smiled. "Let's ask Mac, Catherine's younger brother." He added, "Earlier this year Catherine asked him to check it out, and we met to discuss if I was taking the proper precautions. You, my friend, are not the first person to ask." He spotted the tall, thin man in his twenties chatting gaily with a group of young women. "Ah, the friendly chap. I'll fetch him."

Mac pulled up a chair across the table. "Well, to the matter of a hit team coming here from the Task Force—the possibility is close to nil. According to reports the Task Force enforcement arm has been stripped and most of its teeth pulled. Weekly arrests are in the single digits."

"But what about their off-book prisons? Maybe they have rotated to abducting people and holding them without charges." In response to Mac's surprise, Dan said, "Tom was tortured for three weeks…" He remembered Charles was there. "Sorry, sir."

"No, you're right. Of course, there are no reports about these kind of activities, but I do know a federal task force is hunting down the perpetrators and closing the hidden prisons. There are news reports every week about the ones found. Too often, by the time they arrive, all prisoners are already dead."

"Low-level," Dan mused. "What's being done about the leadership? If they're not dealt with, they can crawl out of their holes in later years and start it all over again."

"That is the never-ending war against sin that will always be with us. But, as best we can, we can at least deal with the groups operating today. A special prosecutor is leading that investigation. It's been ongoing since last year. However, it's carried on behind closed doors. There's no media coverage, and they say all the indictments will be sealed until they are ready to arrest everyone." Charles shook his head. "This is an election year for the current president's replacement. At his second term, he's looking to prolong his control with a close associate."

"Glad I'm not having to hear that every day."

"It fills our news feeds here too," Chaim noted.

"The opponent's not been selected quite yet, but the favored candidate has hinted he will deal with the problem."

"Hinted?" Dan could not mask his disappointment.

"I'm sure Stella knows more about this than I do, but the sense is he's stepping lightly—at least for now. Gone are the days where a Christian candidate could win and where a nominee is helped by standing up for traditional faith."

"So, Mac, your assessment of my risk is…"

"Fair, not likely to face an attack, but I wouldn't make plans to go home soon. Elected in November, but doesn't take office until…"

"Early the following year. The makeup of Congress will determine the success of legislative attempts to reverse the 756 laws."

"Couldn't they dismantle the Task Force? Make it hard for them to pursue infractions?" Chaim asked.

"Not sufficient. Christians would be waiting for the country to turn against them. Those with felony convictions could never be cleared. Keeping it in play would only ensure a reinstituted Task Force could surface again in the future. No, my foundation won't be going forward with this plan until we have a new president willing to sign on to an aggressive 100-day plan." He paused, then added, "The best presidents, like Reagan, accomplished their greatest achievements within the first 100 days of their administration—while they had the momentum and support."

Dan nodded in agreement. "Our prayer. But God will lead us come what may." He turned to Charles. "Thank you again for our reservations at Ashford Castle." He and Catherine were overwhelmed by the Huttons' gift of three days and two nights at one of Ireland's premier resorts in a restored castle with all the modern amenities.

"And you're planning on returning to Dublin?" Chaim asked. "Just checking."

"Of course. You approved my holiday."

"And we will take great care of your folks. Introduce them to our wonderful metropolis."

"Well, do you know where Catherine is?" Ready to slip away, Dan said his goodbyes and went in search of his bride.

CHAPTER 20

WILL FINISHED FOLDING the load of towels, trying not to let his sweat soil them. The on-duty guard loved to find ways to keep them back until they were late for count or a call-out with an officer. A glance over his shoulder showed the guy was busy chatting with the new clerk. He parked the tall cart loaded with fresh towels and headed down the hall to the building's exit, preparing himself for a cold wind.

End of March, early April still had its chill, but nothing like the cold of January. The year seemed brutal in every way. Scampering between buildings without winter gear, he reminded himself running would bring another infraction. He'd already missed two visits with Chris and had just had his phone privileges returned.

Building 2 housed the kitchen, dining room, and infirmary. The mail facility was in Building 3 and the commissary in 4. Navigating between them meant a walk out in the open—rain or shine or heat or snow.

Will shook his head. The nitpicky rules were more than an annoyance. What really bothered him was his inability to move up the ranks as he had done everywhere else. In the beginning, friends with Pastor Rick, he assumed he'd have an office job by now. However, the first warden adhered strictly to seniority for inmate jobs. The Holy Spirit whispered he needed to wait, in the right time, but Will pushed away that thought.

The tile floor, slippery with his wet shoes, nearly sent him skidding. He stopped shy of the main entrance to the dining hall. The line was backed up, and it looked like he'd be at the end of it. Something caught his attention on the warden's line. Choosing his moment, he glanced over. Connors was standing next to the warden on the line. *What is he doing here?*

Warden Foster stood with his executive team three days a week during the lunch meal. Any inmate could talk to him directly about a request or complaint. Will had only seen the other warden stand on the line one time. Foster made himself accessible, but from the beginning he had let it be known not to bother him with frivolous complaints or ridiculous requests.

Things had been easier the year before. Starting with the new year, residents ready for the programs had been transferred in. Will had taken Chris' idea about developing programs for other inmates to Chaplain Rick; he couldn't complain about Rick holding that job. The man had tact and an innate sense in how to influence the administration. He tried to forget the fact that he had been shut out of any part of the development. Instead, he had worked in the kitchen until he had been falsely accused of hiding a shiv in the kitchen and was demoted to the laundry in February. He had hoped working the laundry would be better, but the duty guard was on his case for every little thing from day one. Will tried not to be paranoid.

On top of the problems with the guards, Will had no idea how to straddle the gulf between the inmates from the death camps and those who had signed on to the programs. The mix of doctrinal disputes with outright resentment between the two groups were creating divisions between brothers in the Lord. *Is this how it's always been?* Will wondered. Separating into groups, picking sides, and counting coup meant most were missing opportunities to be a testimony to the other inmates. Will had to admit that he was often too tense to notice an opportunity until the moment had passed. Rick did what he could, but there were too few like him.

As he had understood, most in the prison camps were on their best behavior, not wanting to ruin their early release packages. Many who were transitioned down from higher levels were short—*transients* he'd heard them called by others. Will tried to settle his breathing. It was too early in the day to allow himself to look forward to seeing Chris tonight. He prayed that she could make the trip.

The line slowly worked its way closer to the serving line. Will glanced over again at the same time Connors looked at him. They had been friends for years. Often, Will had been the team lead or in a position of some authority. Today he took in Connors' hard look and steady gaze. A knot formed in his belly. *We are friends no longer.*

Will looked away, focusing on anything but the warden's line. He had to keep it together. He had to see Chris tonight, and prayers went up that she could come.

By the time he filled his plate, most of the tables were full with no open seats near his friends. Will spied the lone empty table. Three moved to join him from another table. He nodded in their direction and resisted the urge to slide down to give them space. Perhaps he could try to connect. He didn't recognize any of them from his former casework.

The wiry, skinny guy looked at him. "New?"

"No, you're the new ones."

"So short you don't want to know our names?" The man blew through his teeth and trash-talked the worship leaders.

Will forced himself not to react. He shrugged his shoulders. "Figure you're the short ones. How short?"

"Nine months. Here to finish up my programs, one last run with the review board, and I'm out."

"Early release?"

"Some, some."

"Better than nothing." Will analyzed the guy without staring at him. Small, wiry, scruffy, with shifty eyes, broken nails and stained hands. "What's your job?"

"Maintenance." His smile revealed gaps between his teeth. "On the short list for *pigeon duty*."

Will nodded. *Pigeon duty* meant scrubbing the walkways. A boring but one of the better paying jobs.

"You?"

"Laundry," he tried to say it like that's where he always wanted to be.

"That's got to be the lowest paid job." He guffawed.

Will nodded.

"What'd you do?"

Will looked at him directly and said, "Crimes. I'm a criminal just like you."

The man collected himself but didn't erupt. A good sign. "How long you have?"

"Too long." Seeing the man expected an answer, he said, "Five years, and I've been in only four months, so I have a-ways to go."

"It'll go by fast."

"Really? Doesn't feel like it from here."

"Get out of the laundry," the man said, along with a string of curse words.

Will set down his fork and straightened his back. He was almost double the man's size. Why wasn't he talking about his faith or sharing that he was a religious prisoner? For some reason, it seemed as if he should just leave. Will began to eat as quickly as possible, not that he was looking forward to two more hours in the laundry.

"You look familiar." When Will didn't respond, the man said, "Been at Oakdale USP?"

"Seen Hannibal."

"This still beats that."

"Yes, it does."

"What'd you do? Embezzle?" His mocking smile bore hints of malice.

Will said with a straight face, "Terrorism."

"Cool."

Will breathed, finished the last bite and rose, but the way the men looked at him set his teeth on edge. Reminding himself to stay focused, he made it to the laundry in time.

Once he was released for free time before count and mail call, Will sat on the edge of his bunk and pulled out his box of books, notebooks and paper. Each day he read and studied the Bible more and interacted with others less. His hunger to learn tamped down growing feelings of isolation and loneliness. Carlos' advanced Bible class was over for the week. Maybe he could ask his questions after supper before visitation.

Boredom was as much a hurt that needed to be dealt with as the isolation from those who cared about him. Fighting the afternoon lethargy, he walked his little area that he shared with Pastor Rick—he still called him that—as he went through his verse memory exercises. His thirst to know more, to understand, overcame everything else—a good way to shut out the reality of his new life.

Eventually, Rick arrived. They stood for count. Hearing nothing, he sat through mail call. Walking with Rick, he joined his usual table, trying to ignore the group that seemed to watch his every move.

Rick walked with Will to the visitor's center, but he was turned away. It was a Thursday. Chris often worked late Thursday to have time to visit Friday evening and Saturday. Deep despair overtook him, and he exerted his will to turn and head for the phone banks. Some feeling told him this would be the last night for a while and he had no idea why.

Digging his hand into his pocket, he worked at not swearing aloud. He always called when she couldn't visit. She'd be expecting his call, but his phone card was back in his locker. Turning around, he headed along the lit walkway back to Building 5—his dorm.

Will heard a scuffle behind him and turned sharply. A flying arm knocked him off the sidewalk but didn't take him down. He recognized the wiry fellow and his two companions. Seeing no one about, he said, "Excuse me, just on my way back," trying to let the man know he could get off easy if they just pretended it had been an inadvertent collision.

"We know you. You're Masters, former FBI."

He was ready for them. The short guy came at him first, and he tossed him aside. He dodged the next fist, grabbed the arm and hurled him into the third. By that time the small guy was on his feet and running at him. Will twisted and let the man run into his fist. He said, "You can keep trying, but we don't want to be noticed, so don't mess with me, and your early release will go along as planned."

Ignoring his suggestion, they planted a few hits before Will took them down. Focusing on the altercation, he didn't hear the guards' whistles or realize a squad had approached. When a hand grabbed his shoulder, he dropped slightly, twisted around, grabbing the fingers and flipped the guy before he realized it was a guard. Game over.

It took three to secure the ones who had attacked Will. Two worked on taking Will to the ground. He spat out the grass, feeling his world collapse. He was made. The inmates had recognized him, and he was headed back to the DU, the hole, the detention unit—this time to stay and not just receive a write-up for infractions. His heart sank, knowing it might be months before he would be allowed to see or talk with Chris.

Three days later Will sat in his single cell with a solid door. The fact he had a shelf with a thin pad, his personal items, a toilet-sink, a shelf, a stool, and that the cell was not thirty feet underground was the only improvement over the Task Force cells. And the food was better, but he was still hungry.

He stared at the bag of personal items. They had dropped them off the night before. Sighing, he realized he wouldn't be sharing a space with Rick either. Five months. He had no idea how he would cope. To burn off the adrenaline, he dropped and did a hundred pushups, found a way to do pull ups and any other calisthenics he could think of.

Finally, tired enough, he unpacked the bag and set the books on the floor. He had the sheets for the Greek and Hebrew, but only had a Greek interlinear. *No more Hebrew for half a year.* He looked at the theology book. Hadn't that been Rick's? He said a quick prayer for the man. Even in the dim light, he could read the Bible through. He had wanted to, but the little chores, line-ups and work duties seemed to fritter away his best hours.

Okay, Lord, I can read Your Word. Help me focus and... He dropped his head in his hands, despair threatening to overtake him again.

He tried not to remember his brief time with the lieutenant heading up the DU. No hearing to speak of with no chance to explain. Upon admission, rules were stated, and participating in a fight, even if you were attacked, required time in detention. Loss of privileges could happen by being late for a recreation activity you had signed up for and forgotten about or being late for count or for any number of reasons. Sometimes he felt the guards made up rules to take away commissary, phone or personal visits. He'd seen them confiscate items or destroy them.

Will drew out his copy of the A&O Handbook—all the rules and regulations the guards were supposed to follow. He would appeal his five months. He requested the forms when they came by with lunch.

They didn't just cuff him up when they pulled him to see the lieutenant about his appeal—they put on a full set, belly chain and all, tightening the chain between his feet. Forced to shuffle, he worked on staying upright.

Lieutenant Wade sat at a long table. Will's handwritten appeal was before him.

"Don't I get a hearing with another officer, sir? You..."

"Accommodations too easy for you?" He grabbed the paper, ripped it into eight pieces, stood, and dropped it into a trash can. "Send him to the hole." Smiling, he added, "Deputy Director B. Reynolds sends his regards. You don't like it? Ask for a transfer and where would you go, G-man? That's right, I'm filling out an order right now to send you to Atlanta USP. Medium's probably a better fit for those who start a fight."

"They attacked me first!"

"Really? Doesn't look like it from the results—three on one, you come out smelling like a rose, and they're marked up? Who's going to believe you, con?" He stepped close to breathe in his face. "Maybe medium's not a good fit either. That's right. You'd have to request protective custody. Hey, better maybe Florence ADX, the supermax. You pick."

Will, stunned, was speechless. *So, I have been targeted.*

"Nothing heard. Take him away. Oh, Masters, you're not going to survive your five years with us. Barrie says hi."

He felt the restraints wear through the socks. But they didn't remove the hardware once they pushed him into the empty box cell with a hole in the floor. Curling up in the corner, he replayed what Wade had said. B. Reynolds was Barrie, his old nemesis at the Task Force. *So, did Kincaid change his mind and is finally going to eliminate me or is Barrie going off on his own again?*

In an instant, he knew in his soul. It was up to God. They could do nothing unless God allowed it. There would be no books, no personal items, no luxuries in the hole. He bent his head and reviewed his memory verses and tried to pray.

Friday afternoon Chris called Butch. She knew he was at work, but she couldn't wait. "Butch, what happened? Will hasn't called in a week. Did he..." Her voice caught, and she forced back the tears. She could not afford to lose it—not with Associate Warden Connors.

"He picked a fight and is in the DU."

"Will doesn't pick fights! Butch, you know him. He's too smart to do something like that!"

"Chris, people change in prison. You do know he's been flouting the rules."

"I am well aware he has been charged with numerous infractions," Chris said, her voice tight.

"I read the report. He took out three on the walkway to his dorm. He's uptight. Sometimes they snap."

"Okay, so how long will he be in detention?"

"Five months."

"Five months! Butch, please, look into it."

She heard his response, but she knew he wouldn't do much. His last statement sent a chill through her heart.

"Listen, Chris, on the inside, I'm the associate warden and can't be seen to play favorites."

She ended the call. Resisting the urge to talk with Irma, she turned back to her day and the six-month plan to retool the training schedule. Focusing, she studied the chart. They were just shuffling the pieces. The real problem was the training itself—it needed the overhaul. She had the time now. Before she left work, she downloaded all the documents and outlines to review that night.

Officer Klueyer had observed the lieutenant's remarks but had not heard the instructions to the officers who had brought prisoner 13678 to the hole. An hour later he stepped through the two doors leading to the inner detention unit and stopped by the guard's mini-office. The TV was blaring, but he couldn't allow himself to be sidetracked. He scanned the board, saw Masters was in cell 8 and headed down the range. He reached the door and pulled back the small window covering to peer in. *Too dark to really see,* he thought he spied a shape in the corner.

"13678, appear," he said.

Will uncurled and tried to stand. Eventually, he worked his way up leaning against the wall. The steel shackles cut through his skin with each step. He stood in front of the door, three feet away, head down. *What more can they do to me?*

"Who's Barrie and Reynolds?"

"Task Force Deputy Director Barrie Reynolds."

"What does that tell you?"

"That this was a targeted attack. They approached me in the dining hall yesterday, but I hadn't recognized them. I assume they were told about my former positions. This was planned all along."

"And you were attacked?"

"I'd swear to it. At first, I tried to let it go, take the hit, but they refused the offer." He lifted his head. "I had to prove I could defend myself. Will Warden Foster sign off on that transfer order?"

"Did you make a copy of your appeal?"

"Yes, it's in my notebook. I wrote it there first, with the revisions. I can recreate it from that." Seeing the officer shut the small window, Will's heart sank again. *How can I manage with a full set on in a jumpsuit?* The man's footsteps faded away. Will visualized his walking down the hall through the four doors and out into the fresh air. Shivering, he leaned against the wall until the cold forced him to pace slowly.

Officer Klueyer walked back to the guards' office. "It's your lucky day. Take a break, then do the hourly checks on wing 4." He picked up the phone, his fingers hovering over the lines. Gathering his courage, he dialed the warden's direct line. "Warden Foster, this is Officer Klueyer in the DU. There's something you need to see."

"What is it?"

"Violations by Lieutenant Wade. He ripped up an appeal. Refused to forward it to Lieutenant Ries and ordered a man put into cell 8 with a full set on."

"And you didn't take this to Associate Warden Connors?"

"I didn't know who to trust, sir. Wade intimated he was taking orders from a Reynolds. 13678 says he's with that Task Force."

"Thank you for bringing this to my attention. Next time, take it to Connors. You can trust him. Now, hold your post until an investigation team arrives."

"Yes, sir. Thank you. I took this camp to get away from such abuses."

"Understood, and I indicated when I came here that we would not tolerate violations. You did the right thing. Do you have the names and numbers for the officers involved?"

"I do. Have his file right here with the officers on duty at the time."

"Excellent. Make sure Associate Warden Connors receives the file."

The warden set down the phone. Not surprised, a little disappointed, but maybe there was still time to hope. Now he would see if Connors could rise to his new position. He punched the second line and lifted the handset. "Connors, get in here."

Butch walked in from the adjoining office.

"What's up with Masters?"

"Sir?" He sat in the hard chair in front of the warden's desk.

"Well? Tell me about Masters. He doing okay?"

"Sir?"

"Why does he have so many disciplinary orders against him? Have you checked them out?"

"No, Wade's a good man. Has a clean record. Just looks like Will's changed. They did pump him full of drugs and almost killed him."

"Of course, he's changed. He's a convicted felon with years yet to serve in a very dangerous place for someone with his background. Now investigate. Officer Klueyer is waiting for a team to assess and record violations against inmate 13678. Remember, Butch, Johnson had my back at Hannibal. I expect you to do the same here. Something's brewing, and it's going to blow if we don't take the right measures. And I'm not referring to tightening the screws or putting the officers through the ringer. Find out what the real issues are and come up with solutions that will restore the delicate harmony of Purcellville. Have I made myself clear?"

"Yes, sir."

―――――∝∞∞∞―――――

Connors printed out a summary of the disciplinary actions against 13678, assembled his team of six and entered the wing. "Officer Klueyer, Warden says you have something for me." He listened to Klueyer's description. Trying to hold an open mind, they stood in front of 8. "Open it. 13678, come out."

Upon hearing the many footfalls and the dim voices, Will prepared himself. He stood, trying not to sway. Thankfully, he was still close to the door. Shuffling out, he tried to avoid Connors. He saw the flash of camera lights as they documented his condition.

Connors, his face rigid, straightened his back. "Remove the shackles. Take him to the infirmary and hold him for a complete workup by the doctor."

"Only the physician assistant's in on Fridays," Klueyer said.

"Have him do the workup." He gave assignments to the team and followed Klueyer out to the DU admin section. "Come with me. We're going to have a chat with Ries." *Delegate, I have to remember to delegate.* He wasn't head of the Detention Unit anymore. He outranked Ries. After Klueyer repeated the story for Lieutenant Ries, Connors said, "I want a report of findings on my desk by Monday with recommendations for the officers involved." His lips curled. Ries nodded.

Connors stepped out in the brisk air, tamping down his inclination to talk directly with Will. He couldn't risk the chance he might be tempted to show favoritism.

―――――∝∞∞∞―――――

Will curled up on the ledge of a tiny holding cell in the infirmary. They had taken pictures and given him a gown but hadn't allowed him to wash. His skin still crawled, thinking of the filthy cell he'd been in. *Is this a good sign or are they expediting my transfer?* Fear, sorrow, self-loathing and anger swirled.

"Be thankful," he heard himself say. Recalling the many verses the Holy Spirit brought to his remembrance, he quoted, *"Giving thanks always and for everything to God the Father in the name of our Lord Jesus Christ,"* and *"Rejoice in the Lord always; but in everything by prayer and supplication with thanksgiving let your requests be made known to God."*[9] Prayers to God for Chris, her peace, and his future poured out. He tried to surrender to whatever God had for him, but the fears rose up like a tsunami. The phrase *"abounding in thanksgiving,"* popped into his head, along with, *"Rejoice always, pray without ceasing, give thanks in all circumstances; for this is the will of God in Christ Jesus for you."*[10] The tears flowed along with wordless prayers—beseeching the Holy Spirit to intercede for him as it says in Romans 8:26.

Time stretched out into eternity. Captured by his inner tension, he fought against a threatening panic that the Task Force could destroy him at any moment—like a cat playing with a mouse, prolonging the agony until the lethal bite. *Think on the good things. Rejoice in the Lord!* His mood oscillated back and forth, and forth and back until the door swung open, causing him to jump in his own skin.

The examination by the physician's assistant was thorough and took a while. He began to shiver, and his head felt dizzy. It seemed as if Connors hovered right beyond the privacy curtain. He heard the questions and soft answers from the assistant. The man entered and checked his lungs for the third time. "Yes, there is a difference. Less air movement in the left lung," he heard the assistant say. "Hold him for observation," was followed by the footfalls of hard leather shoes.

Connors was gone by the time the inmate pushed back the curtain. Will smiled. "Cecil, may I shower? Am I going back to the hole?"

"You're staying here for observation. This way," the older man, a former resident of Rosemont, helped him rise and walk to the shower.

"Where are my clothes?"

"Not yet. Once you're out of observation. You're stuck with the gowns for now."

Will felt the shower restore him a little and clear his head. When Cecil returned to take him to his assigned place, he asked, "Please tell Pastor Rick to pass on the message to Chris—and not in any way they can trace. Half the guards in here are taking orders from Kincaid and Barrie. They're going to get me transferred to a supermax—Atlanta." He described the attack.

Cecil nodded. "Sure thing. And, Will, don't forget to look up. See beyond the walls to the heavenlies."

"Thanks." Will laid down on the bed. Cecil brought the curtains around and returned a short time later with hot soup and crackers.

"You good for now?"

Will nodded. He smiled when Cecil placed a Bible on the patient tray. "Thanks."

The only finding, elevated blood pressure, was entered into his file by the assistant the next morning. "You'll see the doctor when an appointment's set up. Look for the callout." And he was escorted back to Building 6, the DU, but they put him in a small interrogation room. The door closed shut as if it would never open again. The blood pounded in his throat. He worked to keep his heart from racing. A middle-aged man walked in.

"13678," he said, taking the seat near the door, and opened a file. He began to question Will about his first infraction.

"Who are you?"

"Lieutenant Ries. Associate Warden Connors has ordered me to investigate your file. How well you cooperate will determine where you'll end up." Taking a breath, he started again.

Will tried to answer objectively, admitting breaking the rules, even when it wasn't intentional, but he refused to acknowledge he had planted a shiv in the kitchen or verbally abused an officer. He insisted he had been attacked and had defended himself. Ries showed no emotion and seemed bored with it all. Forcing himself to focus only on the questions and not be tripped up by wild theories, he repeated what Lieutenant Wade had said to him. The lieutenant circled back, repeating or rephrasing questions. The mental gymnastics helped Will focus on trying to speak the truth and nothing more.

They put him in a holding cell for the weekend.

Chris received a call from Irma Saturday afternoon with the message from Will. Biting her lip, she thanked her for the information, but she was still at a loss for what to do. Taking a chance, she left her office and drove to the Connors' apartment on the south side of Purcellville. She hoped Jennie would be home and had no idea what she should say to Butch. Vacillating whether to share the whole story with Jennie, she prayed again for wisdom and headed for the third-floor apartment. It was understandable they hadn't invested in a house in this area. The cost of housing had skyrocketed in northern Virginia.

"Hi, Jennie," Chris said. "Can I see you for a minute?" She spied the vacuum in the dining area. "Sorry, didn't mean to interrupt."

"Not at all. Cleaning's not my favorite job."

"Thanks." She accepted the coffee and found a seat in the living room. "Is Butch in?"

"He's at the gym, trying to get back into shape."

"How's it going being back in?"

"He loves it, but I think we had forgotten about the stress. Funny, how we had assumed a camp would be easier than a penitentiary."

"Just different problems, I imagine, but stuff still happens." Her eyes surveyed the gracefully decorated living room and comfortable furniture. Jennie was always the delightful hostess. "How are you adjusting, Jennie?"

"Finding places to volunteer. Looking for ways to share Christ. There's a good church not far from here."

"Funny how it all works out," Chris mused. She couldn't tell Jennie. It wouldn't be fair. "I have to talk with Butch. When do you expect him to return?"

"Anytime. Can you stay for supper?" Jennie's face was open and friendly.

Hating to dampen her spirits, she said, "Sure, if Butch's okay with it."

"Oh, it's about…" Seeing Chris' nod, she sat closer and hugged her.

Taken by surprise, Chris could not hold back her tears.

"I can't imagine what he's going through right now, but every day I pray for both of you."

"Listen, Jennie, I'll leave it up to Butch for what to tell you, but do know things are not good for Will right now." She turned aside to blow her nose. "Anyway, find any good books lately?"

"Not since the move. It's been a whirlwind coming East. I can see why Will never wanted to come back. But it's a real mission field."

"Sometimes when you've lived in a place for a long time, it's easy to miss the opportunities." They talked of ordinary things, skirting weightier issues.

Butch arrived home a short time later. "Chris, I didn't know you were coming." He stopped, gauging the look on her face.

"Hi, honey. I've asked her to stay for supper—that is, if that's all right with you."

"Of course, why wouldn't it be?" He watched Chris' set face.

"Great, I'll let you two talk." Jennie disappeared into the kitchen.

Chris stood by the couch. "I heard the Task Force is trying to get Will shipped out to a supermax. Did they try to have him killed?"

Butch set the gym bag down by the door. He glanced at Chris. "Being in the same facility is harder than I thought."

"Tell me about it."

"Look, Foster's on top of this. Ordered a full investigation, and he's been cleared by the physicians."

"What happened?"

Butch met her gaze. "He was in a fight. They said Will had instigated it."

"Butch! That's not Will."

"Really? His frequent detentions seemed to point to an inability to think clearly. Chris, the drugs and the torture seem to have made him unstable."

"You're wrong." She covered her face and turned away. She picked up her purse, remembering Jennie had put her coat in the closet. "That's it then. I'll be filing that appeal on his behalf. Obviously, you don't have his back."

"Chris, take a breath. We're taking another look at the fight and the other infractions. I had no idea the Task Force could reach him there."

"Boy, you forgot quickly! Did you forget about Foster, about what was done to HCL prisoners in Hannibal, as well as other prisons, because of Task Force influence? Do you deny your part in some of what was done to Hutton there?" Chris turned again, shaking her head. "I'm sorry, Butch. That was uncalled for. I know you've changed."

"Chris, when it was reported that some of the officers were doing similar things, we launched an investigation. I'll pursue it until I find the truth."

"It's been two months since our last conjugal visit. His phone and visiting privileges were just restored last week, and now I hear he's in the DU for five months!"

"He submitted an appeal." Butch stared at her.

"I need to be informed."

"I'll make sure a letter goes out once we've completed the full investigation."

"Is he okay?" She knew better than to ask for a visit, seeing the conflict in Butch's face—reminding herself this was hard on him too.

"He's stable and in a safe place," he repeated.

Chris ran through the slim facts she had learned. Will had been attacked. His injuries were serious enough to send him to the infirmary.

However, she did believe that if Will had sustained serious injuries, he would have been sent to the nearest ED. She nodded.

Monday Butch stopped by later in the day to check on Will. Everything seemed fine, and his personal items had been returned. Butch informed the guards that Will would be kept in the single cell near interrogation for the near future. He lost the nerve to speak with his former friend.

Lieutenant Ries sent a message that the report was ready. Connors told him to come over and present it.

Lieutenant Ries arrived with copies of the report and his recommendation. Since his first talk with Foster, the warden had reminded him again to make sure not to create problems with enforcing minor rules too strictly. "They're tools that allow us to take action, but we don't want to discourage them from cooperating." It had been quite the lecture. Butch was still feeling his way with the different dynamics of a prison camp, instead of the penitentiaries he had worked in. Now the warden expected him to keep tabs on disciplinary methods, making sure they hit the sweet spot.

"I find two infractions stand, but three seem to be frame-up jobs. That shiv in the kitchen could have been planted by anyone. The witnesses for the others had large sums added to their accounts shortly after the incidents. And," Ries laughed as he continued, "the three at first stuck to their story, but I pushed back. They turned on each other fast. I'd say they were waiting for him on that walkway and thought they'd have an easy time taking him down."

"The goal?"

"Get him transferred out if he didn't survive the attack. Either way, it was a calculated hit." He shifted. "Since we can't return the lost privileges, my recommendation is release him back to general pop and call it even. I looked into his history. He could have taken them out, but he didn't. For the officers and Lieutenant Wade, I recommend summary dismissal without recommendations for transfer. I recommend Lieutenant Brackston look at the officers working the laundry. According to 13678, they deliberately kept him late to force writeups, which did happen a few times."

Butch nodded. "I'll forward the recommendation." He paused, seeing Ries' look of surprise. "The warden asked to hear final recommendations. I agree with you. I'll let you know what he says. Prepare the official release from DU and post it. I'll approve it once his new bunk assignment comes through from his case manager."

Connors headed for Foster's office with the interim report. The other issues would be harder to solve. Foster agreed to the recommendation, and Connors approved the transfer and staff dismissals, sending a task to the case manager.

He headed to the chaplain's office and program wing in Building 4. Rick was helping a group with a lesson in a nearby classroom. Connors stuck his head in. "Have a moment, Chaplain?"

"Certainly, help each other out and don't forget to save your work in the computer." Rick led Connors to his office and unlocked the door. "What can I do for you?"

"Have a task from the warden," Butch sat in the comfortable chair by Rick's desk. "We're hearing there's some tension between many of you. I'd like to hear from you about causes and possible solutions."

Rick nodded. "I'm glad you brought this up. We have been praying about this for a while. It wasn't unexpected."

"How so?"

"Some of us didn't cave to the new laws—not even under threat of death or torture. Others signed onto the program, turning in friends, neighbors and others pastors. You know what the Task Force did when they came to arrest us, often choosing to shoot first and ask questions later. Hiding us away for weeks at a time. We still haven't located or accounted for all the missing."

Butch nodded. This he knew.

"Now, there have always been divisions over doctrine and matters of practice."

"I'm finding that out."

"Added to that are the differences between those who compromised and those who didn't at great cost. It's easy to be bitter or resentful when we know we've suffered more, and they seem to be given the same consideration. You know, those months they had Will didn't even help him with his sentence. It's like the wicked win, and we pay the bill in the end. You can imagine the temptation to lash out, and the collaborators are easy targets.

"But I praise the Lord for this opportunity to hold to the path Christ provides. This problem is not isolated to the prisons, but already exists on the outside. It's easier to cover up, easier to explain away, but here it's obvious—forcing us to choose to follow the path of love Christ calls us to embrace.

"So, my recommendation for your administration is to house us together. Break up the cliques that are forming and put collaborators with the rest. Make each pod a mixture of both. At the same time, we will remind them of John 13:34-35. Do you know it, Butch?" Seeing the shake of his head, Rick pulled out a Bible and read, '*A new commandment I give to you, that you love one another: just as I have loved you, you also are to love one another. By this all people will know that you are my disciples, if you have love for one another.*'

"It's natural to want things to be fair, but from our limited point of view, God fails that standard too. He calls one to die for Him, like Tom Hutton; He allowed me to survive Rosemont and lifted me up to this office, for which I am extremely grateful. It's Satan's lie that we should take issue with how things work out for us. And if we can't find unity here in this place among those of us who decided at some point to stand up for God and His Word, why do we think we can have unity out there? But if we can find a way in Christ to love one another the way He calls us to, if we can learn to put that love into action, and if we can worship Him in spirit and in truth as members of the body of Christ, perhaps in coming days, we can have a part of God doing a work in His church.

"I dream of a living, vibrant church that lives love for one another and the community and that we build up the faithful so they do the ministry, hearing the Lord's Spirit telling them how they can love their neighbor." Rick lifted his left arm as he looked at Butch. "It will have been worth it all." Seeing Connor's tears, he handed him a box of tissues.

"So, my friend, that is my prayer and proposal. Do you think the warden will go for it?"

Butch laughed at the mischievous smile and boy-like joy in the man's eyes. "But what if it doesn't work?"

"It doesn't work. God offers us the opportunity to follow Him. It's up to each one to decide, to choose. Some probably will, more or less. There will be the resistors, but in the end, God calls us to be *faithful* stewards in I Corinthians 4:2—not *successful*. Remember, it's all a work of God."

"But you said some can decide not to respond."

"That's correct. Salvation does not *remove* our will; it *frees* it. God doesn't force it. We can set up situations to encourage unity."

"But you can't force a horse to drink—even when you bring him to the water." Butch laughed. "I never saw this job as spiritual."

"Our ways of seeing, our ways of reacting are determined by our worldview. And for a Christian, that makes all the difference. Do you want me to write up something? If you could send me a sample, if there's a form I should follow. I don't think the answer is to create two separate prisons. My team and I have been praying for unity. Now we will begin teaching it and spreading the word."

"No set forms. Just write it up as you explained it and include the verses. Describe why it will be important for their development to be challenged in this way. Include your preaching and teaching concepts that will go along with the billeting changeup. It's common in certain situations to regularly rotate bunk assignments." Butch smiled. "You know, last week I felt I was the wrong person for this job and was wondering why I came here."

"You mean, why God sent you here?"

"Yeah, yeah, but today I know that if I wasn't a Christian, I'd be ready to transfer the lot of you throughout all the prison camps and tell the other wardens to separate all of you. So, it would be collaborators to one camp, the resistors to another and on and on. That's the last thing we need. Well, I'll also ask my wife to pray for this as well as friends in church, maybe?"

"We always rejoiced that other churches and pastors managed to escape the Task Force. We never resented them for it. We coveted their prayers on our behalf."

"How'd they get you?" He looked over. "Hate to say that bill to increase the yearly count for all of you has stalled and probably won't be taken up until the new administration."

"We pray about it when we remember, but it's not a priority. He will release me from prison in His time, and when I see what's needed here, I'm glad to be here. Happy to have a part in rebuilding the faithful. Restoration begins with the house of God. It starts with us.

"Alex Hutton was my best friend. He came to me with his Bible idea. I was one of those who helped find volunteers to preserve the Bibles and pack them. We put some on pallets and shipped them throughout the United States. Between us, we found regional distributors." Rick looked off in the distance. "They killed his wife, and I heard through the prison grapevine that they tortured him, almost to death. Not surprised he only lasted a few years in Leavenworth. But he must not have talked because I only received 20 years for being found with pallets of Bibles. For some reason, the agents didn't seem to see me as one of the organizers. Thought I'd sail through in a prison camp, but then they created Rosemont. I was on the first truck." He sighed. "Some committed suicide by guard."

Butch nodded, wondering, *how many Bibles survived?* Out in the hall, he knew he should head to his desk and write the report for Foster, but the Holy Spirit sent him to Building 2.

Butch tapped on the door to Will's cell, swiped the card lock and pushed the door open. Will was sitting cross-legged on the shelf, leaning against an upright pillow with an open Bible on his lap. The look of fear and panic that crossed Will's face when he stepped in pierced Butch's heart. "May I sit down?" he asked. Seeing the nod, he sat on the bolted stool. Breathing, he said, "I have to apologize. I'm still learning how to do this job as a Christian. Guess I fell back on old habits." He shifted. Will looked at him, unblinking. "Well, we still friends?"

"When you're working, and I'm an inmate, no. That much is quite obvious."

"Look, I admit I tried too hard not to show favoritism and looked the other way when you ran into problems. Foster reamed me out for that. Makes it look like I don't know what my job is."

"Do you know what your job is?"

"I'm learning."

"I gather he didn't hold your hand through the 'this-is-all-the-things-an-associate-warden-is-expected-to-do' manual. Did you head the DU before you left?"

"Yeah, and the problems working with the warden's office made me swear I'd never move up any higher. So, why did I take this job?" Will simply looked at him. "Not making it easy, buddy."

"Do I look like I'm having an easy time? I haven't seen Chris in weeks, and now I can't call her—nothing for half a year! Try living with that!" Will sat back, trying to find his equilibrium. *Why does the guy have to mess me up now?* Resisting the urge to ask him to leave, he waited to see what the man would say this time.

"Listen, Chris dropped by the house." He saw the light begin to come on in Will's eyes. "You smuggled out a message." Obviously, the wrong thing to say. Kicking himself inside, he reminded himself he was here to make amends and get their relationship back on track, not play interrogator. "Don't get me wrong—I'm glad you did. My hands are tied. I can't communicate with her directly. So, it's not a problem. We good?" Will didn't move. "Well," he tried to find a way to turn the conversation back to something positive that could connect them. "I'm still feeling my way in putting my faith into practice, you know?"

"Not easy from this side of the fence." Will shook his head. "You're not the only one with a fail on this one. I never got to square one with those guys, and I thought it would give us chances to share our faith." He slumped back, "Blew that one."

"Believe me. Lieutenant Ries got them to talk, and they were set on either killing you outright or creating an incident to have you transferred where you could be killed. No, you had to defend yourself. So, that time it was the right call."

Will watched Butch's face, feeling his resolve to hold a grudge beginning to dissolve. "I'm sorry too. I saw you on the line and was so humiliated. I used to lead your team. You reported to me in the day." He couldn't not ask. "The five months sticks?"

"I'm heading over to write the report and file my recommendation, but the warden asked for this. It's his decision." Butch felt led to share the rest—what he had talked about with Rick. "You will have a new set of podmates by the time you get out. It shouldn't take too long to shuffle the bunk assignments."

"The warden was aware of the tensions?"

"He's really sharp. Why he's such a good warden and wise enough to know it's best dealt with properly before things erupt. And that would be my cue to return to retirement."

"Miss it?"

"Oh, I was getting bored. The guys with hobbies, like the golfing fanatics, do fine. You can only ride so many 4-wheeler trails, and fishing gets old too. Last week I felt like bailing, but after talking with Rick, I think this is the way to go."

"I think it's what the Lord wants us to do. I'll pray for that. Thank you for sharing that with me."

"Still feeling my way. Can't be too friendly out there."

Will smiled for the first time. "Don't even try. We have to take our roles—even if we don't like it."

"What do you have there?" Butch gestured toward Will's pile of big books and papers. "Reminds me of Tom's stuff."

"Bible, concordance, Greek interlinear and lexicon, and a theology book—the beginner's level." He laughed. "Have my Hebrew alphabet, but that won't do me much good in here. Studying, learning, memorizing." He risked a glance at Butch. "I'm done with law enforcement as much as I used to love it, but God is bending me, literally, in another direction. Being locked up with those giants of the faith has been good for me. Just wish the rest of the baggage was easier to deal with. Didn't have that much time to study and really get into the Bible. And five months locked up, well, that's time with this, so, whatever." He tried to shrug his shoulders and act as if he didn't care, but he did. The burning ache to spend real time with Chris never went away. "It's easier being single."

"I don't want to get your hopes up, but you'll probably have a good outcome, so don't lose faith."

"I can't lose my faith."

"Well, maybe I mean, don't lose hope."

"I'll keep that in mind."

It took a week for the bunk assignments to come through. Foster was skeptical, but Rick's report and Butch's explanation along with his insistence it was the right way to go, clinched the project. "But you keep an eye on it. If things go south, we'll have to break them up. I checked with the Arizona warden. They've already shipped out half the inmates and are rotating into a regular prison camp for long-term level one offenders and short timers."

Foster also gave Butch the names of other officers to investigate and recommend for retention or dismissal. "We have to demonstrate we will not tolerate staff violations either. Funny, the three ended up where they tried to send Masters. Your God?"

"Of course, He has it planned out. We just have to figure out our part."

"Hmm," Foster said, dismissing him with a nod.

An hour later Connors headed for Chaplain Rick's office. The man greeted him warmly.

"Well, don't know if the word has reached you, but your bunk changeup's a go. Make yourself available to work with the case managers for new bunk assignments. Especially keep in mind those who should not be in the same unit or area. And…" He waved the report. "I'd like you to walk through the scriptural mandate you're referring to. Good time?"

"Always." Rick pulled out a legal Bible. "Here, for you to keep. Shall we begin?"

CHAPTER 21

O H, THE JOY! Chris floated through the store, selecting just the right clothes for Will's freedom. *Well, freedom day for more than just Will,* she reminded herself. She had cleaned the house, sorted Will's clothes and, with his permission, thrown out the worn, faded and threadbare items. In a day or so they would go shopping for him. Hugging the bag, she walked to the car, feeling the warm spring day share in her delight.

The new administration had followed through on their election promises. Not only did their 100-day legislative initiative rescind all the 756 laws, but they wiped the slate clean for all HCL offenders, along with charges related to trying to survive the Task Force. The pastors and professors who had fled the country under false documents were granted full immunity.

She paused briefly, wondering why Stella Hutton had not asked her to join the group of pro bono lawyers to represent those returning home. She smiled, remembering reading the news reports of Dr. and Mrs. Smith coming to the States to be one of the first to join Charles Hutton's Faith Hall initiative. *Can the nation be made right again?*

Two Sundays ago, she had celebrated Easter with the Connors and the Fosters. They had many questions concerning faith. And now they were at Freedom Monday. She had never seen the Hutton Center so busy and, at times, so frantic. Carlos would be joining Faith Hall as well.

She had hardly slept, but her excitement made the drive to Purcellville FPC seem to take so long. The visitor's section of the parking lot

175

was jammed. Navigating around a pair of black SUVs, she found a spot up and to the right. It might take a while for the traffic to clear, but no matter, Will would be with her.

Associate Warden Connors, in his sharp, freshly pressed brown shirt, dark brown trousers and tie, stood by Warden Foster. The media, relegated to the side lawn, stood poised, all eyes on the portable podium and mic stand. At the appointed time, Foster stepped up and opened with a few words.

"When DOC Wilfred presented the idea to me of being the warden for a select group of inmates, my first impression was to decline. After all, usually those who require special treatment need special handling. But…" His eyes shining, catching his wife's nod, he continued, "nothing could have been further from the truth." Pausing, he said, "It was an honor and privilege to safeguard their time with us as we learned valuable lessons as well. In the spirit of the orderliness of this group, I will let Associate Warden Connors, my able righthand man, hand out the certificates of release and court documents of the reversal of their convictions along with a letter from the President of the United States."

The crowd clapped and cheered.

Butch read the first name, and the man in an outfit provided by the family accepted his envelope with a handshake. Chris assumed they were releasing inmates by alphabetical order, but after a while she could not discern any pattern at all. Name after name was called. She strained to recognize Will in the small group visible from her vantage point, but the parking lot was still full.

Families joined, hugged, sounds of celebration merging with the voices of many. They headed to their vehicles and made their way out to the main road—media recording each one. Chris looked back at the entrance, reminding herself to breathe. One by one by one. The parking lot began to empty, the waiting crowd thinned. Four men in suits waited by the SUVs, but she didn't have time to process anything—her nerves tumbled within her of fear as well as anticipation.

Finally, she saw Will at the end of the line—tall and proud and happy. He beamed his twenty-watt smile that she hadn't seen for a long time. Inching closer, she worked her way to the roped-off area. They exchanged glances. Waiting for the last two to go through the line was hard. Then he stepped forward, surged past the extended hand and hugged Butch. Taking his envelope, he turned, began to lift it in the air in triumph, but the look on his face shifted, his arm fell to his side. Chris pressed closer and took it from his hand. Sensing something, she turned to see what had stopped Will in his tracks.

The four men in suits stood three steps behind her in a semi-circle. She recognized the stance and placement of the agents. A glance back at Connors and Foster told her this was no surprise to them. The rope, walkways, bushes and the building all funneled Will to them.

The nearest one said politely, "Ma'am, we must ask you to step aside."

Inside she screamed out, "No! No! You can't do this!" but her training kicked in. Deciding to let them arrest Will first, she complied, feeling for her ID, and drawing out her federal court card.

Very calm, very professional, the lead agent said, "Will Masters, you are under arrest for genocide."

While the charge stunned her, she flashed her Secret Service badge. And said. "I am his attorney. Is he going to Richmond?"

"D.C., ma'am."

"Fine, I have the right to represent him at that court. I request to follow you to the Magistrate for his arraignment. Who is the prosecuting attorney of record?"

The lead agent only hesitated a moment. He glanced at the fourth agent, who pulled out the docket details with the names of the prosecuting attorneys.

Butch came by her side to escort her to her car. "No comment," he said repeatedly to the reporters. He said quietly before he closed her car door, "I'm sorry. They forbade us to tell anyone. Probably why they kept the indictments sealed until today."

Chris put the car into gear and followed the FBI agents back to D.C. Numb, shaking, mouth dry as sawdust, she couldn't even pray.

Last month she had renewed her credentials with the D.C. Court and knew where to park. Running as fast as she could, she passed through security into the courthouse and asked the nearest officer for directions.

"Your case?"

"United States v. Masters."

"Are you the attorney?"

"I am."

"This way." He led her directly to the clerk to register as Will's attorney.

"Please have them wait until I am there to represent William Masters," she said, trying not to shake.

"Yes, ma'am," the woman said.

The officer had waited and escorted her to the courtroom. Magistrate Sorens read the charge.

Walking swiftly to Will's side, she tried to ignore the image of Will's hands cuffed behind his back. "Your Honor, I request a moment to confer with my client," Chris petitioned. Seeing the nod, she leaned close to Will. "You heard the charge?" Seeing his nod, she said, "Plead not guilty. We have to fight this."

She looked in Will's eyes for the first time. The wound ran deep, piercing his heart. "Shouldn't I plead guilty or no contest?"

"No, can't take that back. You can change a not-guilty plea later, but we have to try to fight it first. Will, you are innocent; never forget that. Not guilty."

"What do you plead, Mr. Masters?"

Looking one last time at his wife, Will faced the court. "Not guilty, Your Honor."

The lead prosecuting attorney requested remand—that no bail be set. Chris declined to argue the forced incarceration throughout the trial. Instinctively, she knew that was their only option. Before they could pull him away, as the Magistrate gaveled the decision, she threw her arms around Will and kissed him. "I won't abandon you. Never forget that."

The reporters try to mob her, but God again sent angels of protection in the form of court officers. She made it to the car and dropped her head in her hands, her shoulders shaking with the torrent of emotions finally released. Stella Hutton had basically shut her out of the foundation as the months drew closer. She knew the woman had testified at the closed hearings. Images of the phrase—*Architect of Rosemont*—floated through her consciousness. *Have I even lost Tompkins as an ally?* Not having the heart to find out, she forced herself to visualize her next steps as she put her car in gear and headed home.

Discovery—where she would learn what evidence had been assembled, and the list of the witnesses they would call to testify against him. The judge—the one who would shepherd the case through the process, instruct the jury, and be the gatekeeper for ensuring all parts of the trial adhered to federal law. The prosecuting attorneys—her opponents armed with the investigative might of the federal government.

I have to hire a firm—not one attorney alone will do. To hold their own against the forces of the government, she would need attorneys, paralegals, and assistants. Will's defense would be a daunting task. One thing she did know—she had to resign from the Secret Service.

Chris drove to work, picked up an empty box from the supply closet and headed to her boss' office on the fifth floor. No one said a word to her as she passed their desks. Their looks told her they already knew. She headed straight into Walt's office. "I have to resign."

He handed her a legal pad. She wrote a sparsely worded letter.

"You have enough leave and a sabbatical due. Take as much time as you need. We'll find a place for you here when this is over." He put his signature to her leave request and made a copy. "See Nancy for your leave paperwork. I'll transmit the authorization right now." He stepped closer. "I'm so sorry, Chris."

"He's innocent," she said, but she could see the look of disbelief in his eyes mixed with pity. She turned away and paused by her desk, frozen in uncertainty and indecision. *Should I empty my desk or visit HR?*

Pam drew near. "I'll clean out your desk. Go see Nancy. She's at her desk."

As if awakened from sleep, Chris walked mechanically to the second floor and sat by Nancy's desk. Everyone said the same thing. Now she knew better than to try to defend Will at this point. As she waited for the forms to print, she tried not to visualize what Will was going through this very moment as they stepped through the booking process and rendered him another faceless indicted criminal awaiting his fate.

Nancy laid a gentle hand on her arm. "How can I help?"

"Pray."

"Are you going to fight this?" Seeing Chris nod through her tears, she wheeled her chair closer and enveloped her in an embrace. "Don't let that miserable man get away with this. Will is innocent."

"How do you know?"

"Because he always denied Rosemont was a death camp until he saw it, and then they just hurt him and never stopped trying to hurt him. I remember all the lunches where you shared his latest troubles. Of course, he had some great adventures out west. And then sentenced to five years. Oh, honey, I'm praying God's angels guard him and keep him safe. Don't lose the faith." They wept as one.

"It helps to hear someone believes me. He wanted to plead guilty, but thankfully, he agreed to a not-guilty plea for now. Pray he doesn't change his mind. He already feels so bad Rosemont happened and that he had even been part of the Task Force."

She longed for rest. Her body cried out for sleep, but she had to check in with the detention center, make sure she had the rights to see him as his attorney and ensure that he was in protective custody.

After a few wrong turns, she found a space to park and rushed in. Her name was on the list—that was good. They had no idea where he was, and for a short time, panic threatened to overtake her. Standing there, waiting, an officer stepped through and led her to a visiting room. "We'll bring him down," he said.

Chris reminded herself it could be a while. The multi-storied facility in the heart of D.C. was a sprawling complex. It took ten minutes, but Will walked through looking as much in shock as she was. Once the door closed, she wrapped him in a hug.

His eyes were wide and free of tears; his stare vacant and unfocused. "I knew," he said quietly. "The Lord warned me something was coming."

"Did they know? At the prison?"

"No. Butch just said they had some strange requests for the setup and that I had to be released last." He reached for her hand. "Chris, I'm guilty."

"No, you're not," she stated, trying not to raise her voice.

"I'm guilty of stupidity and blindness...shouldn't I be willing to take the fall?" He looked away. "So many—so many slaughtered. There were multiple burial pits where they placed the dead after the trench in the yard filled."

Chris' eyes flashed in anger. "Who told you this? Don't let them mess with your head! Never forget. You didn't order the executions. When you saw it, you tried to stop the killings. You faced death yourself. You know who is guilty."

"Kincaid."

"He is the one who is the real architect of Rosemont."

Will looked at her directly for the first time. "He is the architect of Rosemont—the death camp—what he made it to be. I am the architect of what it could have been." He held her hand and returned her gaze.

"But my dream was fictional—unconnected to the reality that Kincaid hid from me."

Chris saw within those few sentences the outline of the defense strategy. Hope took bud, planted in the knowledge God would be with her through all of it—come what may. She shook her head, pushing through a mental fog. *What does he need to hear now to sustain him through the days ahead?* "Yes, never forget that. I will find a law firm. You told me to pay off my mortgage—that's done. We have the savings from your condo sale. We can do this. Hold tight, stay strong and don't cave to this evil. Pray for me to find the right defense team." She cleared her throat. "Walt accepted my resignation today. Said it would be considered a sabbatical, but I don't plan on going back. Not now. Not after this."

"At least there is one blessing." Seeing her quizzical look, he said, "As my attorney they can't keep you from visiting, and they can't listen in."

"Stay in protective custody. Will, promise me you won't give up."

"I have my Bible and my Bible study books. I'll keep myself busy. After all, I haven't had a taste of freedom for a long time."

Her heart broke, and she could not hold back the tears.

He drew her close. "I'm so sorry to put you through this."

"You are not doing this to me, Will. Don't forget the name of the real enemy."

"God will bring us through."

The firms flocked to lead the defense. Chris, still wondering if even Tompkins would reject her, hesitated to reach out to him for advice. Settling on a fifty-year-old law firm, well known for defending clients in the D.C. Circuit, she set a meeting. They didn't have a lot of time. The judge assigned to Will's case would soon announce the court dates. Suspecting they would try to set an early date, she headed out for the meeting with her evidence and trial strategy outline in her briefcase.

The building was well preserved from the early 1900s. The interior was dark paneled wood, high ceilings and paintings from the Revolutionary era. Tastefully outfitted, a young attorney led her to a first floor conference room, offering coffee. She declined, took her seat and considered laying out her files. Instead, she placed the briefcase close to her on the next chair. Shortly, three older attorneys followed by four more, she assumed were junior attorneys and assistants, filed in and took their seats. The lead attorney was past fifty, his chin overflowing his collar, dressed in a carefully tailored suit. Reaching across the table, he offered his hand to her. "Miss Worden, we meet again."

Now that she saw him, she remembered. He had represented one of her suspects years ago. Quickly she recalled the impression he had given—shrewd, cunning, deceptive were the words that floated up. "Now I remember. Your client's name escapes me."

"Good job you did. We had to take a plea. Your case was too well proven. You were with the attorney's office?"

"No, I was the lead FBI agent. I worked to ensure we brought admissible evidence that would be difficult to refute."

Before she could segue to Will's case, the attorney said, "Quite right. I remember now. You see, that is why you chose our firm. And did I remember to say we will represent Will Masters pro bono?" Seeing her nod, he barely took a breath. "Good move to plead not guilty in the beginning. This will help us maneuver for the best possible deal. That's what we do. So, begin with discovery, hint at exculpatory evidence, let them twist in the wind, so to speak." He smiled, his skin smooth as a snake's, his round cheeks crowding his eyes.

"What is your intention?" she asked.

"Get a deal. I know it's hard to grasp. Don't worry your pretty head about the details. We'll take care of you."

Chris rose. "My husband, William Masters, is innocent and will never take a deal." She grasped her briefcase. "I have some evidence, the trial strategy..."

"My dear, while you might have been an exemplary federal agent in days gone by, defending a person in federal court against the weight, manpower and resources the government has at its disposal would take many experienced lawyers…"

She stated firmly, "I am his attorney of record. I have defended clients in federal court. I successfully argued the reversal of the charges against Warden Foster. I know what it will take. I know how to fight this. Are you willing to take up the challenge with me? Are you able?"

His mouth slack, his chipped teeth in evidence, he sputtered at first, then rose. Clearing his throat, he advised, "That would be a grave mistake," and left the room.

A few glanced her way and gave her a thumbs up. The last junior attorney, who walked her out, stated, "They only want the publicity. It's the first genocide case since the law was passed many decades ago." She paused then added, "free publicity for a landmark case. I wish you all the best. Sorry to miss out. It will be a real ride."

"Thank you," Chris said. "Who are you?"

She handed Chris a business card. "Sheryll Platt, fresh out of law school."

Chris brought out her business card. "Most info is out of date. The cell is mine." She shook her hand and held it. "If you decide to come on board, contact me. I will be funding my defense, but it will take a team and many hours of investigation."

"I know." Sheryll smiled, almost vibrating. "Pouring through what appear to be mundane records looking for that clue—that crack that will seal the deal. How we cut our teeth."

She smiled. "I wish you the best Miss Platt. It is a worthy career that seeks for justice for all."

Chris went home. Stunned, shaking more from anger than fear. By the time she arrived at home and pulled up the list of other willing firms, she realized the news must have already traveled. The law firms refused to take her calls. Fear rose up as if Kincaid's hands were around her throat. Shaking her head, she tried Tompkins, holding her breath as she counted the rings. She released it when the elderly professor answered.

"Well, Christine, I wondered how long it would take you to call. Rumors have it the law firms pounding at your door are only interested in arranging a deal and taking a bow."

"Yes." She had to force out the word.

"It's going to be a brawl. They'll throw everything at your team. You're thinking of defending him yourself, are you?"

"That would be disastrous, but I will have to lead the team."

"You are qualified to appear before the court. Judge Halbert is strict but fair."

"I am aware."

"Well, what about discovery?"

"I don't have a firm to attach to it."

"You don't have time, Chris. You know how to handle documents. Start discovery under your name."

Her eyes roved her small dining area next to a compact kitchen. "Can we meet?"

"Not right now, sorry."

"Understood." She held the phone aside, trying to keep it together.

"But keep your phone close and be ready. Someone will contact you with a meeting. It would be in your best interests to attend." He ended the call.

The chill ran through her again. Kincaid played the long game. He also had an extensive network of supporters and operatives. She perceived if they did not prevail by laying the blame on Kincaid, he would rise again another day to continue his crusade—as true a believer as Hawsley and as blind. *So, it begins.*

CHAPTER 22

C HRIS BEGAN THE process of discovery—the prosecution was required by law to provide the evidence against Will. This was Wednesday; the third day after his arrest.

She headed for the detention center.

The stress of solitary clear in his drawn face touched her heart. He still smiled; the life still there. Chris described the last two days.

"So, while I wait for a firm to contact me, I requested the evidence against you. And now…" She pulled out a legal pad from her case. "Tell me everything Kincaid said to you over the last few years." She listened, taking copious notes. What might not seem relevant now, might reveal its importance later. "Did he ever tell you Rosemont was sanctioned by the administration?"

"Yes."

"He did? I thought he kept you in the dark."

Will sat back, trying to put his memories back together. He rubbed his forehead. "Norton had them pump me full of drugs, a little more than a week, give or take. Let me think." He tried to picture his brief meeting with Kincaid when they first seized him. "Not exactly. He believed the executions would be made legal in the future. Until that time, it was a necessary evil, but I had not heard about the administration's approval. That I heard from Norton."

"Who is dead."

"Yes, quite conveniently. Otis and many others are also dead who could corroborate the fact I knew nothing of the killings beyond rumors." He drew breath and set his gaze on Chris' lovely face. "You believe if I plead guilty, he will feel exonerated and try again?" Seeing her assent, he said, "He talked about the poisonous influence of an ancient book unfit for today. His ultimate goal was the destruction of Christianity and the elimination of all Christians. Remember Joe Lyle spoke of *phases?* First the church leadership and scholars, followed by law enforcement. At that point the people would have no one to lead them who could expose the lies and no one to protect them from a vicious agency." He tipped his head. "That fits the charge of genocide, doesn't it? The directed effort to eliminate a particular class, ethnic, or religious group."

Chris tried to recall Will's boxes in her apartment. "You didn't keep a written calendar, journal or diary?"

"Digital only. That's a problem, isn't it?"

"I'll request all your digital records, including your calendar. Did you enter all of your appearances on the Hill and with senators?"

"Yes, even the last-minute ones. It helped me justify the hours I didn't spend in the office."

"Your cell phone numbers?"

Will lifted his chin, pursed his lips, peered off into the corner, but in the end, he shook his head. "I can't recall."

Chris paled. "How spotty is your memory?"

"Some are jumbled about the past. Many are clear, but unfixed as to when and where. It's slowly coming back. Chris, if God is for us, who can be against us? I have to remember that promise."

"I just pray He's not calling you to a ministry in prison."

"Agreed, but even in that, He will make a way." He held her hand. "Chris, believe me when I say He has prepared me for this. Remember that dust up in Purcellville where they put me in detention? I freaked out at first, but then the Holy Spirit told me to man up and take it."

"*Man up?* Those were the exact words?"

"Not exactly, but that was the gist of it. Like it says in Hebrews 12.

Quit pouting, show up and work the problem—whatever it is." Will smiled. "I do remember a short time later when Kincaid told me to take Norton's undercover op or go to Leavenworth with an insider trading conviction—that his goal was to eliminate all of the Huttons. Larry Hutton was my target."

"Did you infiltrate and meet him?"

"Privileged information, my dear." He scanned the room again. "Yes, but I never admitted to it or gave him up. When Norton grabbed me, he showed clips of me talking with Larry, but I didn't reveal what we talked about. Passed it off as another failed attempt to infiltrate. It's believable. Larry's even-tempered and coolheaded."

"Tell me what Norton told you with the time and place."

They worked through the statements. Chris wrote down all the meetings and appearances he could remember with the range of dates. "Every little bit helps. If I can substantiate your whereabouts for the years you were with the Task Force, it might contradict their evidence."

She started a clean sheet. "Tell me everything about the firm that designed your Rosemont model." She hoped to hear a name or the location of the firm's headquarters, but while Will remembered general details, he could not remember specifics. "Who did you contact with the BOP concerning rules, regulations, protocols, and setup of federal prison?" Then she turned to his signoffs. "You complained you had to sign off on facility budgets and spending even though you had no oversight responsibility. Tell me everything about that—when it started, the document names." She plied him with question after question, until her hand began to cramp and his eyes clouded, his answers increasingly vague or uncertain.

"That's enough for today. I'll be back later." Tempted to list the many tasks still before her, she melted into his embrace.

"I know you'll be more than busy. Focus. Don't worry. Okay?"

She nodded and straightened for a parting kiss.

By the time she reached her car, rush hour was already in progress.

She didn't remember to check her messages until she was on a crowded, narrow street, waiting to get through a light. It would probably take at least one more cycle before she crossed the intersection to stop at the next light.

Eventually, she spied a convenient strip mall with a sub shop. Pulling up her messages, she sighed in exasperation. Someone had called during her visit. "Why not?" she asked herself and returned the call. It was a firm. They could meet tomorrow. She chose a mid-afternoon time.

Chris parked in front of the Maryland office of Nolan, Briggs and Kishner, a venerable D.C. law firm. Tompkins had prevailed on Partner Wallace to agree to hear her case. Arriving early, they led her to a conference room dominated by a large mahogany table. The projector and connections were there, but no whiteboard.

"I require a whiteboard. Perhaps one can be found in a storage room?"

The assistant nodded. Chris set up her laptop, ensuring all was ready. Standing at the head of the table, she ran through the meeting strategy and prayed.

A few minutes late, D. Edgar Wallace walked confidently in followed by a middle-aged man and three younger attorneys. Wallace had the look of eternal maturity and played the part well. Dismissive, impatiently glancing at his watch, bored and with a disdainful eye, he stepped to the head of the room.

Chris extended her hand in greeting and walked forward, pulling out the first chair closest to her laptop and notepad. "Mr. Wallace, a pleasure. I'm Christine Worden." As he scowled, taking the second chair, she waited to see if he would introduce his staff. He did not.

"This meeting is a courtesy for our mutual friend, Fred Tompkins," he stated abruptly.

Chris smiled. "He was always my favorite professor. Well then..." She cleared her throat before continuing, "My name is Christine Worden. I earned my J.D. at George Washington University, have investigative and management experience with the FBI, Secret Service and the Task Force. My husband, William Masters, has been with the FBI and the Task Force. As you are aware, he has been charged with genocide, particularly in regard to the atrocities at the Rosemont prison camp run exclusively by the Task Force.

"This is the case. He is innocent of genocide." She plowed through to her next statement. "His defense must prove beyond a shadow of a doubt that the fact Rosemont was a death camp had been shielded from him." Ignoring the looks of disbelief, she continued, "His plan for the former Boy Scout camp was for a camp equivalent to a level-one federal prison, like Purcellville, FPC."

"Miss Worden, or whatever you call yourself, what have you learned from discovery? On what are they resting their case?"

"Digital evidence of Will's signature on documents relating to Rosemont, as well as utilizing witnesses who had worked at the camp."

"Was he there?"

"Physically at Rosemont?" Chris reflected for a moment. "He had the initial walk-through with the real estate agent while he was assistant to Kincaid. He secured the services of an architectural firm to develop the prison camp according to federal guidelines and specifications. Will did not get a chance to oversee camp development and did not visit until that March when he told Kincaid he was going on vacation and booked a last-minute flight to Minneapolis. Appalled at what he saw, he ordered Tom Hutton released."

"He's responsible for the Hutton fiasco?"

"I'd frame it as the wedge that finally cracked the hold Kincaid's organization had on this country. Yes. Due to a clerical error, the guards failed to execute Tom when he had served his time. He had overstayed three weeks, and Will set him free. Will contacted Kincaid and requested on-site management, completely clueless that Kincaid was directly responsible for turning Rosemont into a death camp. Kincaid ordered him to report back to Washington where he was seized and held for weeks without charge before given the choice to take an undercover op with Norton's Southwest Division or face prison time from a concocted insider trading charge.

"Why would he give a rogue manager an undercover assignment?"

"Good question. In the beginning we were tasked with getting to know and understand our suspects, which including reading the Bible. Even when I tried to put teams together, few agents had sufficient biblical knowledge, as well as the understanding of how to infiltrate successfully."

"And did he?"

"Did he infiltrate?" Chris' lips formed a thin, tight smile. "That is beyond the scope of this case. However, using past practices, the executions he witnessed at Norton's Oklahoma prison complex indicate mass murder was a regular practice with certain Task Force divisions and units. Along with the statements that the killings were supported by the administration, including the President and his Chief of Staff."

"Norton can verify this?"

"While held earlier this year, Will witnessed Kincaid's strike team eliminate Norton and his executive team at an off-book prison. They were about to try to extract information from Will concerning his undercover op."

Chris returned to her PowerPoint. "This is an image of what Rosemont might have been if Will had been allowed to develop the camp."

"Is that the mock-up of the camp?"

"No, that's been lost. He showed it to me years ago, shortly after Hawsley took a plea deal, but Otis wiped clean Will's laptop, phone and cloud storage. Norton's team pumped him full of psychotropic drugs, so he has some gaps in his memory. He cannot remember the name of the firm he worked with."

"Challenges, significant obstacles?"

She resisted the temptation to insist she finish the presentation and take questions later, but the questioning would expose this group's perceptions and orientation. "While the usual standard for defense is to establish reasonable doubts in the minds of the jurors, that will not be enough for this case. The country is shocked, appalled, embarrassed on the international stage, and looking for restitution. Indicting Will, in the public's mind, helps resolve the guilt and blame for Kincaid and the administration. To believe a rogue agent concocted and created a death camp under Kincaid's nose is more acceptable than to expose the fact that top leadership, in conjunction with the blessings of the President's men, were behind the plan.

"We must show, in fact, that Will selected Rosemont to be a level-one camp that would adhere to federal standards. At that time, he truly believed if resistors were treated humanely and given a chance to reflect, they would eventually sign on and could return to society. He had no knowledge of the illegal murders, re-education sessions, or intimidation that was ongoing."

"But he stood before the people of this land, proclaiming all was well."

Chris tipped her head in Wallace's direction. "That was why he was so valuable to Kincaid. Will had a stellar reputation as the FBI agent who could put together a team to bring criminal enterprises to justice legally, by the book, producing evidence for US attorneys that could withstand their high-priced defense teams. He was one of the ones Kincaid used to allay fears about the Task Force, with plausible deniability, while his black-op contract teams did his dirty work in the shadows.

She went to the next screen. "This is the list of journalists and editors who died either by car accidents or mysterious circumstances. Every one of them had been investigating the Task Force." The next one. "This is the list of prominent leaders—senators, congressmen, wardens—who had the misfortune to get in his way. The Hutton Foundation has successfully overturned half of these convictions.

"To get back to the challenges." She navigated three screens up. "Refute the validity of digital signatures. Using digital forensics disprove the validity of such evidence. Find ways to authenticate Will's assertion he intended Rosemont as a safe and secure prison camp and demonstrate he was unaware of Kincaid's black-op teams and their crimes. We do not have to prove Kincaid was the culprit, but we do have to show that Will was not involved.

"The added difficulty is the fact many who could testify to the narrow range of Will's activities at the Task Force are dead, apart from Kincaid and Barrie Reynolds, his nephew, whom I doubt would be willing witnesses." She smiled. "It always comes back to family.

"So, we establish Will's whereabouts for his time with the Task Force. Find evidence and witnesses who can support his true plans for the camp and demonstrate that other divisions also participated in illegal killings, increasing the likelihood that the jury will understand that while Will was working for the Task Force, he was not with them in spirit and not in agreement with their methods. During his final conversation with Norton, he told him that the Oklahoma division had violated every oath and was engaged in murder. Unfortunately, Norton again asserted they had the support of the administration."

Taking a breath, ready to share her confidence in their case and the necessity of it, she froze when Wallace stood.

"I think we have seen enough." With a nod in her direction, he gestured for his team to file out.

"Thank you, Mr. Wallace. I appreciate the time." It had been barely 45 minutes. She realized she should have been grateful. She turned to pack up her laptop after the room emptied.

The aide entered. "Sorry, miss, we don't have any whiteboards."

"Thank you for looking. Have a good day."

Shaking her head, she hadn't had a chance to move to summary, pull the facts together, or excite them with the call that this case would benefit the nation and have a part in laying the groundwork for the future. Time is money, and they had given her almost an hour. She tried to encourage herself with that thought.

Too exhausted and discouraged to visit Will—afraid her mood would bring him down, she headed home.

Later that evening the intercom buzzed. "Hello, dear, this is Irma."

"Of course." She buzzed in her friend. A short while later she opened the door to see both Rick and Irma. They surged forward to hug her.

Teary-eyed, she sat on the couch and told them about her day. "Please pray the Lord provides a team or..." She shook her head; the terror of conviction was all she could see.

"We will pray. That's why we're here." Rick smiled. "I had a good visit with Will today. He's doing well, but I don't think I have the time to visit him often enough to continue his studies."

"Incarceration makes everything difficult."

"I'd like you to add another name to his visitor list. Can you do it through the Internet?"

"Yes, what's the name?"

"Dr. Dan Smith."

"Is he the one who just returned from Dublin?"

"Yes, and with his lovely wife Catherine."

"You must meet them," Irma invited. "At the new building for the Faith Hall Foundation just north of town. They bought an abandoned industrial park with some old warehouses on it."

"You think they'd let me visit?"

"Of course, why not? The center's a little slower these days. Stella asked me to manage it. Rick is the chaplain for Purcellville."

"Volunteer?"

"No, they gave him a staff position."

"They're not closing the prison?"

"No, the programs we developed are working, and many will be transferred in. It's a different mix, of course. I'm still in orientation, but it's an important ministry."

Chris nodded, glad to hear how the Lord had provided for them. She shared the difficulty in finding a willing law firm.

"Why couldn't you get him out on bail?"

Chris looked fondly at the couple. "While we know in our hearts that Will is not capable of this, many believe him to be guilty. People don't return my phone calls—even some who had been close friends. As much as I would love him to be here with me, the detention center is the safest place for him. Believe me, they don't want the publicity that would come with allowing an attempt on his life."

Will looked up from his books when the range door opening sounded down the narrow, short hall. His cell, the size of a closet had all the amenities—a sink, toilet, narrow shower, shelf for a desk and a stool bolted to the wall. Farther up a narrow shelf held his study books. It was a tomb, dim and quiet, for the most part.

The guards stood in front of his solid door and peered in through the small window. He tried to ignore them.

"Cuff up."

He slid his hands through the waist-high slot. They walked him through the floor's command center to the elevator and down three flights. His heart lifted, remembering this had been the way to the small attorney-client conference rooms. They removed the cuffs before they pushed him in. But Chris was not sitting on the other side of the table. About to turn and say he was in the wrong room, he heard the man say behind him, "Mr. Masters, I presume?"

Will stood, undecided whether he would visit with the 40-something dark-haired man in a dark blue suit. "Name and business."

"Paul Chartrand, attorney with Nolan, Briggs and Kishner. Your wife, Christine Worden, presented your case to our firm. I'm here to listen to your side of the story. She made a compelling case. Do you believe you are guilty of genocide?"

"No." Will sat. "What do you need to know?"

"Can we win?"

"Only with Chris in the lead. She knows Kincaid and how he operates. She's led several teams to success. After five minutes with her, Rev. Hawsley took the deal he'd been turning down. And she does have some experience defending cases."

"Defending cases before a judge is very different from leading a defense team for a criminal trial."

"She is well aware of her lack of experience. But as an investigator, preparing background research, ferreting out the half-truths and lies, she's excellent. She will marshal the best resources for my defense. And that, Mr. Chartrand, is probably why she approached your firm."

"Actually, our firm agreed to hear the case as a favor to a friend." Paul sat back, taking the measure of the man.

"Nice suit. I have two like that in Chris' closet. Should I wear them?"

"No, definitely not. It will remind them of the many hours you spent on the Hill, lying about how pure and righteous your Task Force was. And you sounded so believable."

"Because I believed it."

"And that statement is unbelievable. How long were you with that group?"

"More than nine years—too long. Chris encouraged me to apply for the Investigators Manager position as she felt bringing in FBI protocols and structure could help steer them in the right direction. Early on, I dismissed the warning signs. At that time, I believed in the spirit of the legislation and felt the Christians would come around. Before Chris left, she warned me that Kincaid was a micro-manager who siloed and compartmentalized his teams. There were more of us, in the beginning—regular G-men, working to see the law upheld to make the country safe for the average joe. However, as the enforcement methods intensified, Chris and Joe Lyle weren't the only ones who left. I stayed too long. However, arriving at Rosemont when I did enabled me to release Tom Hutton."

"The prosecution will present its case first. The defense follows. It's customary for the defendant to take the stand. Do you feel prepared to do that?"

"I do. I've always been good testifying in court."

"Testifying for yourself, with so much at stake personally is a completely different matter." Paul rose and tapped on the door. "I think I've seen enough. Try to have a good day, Mr. Masters."

They led him out again midafternoon, but to the common visitors' area with glass barriers and a phone. The guard led him to a minicube. Will looked through the glass. "Dan?"

"Warren Bells?"

"You met me under that name, but I am Will Masters. How did you get here?"

"I drove my car."

"No, I mean, didn't you?" He glanced about.

"Oh, yes, returned home same time as the rest, I suppose. Haven't been here long. Wow! I never expected you to be…" He laughed. "Anyway, Rick Carlson asked me to meet you to see if we can find a way to help you continue your education. What's possible in here?"

"Well, I have more time to read. I've discovered that Jeremiah's not in chronological order. I think if I put it in order, it might answer some of my questions. And the millennial sacrifices in Ezekiel. Now I see why you were so interested in that subject. Getting a better handle on the aspects of salvation." Will shrugged his shoulders, smiled and continued, "I want to know God and what He's done and how He operates and what He wants us to do with our lives. In short, I want to know everything—all of it, from Genesis to Revelation, in here..." He tapped his chest, "...and in the world."

"So, when were you saved?"

"The Christmas after we parted."

"Really. That's a surprise. What you said about the program—you were right. Tom was too." He shook his head. They reminisced for a while.

"So, what's Rick up to?"

"He's been hired as the chaplain at the prison. They manage the Hutton Center in town, and Charles Hutton acquired an abandoned industrial park north of town for his Faith Hall Foundation."

"Is he going to call it Hutton Seminary?"

"Never. He said that's why he called the foundation by another name. They wanted me to be president, but I'd rather chair the Old Testament studies department."

"Carlos is wonderful in the New Testament. You should hear his teachings on Romans. Fantastic. And he's bilingual. Really good helping those new in the faith take their first steps. It was a real blessing to serve time with men like him."

Dan smiled. "I'm more personable than I used to be. Never forgot what you had said about not acting like a Christian. So, to make this a proper clergy visit..." Dan smiled broadly, nodding with Will's laughter and shake of his head. "There is hope even for guys like me. I'd like to share something the Lord showed me when I was in Ireland."

"I'd greatly appreciate it."

"That Christ makes us free indeed. And when He tells us we are free, He is referring to spiritual freedom."

"The words of God and His love transcends all barriers, cultures, languages and station. We are free to serve God and live righteously. Romans 8, if we walk in the Spirit, we can."

"Well I see you've already learned that lesson."

"Dan, it's good to be reminded, as the apostle Peter stated. I watched this lived out in the men I lived with in Purcellville. Who did you learn this from?"

"Living with the refugees. Tom was incredible. After he was released from prison, he went back to help those inside. Of course, I inherited the task, along with his vision of building up the believers so they could rebuild when they went home."

"Will you be a part of the rebuilding here?"

"I'd like to be."

"So would I."

It was hard to say goodbye, but Will found himself encouraged, even hopeful as they escorted him back. *God has a plan. I just have to be patient.*

CHAPTER 23

CHRIS ANSWERED THE call. "Hello?"
"Is this Mrs. Christine Worden?"

"Yes."

"I am calling for Attorney Chartrand with Nolan, Briggs and Kishner to set up an appointment with him."

Chris accepted an appointment later that day. While she did not know the man personally, she felt this consultation might be a good sign.

That afternoon, the receptionist led her to a small conference room. Chris recognized Attorney Paul Chartrand from yesterday's meeting. They shook hands and settled in their chairs, observing one another.

"Well, Miss or Mrs.?"

"I haven't had time to change my name," Chris said. "Please call me Chris; that would be fine."

"I will take your case. Mr. Wallace agrees this case has merit, and we have the resources to mount a defense."

"I have to insist on being the lead. Think of me more like the project lead."

"Miss Worden, Chris, with all due respect, you are not ready to present opening arguments, lead in directing witness testimony or cross, not to mention summaries and closing arguments."

"I concur." She smiled. "Even though named as lead, you will be the one to take point, for the most part, in court. I request the right to take cross when I feel I have the advantage. I will pass all motions and communications by you and your team for review, but I cannot afford to sit back and let my husband be railroaded by this ridiculous charge.

My expertise is research, evidence analytics and discovery. Once an agreement is signed, I will need a small office or area where I can work. I will need access to your legal databases as well."

"You don't ask for much, do you?" Paul almost smiled.

"Do you have an agreement ready?"

He pulled one out and watched her read it. She read it through and then again more slowly. The third time through she added changes, made additional comments, and slid it across the table. He lifted his brow slightly as he read some of her requests, glanced over and went through it again.

"Can we agree in principle that we do what is best for Will, the client? I will defer to your judgment on most matters, but I might challenge you on some. What say you?" She waited, resisting the urge to ask if he believed Will was innocent. Her years at law school had taught her that a skilled attorney could ably defend "guilty" clients. In the end, what he *thought* should be moot.

Paul sighed, initialed her changes, and slid it over for her initials. "We will need a retainer."

The funds had been pulled and were available. Chris wrote a check for $50,000. "Will that be sufficient?"

He took in the amount, studied her again, looked back at the check and nodded.

The firm provided a desk and Internet access in their admin area. Chris knew it would be adequate as she could use any of the small conference rooms along an inner wall. She met her team—two junior attorneys and a paralegal. She called a meeting immediately. Paul countered with one for the next morning. "You need to get your presentation together, but first you have to transmit your discovery files."

Chris nodded and went to work. She handed a stack of documents to Stan, the paralegal for scanning and upload. Perusing what they had, analyzing tasks, she approached Stan. "Who would you pick to do the IT analysis of the digital evidence?"

He smiled. "I'm the guy."

"Fine, let's go to 3, and we'll talk about what they have and what you need to discover." In the room, behind the door, she described how the Task Force had falsified records to convict Foster. Thankfully, Stan already had programs to ferret out the truth from the data. "We need to know where and when. If we can identify the computer, all the better." She added, "I will forward the spreadsheet of Will's location and duties for his time with the Task Force."

Stan stared at the spreadsheet. "You assembled this?"

"Yes, from the digital files sent from the attorneys correlated with Will's statements. We have to be fleet of foot here."

"Has the date been set?"

"No, but we need to find as much exculpatory evidence as possible." A hope had been growing that perhaps a jury trial could be avoided without taking a deal. She knew and had worked with US Attorney Nat Summers. Perhaps, if things broke their way, he could be approached. "I will check with you to see how it's coming. Let me know if you need anything. Don't wait until you're done. I will be interruptible. Call me if I'm not in the office."

Paul had made it clear the junior attorneys would be available to help with motions but also had other duties. She would contact them after their meeting the next day. She sat back at her desk, running through the witness list. She had already completed the initial workup and began to consider the ones they needed to interview.

A call came through. Chris answered and heard, "Hello, Miss Worden. This is Sheryll Platt. We met outside of Radson and Clarks."

"Of course, Sheryll, I remember you. How can I help you?"

"I think it's what I can do for you. Can we meet?"

"Yes, of course." Chris named a coffee shop nearby. "Are you available now?"

"Definitely."

"I'll be waiting for you." Chris packed up her laptop, slid it into her case with a few files and headed out. Stan was busy with his assignment, and she was mostly ready for tomorrow's meeting.

Sheryll walked through the door an hour later. "Traffic," she explained, "and parking."

"Always a challenge. Are you still working for the firm?"

"No." She looked at Chris. "Are you familiar with the phrase *glass ceiling*?"

Chris smiled. "I assume it's pretty low there—as in scan, make copies, mail letters…"

"Bring the coffee service." She sighed. "I've paid my dues, Miss Worden…"

"Call me Chris. I understand. Do you have a proposal?"

"May I join your team? I heard what you had to say, and I don't believe what they say on the news."

She had checked into the young woman and hadn't seen any red flags. "You understand this will be a short-term assignment."

"It might be a while, right? If it goes to trial, that could be months."

Chris nodded, and they came to an arrangement. She didn't want to pull Stan away from the digital evidence. "You ready to visit Will?"

"Yes." She looked at her purse. "I didn't bring anything with me."

"I have notepads. You'll have to use your own computer, but first, let's find a place for you at Nolan, Briggs and Kishner."

"They took your case?"

"They agreed to assist me with the case."

At the detention center, Chris and Sheryll waited in a client-attorney room for Will to appear. She filled her in on the broad details of the case. "Will was tasked with finding and developing sites for Task Force prisons. He spearheaded the approval process with the Department of

Justice, demonstrating the facilities would adhere to federal standards. We need to find proof of the installation of appropriate protocols and procedures, and that he never intended Rosemont to be a death camp."

Will walked in and smiled broadly. "Someone new! Second day in a row."

"I heard about your meeting with Chartrand. He'll be the lead, for the most part, at trial." Chris introduced Sheryll. "She will be assisting me."

"Glad to meet you, Mr. Masters."

"Just call me Will."

Chris watched as Will's charms helped Sheryll relax. "Now, you need to describe every conversation you had in the beginning about your goals and dreams for Rosemont—before the rumors and accusations started. How and when did Kincaid start the process for the Task Force to run their own prisons?"

"Well, right after my promotion and you left for the Secret Service, Kincaid and Otis met with me first. They asked how I thought HCL offenders were doing in federal prisons, giving me the impression that they were as concerned as I was about the assaults and attacks on these particular prisoners."

"They didn't mention any other reason for having your own HCL prisons?"

He shook his head. "They asked the question and let me ramble about the unfortunate incidents in detention and in prisons. Sending pastors to penitentiaries didn't work well for some."

"And they agreed?"

"They seemed to. While I suspected their desire to gain access to inmates after conviction, I considered the guidelines I had set in place would ensure inmates' rights were protected. I had never heard of plans for re-education and death camps. The thought never entered my mind that anyone who had ever served in law enforcement would ever consider it acceptable to assassinate prisoners."

"Who did you meet with daily?"

"Three admins on the third floor: Tammy, Deb, and Amy-Sue, and I convinced Kincaid to let Joe Lyle assist me. Tammy organized the BOP regulations, protocols, training and rules of engagement for prison staff. Deb had been a realtor and helped me find the right locations—distance to major highways, smaller cities with adequate infrastructure, all the parameters one had to consider. She also created the initial list for possible architectural firms. Amy-Sue worked with Lyle on everything else. They were the ones who knew what Rosemont was supposed to be. It's too bad, Lyle was a talented young man who could have gone far in the right agency."

"Didn't you meet with Kincaid, Barrie and Otis?"

"Kincaid was often at the White House. He had meetings with the managers—investigations, outreach, you remember the divisions. I rarely met with him as I was tasked with creating facilities acceptable to the DOJ, the Department of Justice. And he gave me a short timeline for such a massive task—not only find the locations, develop the facilities, create rules and regulations, training programs, with all the other details."

"Didn't the prisons have to be ready to go for approval? It's curious that Rosemont had not been renovated."

"Somehow he managed to bypass that step. I wasn't a part of it. I worked furiously to push through permits, funding and contracts as soon as possible to meet the timeline, but there were always roadblocks. Now that I look back on it, they were obstacles Kincaid created. Then one day Otis walks in with the signed approval. He actually said we had the green light and could proceed."

"When did you become Northeast Director? During this process?"

Will furrowed his brow. "Wait, it seems that I was transferred out shortly after our approval went through. Even though Kincaid hadn't officially named me as prison director, it was still my project. He assured me that my current position covered that."

"Hadn't you already hired staff and started training?"

"We had collected résumés and had completed the initial selection process. I did not interview or hire anyone. Otis did that. Once I became a regional director, Otis ran the prison project and Barrie came on board to run the training sessions."

"Do you remember the names of the firms?"

"I can't. I've tried."

"That's okay. We'll keep digging and see what we can uncover." Chris looked at Sheryll. "Now we have to locate your assistants and take their depositions." She glanced back at Will.

"Yes, go. I know you've got to be in the fast lane. At least, I can pray for you." He hugged her briefly when she stood and whispered in her ear, "Someday, we'll be like a normal couple." Laughing lightly, he released her reluctantly. "Nice to meet you Sheryll. Good hunting."

Chris winked at Sheryll right outside the detention center. "Never forget to ask the secretary," she said. "Kincaid pushed me out of his organization. I'm so glad he did. Now it's back to the office, locate the staff and take their statements. And we need to get it done in two days."

Tammy lived in Pennsylvania and agreed to provide a statement later that afternoon. If it needed to be officially notarized, she could go back later and complete those steps. Chris tried not to give in to disappointment when Deb refused to meet, even though she lived nearby. "Hope is on Amy-Sue then," Chris mused.

Amy-Sue was more difficult to locate. Chris left Sheryll at the office to search for the third assistant, while Chris drove to meet Tammy. Her statement was helpful and informative, clearly establishing Will's goals and intentions for the prisons, but she couldn't recall the architect's name.

Chris, on the road back, answered a call from Sheryll.

"You'll never guess where Amy-Sue is," Sheryll stated. "She moved back home to Atlanta. I'll text her contact info."

"That's great, Sheryll. Clock out and have a good evening. I'll let you know if we're going on a trip or not."

"Did she know the name of the architect?"

"No, said Deb knew."

"Well, that's that."

"Keep praying," Chris said before she could take it back. She didn't even know if Sheryll was a Christian or if she was hostile to the faith.

Sheryll paused and then said "I'll pass it on my mom. That's her specialty."

Chris' eyes teared. "That would be so encouraging. Knowing others are pulling for Will. It's…"

"Never easy, but it's always good; that's what she says, anyway."

"Well, have a good evening. Thanks for the good work today."

"I had a blast."

Amy-Sue agreed to make a statement, and Chris wanted to make the eleven-hour drive to Atlanta directly after updates were heard and assignments handed out. Paul consented to a working lunch when she offered to cater the meal.

Stan had made good progress with the digital evidence. Sheryll volunteered to help match it up with Will's schedule and assist in the analysis. Chris listened to the motions that had yet to be filed and additional evidence requests. The junior attorneys could handle those.

"So, anything else?" she asked, waiting to see if Paul had any further directives. Hearing none, she asked, "With what you have heard so far from the deposition and Stan's discoveries, does it sound like we're making progress?"

No one jumped in. After an uncomfortable pause, Paul stated he was somewhat encouraged but reminded them that everything would be subject to intense cross, and they would have to work to make the point that the digital evidence did not prove the charge.

Chris nodded. "We cannot win this case solely by damaging the digital evidence. However," she paused for effect, "with Tammy's statement, and if Amy-Sue is as good, we might have a chance to see a nolle prosequi from US Attorney Summers." She held back her laughter with the look of shock on Paul's face. The others stared at her as if she were crazy.

A nolle prosequi motion had to be filed by the prosecuting attorney, indicating his desire no longer to pursue the charges due to fatal flaws in the evidence or new evidence showing the defendant's innocence.

"I've brought several high-profile cases to Summers. We had worked very well together. In fact, he occasionally brought me in for advice, even sent an investigation to one of my teams. He's thorough and topnotch; it's rumored he could be the US Attorney General someday. He's fair, honest, but meticulous, demanding and can be impatient if played. We must not forward any of these findings to him until I am ready to present them to him in person."

Before Paul could state his objections, Chris continued. "In some sense, everything is political and even more so with this case. Believe me, the idea to charge Will with genocide originated with Kincaid a long time ago. Will overhead Kincaid telling the guards he was to be kept alive because there was 'a purpose for him.' This is it. When I present the evidence, I will also let Nat know that when my husband testifies, he will name names. Will had conversations with both Norton and Kincaid where they unequivocally expressed their support and direct involvement in the death camps. Once they realize that laying the blame on Kincaid will also point the finger at the former president, the chief of staff and department heads, I believe the desire to prosecute this case will wane."

"Summers will not admit that to you."

"Probably not, but I can plant the seed, nonetheless."

"If he doesn't go with nolle prosequi?"

"With the help of our team, I believe our chances of acquittal are increasing by the day." She smiled. "I leave immediately for Atlanta.

Oh, and the names and locations of these new witnesses are to be kept strictly confidential. I will try to withhold their identities for as long as possible. Kincaid still has some contractors at his disposal. That is why I am making video and audio recordings to go along with the signed statements. I should be back by late tomorrow."

Chris waited in her car a few doors down from Amy-Sue's compact ranch. The drive had been uneventful, the motel quiet as it was mid-week. Chris slept in and went to breakfast. She processed files on her laptop until it was time to head out for a leisurely lunch at a local strip mall with coffee shop, stores and restaurants. Amy-Sue said she would be home around three.

Feeling almost rested, Chris watched a late-model Toyota compact pull into the drive. Once she identified her witness, Chris exited the car, her large tote over her shoulder, and headed up the sidewalk.

The large black woman in flowing skirt and braided hair turned her way. "Well, well, I remember you now," she greeted, pulling Chris into a hug.

"I'm sorry, but…" Chris tried not to stutter.

"Understandable. Didn't see you but one time on the third floor. When did you leave the Task Force?"

"I stayed long enough to get Hawsley to take the plea deal. Didn't want the ladies to have to testify against him in court."

"He was a bad one. I'd not like to be him on judgment day."

Chris stopped and faced her. "At the time. I wondered how a Christian could do such a thing."

"Not all's that says they're saved are."

"Agreed, and now I know that even after salvation, we can still get trapped by sin. He's on my prayer list, whether or not he knows God. Many in prison do find God."

"Or get back with Him." She glanced at Chris' tote. "Need help?"

"I'm good. Have a video camera, if you don't mind? That way they can see and hear your testimony."

"I can go back to testify. I'd be willing."

"Thank you. I will surely keep that offer in mind. We're still in the planning stages." She followed her into the long, narrow living room. "Where should I set up?"

"Let's get some sweet tea and take the weight off our feet."

"Sounds good." Chris put her tote on the couch and sat on the end near the kitchen, just on the other side of a short wall. "Still warm here. Getting chilly in Maryland."

"You know, the district was fun—for a time." Her eyes rested on Christine's rings. "Miss Christine Worden or are you married?"

"Will Masters is my husband."

"Oh, that's hard to handle. Knew you were close—worked so well together, and he always had such nice things to say about you. Mr. Masters was a fine gentleman. He'd let the babysitter drop off my two boys if I needed to work late and let them play in a conference room or his office. And he didn't ask us to stay late too much. Real considerate."

"So, did Will talk to you about his plans for Rosemont? What kind of a prison it was supposed to be?"

"Supposed to be a real nice place. After I talked with that young woman…"

"Sheryll, my assistant," Chris said.

"I went downstairs and found my box. I'll get it." Amy-Sue returned with two boxes and set them by her on the floor. She opened the first and pulled out a miniature model.

"Rosemont!" Chris said, putting her hand to cover her mouth. "That's Rosemont, isn't it?"

"Yes. You've seen this before?"

"Only as an image on his notepad. What an answer to prayer!" She reached out to hold the woman's hand. "What an answer!" She leaned closer to read the nameplate: Wilkins, Marsh and Terry. "Do you happen to remember the architect's name? It seemed as if Will worked closely with one."

"Mr. Daryl Sanford." Amy-Sue opened the other box and placed three piles of paper on a nearby coffee table. "Training manuals, fashioned after the federal codes. Staff paperwork with their positions and duties. And the prison specifications for all seven. Will gave me the Rosemont model to take care of when he became regional director. Otis never asked for it, and I like to keep copies at home—just in case something goes missing at work."

Chris nodded. "How long did you stay?"

She looked aside. "It hurt my soul when I heard they'd killed Joe. We worked closely together. A fine young man." Amy-Sue looked at Chris. "I pray you win and win big. Bring it out into the light. The training schedules, documents and forms had been developed. Joe worked on that. Mr. Masters spent a lot of time with the budgets, securing the money to start construction, but everything changed after the approval, and they promoted him. I left shortly after."

"What caused you to leave?"

"Otis and Kincaid's nephew." She shook her head.

"Barrie Reynolds?"

"Yes, Mr. Reynolds took over the training, but they changed it. I was supposed to help with the meals, clean up—stuff like that. Not like with Will and Joe. I could've put up with Reynolds and Otis until I could transfer to a different department, but then they changed the program."

"How so?"

"The manuals were replaced with the three-step plan." Amy-Sue pulled out a thin stapled booklet. "First, they sit in cages with two meals and no privileges. To earn a spot in a level 1 camp with regular meals, infirmary and commissary, they have to agree with the new laws and turn in their friends and neighbors. It was bad, reading that. After a month or so, the ones who refused would be sent on to the other camps..."

Chris reached for her hand. "That's okay. You don't have to go into specifics. What I need to record is your statement that this…" She held the first training package. "…was Will's plan, and the three-step plan was not. Mrs. Johnson, who supported the new plan?"

"All of them. They never talked about it in front of Will, Mitch, or Sandy, but everyone else on third floor was in on it. That's when I took my exit. Came home and lived with my mother until I found another job."

"That was a good move." She glanced at the piles. "Anything else?"

"I think that's it."

Chris explained the process, set up the camera and they recorded the statements with the evidence. "May I take the model and the documents? I could make copies. Is there a place near here?"

"My copier's downstairs. With a printer."

"Great. I'll video your statement, transcribe it and we can go to the Merchant Bank not far from here to have it notarized."

Chris praised the Lord that Amy-Sue was direct, articulate and thorough in her statement. She quickly transcribed it, and Amy-Sue printed three copies.

"Where are your sons?"

"They're in high school now. Staying with friends. They were eager to play video games over there."

"I think we can make the notary in time if we leave soon. May I take you to supper? Do you have a suggestion?"

"Just my favorite place for good homecooked meals."

"Let's go." They headed out in time to catch the notary. Chris brought her bags and the boxes with her.

She followed Amy-Sue to a white, two-story clapboard house on the outskirts of her area.

"Momma's Kitchen—my place to go. You like Southern food?"

"Some of it. Not very experienced." Chris laughed. "Looks good with plenty of veggies."

"Also, the best pies."

Chris found it easy to talk with Amy-Sue about her faith. She shared about Will's struggles. "He's a Christian now, and that makes all the difference."

"I can at least write him."

"He'd really appreciate that." Chris wrote out his address and number. "Remember, all letters are read, so no confidential information, but quoting verses and prayers would be acceptable."

"Always looking for chances to talk about God and His glory. You driving home?"

"Tomorrow morning. Have one more night at the motel."

She left copies of everything with Amy-Sue. They prayed over the house. She prayed for Amy-Sue and her sons, that the Lord would send His angels to guard them. Amy-Sue prayed the same for Chris, Will and his defense team. Before she left, Chris hugged her, thanked her one more time, and said, "If you're in the area, let me know, and we'll get together. God bless you."

Chris went to bed early and rose before dawn. She planned on being at the firm by mid-afternoon.

She found Sheryll and Stan in the admin area.

"How did she do?"

Chris beamed. "Scored. Who's about?"

"Chartrand's in court, and the others were called away to work on other cases."

"All right. I'll wait for Paul to return from court. Catch me up to date. Anything new?"

It took Stan about ten minutes to update her. They were making progress, but there were no breakthroughs to speak of—nothing to the extent of what Amy-Sue had to offer. She checked her texts but was not surprised when Paul did not reply.

After stowing the camera and boxes from Amy-Sue, she said, "I'll catch a quick visit with Will and be right back."

The videos were already on her laptop, along with a copy of the documents in her briefcase, she headed to her car.

Will wrapped her in a hug. She melted into his embrace. "I have something to show you. Deb wouldn't tango, but Tammy's in Pennsylvania." She played the first video.

Will nodded. "This will help."

"Amy-Sue's in Atlanta. She remembers you, had many kind words." She smiled when Will stared in shock at the mini model in Amy-Sue's hands. His smile widened as she worked through the timeline to when he stepped away from the prison project.

"Remember nolle prosequi?"

"Maybe, fill me in."

"It's the motion a prosecuting attorney files when he's discovered the evidence is flawed or learns of new evidence that proves the defendant innocent. I plan on personally bringing the new evidence to Summers and perhaps he will file the motion." She smiled. "And I'm also going to tell him that you will testify that Kincaid and Norton supported and developed the death camps for all to hear in a public trial."

He grasped her hands. "We have a chance! There is hope!" Will paused. "What if it's God's will for the trial to go forward to expose Kincaid?"

"While I'd have to accept that, I'm still praying for the motion. God will be with us—no matter how it breaks. Are you glad now you didn't take a deal?"

"Yes, because you stood up for me."

"Anyway, I want to talk with Chartrand when he returns from court, but I had to show you. Keep praying. God's not done with us." She planted a kiss and knocked on the door.

"Hey, Chris, did she give you the model?"

"Yes, it's small, but you can't miss the fact it doesn't match what they Rosemont became."

Back at the firm, while she waited for Chartrand, she placed a call with Laurie, Attorney Summers' main associate. "Hey, Laurie, it's Chris Worden. I have some evidence to bring to Summers. When would be a good time?"

"Which case?"

"Masters."

"Oh…" Chris recognized the now-common response. "Well, how long might it take?"

"Under an hour."

"I can give you 30 toward the end of a lunch break Monday. Will that work?"

"I'll make it work. Which judge?"

"Cary, he's pretty regular with his lunch breaks—sugar levels. Say, one sharp. Oh, and Chris, I was sorry to hear the news. Tough break. But just so you know, I'm not assisting with that one."

"Thanks for the info. See you Monday. I'll be sure to text if I have to reschedule."

CHAPTER 24

W HEN PAUL CHARTRAND heard about the Monday meeting with Summers, he wanted to go with her, but she reminded him, "He won't be expecting me to push him. You walk in with me, and he'll be ready. I wouldn't insist on it if it wasn't necessary. Do you have time to give an update?" She noticed the tiredness seeping around his eyes. "Hey, we've both had long days. Tomorrow, morning?" Seeing the nod, she headed home.

She only had to bring new evidence—information they surmised the prosecution did not have. To avoid revealing their trial strategies, Chris went over with Paul what she should and should not say. Eventually, they settled on a plan, and Chris brought only what was required and no more.

The model and the documents had been tucked in the safe. They had digitized everything else. Files for Summers were on a common thumb drive.

Arriving early, Chris entered the large offices for one of the top D.C. United States Attorney. Laurie waved her over to her desk. As usual, she was halfway through a sub, pieces of lettuce threatening to fall on an open file.

"Having fun?" Chris asked. "It's been too long."

"So, let's see it."

"What?"

"The rock he gave you. All the good gals are hitched." She reached for Chris' hand to see the rings.

"Hey, we can still get together." Chris paused. They would have to change the venue. "But not at a bar. I'm into coffee now." Not knowing how much time she had, she added, "That new place down on C?"

"I heard they offered you a package to work for the Director of the Secret Service. When does that go through?"

"I resigned—for this case. We need to catch up." She looked to the door when Nat Summers walked in followed by two of his associates. They stepped past and into his large office.

Laurie, wiped her mouth, threw out the wrap, and said, "Give me a minute to feel things out. You ready?" She surveyed her friend. "Of course, you are."

Chris watched Laurie return five minutes later and heard her say, "Go in when the associates come out. He'll give you what time he can."

She nodded and prayed.

"Well, we have some time. You married William Masters. That's not a surprise. The mess he's in—that's the whammy." She leaned forward, "You're really going to fight it?"

She tilted her head with a taut smile. "I have to talk with Nat first. Not sure what I'll do when this is over."

Laurie flicked her eyes to the closed door. "You know why they gave it to him."

Chris nodded. He was the best, but he was also honest enough to admit when he'd been dealt a losing hand.

"All right. I know you won't talk." She tilted her head, taking in her friend with a laser-like focus. "What's so different with you?"

"I have my law degree, and I'm a Christian. My faith in Christ is getting me through this time with Will in detention facing these charges. Laurie, don't forget what kind of agent Will was and what kind of man he is. He's not changed for the worse, but for the better. And that is all I can say for now."

The large doors opened. Chris stood, clutching her briefcase. By the time the second associate had cleared the threshold, Chris held the edge of the right door and slid in. "Sorry, to be right on top of your session, but I have evidence we need to provide. I thought I'd deliver it in person."

Nat waved her in, his eyes still scanning the document in front of him. Slipping his glasses aside, he sat back and met her gaze.

She froze. Her mind went blank. "Attorney Summers, I have depositions and copies of evidence to submit for *United States v. Masters*." She cleared her throat, and prayed he'd agree to watch Amy-Sue's video testimony. She handed over the USB drive. "I'd like you to see video 1 while I'm here. That way if you have any questions, I'm here to answer."

She sat, praying.

He leaned forward, trying to keep his balance, fumbled for the open USB port and inserted the drive. "Video 1?" Seeing her nod, he started it, listening to Chris authenticate and document the witness, time, place and relationship to the defendant.

Chris tried to observe his reactions without staring at him.

"Who is this again?" Setting his hand on the desk and pushing against it, a common tic, he closed the video and looked at the file names on the drive. "The other documents?"

"Go along with the testimony of two new witnesses. Masters worked with three assistants and Agent Joe Lyle to develop Task Force prisons following federal prison standards. Amy-Sue Johnson and Tammy Walters worked with Masters on this project and can document his plans and intentions for Rosemont. I have also provided Lyle's testimony provided to Ireland. When we add additional witnesses to authenticate their testimony, we will provide that information as well. The attached documents should explain themselves, but I can answer questions anytime." She also relayed the substance of Will's testimony. Then she paused, resting her case.

He glanced at her, opened one and scanned it quickly. "Looks like right out of the BOP's A&O manual."

"Masters worked extensively with his contacts at the Department of Corrections to ensure Task Force prison regulations adhered to federal standards." Tempted to react to his smirk and rise to Will's defense, she added as evenly as possible. "Transcripts are provided for the videos. Miss Johnson has agreed to testify in person. Assuming everything goes ahead, we will most likely be adding her to the witness list. Like I said, Masters will testify to his true intentions for Rosemont and repeat statements from Norton, Kincaid, and others, that indicated their involvement in the prisons." She leaned forward. "Both Norton and Kincaid told him the President and his administration approved the executions. He is looking forward to the chance to clear his name." Fearing she'd said too much, she rose. Tempted to ask about the date, she decided to stand, see what he said, and watch to gauge his reaction.

He shook his head. "Unbelievable." He flicked his eyes up to meet hers. "You will be hearing from me."

"Thank you, Nat. I greatly appreciate the courtesy. I didn't want you to be caught unawares." They both nodded, professionals who respected each other to know when to say no more.

Later that day, Chris looked up from the data set she was examining. It had been a long day. They were still slogging through the digital evidence, and Chris helped Sheryll run the analytics. Mike, one of the other attorneys, approached and handed her a transcript.

"What? Who is this?"

"The head Rosemont guard." He pointed to the fourth line. "He will testify that Will personally interviewed and hired him for the job."

She navigated to the spreadsheet for Will's schedule to match the date. "Does he say where this happened?" She furrowed her brow. Will had been in the office that day, but then she remembered something about a nearby facility in the outskirts of Minneapolis.

He reached for the transcript. "Yes, here. Says it was in the office."

"Which office?"

"Which office?"

"Task Force headquarters had a building north of D.C. Will's offices for the Northeast district were there as well. I remember seeing somewhere that the prison division had an administrative office in part of an industrial building in the northern section of Minneapolis-St. Paul. I never went there, but Will was definitely in Maryland that day. Where was the guard? We need his location for that date."

Paul stood, listening to the exchange. "Something they would have to verify with a known metric."

Chris smiled, seeing they had been given the witness' cell number, asked, "Do you have access to historical cell phone tower records?"

"It was how many years ago?"

"Four." She glanced between Paul and Stan.

Paul looked at Stan. "Do we?"

"Yes, of course. Date and number?" He activated the program, entered the data and they waited. He leaned forward and said, "Looks like twin cities, then heading east. Definitely nowhere near Maryland."

Paul smiled at Chris. She nodded. "I'll write it up and send it on to you, Mike. Do you have a format for trial notes? I think we'll be asking that witness some questions and maybe…" Seeing Paul's nod, she added, "discredit his testimony."

Paul added. "Mike, make sure you and Sara forward all the witness transcripts to Chris. I think it would be good for her to see if we can find other flaws in their evidence." He stepped aside. "Oh, Chris, I have a little time."

She followed him into his office, shut the door behind her and sat in the chair across from his desk.

"Well, hear from Summers yet?"

"No, but that's not surprising. He's lead attorney in a big case right now." She watched Paul nod. She was glad to see he did his homework. "I asked him to watch Amy-Sue's video testimony while I was there. I also gave him a brief summary of Will's testimony concerning Norton and Kincaid. He was clearly bothered. I'd seen that look before when he realizes a key witness has been caught in lies. The fact the head guard will be put forward to lie about Will hiring him would not break their case, but will sow seeds of doubt. Amy-Sue and Tammy's testimony does damage it greatly."

She took a breath. "Will and I are now Christians because of our time with the Task Force. We met real Christians and saw true faith in action. God is real, and He will be with us, whether we go to trial or Summers chooses not to proceed. Either way, we will do our best, and I will be here every day—for as long as it takes to give this our best shot." She cracked a smile. "And if they take this to court, and we win…"

Paul nodded. "We win big. But don't bring this up again. We want the team to focus on the trial prep."

"Of course. Next steps?" She smiled. Perceiving that Paul was accepting her input felt good.

The week dragged on with nothing heard from the US Attorney's office. She assigned some legal research to Sheryll and watched her navigate the firm's legal databases like a pro. The days were long. She tried to remind herself to take breaks, but there was always one more piece to verify, one more fact to disprove. She should have seen the workload as a heavenly distraction since visits with Will were growing harder to bear—the agony of separation increased each time until she skipped a day, only to toss in bed that night, regretting the decision.

Trying to decide the best time to visit Will, knowing she didn't have anything new to share or questions to ask, she sat back and rubbed her eyes. Just as she bookmarked her place and closed the file to reach for her purse, Sally-Ann walked over to Stan. He rose and gestured for her to follow him into Paul's office.

"Sir, the Attorney General's office is on line 3. They want to meet with you and Mrs. Masters."

Chris stepped aside to let Stan past. "That's me. I probably should make it official but haven't gotten around to change my name." She smiled. He nodded and closed the door. *Am I now Mrs. Christine Masters or am I Christine Worden-Masters?* She shook her head. She actually liked the ring of Mrs. Christine Masters.

Paul hung up the phone. "They're calling a meeting in Judge Halbert's chambers tomorrow at three."

"Could it be?"

"Possibly. Could be any number of reasons, but it's probable."

"What do we bring?"

"They did not state we were required to bring anything."

"The motions we've prepared?"

He thought a moment. "Next meeting or we call it."

Chris smiled. "A little show and tell, however." She leaned forward. "I bring the model and lead with that."

Seeing his agreement, she said, "Well, I'm going to call it a day. It's late enough. Should I send some of them home?"

He breathed. "Yes, sometimes it's tempting to work so hard you don't have anything left for the trial."

"Tomorrow then." She heard his assent and goodbye on the way out. She would visit Will even if it might interfere with his supper.

Judge Halbert's chambers were moderately sized for a federal district judge. Half the large office held his mahogany desk with floor-to-ceiling bookshelves along the corner walls. Padded chairs formed a ring in front of the desk, with more chairs pushed up against side walls, just under tall windows.

The judge's chief clerk escorted Chris and Paul Chartrand to the large doors. "They're waiting for you."

Chris stepped through, holding a white box in her hands. She recognized the judge from her research and two of the three attorneys sitting in chairs in front of the desk. The man seated directly in front of the judge looked slightly familiar. After a moment she recognized him as the deputy Attorney General. The three chairs formed a semi-circle facing two that had been pulled away from the outer wall. They rose as one when Chris and Paul stepped through the door.

The judge said, "Welcome to my chambers, Mr. Chartrand. And you must be Ms. Worden?"

They nodded and headed to the two chairs facing the group. Chris said, "It is a pleasure to meet you, Judge Halbert."

"You know US Attorney Summers and US Attorney Russell." She nodded at Russell who had prosecuted Hawsley. "Acting United States Attorney for the District of Columbia Drummond." Chris observed Paul knew Drummond well. "And Deputy Attorney General Hallen." Several stated it was good to see Paul.

Chris prayed for guidance. Seeing the nod from Chartrand, she pulled out the model. "We have uncovered new evidence. This is a model of the plans for Rosemont as it should have been." Fearing she had overstepped, she smiled and sat.

"Interesting," the judge said and looked at Summers. "Do you have a motion for me?"

"Your Honor, in light of the new evidence provided by Attorneys Chartrand and Worden, I am filing a motion for nolle prosequi."

"Based on a model?" Drummond asked.

"Based on two new witness statements. The model corroborates their testimony." He hesitated. "Based on the evidence they have provided a successful prosecution is in doubt."

Chris knew he was phrasing his words carefully. There was no real exoneration of federal charges with the motion and no statute that allowed expunging a record even if there was proof of innocence. The only way to clear a name was to win at trial.

"Anything else, Mr. Summers?"

"Counsel has indicated that the defendant will testify on his own behalf and that he will testify to statements made to him by Kincaid and Norton, that they developed the death camps, supported the execution of prisoners, and that they had the support of the President, his administration and the chief of staff."

Stunned silence filled the room. The judge, after a moment, glared at Summers and Drummond. "Is it credible?"

Summers cleared his throat. "I believe it is."

Drummond began to rise. "We will get to the bottom of this. Mr. Masters is the architect. We will examine it carefully."

When Paul rose, Chris stood beside him. She placed a hand on his arm. This was her fight. "Gentlemen." She reached for the model, cradling it in her hands. "This is the architectural rendering of Will's vision for Rosemont. It was to have been equivalent to Purcellville FPC, where he was recently held. He envisioned a place of retreat for pastors and church leaders to reflect, giving them time to accept the new laws. Masters had nothing to do with the Rosemont Kincaid created or the cremation chamber used by Norton in Oklahoma.

"The stories you have been told are false. Who ordered Lyle and Hutton executed? Will had nothing to do with that. Who ordered the killing of journalists? Who instigated false convictions for those who tried to stand against the Task Force? I have personally assisted in efforts to overturn the convictions of Foster, Branton, Wray and Lesters. Will had no involvement in any of these illegal actions.

"Believe me. We are sifting through every piece of evidence we have received through discovery and are finding inconsistencies, misstatements and outright lies. If this motion is denied, we look forward to exposing the lies and to Masters speaking on his own behalf in open court."

She had to stop before she went too far and ruined the moment. However, many averted their eyes.

Paul nodded, standing by her side. They faced the judge and lawyers.

Judge Halbert stated, "You will be hearing from us."

CHAPTER 25

Chris led the way out of the judge's chambers. She paused at the top of a long flight of stairs, trying to keep from shaking.

"I can carry that," Paul offered. "You were very brave."

She nodded, "Thank you. This is my fight. No sense in ruining any more lives. Mine's already…" Stopping, she breathed, tried to compose herself, and took the next step.

Thankfully, Paul's chauffeur was waiting for them. In the back seat, she asked, "I thought the nolle prosequi was the prosecutor's call."

"It is, but he has to answer to his overlords."

"I'm still confused. If they can force him to continue with the trial, wouldn't that discussion have been held in Drummond's office?"

Paul laughed. "You're not the only one playing politics to force a consensus. If I were a betting man, I'd say he hoped you would rise to the occasion and lay out the dangers of going to trial. The only shame of it is this will always be on Will's record."

"I know, but going through the months of a trial…" She shook her head. "And you know how irrational juries can be, especially with such strong public sentiment against the defendant. You heard Hallen. At least he didn't call Will the butcher of Rosemont." She turned her head and blinked away a few tears, trying to forget her brief confrontation with Stella Hutton when she told her that her assistance was no longer required at the Foundation and that she would not be welcome at the center. "People I had considered to be friends no longer talk with me or return calls."

He patted her hand. "You did very well."

"How long before we hear?"

"This is new territory for me."

"Me too." She tried to laugh and clear the air. "What do I tell Will?"

"Tell him what happened. Will he understand the terms?"

"He has a law degree from Georgetown. Finished right after he completed his training with the FBI. Said he wanted to know what the lawyers needed to make a case go through and not be thrown out. He was also tired of lawyers running rings around them with ridiculous requests. Some seemed afraid to go forward with a case and make unreasonable evidence requests."

"That's interesting. He never practiced law?"

"No, but put it to good use in his years with the agencies. That is over. He told me he will never work for the government again."

"I can see his point."

At the office, Chris stood by the curb, watching the chauffeur drive away.

Paul said, "You can call it a day. I'll put the model in the safe."

"Tell them what happened." Chris couldn't keep disappointment from her voice. The weight upon her threatened to take her breath away.

"I'll walk you to your car."

"Thank you."

Pushing against her desire to curl up and never leave her room, she drove to the detention center to see Will.

She couldn't hold back the tears when she described the meeting.

He held her in an embrace. They said nothing for a long time.

Chris stood back and wiped her face. "In God's hands." She wanted to say it confidently, but her voice squeaked and trembled.

Will held her hands. "In God's hands," he said confidently.

"Your name will not be cleared."

"It is in God's courtroom," Will said, his eyes taking in the figure of his wife, tall and brave.

———— ⌘ ————

The next morning Will ate his breakfast, keeping Chris in constant prayer. He reached for his journal and Bible to begin his morning devotions, but the sound of many feet walking quickly grew louder. He rose, wishing he could see through the door. Tempted to stand closer to hear, he jumped back a little when they opened his door and ordered him out.

The guard shoved him up against a wall, and two others put on a full set of chains. He couldn't make out what they were saying, and no one would answer his questions.

They marched him to the infirmary where a nurse looked at him quickly, took his blood pressure and his pulse and confirmed him fit to be moved.

Will's mouth went dry. Yesterday Chris had dared them to go forward with a trial. They knew he could point a finger all the way up to the White House. *Does Kincaid's reach extend to the federal prisons? Are they handing me over so I can be erased?* Holding onto an inner thread of hope, he battled against the nameless unknowns.

They marched him down corridors and through locked doors to an underground garage to a black van with the side door slid back. When he didn't step fast enough, they practically lifted and shoved him into the second seat. A slim guard secured his shackles to the floor. Thinking he would be whisked away—fears of never seeing Chris again rose up, almost drowned him with sorrow.

Indistinct voices, some angry and impatient, seeped through. The van did not move. He couldn't see the driver's compartment due to thick tinted glass. *I'm in a moving tomb,* his mind shrieked. Will twisted his wrists against the cuffs, wishing this was over, wishing things were different, fearing the end.

He heard the back hatch open, felt a whiff of cold air and the sound of items being dropped with a thud. The hatch closed, the air once again became still and suffocating. Then the vehicle lurched forward, and he focused on remaining upright. Blind, he could not see. Eventually, he found his center in Christ and tried to hold it.

The process was reversed. He stepped through doors and walls and long halls, but it was not a prison and was not underground. At the last door, they pushed him into a large space bounded by dark paneling, crafted wood railings and tall structures on his left. He didn't dare raise his head or he would stumble and fall with the shackles. Hearing a slight sound, he looked to his right, and his eyes widened.

Chris stood next to their lawyer. She wore her best pantsuit, but her face was drawn.

The bailiff who stood behind him said, "All rise for the honorable Judge Halbert."

Being this was a closed session and everyone was already standing, the statement was a mere formality.

Judge Halbert, middle-aged with a receding hairline, was still fit and handsome with dark hair and eyes. He set his gaze on the prosecuting attorney. "Do you have a motion, Mr. Summers?"

"I do, Your Honor. In the matter of *United States v. Masters*, I wish to file a nolle prosequi motion."

"I accept your motion, Mr. Summers." The judge looked at Will standing there in an orange jumpsuit, unshaven and his hair a mess, with a full set of chains. "Mr. Masters, a nolle prosequi motion means Attorney Summers has chosen not to go forward with your case; however, at any time in the future, given there is no statute of limitations for the charge of genocide, pursuant to U.S. Code 18 Section 1091, the United States may, at any time, go forward with this case."

"I understand, Your Honor," Will stated.

"Bailiff, you may release the prisoner." Judge Halbert gaveled the decision, rose and left the court.

Two guards entered with Will's personal effects and directed him to a side room to change.

Trying to reduce the wrinkles in his street clothes, he gladly removed the orange jumpsuit and dressed. He followed the guard through a side door to a hall where Chris and Chartrand waited.

He didn't know how long they held the embrace. Eventually, he stepped back. "Attorney Chartrand, thank you." He shook his hand.

"Thank your wife. She delivered quite the performance yesterday."

"I know. She told me."

"We can start working on trying to clear your name."

"We'll let you know. For now, I'd like to go home."

"My driver is waiting to take us to the office. I'm certain the team will want to hear the good news, and you folks can be on your way."

Will followed Chris and Paul to the third-floor offices. Meeting and thanking each one individually, they circulated through the large work room. Chris cleared out her desk and spoke briefly with Sheryll.

Stan, after answering a phone call, walked over.

"Chris said you did good work analyzing the digital evidence."

"She knew where to start looking."

"Nothing new under the sun."

When Chris returned with a partially filled box, Stan said, "Mr. Chartrand can see you at three. Would that work? Settle up and discuss next steps?" He glanced at Will.

Chris stared at the room at the empty desk where she had worked countless hours just the day before.

Will reached past and shook Stan's hand, "Of course. Will give us time to go home and get myself presentable." He reached for the box. "I think I can carry this for you. Come along, Chris, I'm sure they have other cases that need their attention."

They brought his bags up to Chris' condo. She pushed the door back. "It's done. I had no idea they'd act so quickly."

"Guess Summers won the fight." Will stopped. He really didn't care who drove this charge against him. He only wanted to forget the last few years.

"I'll make a big breakfast. Want to shower?"

"That sounds wonderful." Will froze. This had been Chris' place, and he had only been in it a few times over the years. A wave of disorientation swept over him.

"I forgot. This is not my place. It's our home, together! Let me show you where your things are." Chris stepped into the walk-in closet and stepped to the right side. *Has it been just six weeks since his arrest? Since I purchased a few items for him?*

Will reached past to pull a pair of jeans from a shelf. "New?"

"I bought some for your…" The tension dissolved, and her shoulders shook. "Is it really over?"

"I hope so."

Chris led him to a long bureau. "I cleared out the left side for you." She stepped back, letting him discover. "I thought we'd do some shopping." She laughed with a hard edge. "I don't even know what type of clothes you're going to want or what you like." She sat on the bed. "What are we going to do?"

"Give ourselves time to adjust. Remember, have a normal life. I think we're due a vacation. Sleep in, shop."

"Go out to your favorite Italian restaurant." Chris watched the shadow cross his face. "Or another restaurant."

"Let's go on a road trip to thank Tammy and Amy-Sue but take our time. Drive the back roads." He twisted about, his mind feeling overwhelmed with the thinking required—what to wear, what to eat, what he should do next. His brain was tired.

Chris handed him a small decorative box with a felt-covered lid for putting pocket items. She pulled out a small drawer with Will's ID.

He reached for the packet of cards. The Wyoming driver's license was still good, but he handed his FBI cards to Chris. "I don't care what you do with them."

"I can see that we have a lot to do. I'll take some time before going job hunting."

"Not going back to the Secret Service?"

"No. Now I'll make a big breakfast, and you take a shower."

He paused just inside the standing shower. Chris had purchased some men's bath soaps and shampoo.

While it seemed they accomplished very little, the day raced by. Went to the bank to create joint accounts and order a credit card for Will. They reviewed their investment accounts. Before they could head to the mall to shop, Laurie called from Nat Summers' office.

After the short phone call, she said, "Attorney Summers wants to see me today."

"Did he say why?"

"Laurie didn't say. He's working in the office today, so I can drop by anytime."

"I think I'll tag along—for your protection." Will added, "He probably wants to hire you."

"Me?"

"Yes, and if I were him, that's what I would do."

"Good he doesn't know me as well as he thinks." Chris thought through the plan. "We drop by before the meeting with Paul. Gives us an excuse to cut it short if necessary. Needs to see us at three to go over your options, and we can settle up. I gave them a retainer." She glanced at Will. "So, lunch, shop and head over?"

"Lunch at home and nap. I never had a chance to read my Bible today or spend some quality time with you."

They said little on the drive to the US attorney offices. Will tried to hide his apprehension. *Is this a trick?* Shaking his head, he held the heavy wood door open and followed Chris in. He tried to ignore the look of shook on Laurie's face when she saw him.

"Oh, Chris…and Will. Glad to hear of your release. He said to walk right in." She glanced at Chris. "Will can wait here. I'll send him in if he needs to see both of you." Tapping a solid wooden chair by her desk, she smiled. "What's your favorite coffee blend?"

"Dark French roast." He sat in the chair, studying the family pictures on her credenza. "Growing family?"

"Mostly," Laurie returned with two mugs. "These one-pot machines are fast. Mostly, mine. He had a daughter with his first wife, and I have my two sons."

"I was sorry to hear about your divorce."

"It's a rough town to build a marriage. Some do fine, but we each had our careers and drifted away over the years. He's been very reasonable, and Matt and Ron love Earl." Her eyes rested on Will's left hand. "You and Chris make a good couple."

Will met her gaze, amazed he was speechless. What he wanted to say and what he should or could say to the lead attorney's main associate and brilliant office manager swirled in his mind.

"It takes time, patience and lots of saying 'I'm sorry' and not saying 'Told you so.'"

Sighing, he nodded. Laurie kept the conversation going, encouraging and helpful. He listened and talked little until the door opened, and Chris stepped through. She shook hands with Nat. After tilting his head in Will's direction, a gesture Will remembered well from working with the attorney, he headed back into his office.

"Ready?" Chris asked. "Thank you, Laurie. I don't know if we'll be seeing each other here, but…" Her eyes took in the familiar office as she paused. "Let's keep in touch, shall we?"

"Of course, we're up near Frederick now. Nice neighborhood."

With smiles and nods, they walked through the doors. Chris didn't speak until they sat in the car. "Well?"

She looked at him. "You called it. He made a job offer. It was pretty good—by government standards."

Will laughed. "Guess he realized he'd rather have you working for him than sitting on the other side of the courtroom, objecting to his questions and motions. Did you take it?"

"What do you think?" Chris sighed. "Not the best thing to say. No. I said no, and I wasn't even tempted."

He resisted the temptation to say, "That's my girl," and instead said, "I want you to be happy—even if it is working for the United States government."

"Don't forget I have my regrets concerning the Task Force. If it can happen once, it can happen again. I never want to be in Nat's position where he's forced to prosecute someone who is innocent. I shouldn't have been surprised to hear of the political pressure to convict somebody of the whole travesty to show they've dealt with it."

"On to the firm."

Chris drove around one time before she found a spot in the underground garage. They walked up the steps and to the back end of the third floor. Chris spied the media center with copiers, a shared printer and paper cupboard. *Will I miss this place? It seems to have reverted back to when I first began to work with the firm—the associate attorneys working away in their cubes, the admins in their section diligently completing their tasks.*

Sheryll looked up from the floater desk she had been assigned to. "Chris," she beamed. "You're a little early. Coffee or tea?" She glanced at Paul's office door, seeing the figure of a woman gesturing with her hands as she talked. "One of his clients had to see him right away."

"You're here?"

"Yes, have a seat." She pulled over two chairs, sat and leaned over as if to talk.

"Let's grab room 2."

Once in the small conference room, Sheryll said, "I've accepted a job offer with Mr. Chartrand's staff, but I can also work for other attorneys while I figure out a specialty. They have internal training programs. I can learn more about real estate law, bankruptcies, divorces, family law, legal guardianships. It's…"

"They are a good firm, Sheryll. I'm pleased for you. Send your hours, and we can settle up."

"It looks like she is heading out. Ready, Chris?"

Will followed Sheryll and sat near her desk. "Will he make her an offer?"

"Oh, most definitely."

"An hour ago, she turned down one from the US Attorney's office."

"I'm looking forward to working with her." Sheryll lowered her voice. "Mr. Wallace, one of the senior partners, marched in and told Paul to hire her."

Chris emerged beaming.

Paul walked to Will. "I know it's bittersweet having the prosecutor decline to pursue your case without clearing you name, but I think you can live with that."

Will agreed. "With the media spin and the mood of the country, this would not be a good time to leave it to a jury." But he also knew what it meant; the case could be reopened anytime.

"Well, let's have a tour of the firm, and Mr. Wallace would like to meet with you."

"Should I?" Will asked.

"Both of you." They rode the elevator to the first floor, and Paul introduced them to the attorneys and staff for each section, grouped by legal specialty. The partners' offices were on the fourth floor. He followed the couple into Ed Wallace's office, as spacious as a judge's chambers. The four sat at a compact square dark word table.

Wallace welcomed Chris to the firm, expressed his assurances that she would be a valued asset for Chartrand's team and dismissed him with a nod.

It was the three of them. Ed Wallace studied Will.

"You've had a roller coaster ride with the agencies. At one time good money would have bet you'd be two steps just under the FBI deputy director." He shook his head. "It's unconscionable that the attorney's office would cave to a thug like Kincaid. He's ruined so many people—senators, congressmen, lawyers, wardens." He nodded in Chris' direction. "Brilliant work getting that warden cleared." He leaned toward Chris. "What did Summers say? Reveal who pressured him to go forward with such a ridiculous charge?"

Chris looked at the elderly partner. "He didn't say much but did allude to tremendous pressure without naming the sources."

Will laid a gentle hand on her arm. "His associate was more forthcoming. She told me the order to prosecute came down from the Attorney General himself the day after he visited the White House."

Chris looked at Will. "Wouldn't you expect him to have some business with the White House?"

"Yes, of course, but the timing is suspect."

"That bluff that he had conversations with Kincaid that implicated the President." He shook his head.

"That wasn't a bluff," Will stated. "I couldn't believe the charges leveled against the Task Force because I never imagined they would be able to get away with such atrocities. Mr. Wallace, how else do you think he had the cover to run operatives on home turf and turn abandoned facilities into secret prisons?" Seeing the comprehension in the man's eyes, "Yes, it was condoned, protected, and enabled by the President, some members of his staff, as well as Senator Roxston."

"This is not over."

"No, it's not, but they will have a harder time getting to me."

"That's why I wanted to meet with you. Pro bono, we need to take the steps to clear your name."

Will shook his head. "It's nolle, and they could conceivably bring the case back to life, but I am innocent, and eventually, the truth will become evident in time."

"You sure about that?"

"No, but I have to find a way to leave this chapter of my life behind. Pursuing further legal action will only keep it in play for years."

"Well, then, I wouldn't wait, but if that's your decision, I wish you the best of luck. And…" He patted Will's knee. "…you could sign a book deal. They'd line up at your door with a big, fat check to publish a tell-all book. And it would sell."

"I'll take the suggestion under advisement. I appreciate your time and will remember your advice," Will acknowledged. They rose and shook hands.

"Thanks to Tom Hutton, it's been stopped for now. Had you ever met him?"

"I set him free from Rosemont."

"Ah, another damming fact."

"That they were ready to explain away as Will's attempt to assuage his guilt over having created Rosemont," Chris stated forcefully.

"Yes," Wallace conceded, "perhaps it would be best to let things lie for now. Stay in touch." He placed a gentlemanly kiss on Chris' hand. "Welcome to the firm. We look forward to the many contributions you will make and experienced wisdom you bring to the table."

"I look forward to learning, taking up the challenge to defend those the courts have decided to persecute."

They made their way to the car. "Charmer."

"He is," Chris agreed. "I had forgotten how thoroughly Kincaid had been able to control the narrative. Do you believe he truly did not know the former president approved the measures?"

"His ignorance of the situation should not have surprised us—just as the attorney's office accepting his excuse that these unethical measures had been done behind his back and without his knowledge shouldn't have surprised us." Changing the subject, Will asked, "When do you have to start with Nolan, Briggs and Kishner? Do you like the sound of that?"

"Yes. I told him I'd need at least two weeks. And you have to transfer your driver's license, get a car, and figure out what you're going to do with your time. I'll be busy most days."

"I already expected that."

Back home, Will activated his cell phone and called Dan. "Hey, I'm out. When can we meet?"

"Come over for supper."

Will walked to the kitchen. Chris was trying to figure out what to cook. "Dan invited us over for supper."

"Ask him if the Huttons are in town."

Puzzled, but figuring he could ask her later, he relayed the question. "Fine, seven will work." He ended the call. "What was that?"

"Stella Hutton bought the lie and basically told me my services were no longer required at her foundation."

"Oh, we'll have to pray about that."

"I have been, but I don't see any hope of reconciliation at this point."

"Maybe she needs to hear the whole story."

"Maybe she's already made up her mind. Anyway, is this the Dan whom Rick Carlson recommended?"

"Yep, we have history. I'll tell you the story." He held her hands. "Those days I was working undercover in Texas, I couldn't tell anyone names or places or what happened. It was bad enough they were after me. Dan's the one they sent to Ireland who worked with Tom in Dublin. I protected him for the months when I was undercover. We have a lot of sorting to do. I'd like us to be close friends who fellowship together. I think Dan will be part of my healing."

They had so many things to learn about one another. Chris nodded, walked to the cupboards near the wall, opened them and began to plan. "We need to make a shopping list, but I have no idea what you like. Spill the secrets. What are your favorite cereals?"

CHAPTER 26

WILL TOLD CHRIS everything he knew about Dan, but it wasn't much. Chris shared she had read that Tom's fiancée had married another refugee. "This is *that* Dan Smith?"

"Do you know where they're staying at the center? I have never seen it."

Chris didn't respond. She drove, tight-lipped.

Will figured it would be best to figure out how to reconcile with the Huttons at a later date.

"Irma will know where they are staying." However, Chris did not see her in the sitting or dining area.

Will was about to offer to send a text when a tall, young woman with flowing red hair and green eyes approached. "You must be Christine and William?" An Irish lilt embodied her melodious voice.

"Yes. Catherine?" Christine questioned as she extended her hand.

"In the flesh, so to speak." She giggled slightly, but hesitated. "Sorry, still getting used to living across the pond." She shook their hands. "They've provided a lovely suite and let me manage the place now that the Carlsons have a place of their own."

"Irma's not here?"

Catherine smiled. "They needed some time together without the interruptions." She laughed again. "I used to administer a refugee center. Interruptions make my day! Anyway, here we are."

The small suite looked more like an apartment. "We made do with just a bedroom as I have the former manager's office, and Dan has his library at the hall." She tried not to make a face when she saw the table filled with Dan's books and notes. "Mostly keeps it at the hall."

Dan rose. "Christine! I've heard so much about you."

"Really?"

"Irma mostly. Haven't seen you around lately."

Before she could respond, Will interrupted, "So, you brought your bride with you. Congratulations! It's a big adjustment."

"It is, but we are so excited. The center is even busier now as more inmates are coming to Purcellville. Irma helps with the Bible studies and some programming, but it keeps me occupied."

Catherine glanced at the table. "Dan, can you set the places? Chris, let's see if the stew's ready. Irish stew okay?"

"Of course, we'll give them some time." Chris joined Catherine in the kitchen.

Will knew better than to try to help Dan pile his items and set them on a nearby end table. "Thought you had an office at the hall."

"It's harder to justify spending every waking minute in my study when I have such a lovely wife. I take a project home when I can so we can at least be in the same space—even if we're working on different tasks."

They sat on the couch. "So, taking up construction?"

Will recognized Dan's jab. "Not really, but open for suggestions. Tell me about this hall of faith."

Dan relayed the background and described the facilities Charles Hutton had acquired. "We could use your help. I've heard you're good with project management, as well as being a good spy." He couldn't resist one more jibe.

"I would love to be your first seminary graduate, but not sure how the Huttons will respond to my offer to help."

"Why? Charles Hutton is willing to accept those with felony convictions, and yours have been cleared."

"Not with a nolle prosequi."

"Isn't that the same as a dismissal?"

"No, it simply means the evidence wasn't good enough to convict, which means the FBI can keep looking for better evidence and start the process all over again. No, according to Chris, Stella Hutton believes Rosemont is my fault. She blames me. Kicked Chris out of her foundation. We wouldn't have come if we knew the Huttons were in town. I'm sorry. Wish things were different, but I don't think either of us are welcome here or at the hall." He breathed deeply.

The man stared at him. Trying not to blabber under his direct stare, Will looked away.

"We can't let this stand. Will, we have to pray you both can reconcile with them—for your own sake as well as for Charles' initiative. I think you'd be instrumental in the ground floor development. I take it you're not going back to the FBI." Pausing, he added, "Will, we have to beware the root of bitterness that will destroy us and those around us."

Will nodded, but still looked away. "I wish it were so. Maybe, in time—but not right now." He rose, wanting to walk away and leave. *I am only kidding myself.*

Catherine called that supper was ready. She filled the bowls, and Chris placed freshly sliced bread and butter in the center of the table. Dan led the prayer.

"I've grown to love her stew," Dan said. "Chris, could you share with us your part in Warden Foster's exoneration?"

"Of course, I'll be glad to. On the surface the case appeared to be solid, but a thorough investigation revealed the evidence had been twisted or fabricated. The case was assigned to a reasonable judge, and he threw out the conviction, acquitting the warden."

"Are you still helping with the Hutton Foundation?"

"No." She looked between Dan and Will.

"He knows. I told him."

"Well, Dan, the last time I saw her, she made it clear she didn't want to see me around the foundation office or this center."

Catherine leaned forward. "She's dealing with her own grief and is in the hard phase. In Ireland, right after, she was as calm as a statue, but in time, grief has its way. Hold her close in your prayers."

"Honey," Dan said, "Would you agree that the Huttons highly respect Irma and Rick?"

"Oh yes, everyone does."

Dan looked at Will and Chris. "We can't go forward with the Lord if we have something against a brother, or if they have something against us. Will you agree to pray with us that the Lord will show us the way to bring reconciliation between you and the Huttons?" He added, "And if you agree, I'd like to discuss this with Rick so we can arrange a meeting."

Will recognized Chris' set look. He reached for her hand under the table. "We can pray for reconciliation and for them." He added, "Chris, they've lost their only son and half their family. Unless we can help them find family with other believers, they will be in a dark place too."

"Just like us?" Chris couldn't hold back. Through her tears, she said, "It's not just Stella. My friends are very few right now." She looked at Dan and Catherine. "It really helps that you still want to talk with us." She wiped her eyes. "In two weeks, I'll start with a law firm, working at least 80 hours a week. That'll keep me busy."

Dan would have reacted to Chris' last comment, but he noticed Catherine tip her head with a slight shake.

"And during these two weeks, are you taking a holiday—a honeymoon?"

"Something like that." Chris fingered the wedding ring on Will's left hand. "We'll take a few days, get some chores done and then we were thinking of visiting a friend in Georgia."

"Wish we could go, but Dan's busy already and weekends are full for me. But maybe we could visit your ocean. I miss not being closer to the water."

"Were you close to the Atlantic?"

"No, we were on the east side facing England. That's the Irish Sea."

"Sure! Will, I'm sure we could make that work. Let us know when you're free."

"Mondays are usually good."

"This Monday then." Chris smiled. "I have my favorite spots."

"And maybe you could introduce Catherine to your favorite stores. It's quite different here."

"Tomorrow?"

They talked. They laughed. Catherine shared some funny missteps since coming to the States. Dan related his surprises while living in Dublin. Talking about something other than court or jail was good.

"Oh, the Fosters have been attending church with the Connors." Dan remarked while Will and Chris were getting ready to leave.

"Passing the torch," Will said. "Good to hear."

"Hope you can come this Sunday."

"Of course." Will glanced at Chris. "I think it would be a good idea."

She looked away. "I really shouldn't care what they think."

"We'll save you a seat. Look for us. Early service and the teaching to follow. Dan's working through Joel."

"Look forward to it." Will smiled at Chris. "Dan's a superb lecturer."

"Right! Supposed to be a Sunday school class."

The next evening, retiring after a packed day of rebuilding his life, Will sat up from the couch when the intercom sounded.

Chris extracted herself from the afghan and asked, "Who is it?"

"Irma, dear. Have a moment?"

"Of course." She buzzed her in.

"What's up?"

"Not sure." She opened the door and Irma walked in, followed by Rick. "Is it cold?"

"Getting nippy." Irma walked over to Will to give him a warm hug. "And you too, dear. It's been so long since we've seen you."

After greeting them, Rick said, "Sounds like we have a lot to catch up on."

"Of course, we do." Will cleared the couch and sat in a recliner. "Tea? Coffee? Something hot."

"We're fine, dear," Irma said. She glanced at Rick.

Chris pulled a chair around from the table. "Now that we're probably going to have company occasionally, we might want to add another chair." She paused and sat.

"Yes," Will answered as he looked at the couple, wondering why they were here. "Lots of changes."

"It will take a while to settle. It's been more than a month." Irma held Rick's right hand.

"It's been that long since the pardons?" Chris shook her head. "How did you find your apartment so quickly?"

Rick beamed. "Irma found it once she had the release date. The family brought what we had put in storage, and it's like starting over again—after ten years!"

"That long!" Will shook his head. "It's amazing you survived."

"That is of the Lord, son. We love you both as if you were our own. In a sense, because we belong to Christ, we are family. And when family is hurting, you help. We'd like to help you."

Will knew what was coming. He'd seen this when Pastor Rick gently admonished another Christian. "What else can we do? I don't want to sound like we have to go through the case all over again."

"Will, she's only seen what the commission was told and what they were supposed to see. Maybe we do. Maybe we need to show them." Chris rose and retrieved the model. She described the night when Will showed her a picture of the vision for Rosemont. "Of course, the Rosemont you experienced was far different." She looked at the couple. "If you were in our shoes, what would you do?"

"Pray for them—not against them. Thank the Lord for them and asked Him to bless them. Pray for a chance to meet, presenting your side of the story." Rick lowered his voice. "She might not have realized that you are the one who released Tom."

"It might not matter with the way they presented the scenario. It could be argued that Will was simply acting out of guilt and remorse for a tragedy of his making." She nodded. "There's always a risk with such slanted views, that a jury still would have convicted him. We'll take the nolle and live with the stigma." She relayed the reality of a decision to stop prosecution.

Irma reached for her hand and tenderly caressed it as she implored, "Chris, believe in God, that He rewards those who diligently seek Him. We will plead with the Lord to bring the four of you together. We see you both having a part in their faith hall. Please don't let the Devil get the win. Seek to reconcile and love them no matter how they respond."

They shared their favorite verses and encouragements from the Lord. The friends wept and prayed together.

"So, Will, what's the next step?"

"I'll work with Dan to see what their schedules are like. Keep us in your prayers."

The next day, when Chris drove into the city to complete her application and fill out the employment forms, Will drove his new Tahoe to the center and followed Dan to the industrial park. Wide, mostly straight roads with some functioning warehouses and distribution centers dotted some of the lots closest to the main county highway, a half mile down from an interstate on-ramp. "Build-to-suit" lease and for-sale signs dotted most of the overgrown lots in between active businesses.

He followed Dan down a short side road with badly cracked pavement. A large building on the left looked like simple steel construction with a slight, sloping metal roof. A smaller building with a short brick front that might have held offices sat to the near right.

Dan walked the three lots Charles had acquired that occupied the end of the road. "He has options to buy two more but is waiting to develop this first."

"This is going to be a Bible college?"

"Actually, the board and a select group of friends have agreed to meet regularly to pray about what kind of school it should be."

"I thought it was to be a seminary?"

"Well, part of it." Dan headed back to the smaller office building and drew out a key. "In Dublin there was a fairly good online unaccredited Bible school that taught the basics with some excellent courses on selected books of the Bible. Practically self-funded by a group of churches, it laid the foundation. In fact, I have copies of their coursework and their permission to use it here. Everyone going into seminary needs to attain a certain level of Bible knowledge before starting. I think requiring the same foundation courses for the undergraduate college would be good. But why should we insist on seminary and masters level work if that's not what the Lord wants this place to be? So, we're praying about whether we shouldn't begin with a high-school level Bible school."

"Why not do all three levels to start with?"

"That possibility has been suggested. Hey, if we can work it, maybe you could join us?"

"I'd like that. I thought I'd be your first M.Div. graduate."

"Well, that possibility is probably quite far down the road. The Masters of Divinity degree is one of the most difficult to attain and often requires as many credit hours as a law degree." He noticed Will's smile. "Yes, I know you are ready. Should I start looking for a good online seminary?"

"Well, I do need to pray about what God really wants me to do. Make sure it's not just me. You know. Things can get confusing."

"Don't I know it." He paused, watching a dark Lexus drive down the road. "That would be Charles. Well, God has intervened."

"Rick and Irma visited us recently. I needed that reminder. It was something else to have been his roommate for several months. I really struggled in there. God humbled me, and I didn't always handle it well. Never took offense but always challenged me to reach higher and seek God, no matter what."

They waited for Charles to emerge from his vehicle. "Dan! Will Masters! I have been praying for you. I have been waiting for you to contact me. Congratulations on your dismissal."

"Nolle prosequi."

"Right, that's what Stella called it. Doesn't that mean 'case dismissed' in fancy Latin?"

"No, it's fancy words for 'case shelved' until they find better evidence. Not cleared. Think of it as being stuck in no man's land with no possibility of an exit. That's a nolle."

"Oh, so that's what she meant." He shook Will's hand and stepped forward to hug him. "But that gets you out of detention, and we had some ideas of how you could help." He smiled at Dan. "Yes, we have plans for you."

"But, Mr. Hutton…"

"Call me Charles, and I'll call you Will. Settled?"

"Of course. Charles, I think we need to run this by your wife first. I wouldn't want there to be any misunderstandings."

Charles looked at both of them. "Let's go inside, and we can discuss things where it's warmer."

Part of the lower floor had been gutted, with two front offices left untouched. Charles entered the right-hand one and sat behind his desk. "Coffee, tea? We have water, and there's instant if you don't mind it."

"No, thank you."

"So, nolle prosequi? What does look like to an agent? How did you handle it?"

"Well," Will reflected, "I remember four cases with a nolle over the years I was actively doing investigations before I moved up. Two we continued to investigate and eventually uncovered enough hard evidence for a conviction. One we lost due to a short window from a five-year statute limitation. For the fourth, the offender was completely innocent. I was lead, and before I could stop two of my less knowledge-able agents, they gave immunity to the wrong guys. Looks like they had brought in someone to be the fall guy all along. So, they bring him back in and try to get him to confess. I stopped it, brought him into my office and said, 'Just the two of us, no cameras, no mics. You were there.' He admitted to it. 'When?' I asked, and he gave me the times—totally outside of the time when the crime occurred. With a little digging, he admitted to cruising four bars and ending up in some gal's apartment. I sent the agents out to find video recordings, and we proved he had been knocking back several while the robbery of their drug dealer went down, along with the shooting of three people. I should look him up. He was young, hanging with the wrong crowd at the wrong time, so he bolted when he realized being with these guys was a mistake."

"What of his *wonderful* friends?"

"Well, we couldn't get them on the brilliant hit of a drug kingpin. You can always hope, now, not pray, that someone else gets them before they hurt more people. But they moved to Pittsburgh and set up shop. I put out my feelers and found some undercover police, working with DEA agents, who were very happy to receive intel on those two. About six months later, they had enough to put them away for twenty years, and in the federal system, you basically serve all your time." Will remembered his name—Jeremiah Towers.

"So, from an agent's perspective, what kind of nolle is your case?"

"Frame-up job by the real perp and he's pushing for immunity. I thought I'd see where he was at, but the Lord wouldn't let me. I have to just stop, turn around, pray for him and walk away. That's all I can do. I believe the prosecutor knows that. I assume so."

Charles nodded. "He is probably under tremendous pressure to get a conviction. It bothers me that there have been so few."

Will measured his words. "This group started eliminating those who could take a plea and testify against them. I personally witnessed a strike team take out a director and his executive team. When you try to find someone to corroborate what happened at the Task Force, you will find many of the most prominent agents are dead." He nodded. "I was thankful, after the fact, that Chris left when she did. I should have left earlier."

"But then Tom might not have been set free."

Will nodded. He took the chance. "I think Chris and I need to meet with Stella."

Charles looked aside, drank his coffee, and rose to pace the room. "She had a really difficult time when Tom left for Bible college. I was still angry at Christians, blaming God for breaking up the family. But the separation was my doing, my fault. All those lost years I could have had with my brother."

"Well, I can tell you right now that the only reason the Task Force was not able to touch you was because you had had no contacts with anyone else in your family, including Tom. If he had come home after prison, they would have been able to find a way to seize your assets, at the very least."

"And their absence drove us to God. In the end, to save the marriage Stella found solace earning her law degree, but that only helped for a short time. Then there was the expansion. But her foundation is stalling because she's having a hard time accepting Tom's death. Her initial vision has been achieved. A smaller number of cases need to be examined to see if they can be overturned. Some were legitimate convictions."

"We can wait—if you think that's a good idea."

"No, sooner is better. We've let this fester long enough. Tomorrow. Rick talked with me and I agree that we need this settled because I think we need you on our team, and God has released you from prison. I've rented a place not far from here. I'll text the address. When would Chris be available?"

"She's taken two weeks, so we are fairly flexible. Once she starts with the firm, she'll be very busy."

"Glad to hear she found a good offer. Stella's coming in tonight. Tomorrow at ten."

"We'll plan on it."

"Enough of the past. Let's find the future." Along with Dan, they shared their vision as they walked the buildings and the lot. He finished, "So, you a carpenter?"

Will laughed at Dan. "Very funny. No, but I might know someone who is."

That afternoon Chris stared at Will as if he had betrayed her. "I think our little honeymoon will be better if we're at peace with the Huttons."

"I know, but…" She turned away. Chris knew she had to do this, but her heart rebelled. Breathing, she faced Will, nodded and said, "At least I'm not facing her alone."

"Charles will be there too. I perceive he's a peacemaker."

She melted in his arms. "So, this is what it's like? We have each other for the hard days and the good days. I pray we always have peace between us."

"Amen."

CHAPTER 27

DRIVING BACK HOME, Will glanced at Chris, trying to stay awake. "Hey, navigator. Don't wink out on me."

"Yeah, we had to stop at one more beach."

"It was worth it!"

"I know." Chris allowed the warm darkness to envelop them. "We push to get home even if it's late. I think we can sleep in."

"Planning on going to church again?"

"Yes." She nodded. The time spent with the Huttons and getting things right with Stella had helped. "I didn't know thinking Stella was against us had upset me so."

"You ready to begin your legal career? Would that be your third, no fourth career change?"

"Yeah, yeah, agency hopper. Jumped out of one bucket and into another. Amazing what God can do." She glanced over. "Find a seminary?"

"Well, that's on hold until we can get Faith Hall, the physical plant, built."

"How can you plan the layout if you don't know what kind of school or college or advanced seminary you're going to have?"

"Because whatever level it is, it's still an educational institution. I've been looking into the science of building schools, searching for basic plans that can be customized later. And it's going to be strictly for Bible and ministry training and that narrows it down. I don't know what God has in store for me, but it has something to do with Faith Hall. Guess we'll find out in time."

"In time. Are you ready for me to work those crazy hours?"

"Like we used to pull at the FBI?"

"Well, it went in stages. But this is how I establish myself. In the beginning, I will have to be all in."

"Wouldn't want it any other way." He looked over, enjoying the size and power of his Tahoe. When he demonstrated the large cargo space and the ease of loading, she agreed they could take his SUV. "I'll be putting in the hours on my studies, along with the renovations, so I don't mind not having you home to bug me."

"Oh, so now I know. You married me for my living space!" They laughed, and the miles rolled along.

Jeremiah Towers was the name of the man who had been framed by two men he thought had been his friends. Will knew he had to locate the man. Will's stomach churned each time he caught himself longing for the kind of access the FBI had. Agents from the D.C. office had tried to bring him in for questioning—the usual tactics. "Can you come in? There are just a few things we'd like to clear up." Chris contacted an associate in the director's office to relay the message to leave her husband alone. His skin crawled. *There's no going back.*

Eventually, he thought he had located Jeremiah and his home right across the border in West Virginia. Will didn't make any plans the Monday Chris started with the firm. He cooked supper and set it in the fridge, knowing he could reheat the meal quickly when she came home. "Don't fuss," he'd said. "You get home when you get home. I'll be here."

"Well, not sure how's it's going to go the first day."

And he waited, diving into the latest book from Carlos about the doctrine of salvation. He'd told them he would be in Tuesday for an early meeting to flesh out plans and set timelines. It was hard to establish an organization when they didn't even know what they were supposed to be. Will had thought Dan would be more help, but Catherine told him Chaim at the Hebrew Centre had given him clear objectives. The direction, vision, and planning already had been established.

After dark, Chris returned home with a dazed look. She hugged him and shook her head. "You'd think with all the places I've worked, the first day would be easier."

"Well, sit back. Here's your herbal tea, and I'll get supper ready."

"Oh, the bliss!" She laughed.

"Don't get used to it. I'm going to get the Faith Hall project going tomorrow."

"Do Dan and Carlos know what's coming?"

"Probably not." He handed her a study. "Found this about designing a college. Gives us ideas about what to do first."

"Meaning?"

"We're going to need an architect and a contractor who can pull permits, but that comes after we design the place. Charles wants us to do it ourselves, and I understand his point. Your professional is going to give us the standard format."

"Sounds like you need to decide what you're going to be first. Aren't you trying to put the cart first?"

"Let me say three words—analysis by paralysis."

"Meaning?"

"We choose something in a few weeks, but we have to at least create the admin working space in the office building."

They talked through the possibilities while Will set the table and served the meal. "My best, but I hope my range of recipes will improve over time." He looked her way. If those comments hadn't brought a witty comeback, she was definitely past tired.

After supper, lounging on the couch, Will asked, "You have an idea of your hours?"

"Their work-life balance is better than I thought it would be. Put in the hours during the week, so it's mostly a half day on Saturday, and you're not expected to come in on a Sunday unless you're working a trial."

"So, this day might be typical?"

"I guess so. Do you have something in mind?"

"I found Jeremiah Towers."

"Was he the one with a nolle?"

"I'm thinking of trying to contact him just to see how he's doing. His dad used to have a small construction firm. I'm wondering if he ever worked for his father."

"What crazy idea are you thinking? You're liable to scare him half to death. The FBI agent who almost put him in prison is poking around again?"

"I'll let him know it might be a job—a legal job."

She sat up and looked at him. "Why are you really trying to find him?"

"It's the first case where I think I heard God. I didn't know it at the time, but I was watching two agents trying to get him to confess and nothing worked. He restated his assertion that he bailed on the crew and went barhopping. My gut told me he was innocent, and we should just drop the case after the prosecutor decided not to pursue."

"Oh, that case." She nodded. "I remember how angry you were. They gave immunity to the ones who actually did the crime. That's when you hate your job." She rolled to the side and leaned against him. "I'm sure I'll have my moments when I feel that way."

"When you lose a case?"

"Yeah." She didn't want to think of all the ways being a trial lawyer could go wrong. Not today. "Did you ask around at church? Talk to Cliff, my old fellowship leader—the one with the family?"

"Yeah, and I discovered there aren't many skilled tradesmen in our circles. And I don't think putting out an employment ad is a good way to go."

"Well, if you need to go, send a text with your destination details, contact info and approximate timeline." She lowered her voice. "And if you are detained and I don't hear from you, I will send them after you."

He smiled, mumbled his assurances and leaned closer for a kiss.

Will reminded himself not to be impatient. He had refined his plan while trying to sleep the night before. He brought his book bag and laid out his current study on a folding table near a space heater. Getting to the office early felt good. However, he knew it might be a while before Carlos arrived after dropping off his kids at school.

Dan nodded and headed into his office. Will gave him time to settle in before he asked for Charles' schedule, including the virtual meeting dates. Top priority—find a reliable Internet service and price out fiber-optic cables for greater capacity. Whatever this organization decided to be, they would need better Internet than what they currently had and was probably why the more recent development had been on the newer roads.

When the brief daily meeting was called to order, each person described his day and the tasks at hand. Will held his peace, saying little as Carlos and Dan fleshed out their latest topic of study and research. Carlos pursued some aspect of soteriology. From the brief discussion between the two, Will surmised the topic was controversial enough that many were locked in disagreement. Dan, with bright eyes and excitement in his voice, described his latest finding—a discrepancy between Kings and Chronicles. Lifting his brow, he added, these supposed discrepancies often yield valuable insights. Carlos concurred, and they looked at him.

"Well," he hesitated about saying what he was thinking—they had a seminary to create from scratch. However, he sighed. "Work on planning this building and hire the workmen to do it."

"Construction not your thing?" Dan couldn't resist. "Sorry, that was uncalled for. Sure, but how can we decide on a layout if we don't know where we're going?"

Their catch-22, their conundrum—the ever-swirling circle of doubt and the unknown—had been voiced. He had determined, though, they had to take a step—even if in the wrong direction. At this point, they could shift it, refine the target, but they had to at least make a decision. "We need a decent place with the proper facilities to make a launch possible." He didn't need to say that unless they made headway soon, Faith Hall would be another failed foundation set up by a wealthy patron, who upon seeing little progress, would let it shrink due to neglect amid the pull of immediate concerns. "Anyway, I'll be out of the office this afternoon, but I should be back tomorrow."

Will left for lunch, resisting the desire to seek the solace of home. He liked the ring of it, especially knowing Chris would be there each night. He headed to an ATM, pulled through a drive-through, and balanced his Bible on his lap while he ate a burger. *Lord, You have to help me. I can't do this on my own.* He rubbed his forehead, feeling as if the weight of the project rested fully on him. Already Dan and Carlos looked to him for direction, but they didn't seem too eager to follow through when he needed their input or assistance. Shaking his head, he understood intellectualism, and they were professors through and through. Their intense focus fueled their drive that would yield solid scholarship and add heft to their seminary. He had to work with what the Lord provided. *Lord, give the Towers a heart to hear me out.*

Technically, the hour was early, but he turned north on a county two-lane to intercept the interstate into a small wedge of West Virginia bounded by Maryland to the northeast and Virginia to its south, sort of.

Jeremiah Towers' address was a trailer on a corner lot in Charlestown, West Virginia. While they called it a city, it was no more than a village turned into a bedroom community for the sprawling government and related industries. No vehicles could be seen in front or on a short drive leading to a detached garage-like structure that appeared to have more square footage than the home. Out of habit, he parked around the corner and strolled past the trailer. The neighborhood, while not wealthy, seemed kept up and orderly.

Though early, he approached the righthand door—the only one with a small set of stairs leading up to the door in the center of the long side. He tried the doorbell and knocked, taking a step back.

"Hello?" A young black woman with close-cropped hair and a toddler clutching her knee stood right inside the closed screen door."

"Hello, Mrs. Towers? I'm Will Masters. I was wondering if Jeremiah is home." Will watched her glance to the right with an inpatient look.

"He's not here," she said, shaking her head.

"When do you expect him back?"

"Well, maybe suppertime, if the trip goes as planned." She looked at him closely.

He hadn't remembered a girlfriend and hoped she didn't recognize him.

"What do want with him?" She looked down at his hands.

"Oh, I was wondering if he wanted a job renovating an old office building near Purcellville, Virginia."

"That's not near here. How'd you hear about Jeremiah?" She studied him closely.

"I met him years ago. He made quite an impression on me. Anyway, I remember he said his father had a construction business and assumed he had trades skills."

"Yeah, but the business is gone and it's hard to find regular work in construction." She pursed her lips and added, "For him, anyway."

"It could be just for the office renovation. He wouldn't have to make a commitment."

"No traveling? He could be home with us at night?"

"Yes, and there's a nearby center where all of you could stay for the week. No charge." He smiled at the boy staring at him. "They have a pool."

Her eyes flashed. When it seemed as if she were about to send him away, a child's scream erupted from the darker living area. She pushed open the screen. "Come in."

Will stood in front of the toddler who stared up at him.

"You're big," the boy said.

Will crouched down to his level. "Let me tell you a secret. Someday you'll probably be as tall as your father, and he's about as tall as me. What's your name?" He extended his hand.

The boy shook it as he answered, "Marlin." He leaned forward and whispered, "Cause Daddy always talks about getting a marlin. Do you know what a marlin is?" His eyes wide, he extended his arms as wide as they can go. "They're huge!"

"You're right. Maybe someday you can go fishing with your father and catch a big one."

"Not in this lifetime," the mom said, having settled the squabble.

"Are these all your children?" Will asked, as he stood. Three played on the floor, and two were on the couch.

"That girl on the couch with the doll, Sandy-Patty, and Marlin are mine." She smiled. "With the cost of childcare, it only made sense to quit my day job and watch kids. What I earn pays for the groceries." She headed back toward the small living room. "Okay, kids, clear out. You have a playroom."

Will took a seat in the chair she pulled out for him and accepted the proffered iced sweet tea. "Thank you. We haven't been introduced."

She looked in his direction and replied, "Virginia Towers."

"Had you known Jeremiah for a long time?"

"We met in teen group. He was kind of wild, but he went forward, and I thought he'd be the one." She poured a glass and sat across from him. "How do you know him?"

"I met him years ago—before the Task Force."

"You're an agent."

"I was."

"What's the job?"

"I want him to help me renovate an old building and warehouse into a seminary."

"Christian?" Seeing the nod, she said, "In Purcellville? Does this have anything to do with those pastors who were in prison?"

"Everything. We're trying to rebuild." She leveled her gaze at him. He gave a quick explanation.

"Jer doesn't like feds. Won't have anything to do with them."

"I feel the same way." Her eyes tightened. "I have a nolle over my head too."

She said, "I think you'd better leave, mister. Like I said, he'd flip if he learns I let you into the house."

Will rose. "I understand. I'll wait outside and give him the offer. If he says no, you'll never hear from me again." Heading for the door, he froze when it opened, and a large man stepped through. His sharp eyes settled on Will. Being proactive, Will stepped forward and extended his hand. "Will Masters, I stopped by to see if I could hire you for a construction job. I need the help."

"Go on," said the slim black man with close-cropped hair.

"We're trying to rebuild after the 756 laws were overturned—starting a seminary. They purchased an old warehouse and office building that need to be refitted. I need someone who can help me with that."

"Do you believe in Christ?"

"I do."

"This job include travel?"

"No, it's in Purcellville, but we can provide housing for the family during the week." Will watched Jeremiah look at Virginia, and she shrugged her shoulders.

"Maybe you should hear him out."

He looked back at Will. "All right. Let's sit."

"Virginia," he said in a lowered voice, "Carl says he has no work for the next two weeks." Jeremiah looked back at Will. "Maybe this is God. Maybe it isn't, but as I see it, we don't have any other options."

They sat on the couch, and Will described Faith Hall Foundation and the property. He also said, "Virginia, I would also be interested in hiring you as my administrative assistant. There are some people at the Hutton Center who could watch the kids."

"You might as well stay for supper," she said, not quite yet ready to commit.

"If it's not any trouble, I'll let my wife know."

"You're married? Have kids?"

"No kids, just married over a year ago. She just started with a D.C. law firm."

"Hey, Jer, he says he has a nolle too."

Jeremiah looked at Will, and his face hardened.

"Jeremiah, I'm the one who stopped your interrogation. I'm the one who brought you into my office, and after you told me what happened, I said that I believed you. After you left, while I couldn't fire those agents, I did demote and transfer one to Fargo and the other to Fairbanks. I was wondering how you managed with a nolle."

"It's not fun. Being innocent, I can't get it cleared. Hard to get any decent jobs where they'll pay you regular. But it did keep me on the straight and narrow."

"So, God used it for good?"

"What's yours?"

"For genocide."

They just looked at him. Gathering himself to flee, he waited.

Jeremiah shook his head. Almost laughing. "Framed?"

"Definitely, my wife led the defense. If she hadn't stood up for me, I probably would have taken a deal. I'd be in a supermax by now."

"God works in funny ways."

"He does. Listen, come visit us at the Hutton Center in Purcellville for the weekend. I'll show you around, you can meet everybody and drive home after church on Sunday."

Will watched Jeremiah keep the kids occupied while Virginia made supper.

Will read a story. After it was over, he said, "I'll tell you a secret.

Did you know there are no grandchildren in heaven? Everyone is adopted, chosen by God Himself to join His family. You can't get into heaven just because your parents believe in Jesus. You have to ask God to make you His child." He glanced at Jeremiah. "When did you accept Christ?"

"At teen group." He glanced at Virginia in the kitchen. "But I walked away. And you?"

"Took me too long. While I was with the Task Force, I really fought against the pricks of the Holy Spirit. And when I did find God, I realized I'd been a fool to wait so long." He looked at Sandy-Patty, "So, when God calls, listen and follow. He has great plans for you."

The parents came for their children. Will enjoyed the fellowship with the family, settling on a time for them to arrive.

Jeremiah, Virginia and the kids arrived early Friday evening at the center. Will met them at the door. Catherine led them to their suite. "Get your bathing suits. Do you like to swim?"

Sandy-Patty giggled, and Marlin screeched. Virginia smiled and took them into the bathroom. Irma and Rick met them in the hall to the pool, welcoming the children and inviting them to join the four kids frolicking in the shallow end. "We can keep an eye on them if you'd like a tour," Irma offered, already holding Sandy-Patty's hand.

Catherine and Chris led the tour for the Towers. Will and Dan trailed behind. "I stayed here quite frequently. At one time it was mostly the pastor's wives, but now we have a more diverse crowd," Chris said.

After a brief tour of the small city, Catherine and Maria hosted a snack in the conference room.

The next day Will drove Jeremiah to the industrial park. They stood in front of the buildings. Jeremiah walked around both structures and poked his head into the mostly empty warehouse. "Good, they haven't divided up the space yet." Will followed him in. "Solid structure."

"Now for the building. We have to refit that first." Will led the way to the building on the right. He could see Dan and Carlos were at the respective folding tables. Internet ethernet wires snaked to their laptops, extension cords snaked around the room.

Jeremiah looked at Will. "Yeah, you need a refit!" Will took him through the structure, including the second floor and utility room. "Only way to do it is to gut the whole property and start over."

Will handed over his rough floor plan.

Jeremiah pulled out a measuring tape. "Let's walk it."

Nodding, he headed for a series of tables pushed against a wall with tool belts, a small toolbox and some boxes.

Jeremiah surveyed the men in the main area. "They will have to relocate. Won't want to be around once we begin."

"I figured. Dan can work at their suite at the center, but Carlos has three little kids at home. Maybe he can use a room at the center. I'll ask Catherine." Will looked at the area with partly painted walls, dangling wiring, littered with old, discarded office furniture toward the back.

"Gutting means everything goes."

Will nodded. They walked the sections, writing down the dimensions. As he answered Jeremiah's questions, he jotted notes.

They walked to a table toward the back. Will turned on a standing lamp and the laptop. "Paper or spreadsheet?"

"Paper for now." Jeremiah pulled out several sheets of paper from the notebook and began to draw each room, marking up the first floor draft. Adding dimensions, he pulled out a small pocket calculator and began to make a list.

Will's heart quickened. *This just might happen.* "When do you think you could start?"

"Everything begins with the plans. I know a good draftsman. Planning on hiring a contractor?"

Will shook his head. "Charles wants us to lead, for this building. So, we'll need subcontractors."

"Need building permits. Lucky for you I have my Virginia contractor's license."

Will brought up the offer of employment letter and printed it out. "We can assume you start today. Here is what Charles Hutton can offer."

"Who is Charles Hutton?"

"The owner of Hutton Family Furniture Stores."

Jeremiah stared in shock. "You're kidding. He's funding this? And you're supposed to run it?" He shook his head. "Does he support it, really?"

"We'll find out." Will pushed back his chair. "I'll give you a chance to read it over." He ran his fingers through his hair and walked over to the professors to tell them they'd have to relocate until the first floor rebuild was completed. Jeremiah had said aloud what Will feared—once the college was formed, and on its way, there would be no place for him here. He tried to remind himself his plan had been to be one of the seminary graduates and take a church. But his heart tugged within anyway.

"Okay, think this will work. Ginnie will know how long it will take to help her clients find another daycare. I'll commute until we can move here. The trailer's a sublet from a friend, so I can give notice anytime. She mentioned you needed an admin?"

Will nodded. "Let's talk outside." The weather wasn't too bad yet. "Dan and Carlos will anchor the New and Old Testament departments, but they're not the kind to plan or develop. I'm trying to push them to establish some kind of a Bible program to get things off the ground. Dan was given permission to use a Bible study program developed in Dublin, Ireland. We only have to pay royalties. Local churches and church-plants could use the materials for their Sunday school classes or Bible studies. Virginia could help Catherine run it—finding groups and fellowships, taking orders, shipping, tracking grades, for example."

"Sounds good to me. Ginnie does fine with the kids, but they drive her crazy. I think she'd like to get back to office work." He led Will back into the building and to the table piled with various tools and hardware. "This it for the tools and supplies?" Seeing the nod, he thought aloud, "I have most of the tools, but is Hutton willing to invest in the ones I don't have?"

"Yes, we have a relatively good budget. Just need to have documentation for everything, with invoices and paid receipts. I'll get your employee forms done now." He stared at the floor plan and growing material list. "Have a rough estimate of how long this might take?"

Jeremiah sat back. "Depends, everything begins with the plans."

Will spread out his rough plans and they discussed the design for the first floor.

An hour later, Will smiled at the sketched drawings, lists and tasks. Progress. "Maybe we should take some family time, then." Will walked over to Dan and Carlos. "We're finishing up his paperwork and will done by lunchtime. Want to join the gals?"

"Didn't Maria tell you? She's hosting a party at our place this afternoon. Why we were kicked out. I usually don't work on Saturdays." Carlos laughed. "Don't expect us to put in lawyers' hours. Chris said she could be there by three."

"Right."

A week later Will reviewed the upcoming visits to meet the electrician and plumbers, while waiting for their permits. He navigated to the list of code requirements, picked up his cell and called Charles.

"Hi, Will, how is our new employee doing?"

"Awesome. Have the drawings, pulling permits. Looks like we'll have to install sprinklers for fire suppression."

"I would imagine so. Who are you looking at to subcontract?"

"Local electrician and plumber, but do you have any firms you'd recommend?"

"Local is better, but make sure they can handle the job."

"Absolutely. Jeremiah and I will visit their worksites soon. While we wait for the permits to go through, we'll finalize the bill of materials and send them out for quotes. There are, at the most, three suppliers in the area. Would that be enough for you? While we might be able to save some money on price-shopping, working with one supplier will simplify the process once we're in the building phase. I'll also make sure they understand that if they do right by us, there will be a larger order in the future. Does that sound acceptable?"

"Excellent. Keep me in the loop. Sounds like you have good help. Oh, Will, I'd like you to plan on attending the next board meeting in Pittsburgh with a progress report. I'll send the details. Oh, and I didn't get a copy of Jeremiah's Virginia contractor license."

Will breathed. At least that had broken their way. The process in Virginia to obtain a license took over two months. "He holds licenses for Maryland, West Virginia and Virginia. I'll send scans. Sir, is the board meeting about the physical plant or something more?"

"Well, they want to see how the refit's coming."

"That's one of the obstacles I've run into. Hard to create plans when you don't know what you're planning for. We can refit the building for generic office use, but they will have to be more specific before we can touch the warehouse. By the way, Jeremiah says the large building is sound."

"Bring your ideas. I think it will be good for them to get to talk with you about these concerns. At least it sounds like you have a good start.

CHAPTER 28

THREE WEEKS LATER Will pulled into the convention center north of Pittsburgh. He didn't have a pretty model, but he did have drawings and pictures ready in a presentation. After weeks of thrashing through the details, the project morphed into overdrive. Some days, he put in more hours than Chris. They relocated to the Hutton Center and transformed a conference room into the main office and printing center. Dan and Carlos contacted nearby churches to promote the Bible course program. Copying the setup of the Dublin online school, Dan headed up that initiative. Carlos began to translate requested courses for Spanish classes. Virginia was Will's able assistant keeping a supply of copies, shipping and tracking completion records. It was a beginning. Where it would head, God only knew.

The board consisted of Zachary Taylor from Colorado, Merle Washington, the man he had met when he was undercover as Warren Bells in Texas, two others Will had never met, as well as Dr. Sal Larkin, and Dr. Bertrand Louden. Charles Hutton was the chair. Will tried to settle his nerves, reminding himself he would most likely spend more time listening than presenting.

Hoping it would not be out of place, he brought his expensive suit, along with more than enough show-and-tell items. He headed to his room at the hotel and readied himself to meet Charles in his suite. *Who else will be there?*

Charles let him in and gestured for him to take a seat on a short couch. "Coffee?"

"Thank you."

"They'll bring up the meal when we're ready. I like to have a preview of your presentation before the board sees it. Part of my management style—I hate surprises."

"Of course." Will set up his laptop. "It's really a slideshow at this point. When you're ready."

Charles brought two coffees and sat on the couch. "Okay."

Will stepped through the progress for the building and the church outreach program. "However, the direction of Faith Hall's higher learning divisions will require direction from the board." He took a breath and put his thoughts into well-chosen words. "If we want to serve the continental United States, we must reach past our small circle to other areas of the country and ask them what needs they feel we could meet. Given that certain parts of the country lost many experienced pastors, should we have an undergraduate program for church leaders? Since some might be called after having obtained their degree, should we also add a few master's level degree programs?"

Charles nodded. "Since I have begun working with these fine men, I have also come to understand the necessity of adopting a doctrinal statement."

"May Dr. Smith and Dr. Rodriguez be a part of that?"

"I wouldn't want to do it without them."

"The more specific their plans—departments, degree programs— the easier it will be to move forward with the warehouse design."

"You will need to hire a general contractor for that part."

Will nodded. Jeremiah was doing a superb job on the building. Will assisted him daily. However, transforming the warehouse space would take an experienced firm. "What about Jeremiah?"

"Oh, he's going to be more than busy staying on top of the contractors. He will serve as your eyes and ears, making sure they build to plan, follow the specs, and comply with code. Both of you will need to make sure all the pieces come together in a timely manner. You can't leave it to the general contractor to remember to let the elevator company know when the shaft is ready."

"Elevator?"

"I assume it will be two floors and, yes, an elevator, probably attached to an outer wall will be required for code. And it helps with moving property and supplies."

"Will we need two?"

"One large enough for general purposes should be sufficient. You're not manufacturing, so you should not need a freight elevator." Charles sat back, tapping his middle finger on his lips. He looked at the last slide of the closing shot—the group standing in front of the building spruced up with new paint and a sign, Faith Hall Foundation. From left to right, Rick Carlson, Dan Smith, Carlos Rodriguez, Will Masters and Jeremiah and Virginia Towers. "Pastor Rick?"

"He's like our pastor, our spiritual adviser, sounding board and prayer leader. How he appears exactly when we need a little exhortation or encouragement is amazing! We have to find a place for him."

"Of course." Charles, who was deep in reflection, jumped slightly with the knock on the door. "Our meal. Will?"

He rose and opened the door, pulled in the cart and set the table with the plates and service. Everything was there. He sat, waiting for Charles.

The older man reached over to hold his hand while he prayed. As they selected their utensils, Charles said, "Tom was such a good son. I regret barely spending time with him. I hardly knew him. I will never forget the final few weeks with Catherine and him in Dublin. He often said that someday things would change, and Christ would rebuild the church in America. While he never mentioned his part, I had always assumed he would be here." Staring off in the distance, he added, "But Tom is safe. Where God wants him to be. I have to accept His plan." He looked at Will. "Let us make this project a reality with God—not running ahead or trailing behind."

"Exactly! I want to propose a prayer gathering—a brainstorming session, so to speak, at Merle Washington's Mesa Ranch. I'd like to invite any of the board who would like to attend." He laughed. "I'd be inviting Merle to attend an event at his ranch. I know that borders on brazen, but it's the perfect place. I'd also like to invite pastors and Christian laypeople. Here's the list—many of them are believers today because of Tom or worked closely with him. Some I have met. Giles, Merle's horse wrangler; Larry Hutton, your nephew; I hope Zackary Taylor would come with Bruce, his foreman; Todd became a Christian in Hannibal and is now leading a fellowship in his hometown; Jordan and Riser served time with Tom and were close friends with Tom. And of course, Dan and Carlos. If you think of anyone else, let me know." He waited. Charles sat unmoving and looked away.

He nodded. "Make the proposal and see what they say. I assume they can add to the list. What about accommodations at this ranch?"

"It has a bunkhouse. That's the point. It's not luxury, but it can be comfortable. Dan and I hid there for a month with Giles and his wife Alexa. She recently died of cancer. Dan helped her reclaim her faith and had a part in Giles' coming to Christ. I will never forget that time of watching them grow in Christ when I couldn't stomach the thought of believing."

"Who would lead it?"

"I would get each session or time block started, but then let the Holy Spirit move and see what He does. I had a chance to attend a ten-hour prayer meeting for persecuted Christians throughout the world led by a missionary who works in the Middle East. It was a moving experience. We had a taste of the hatred of the Evil One toward believers. We might experience that again and most likely will. Let us pray what we do here is part of God's plan for preparing the church for the years to come."

Charles didn't hide the tears. He reached for Will's hand. "You open in prayer, and I'll follow."

———⚬⚬⚬⚬———

Will dressed in his shiny thousand-dollar suit with a dust blue paisley tie Chris had given him. His black shoes shined, his hair groomed, and cufflinks in place, he looked the part on the outside. Trying not to stand too stiffly and maybe staying closer to Charles than the man would have liked, he worked through the introductions. He had briefly talked with Zackary Taylor and had not talked with Larry since that day in Amarillo. Stepping aside, he walked closer to Merle Washington. The man extended his hand. "Please forgive me for having to deceive you."

"I understand it was necessary and that you did not betray us."

"After seeing Rosemont, I'd rather die first."

"And from what I hear, you almost did."

"Do you still own the ranch, including Mesa?"

"Oh, yes. Now I have more time to invite friends for hunting trips, though I can't seem to convince my wife it's worth the drive. She's more partial to Albuquerque, the city life."

"Understood," he said, extending his hand to Cal.

"Should have trusted my instincts with you, but it worked out."

"So, I really hadn't convinced you."

"You reminded me too much of myself. Figured you were a military-type carpenter. Good we hadn't asked you to replace that roof?"

"Exactly. But we're past that for now. I hire carpenters. Don't even want to go there."

"Sorry about that charge. Incredible."

"Incredible that I'm here and that I was asked to be a part of this." He stood by Cal's side as he had at the ranch. "And you?"

"Well, I just make sure he gets where he's supposed to go and stays in one piece. But, yes, it's great to work for a person who loves and respects the Lord."

When the two professors walked in, Will waited for Charles to introduce them. If Louden recognized him, he didn't tip his hand. Dr. Larkin looked him in the eye with a warm greeting. "So, did you know Tom Hutton?"

"I met him twice." He noticed Charles had moved aside to talk with another group. "I interviewed him at Hannibal years ago when I was with the Task Force and ordered him released from Rosemont."

Larkin nodded. "A sad time in our history." He surveyed the crowd, "And may we meet the challenge in the Spirit of our Lord, looking forward—not back."

"Amen."

Charles led the morning meeting, opening with prayer. He stepped through the financials first before the discussion concerning fundraising. They all relayed how the Lord provided funding without a media campaign. They stepped through some housekeeping amendments and then came Will's turn.

Stiff and awkward, he tried not to fumble attaching his laptop to the network. Praying all the technology worked, he stepped through each frame, showcasing the progress. "Starting small, but with room to maneuver once we discern God's leading." He glanced at Charles and seeing the nod, plunged into the most pressing need—a vision from God.

Will had memorized an outline, but feeling the Holy Spirit take over, he said, "Christ said during this time of the Gentiles the gates of hell would not prevail against the church, the body of Christ. Even though, sometimes, it seemed as if evil was winning…" He had to breathe, turning away from images of detention in the cramped cell. "But it did not. Even in what looked like defeat, God remained victorious for He will never leave us or forsake us. Christ sifted the church, allowing it to go through dark valleys, but we were never alone. For us to come alongside His efforts to restore, renew, and rebuild, we must ask to do it with Him—in His way.

"I propose a two- or three-day retreat, if Mr. Washington would consent, at his Mesa Ranch facility for any of you who would like to come for days of prayer, reflection, and fellowship to seek God's leading and direction. I have shared a proposed list with Mr. Hutton."

Charles said, "You may share the list, Will."

Will read the names, blinking back the tears. "All of these men are invested in Christ and His church. Let us see where this takes us." He faltered, feeling led to say nothing further.

Charles rose and led discussion. Will fielded questions. Will turned to step aside. Charles stopped him. "I don't know if some of you have heard Will's story, but I assure you, I have full confidence in this man's faith, integrity and honesty. The accusations against him were groundless, and the US attorneys could not bring his case to trial. I hope you take advantage of this time to get to know him better. Thank you, Will."

While Will would have liked to visit Mesa Ranch in good weather, he agreed with the decision to have the retreat as soon as possible. Merle chose Cal to set it up and make the arrangements. "I wear many hats," he said with a laugh.

"Good to know. I'll send you the list and the contact info for the ones I have. What about the invites?"

"I'll let you handle that."

"Then I'll need some contact data from you."

Snow snakes flitted across the road. The Tahoe's heater hummed, more than able to handle the sudden drop in temperature that can happen in December. His cab was full, and Will's heart sang as he drove Dan, Carlos, Jordan and Riser to the big house on Washington's ranch. They would pack and convoy to Mesa Ranch together. He had driven to St. Louis and stayed with Riser. Jordan had joined them. They had a straight run to the ranch house northwest of Amarillo. Cal assigned him to the bungalow he had shared with Dan along with Todd. He met the man for the first time.

A few months before, Butch Connors had taken him to St. Louis to meet Jordan and Riser. Butch couldn't come to the retreat, but the men of the church had prayed over them before they left. Holding close the fellowship with Rick and many others, they all rejoiced with the Fosters' baptism.

Todd shook his hand firmly and looked at him with piercing blue eyes. "So, you knew Tom?"

"Met him twice. But I've heard much about him."

Todd relayed his stories from Hannibal. "He stayed with me a short time. Learned a lot. That Bible college you're heading up..."

"Think of me as the organizer. I don't have the creds most of you have, though I'm learning. Get into Greek yet?"

"Pretty busy. Want to, but I think I'm going to have to take classes. That will force me to learn it." He shook his head. "I'm really glad you invited me."

Will nodded and smiled. "Hey, don't want to miss supper."

The drive to Mesa was different from the time before. A cold front with a storm had coated the Texas Panhandle with pristine whiteness that dipped and rose with the hills and gullies. Sparse vegetation poked through, and he remembered the staff's talking about a thaw coming in a week. He looked forward to seeing Giles again.

They fasted, prayed and shared. The meals were simple. Will had a rough outline, but he let the Lord lead and set the pace. The love of God for His church came through. Each sang from his heart—the depths of his soul. And they shared what came to mind of going forward with a grounding of God's Word, wrapped in the cords of love. Truth with love, setting aside pride, arrogance and vainglory of puffed-up knowledge that divided instead of healed.

Charles spent many hours listening to the stories of those who had spent time with Tom. Will could see the healing occur before his eyes.

Will felt he heard a whisper saying, *Find the lost ones.* Focusing on the Scripture Todd read, he thought he heard the message again.

The last day. The last meal together. As they cleared the table, Will walked to the head of the room to an easel with a large pad. He nodded at Larry and Zackary, waiting to see who would chair the sounding of the hearts, record the words and set the vision.

Larry said something to Zack, who walked to the easel and shook Will's hand. He said to him, "Carry on."

Will gathered himself, smiled, feeling poorly dressed and unfit to direct this session. "We have gathered to fast, pray and seek God's face for our nation, for our church and for our families, for Faith Hall. Now is your turn to share. What have you learned? What do you see that we need to do to rebuild?"

Silence hung in the air. Will prayed. Hadn't they made it clear from the beginning that this retreat was for finding a way forward? Forcing down his disappointment, he heard a rustle toward the back.

Bruce stood. "We need to forgive and come together. Stop asking, 'What did you do during those years? Were you against us for a time? Were you with us?' We need to find a way to reconcile and forgive." In large letters Will wrote *Reconcile.*

Dan rose and answered, "By the path of love—love our enemies."

Will nodded and wrote *Love.*

Dan added, "That we see past the outer person to the inner soul for whom Christ died. As Bruce said, reconcile. We must bring them in and accept them, making no distinction."

Will paused, waiting to see if any had heard what he had felt. Zackary Taylor stood and surveyed the group. "Not to criticize this meeting, but we seem to represent only a segment of our country. Most of us are from the central corridors of our nation. What of the rest? Each area had a different experience; some seemed hardly touched while others suffered cruelly. What of their voices?"

Smiling, Will wrote *Find the lost ones.* "This is what I heard. I concur, Mr. Taylor." He flipped the page to the next one with an outline of the continental United States drawn in rough lines. "Not an artist," he said. "As Mr. Taylor said, most here are from the center of our nation. If we divide the rest…" He paused to circle in red the North and Southwest, then selected green for the Northeast and Southeast. "These are broad areas, but I propose a small group reach out…" He tapped the western sectors. "…to these groups. Who has connections to groups in these areas?" Will recorded those who raised their hands. He worked through the groups. However, no one seemed to have connections with Northeast fellowships.

Will was about to elaborate on the phrase he had written, but Charles rose, stepped to the front, nodded and closed in prayer.

Will sat near Bruce and Todd. They had bonded during the retreat. "Come visit when you can."

"Come to Colorado," Bruce said. "We have horses on our ranch."

Will smiled. "I'd love that. But we'll have to wait until Christine has vacation time."

Todd smiled, "And don't forget the children."

"I think we missed that calling, but if the Lord puts some arrows in our quiver during our old age, I won't object." He laughed.

Larry approached. "Thank you for helping my aunt and uncle. It's so good to see Uncle Charles working for the future."

"Visit anytime. See the center and the hall, such as it is. Not much to look at right now."

"We will."

Giles walked up, and Will said to Larry, "And bring our friend with you." He winked at the horse wrangler. "Think you can handle being out East?"

"Only for a visit." His eyes scanned the horizon. "The open skies are my home, but I can visit."

———❀———

Will packed, gathered the names of those with contacts. Larry helped take down the easel. "Keep me in the loop for the Western conference. I'd like to have a part in it."

Charles came by his side. "Stella and I will meet you at the center as soon as we can arrange it."

Will took him aside. "No one said anything about Faith Hall."

Charles tapped his upper arm. "Reconciling the body of Christ must come first. You wrote, *Find the lost ones.* What did you mean by that?"

Will stared out the window. Icicles dripped and bare ground had expanded to surround the remaining clumps of snow. The thaw had come as quickly as the snow. "We're fractured, divided, leaderless—frothing and churning without direction. At the prison camp in Purcellville, Pastor Rick led reconciliation between the resistors and the collaborators. But there is more to do—the reconciliation of the churches and with our nation." He looked at Charles. "The Task Force agents committing violent acts caused some fugitives to remain in hiding. Shortly before Chris left the foundation, she told me there are still many missing and unaccounted for. We have lists of the missing Christians, but I suspect there are missing Task Force members as well. Kincaid's strike teams might have and might still be eliminating those who could expose them. I believe there are lost ones on both sides. We need to keep searching for them."

CHAPTER 29

W ILL DROVE BACK deep in thought, hardly hearing the conversation flowing around him. After spending the night with Riser, the three would head out the next morning. He sipped more of the thick coffee Riser was known for brewing. Will thanked the Lord for the bitter brew as Dan and Carlos napped, instead of helping him stay awake.

While the retreat had been a spiritual high, Will's sense of unease grew with each mile taking them back to Purcellville. They had a direction—but nothing related to Faith Hall. He battled within himself, trying to find the patience Charles had tried to convey. Will ruminated on the two competing tasks—find the lost ones and raise up a school from the ashes.

From the ashes...*ashes of what?* A broken church? Divided families? A nation torn and drifting? Charles had been right. He had been right. There were more lost ones to find. He swallowed, realizing probably more graves and death to be uncovered as well.

However, he had a video meeting with Larry in a few days. They would organize the Western conference. *Is the Lord telling him to focus on that task, letting Jeremiah head up the building renovation and the others the Bible study course program?*

Resisting the urge to try to do it all himself, he began to pray through his next steps—the Western retreat and networking with church leaders on the East Coast. The phrase, *the lost ones,* sounded endlessly with the hum of the tires.

Will flew directly to Phoenix. A young man from Glendale Community Church met him at the baggage claim area to take him directly to the church. Larry was scheduled to arrive the next day, giving Will a chance to meet the pastors.

A large, winged brick building occupied what looked like a ten-acre lot. They drove up the large parking lot to the covered main entrance. Friendly and helpful staff led him to a side wing with a large meeting room. "How many are attending?"

The woman smiled. "Oh, we sent out invitations to everyone, but under one hundred responded. We were thinking of making it virtual so those who couldn't make it can follow along."

Will's head spun. This was not what he had envisioned. Trying to curb his emotions, he left his luggage in a side closet and followed another young man to the pastors' offices. The church had a senior, associate and youth pastor. Will entered the large office with bookcases, dark wood furniture and a seating area.

"Coffee?" the man asked.

Will's eyes lit up. He had taken the red eye from Dulles and was still bleary-eyed. "Yes, thanks." He took in the three men sitting on short overstuffed armchairs—guessing the grayish one was the lead, the slightly thinning, black-haired one was the associate and the youth pastor was a wiry, black man with braids.

After introductions and shaking of hands, Will sat, cradling the coffee in his hands.

"Good flight?"

"Yes." Before they could begin the twenty questions about his past, he launched his. "You have a large church with a building. Impressive. How did you keep it going during the past ten years?"

The senior pastor cleared his throat. "We were in the no man's land between the West Coast and the Oklahoma divisions. A nearby church became the recycling center for the region. Our people gave cash, and when we filed the returns each year, we had only anonymous donors. If it had continued and if not for the bravery of Tom Hutton, we would have eventually come to their attention."

Will nodded. "I'm thankful you didn't have any sent to Oklahoma."

They shifted. "Well, we still had our losses. When they added the speech codes, some were arrested, and some have been identified from the Oklahoma site. We were wondering where the rest are."

Now came his turn to shift uncomfortably. Gathering himself, Will said. "Director Norton used a cremation chamber." Seeing the look of shock on their faces, he continued. "Didn't they tell you? Thankfully, he didn't send them in their alive, but..." He gathered himself. "I observed the execution procedure. They were shot and pushed into the box. They kept the ashes, assuming Congress would soon add the death sentence for more serious HCL offenders. We have learned that Norton ordered the ashes mixed with trash and sent to landfills. But..." he added without taking a breath, "they are safe now in heaven with Christ Jesus. I understand finding closure in situations like this are much harder for the families."

"There were prison breaks, weren't there?"

"I wouldn't know. I was never assigned to Oklahoma. Have you pursued this with Texas Ranger Larry Hutton?"

"We look forward to meeting him tomorrow."

"Who did you network with?"

"No one. That's how we stayed off the radar," a man who was standing by the door offered. "Sheriff Walters," he said walking forward to shake Will's hand. "We understand you have quite the background as well."

Will smiled and navigated their questions, which were more probing than accusatory. "Have you contacted the Hutton Foundation to find your missing members?"

"No, tell us about this."

Will provided the extended story. "They use DNA matching. If a family does not have any genetic samples, they provide blood samples from close family members. It can be typed with the remains for identification. Do you have a coordinator or contact person? They can contact the Foundation through their website."

"And what of the rest?"

"What was left of the Task Force files are housed at the FBI's D.C. Field Office. Once your list is narrowed down, you can forward the data on those still missing to that office. They will most likely assign it to the nearest field office and resident agencies."

"Some entire families are missing," the youth pastor noted.

Will nodded. "If they fled to a remote area, they might not know the laws have been rescinded. Finding them will require delicate handling. If they think a team is coming for an assault, they might resist. I would recommend that you establish a liaison with any law enforcement efforts to locate them."

"We would try to do it ourselves. Just use federals for information and possible locations."

"That would be a wise idea. If the FBI in charge is shutting you out, leave no stone unturned to insist they provide data only. Some will assume it is all federal, but push for local control." Will saw the assent and understanding in the sheriff's eyes.

He shifted. "Our first retreat was with a small group to seek out the Lord's will and direction for Hutton Faith Hall Foundation. Have you heard about this endeavor?"

After Will explained the initiative, the listeners pushed for greater detail even though he tried to make it clear that seeking the Lord's direction was or had been the intended purpose of the retreat.

"Do you have a schedule and plan for the sessions?"

The pastoral team smiled, handed out the packets, and the associate pastor worked them through the programs, breakout sessions and free time.

Will tried to suppress a groan and kept his misgivings to himself. The

Holy Spirit whispered that there were as many different ways for a fellowship group to look like and function as there were varieties of fish in the sea. "Do you have any representatives coming from coastal fellowships?"

"Yes, some prominent groups were decimated, but they are rebuilding and will be sending some delegates. We are very excited to be a part of this association."

He bit back the reply that they were seeking to build broad consensus. Will prayed for a chance to discuss these matters with Larry the next day.

During a midmorning break from another organizational meeting, Will sat on the bench right outside the main entrance. He smiled when he saw Larry drive in. Walking over, he greeted him quickly and said, "We have to talk. Are you aware this retreat is going to be vastly different?"

"Relax, this group has always been independent, innovative and with a mind of their own. It's as if the Lord put a dome of protection over this area, for which I am very thankful."

"Of course, this is great news, but they do have lists of missing." Will quickly described yesterday's meeting.

Larry pulled out a small satchel and patted Will's arm. "Relax, sit back, and see what the Lord does with this. I don't think we have to worry about running this one. Enjoy the event. Maybe we'll learn something."

"Of course."

The leadership selected Larry to run the last session recap. Will was glad they had not asked him. Most testified of the grace and goodness of God. He wondered if they would have sounded a different note if they had experienced true loss. Then the Lord reminded him of the three-page list of the missing. They had not lost their vision, but he had gleaned a few leads for the future.

In the end, the senior pastor ascended the four steps, thanked Larry for spurring them on to host this conference. He raised his left arm, with his right around Larry, "Let's do it each year, shall we?"

Instant anger morphed to a vision of what was to come. Will shook his head. Couldn't he see God showing him before his very eyes, what the near future held—a living, vibrant church, loving and adaptable and secure in and because of the power of God? Then the pastor called him to the front.

Will weighed his words. *What should I say?* He hardly knew as the Holy Spirit seemed to speak through him—joy about those sheltered from the troubles of the past ten years; the reminder to continue to love, share and serve that those might know God's love as well; and the charge to make disciples.

He left the podium and sat near Larry.

"I see you've reached past your conflicts. Remembering to rejoice with those who rejoice as well as weeping with those who weep is good."

"Actually, it feels great." He smiled. "I hear your family's meeting with your aunt and uncle for Christmas."

"Just after. New Year's was the best I could get, and my sister Karen was able to find a replacement as well."

"Sounds great. In Ohio, I assume?"

"No, actually at Purcellville, in your backyard. I perceive Aunt Stella's foundation's job is still not done."

"It won't be for a while."

Will flew back. Charles called him that evening to set up a recap session at their place right outside of the village. "Oh," he added, "I would like you and Christine to come for Sunday dinner after church. Could you make it?"

"Yes." Will put the cell on the table. He prayed and made a mental note to let Christine know.

The week flew by. Jeremiah was making good progress on the building, and Will helped with some of the wall assemblies. He explained the timeline and the subcontractors who would put in the wiring, including ethernet, plumbing and water sprinklers.

Will and Chris said little on the drive to the Huttons' home.

The smell of a roast wafted through the door. Charles greeted them. Stella stood by the foyer and led them to the living room. Sitting close to Charles, she said, "I have to ask you to forgive for my manner toward you. I grew bitter so fast, I hardly realized until…" She dabbed her eyes. "I chose to turn away from bitterness. It took a while, but," She smiled. "I dreamed last night that Tom was in heaven—happy and wanting us to go on with our lives. I'm thinking of disbanding the foundation." She glanced at Charles.

"Mrs. Hutton…"

"Please call me Stella. We are and will be friends, Will."

"Stella, please keep the foundation going. I just told a large congregation to contact you for their missing. While we had assumed the work of the foundation was well known, perhaps other areas are still uninformed of how you can help."

"Really? Tell me about it."

Will described the session. At the end, he said, "While it was totally opposite of what I had hoped or expected, it was almost as if I were seeing a vision of where we might be in years to come. That was encouraging."

"Nothing about the college?"

"Not even on their radar."

"Maybe not as a corporate group, but I can't stop thinking there will be a place for Faith Hall College and Seminary," Chris said.

After dinner, while Chris and Stella cleaned the kitchen, Will sat with Charles.

"Will, we have good contacts for a Southeastern retreat, more like the one in Texas, but there's nothing from New York and the North."

"Nothing?"

"Not a peep." Charles hesitated to describe the words he had for the existing churches in the Northeast. "I could not find one work that wanted to associate with our group."

Will nodded.

"However, we can leave that for the moment. Pastor Rick would like you to help him lead the Southeast Retreat in February in Raleigh, North Carolina. It will probably be more like the Phoenix event."

"Now I am thankful the Lord has prepared me. It will be fine. I'll network with him. Do you have the dates?"

They left further planning to the next day when the ladies joined them in the living room. Talk of the upcoming visit with Karen, Larry and his family, dominated the conversation. Chris smiled broadly as Stella glowed about having family over for a holiday.

"And you come too. You are family now!" Stella said, squeezing Chris' hand.

CHAPTER 30

Larry walked into the building and whistled. Will emerged from the main office—one he officially shared with Charles. "What a transformation!" He surveyed the literature and media center, greeting Virginia warmly. "Tour?"

She smiled and walked him through the correspondence, shelves of printed courses, and bank of computers for managing the online students. "Catherine helps a great deal. So far, we can manage."

Will brewed coffee for Larry. "So, you said that we had something to discuss?"

Larry evaded the question. "Heard about the Southeast Retreat, a little different, but not much from the one in Phoenix. They going to make it a yearly event?"

"Not exactly, but we did receive good suggestions for Faith Hall—enough to move ahead with development. Jeremiah and I will be visiting some contractors in the near future with rough plans. I've had more time to study college layouts and there's enough commonalities, we don't have to have a settled program before we begin renovation."

"What did they suggest?"

Will smiled, "They want everything. They loved the Bible study courses for their membership. Carlos and Dan did a great job demonstrating how that fits well with adult Sunday school programs and small group Bible studies. We haven't considered entering the market for the younger years as there are already good programs to choose from."

"No need to duplicate."

"Exactly. The board has started the hunt for the president." Will stared out the window. "I've had some time to get back to mastering Greek and learning Hebrew." He needed to lay the groundwork for his future. "So? I hear the West Coast is taking care of their own investigations for finding the missing."

"Yes, and there have been some developments there as well. During the last year, a small group of agents decided to bypass the courts and prisons. More mass graves have been found."

"Larry, did the FBI indicate whether or not they had closed all of the off-book prisons?"

"They think they have, but I'm sure some slipped by." He gauged Will's face and prayed if he should share the other half of the equation. "I only ask this because we've come as far as we can with what we can uncover."

"I thought Scot up in Gillette was helping with the FBI searches."

"He has been, but D.C. has Task Force files locked down tight. He spent two months learning they're not letting it out—not even through their intranet to secure field offices."

"Like Denver?"

"Will, what are they afraid of?"

"Americans discovering that the administration approved and encouraged these measures. Same reason they nolle'd my case."

"So, you can understand my problem. We've obtained the barest of information concerning the Christians in the Northeast."

"Scared? Hiding?"

"It's like they're gone." Larry hesitated to list the ten areas scattered throughout the upper Midwest and along the coast where organized Christianity seemed to have disappeared.

"So?"

"We need you to go to the field office and run the searches in their air-gapped room."

Will wanted to shake his head, but he could not move. He released a long held breath. "You do know, to a federal agent, a nolle'd case is like wagging a juicy bone in front of a bulldog. The agents are just looking for a chance to prove I'm culpable. We almost had to put in a court order to force them to leave me alone. I don't go near them. I don't talk to them. I don't even think about them."

"I know. I understand. It's what I told Scot, but if you don't, we might never find the lost ones in New England."

The last phrase smacked him between the eyes. *The lost ones...the lost ones of New England.* "Fill me in on what you have."

Larry reached in his pocket for a small drive. "This is all we have, and it's not much." He walked him through the slim data set. "We have identified that the distributor was someone called 'the Bard of Chaucer.' We have no idea about his identity, but you see why we need something more to go on. A few works are getting started, but there are many more with missing..." He paused, "...on both sides."

"Both sides?"

"You know what the Bible says about those who live by the sword?" He watched Will nod.

"They will die by the sword. I know that, Larry. I've seen it."

"Okay, so you understand why I'm asking."

Will glanced at the clock. "You have a supper date?"

"No, had the time and managed to book a late flight."

"I'm sure Chris would love to see you. I'll ask her about 'the Bard of Chaucer.' That used to be her favorite genre. Drove me crazy with notes written in Old English. Didn't make a lot of sense."

"Don't you have to check with her?"

"Ah, I'm the house husband and manage most of the meals. It only makes sense for me to plan suppers. Gives us more time to spend together—the little we get now that she's assisting with two trials this month. Tonight's fare will be the best our little takeout place can provide. You prefer beef and broccoli or General Tso's chicken?"

"I'm partial to beef."

———⌘———

They drove to the condo and ate. "I'll fix hers when she comes in."

"Court runs this late?"

"No, but after slogging through the day in court, they have their debrief and strategy meeting. It could take some time. Still, she thought she'd be home soon."

"Can she handle it?"

"She's loving it. I didn't have much patience for court shenanigans. But Chris has the instincts for trial planning and strategy. She is the reason I'm not sitting in Florence ADX right now."

When Chris arrived, Will let her decompress and revive herself with their favorite dishes. "So, Chris, now that you've had a chance to relax, do you remember a 'Bard of Chaucer'?"

"Sure." Chris sipped her tea. "Her name is Dr. Eliza Cummings, a Harvard Old English professor. She hadn't been chair of the department at that time, but she probably is now."

Will brought over his laptop and typed in the search. He furrowed his brow and turned it to Chris and Larry. "She's missing and presumed dead. Five years."

"Wait? You don't think?" Chris shook her head. She gestured for the laptop and navigated to several videos of Eliza's performances of Chaucer and other Old English authors. "I found her speeches stimulatingly hilarious as well as colorful and irreverent. You can slip a whole lot of naughty into lectures from that period. It wasn't exactly a sweet and genteel time."

Larry explained, "One of the few clues to the underground network in the Northeast has been linked with 'the Bard of Chaucer.' We always assumed it had been a man."

"Of course, you did."

"Well, progress…" Will said.

"Micro-progress. She's missing." Larry looked at Will, raising an eyebrow.

Will breathed and turned to Chris. "Larry has a request, but I'll let him tell it."

Larry repeated the gist of what he had told Will. "So, we either quit, or Will goes to the D.C. field office to find some leads."

"Then Larry, you must go with him." She looked at Will. "Tell him what they tried to do."

"I explained the situation."

"I need to know when you are in the offices, and I will expect check ins or I will send in the troops to extricate you."

"You know when I'm in the air-gapped room, I'll have to leave my electronics behind."

"Yes, but Larry can stand guard. I'll be counting on you."

"Agreed." Larry settled back. "We head in tomorrow. See the in-charge agent at ten."

"Really?" Will and Chris exchanged glances.

"You were that sure of yourself?" Chris asked.

"I was that sure of your dedication to finding the lost ones."

Will and Larry followed Chris into the D.C. metro area. After a quick tour of her firm, Will drove to the FBI D.C. Field Office. He led Larry to a corner coffee shop.

"Don't want to be early?"

"No." Will stated, not looking forward to the task, but he knew there was no other way. When the time came, he said, "Ready."

Upon entering the building and stepping through the security area to the inner section, memories flooded back. It had been so long ago, Will doubted he would recognize any agents. They headed to the section led by Special Agent in Charge Sabers. A young agent went to Saber's office and tapped on the doorframe. "Your ten o'clock, sir. Masters."

Will recognized the middle-aged agent.

Sabers smiled at the man with a white Stetson. "Texas Ranger Hutton, what a pleasure!" He extended his hand, acknowledging Will with a nod. "You, as well, Will. You look fit," he studied him closely.

Will met his gaze.

"Well, let's go into my office to go over the ground rules."

"We can do that here," Will said, trying to keep a neutral tone. "I have my pen and pad. The rest will stay with Texas Ranger Hutton. Please lead the way."

"Oh, it won't be that easy, Will. You know that. Special Agent Healy will assist." Sabers gestured for another clone of Sabers to join them.

Healy led the way through a back corridor, turned right and stopped by a locked door with biometric sensor. Once his identification was complete, he stated for the record: "Special Agent Healy with supervised guest, William Masters, access approved by Director in Charge Atkins." He read the day, date and time of their entry.

The door swung open, compressed air slipped out. Will nodded to Larry who stood guard by the door. "Check in no later than noon."

"Confirmed," Healy said.

Will hoped he could find what he needed before that. His skin crawled. At least he had a forward observer who could report if something happened.

Healy insisted on a thorough pat down once the door closed and sealed behind him.

"Satisfied?"

"Yes," the man grunted and let Will step past to the short folding table with a computer and monitor and printer."

"May I print?"

"Selected data, at my discretion." He ordered Will to stand aside in front of him and turned on the computer and entered the passwords to open the Task Force files. He stood up, sat in a nearby chair and opened up Solitaire on his phone.

Will stared at the man. "Get that device out of here." Seeing the man's attempt to appear surprised and puzzled, he finally stood up. Once the man exited the area, Will stepped through the first set of screens, familiarizing himself with the layout. His hands were in his lap when SA Healy returned.

Will plowed through the first level down to the staffing files searching for agents assigned to the Northeast. One name stood out. Will jotted down the name and navigated to the agent's reports and filed cases. Pursing his brow, he saw few, if any cases, but multiple file attachments. He opened and read each one, jotting down names of contractors, towns, locations and numbers. Few names of offenders were listed, only counts.

It felt like hours had passed, but he doubted such was the case. Remembering a shortcut Otis had built into the system, Will searched for New Hampshire and New Ipswich. Tight-lipped, he watched an assault on what looked like a remote home involving the murder of an expectant mother. He paused the video and tried to identify the man pulled out of the brown-shingled house, but the image was distorted.

Will also searched under the names of the contractors and jotted down time, place and the count for each incident reported in text files. However, the name, Eliza Cummings, did not link to any file. Will was puzzled since it seemed the Task Force had hit her home. Will sat back, trying to remember other places agents liked to hide files. A snatch of a conversation emerged from old memories. "Red brick" referred to the Carolinas. *What code did they select for New Hampshire? White.* Inputting the word brought up ten more files. Will took notes from each one.

If he had access to the standard FBI databases, he could do a thorough search on each one. However, Scot also had access to that. Perhaps they had enough data for a warrant for Cummings' New Hampshire home.

Will glanced at Healy. "Done. Do you want to shut her down?"

The man glared at him and shook his head. While the computer ran through the shutdown process, he held out his hand for Will's note-book and glanced through the pages. Not seeing any red flags, he returned it.

Larry joined Will when they walked through the door. He smiled, seeing the wink, but Will said nothing. They followed the agent out to the first-floor reception area. "Was it as bad as you thought?"

"No, not like the last time when they tried to get me into an interrogation room on the precept on needing my help to nail Kincaid. I almost fell for it."

"How did you know?"

"I recognized the agents." He walked out the door, down the street and around the corner to a diner. "I'll buy you lunch, and we can decide our next steps."

Once in the booth and after sending a text to Chris, he started his music and said with lowered voice. "They have video of an assault on her home on Green Farm Road. Murdered a pregnant woman and dragged a good-sized man out of her house. I couldn't find any filed arrest or conviction reports, but I did find several text files of assaults throughout the area with counts and few names. Only four agents seemed to have been assigned to that area, one for each state or area: New York, Connecticut/Rhode Island, Vermont/New Hampshire/Maine, and Massachusetts. However, they probably worked with contractors whose names you will never find in their employee records."

"Kincaid's old military pals?"

"Most likely. I have some full names. If we had access to the FBI general database, we probably could start with the names we do have and work through their known associates. I don't feel right asking Esterly."

"Do you have a friend in that office?"

"I doubt it. We can check with the Hutton Foundation for their FBI contacts who might be willing to run these searches. In the meantime, we do as much as we can on our own—find enough evidence for warrants and take a team to search Cummings' farm. We would need cadaver dogs or ground-penetrating radar." Will thought for a moment about the analysts Chris had worked with at the Hutton Foundation. "If your Aunt Stella would allow us access to her foundation's resources, we might be able to establish if the names in my notebook match any reported missing."

"We can also check the names of those who lived around her Green Farm Road property who are also missing," Larry said. "I'll call her now."

"First, ask if she has a friendly in that building—as long as we're in the neighborhood."

Their lunch came, and Will listened to Larry chat with his aunt before making the request. He handed the phone to Will. "Wants to speak with you."

"Hi, Mrs. Hutton? Okay, Stella. Yes, I have some info from the old files. Don't want to request the warrant to investigate until we have more." He hung up and handed it back. "She'll let the staff know. She'd like to see what we have. Plans on being there in two days. How long do you have?"

"Officially, a week, but my command is behind this. I can request more if needed."

"Great! I assume she didn't have an agent to recommend." He watched Larry shake his head. "Then we travel on to the office in Reston, Virginia."

Within a day they had enough evidence for warrants. They met briefly with Stella the next day right before leaving for New Hampshire. The county sheriff had a forensic team with a cadaver dog. After adding some shovels to their gear, they headed up the interstate.

The congested multi-lane interstates passing through dense population areas gave way to twisting two-lane county roads. They climbed the hill and rounded the curve to the local sheriff's office in New Ipswich,

New Hampshire, a scenic place where trees filled every available space and hugged the edges of the roads, obscuring most homes.

Will shifted his vehicle into four-wheel drive to climb up the short incline to a tattered brown-shingled house. He recognized it immediately from the low-resolution video. The sheriff removed the aging yellow crime tape and walked them through the house. In the lower walkout area, bookcases dominated from floor to ceiling with books pulled out and strewn about. A Franklin stove in the middle of the room overflowed with ashes and partially burned books and paper on the floor. Marks of charred floorboards formed a semi-circle in front of the mouth of the stove.

"House didn't burn?"

"Someone put it out."

"Fire and rescue?"

"No calls were logged." The sheriff nudged a pile. "This is how we found it a week after we responded to a report of a noxious odor and seeing no one home for a while." He met their gaze. "She was a Harvard professor and could be eccentric—often gone for a month or more. Didn't log it until after learning she hadn't checked in at the university either. But the FBI shutdown the investigation."

Will walked the area in the video. "I saw a video of an assault team shoot a pregnant woman in the gut with a shotgun, followed by a pair dragging out a large man." He studied the ground. "Four years ago." He looked over the descending slope. "What's over there?"

"She had a back garage and drive along a road to an adjoining property."

They turned to see a k9 SUV pull up, and a man exited with a dog. He didn't find anything at the area, but the handler walked the dog around the yard.

Will and Larry headed down the hill to the lower garage. A deputy opened the garage door and yelled, "Bring the dog." Bodies were piled alongside a late model, light-brown Saab sedan.

Will looked at Larry, "Let's check the neighbor." He consulted his notebook. "Lott Sarkin's place."

"Our warrant's just for Cummings."

"I know, but we can look around. They might have been neighborly." The spring was late and winter dogged hidden paths that saw little daylight. Skirting slick ice-coated mud, they heard the crunch of dry pine needles under their feet. Piles of shriveled vegetation in spots along the road indicated little traffic if any at all. The small rectangular unpainted house looked deserted. A squirrel worked its way out of a hole on the side near the roof and jumped to a nearby tree branch. They knocked anyway. "Maybe he's in the pile."

"Let's see if the sheriff has cause for entry."

Within the hour they followed the sheriff and deputy down the lane. He knocked, called, "Mr. Sarkin." They walked around the property. The back window was broken, and the door ajar. They followed them in.

Will noticed more books and walked over to read their titles. "Interlinear, theology of the cross, eschatology, biblical ethics. From the look of his books, Mr. Sarkin was a pastor."

They negotiated collecting DNA samples from the remains. Knowing the forensic team would take hours to deal with the bodies, Will and Larry headed to the lower level to search for clues.

Larry looked at the remnants of books and papers near the stove. "Looks like they tried to burn *Chaucer's Canterbury Tales, Peterborough Chronicle,* as well as *Beowulf.*"

Will searched through a desk, spied a shadow behind it, and pulled it out to reveal a cubbyhole. Pages pulled from a book, poetry, with handwritten letters and numbers running down the side. Underneath the pile was a thin notebook with most of its pages removed. Opening it, he read: *My name is Clyde Baxter, and this is my confession.* Will's eyes moistened as he read the story of a contractor torn by what they were paid to do, trying to leave. He described an underground prison, and the van that transported him. Unable to talk, swallow or eat, he escaped when the van slid on a patch of ice. The van ran off the road and rolled down a steep incline, killing all but Baxter.

The Lord indicated I could take the luggage that landed beside me. It had clothes that fit, but nothing else. I changed and buried the prison rags. As if led by an invisible hand, I walked, avoiding all dwellings, and found myself, cold and starving, in a chilling rain, stumbling into a barn. The owner came with a floodlight, a dog, and a shotgun. I held up my hands but could not speak. After several gestures, he brought pen and paper. I wrote that I was Christian, tortured and hunted. Expecting him to turn me in, he lifted me up, embraced me and said they would shelter me.

And they did. I married Eliza Cummings, who is now the love of my life. I cannot imagine any other. My heart is sad when she is away at Harvard, but when she is here, we have sweet fellowship together. Pastor Lott teaches me very patiently about this faith and how to live it. It is as if we exist in a different world, and I pray God continues to shield us from those who seek to harm us.

They grow closer in our area, and as she is the one to hide the Hutton Bibles, I go with her for her safety. In the world she is known as 'the Bard of Chaucer' and travels widely throughout New England with her witty stories about life and the literature of the Middle Ages. While she has changed her act slightly since her conversion, she maintains it, as much as possible, to distribute Bibles under cover of her travels.

The most amazing thing. To us, in our middle years, we are granted a new life. The doctor says it is a boy, and I am praying for his name.

The writing stops with a slash across the page. The cover is torn from being thrust under the pile, and the desk pushed back. Will imagined his terror when he perceived they were under attack. He stopped by a framed photo of a large tan-black German shepherd.

Heading down to the hill, he sees the bones laid out on a tarp. "Is there a large dog?"

"Yes," a tech replied.

"There's a picture of a German shepherd in the house." Will shook his head. *Was Clyde Baxter among the dead?* He couldn't explain the affinity he felt for the one whose story was similar to his, and he wondered if someday he and Chris would also be gifted with a child.

While waiting for the genetic results to come back, Will and Larry, along with the Foundation's private eye, scoured the Internet for clues. They pieced together what they could find relating to the names. Clyde Baxter was missing, and they gleaned a little of his past. Someone worked his magic, and the Foundation soon received reports and summaries of Baxter's service. He had been a SEAL—a Navy special operator for overseas covert missions. He had high scores in marksmanship, hand-to-hand combat, survival training, and navigation. If he was not among the remains, perhaps he had escaped.

Will had an idea. He asked the staff in their spare moments to run checks for the past four years on reports in an ever-widening circle around the home for reported break-ins, particularly of seldom used hunters' cabins or any missing items. Will traced the smaller streets away from the property, towns and well-traveled highways. Dense, sparsely populated forests, just north and west of Ipswich might have been good places to hide.

The genetic matching service identified the remains faster than the lab used by New Hampshire. The expectant mother Will had seen murdered on the video was indeed Eliza Cummings, along with the remains of an unborn baby that had been hers. The staff had reached out to relatives for Lott Sarkin, and one submitted sample matched his.

One person was identified through a military database, but the others had no matches. However, general descriptions and the time period should lead to matches with those reported missing.

Larry was about to head home when Will, tracking a series of break-ins, found an image of a person matching Clyde Baxter's description searching a dumpster behind a restaurant in the early hours before dawn. As he had with everything else they had uncovered, he forwarded the stills and analysis to Special Agent Murray, head of the Task Force Recovery Team.

Will went back to the satellite images they had been given access to and methodically searched the area in an outward circular pattern. He identified a remote cabin not far from a free-flowing stream that might be a good place to hide. His cell rang at the same time as Larry's. He assumed he had been asked the same question: are you interested in joining the team to locate Baxter?

Their eyes met, and they both said yes. "We're in," Will said, still incredulous.

"Well, we're attached as limited task assets, but we can still be there." Larry studied Will. "You ready to be back with a team?"

"In some ways, yes. But we have to be there to try to make contact with minimal bloodshed."

The both knew what was at stake.

Will texted Charles that he would have to miss the next board meeting due to the New Hampshire operation. They drove to the Hancock Fire Department facility, the staging area, arriving in time to listen to the update on Baxter's movements. The joint operation involved state and sheriff's officers assisting the FBI strike team. Will's unease grew as he listened to the lead agent describe Baxter as a lethal, rogue operator and fugitive from justice.

Are they going to pin the murders on him?

Donning vests with spare clips, carrying rifles and pistols, and equipped with night goggles, the teams moved out and set up a perimeter. A report from one on the eastern side indicated Baxter had spotted the scout and was moving toward the cabin.

In the time of the dawning, the transition from dark to light, Will slipped around the command tent, down a side trail and worked his way around a bored sentry. Once past the line of fire, he moved as quietly as he could to the cabin. Hearing a splash in the stream, he whispered, "Clyde. Clyde Baxter."

The man was on him in moments. He dodged the first charge but lost his footing, and Baxter sent him tumbling down the path. Grabbing Will forcefully, he dragged him to the cabin and threw him against the wall. "What do you want? Who are you?"

"I am William Masters." He had no time to dodge Baxter's fist driven into his side.

"*You!* It's your fault. You reported to Kincaid. You gave the orders."

"No," Will gasped for breath. He had felt the ribs crack and tried to breathe through the pain. "God sent me to find you. It's over. The laws are rescinded. The Task Force is dissolved."

"Where is Eliza and my son?"

"I found your confession. If you believe in Jesus, you know they are in Heaven waiting for you." The fury and agony evident on his face, Will waited for the next blow. "If you know Christ…"

"What good did it do? Why did?" He stepped back from Will and sobbed, almost pulling his hair from his head in agony of soul.

"And what of that time with Eliza? What of the good you did helping her distribute the Bibles? Do we take the good from God and not the bad?"

Clyde turned. "Job said that."

"He did. Sorry I can't quote the chapter and verse, but Clyde, let us bring you back to the light. My story is not that different from yours, and I have a place again. A home."

"She's gone."

"She went ahead. I know it's hard. Many have died. Many are like you with their loved ones gone, but only for a time." He held out his hand. "Please walk out with me. I don't want them to compound their error by adding your blood to the rest."

"Where? Where did they put her?"

"We found several bodies near the Saab in the lower garage." Will waited for the anger to work itself out, the tears to fall, the grief to run its course. Feeling lightheaded, he tried to shift, but the pain in his side caused him to groan. He tried to hide it, but Clyde turned to look at him before he turned away.

"All we like sheep have gone astray. We have turned everyone to our own way and the Lord laid on Him the iniquity of us all. There is therefore no condemnation for those who are in Christ Jesus. For the law of the spirit of life has set you free in Christ Jesus from the law of sin and death.[11] Clyde, let us help you live in the light of Christ. If you are a believer, you are forgiven, totally, completely."

Will tried not to flinch when Clyde knelt down to examine his side. "They took me to a hidden prison and nearly killed me," he explained. "Some of my ribs were shattered, so I have to be careful."

Baxter helped him stand.

"I can walk, but not very fast."

"Probably better. How far out's the perimeter?"

"Half mile or so." Will set one foot in front of the other, keeping an eye out for the line. Eventually, he saw figures ahead of them. "This is Will Masters with Clyde Baxter. We are unarmed. Do not shoot." They froze when they heard them advance, rifles pointed at them. "Stand aside."

Will, following instructions, lay down next to Clyde. When they lifted him up, the pain increased, and collapsing, he fell into blackness.

He heard and smelled the emergency room before he opened his eyes. Trying to assess his situation, he drew breath, feeling the pain shoot up his chest.

"Mr. Masters," he heard. Will opened his eyes.

"You have a collapsed lung. We are inserting a chest tube. Lie still."

Will nodded. His eyes took in the bright lights and sounds of movement in the large room.

Once the doctor had secured the tube and stepped away to check his vitals, Will asked, "How long have I been here?"

"Not long, but they took a long time getting you here."

"We were not close to anything," Will said. "Is Larry Hutton here?"

"Yes. He can see you now."

Will watched Larry's face go from concern to worry before he smiled. "And I thought I was the maverick. *What was that all about?* They could have shot you."

"I didn't like how he prepped the team. Was afraid…" He tried to catch his breath; his throat felt so raw. "Afraid they'd be trigger happy. Afraid that Baxter would react badly, and they would overreact. I went in unarmed. I had to. It was the only way to bring him home. They treating him okay?"

"We assumed he assaulted you."

"His Task Force commanders told him to kill people. He recognized me and thought I had given the orders, but then I was able to talk him down."

"They've taken him in for processing and interrogation."

"Larry, you have to help him. Find someone to stand up for him. He knows what happened up there. We didn't have time to talk too much, but the little he said…they need to know." Will lay back, exhausted from the effort.

"What did they do?"

"Like a scorched earth. You described it—areas where no one was brought in, but murdered instead. The agents didn't want to deal with the courts. Remind them of the notebook we found."

"Well, rest easy. As soon as they release you, I'll be driving you back home."

"That sounds great."

"You are crazy!"

"Hey, just doing the job." It felt good when he saw Larry nod in understanding.

"They're admitting you for observation. I'll stay until you're settled in a room. My hotel is a few blocks away. Think you can handle an overnight in this place?"

Will woke, feeling the effects of the medication. He shifted carefully before he opened his eyes, still utterly spent and tired. Before he could drift back to sleep, he heard the sounds that had awakened him—footsteps, shuffling, pen on paper. He opened his eyes when a phone chirped. Men stood around his bed.

The one closest to him nodded and turned on the bank of lights above the bed, almost blinding him. Will felt for the control to raise the head of the bed. "Yes?"

"Atkins," he said and extended his hand.

"You over the Task Force teams?" The man was so high up he was surprised to see him at a small rural hospital west of Concord."

Atkins pulled a chair around, nodded at two who stood by the door and the agent closer to him fumbled with something in his pocket. "Well, Mr. Masters, we have been trying to have a conversation with you for a while." He watched Will look toward the door. "Hutton's still asleep in his hotel."

The Holy Spirit reminded him to be civil. He shifted to find a more comfortable position. "What..." his voice cracked. The pain separated and he could feel his raw throat. An agent handed him a mug of water.

"We need a statement for Baxter's assault charges."

"No," Will shook his head. "He had no idea my ribs had been shattered. He didn't intend to harm me. Hear him out before you file charges." Will tried to lean forward, "He could be your best source yet. He knows who gave the orders and what they were told to do." Sitting back, he added, "Kincaid ran his teams like covert, black-op missions. Otis was his righthand man. Specializing in computer data and cloud storage, he designed the system as a complex maze. Despising passwords, he created backdoors accessible by series of complicated keystrokes. If you know them, you can navigate the files and run searches."

He looked at the agent by Atkins. "Have paper or a notebook?" The man fumbled in a slim case. Will pulled the patient table around and outlined the Task Force data structure.

"Wouldn't he have a kill code?"

Will shook his head. "No, he didn't want the evidence destroyed, but hidden." He met the man's eyes. "He's ambitious." Will sighed, "Oh, and have your best people scour cloud storage. Otis liked to hide things at remote server farms. Don't discount innocuous mom-and-pop companies." He handed back the paper. "Atkins, you have the agents. Utilize their talents and you will discover what you need to know." He had to add, "Debrief Hutton for other pockets of missing contractors as well as citizens."

"How did you know he wouldn't kill you?"

"I didn't."

"Why risk it?"

"I heard the briefing and realized their aggressive approach would most likely result in bloodshed—Baxter's as well as maybe some of the team members. Remember, the last thing he saw was the body of his murdered wife and unborn son. I had to tell him the laws had been reversed, and they had come to rescue him—not kill him." Will added, "He told me that when he refused to commit murder, the Task Force nearly killed him."

"You could have a spot on my team as a consultant. Help avoid tragedies, like you did with Baxter."

Will smiled, "You have the talent. Use it. Trust it. There still are those who joined the FBI to fight for justice. God has given me a different task—to raise up Christians who can be light and salt to our nation."

CHAPTER 31

CHRIS MET THEM in the parking lot. He could tell she vacillated between anger and relief. "You..."

Will tried to hug her, but his side screamed, and he stepped back against the Tahoe.

"Come on." Larry followed with their bags.

"I couldn't believe my ears when he called to say you approached the suspect by yourself."

"Honey, what if there had been a manhunt for me, and you had heard the CO telling them how dangerous I was? I knew they would kill him. Remember Hawsley? You knew you had to go in so you could rescue the hostages." He didn't say he thought he heard God tell him everything would work out. "Believe me, I'm not going on any more of those operations."

"And that's the last time you'll be invited."

Will looked at Larry who was trying not to smirk.

"Yes, you deserve that and more. Gave us a real fright—even the CO. Knew it would be his last assignment if something had happened to you during his watch."

Chris opened the door to their home.

"The debrief? Can you get in there and make sure they do it right?"

"Will, this is not our jurisdiction, and it's not your job. If you're that concerned for him, pray for him and write him a letter when you find out what prison they'll be sending him to." Larry followed them through with the bags.

"I'll be calling Tompkins to see if they can help with his defense. They tortured him and murdered his family in front of him."

"Yes, you can do that, but not today." Chris interrupted before listing, "Hot herbal tea to help you sleep, warm soup, and maybe crackers if you behave."

"Larry," Will said, straining to stay awake. "Thanks for going with me, for hanging in there. We found one of the lost ones. We brought him in."

Larry nodded. "I'll be staying at Aunt Stella's and flying home as soon as I can book a flight."

"Let me know. But if it's soon, goodbye, but not for too long. Honey, we need to visit him in Amarillo. It's beautiful."

"Okay, adventure boy. Bedtime for you." Chris looked at Larry. "I'll drive you there after he's settled."

"Actually, they're coming by to pick me up. Said they have something to tell Will."

"Oh, in that case…" She helped him rise. "Get into the bathroom and make yourself as presentable as possible." She smiled and winked at Larry.

Will's brain was too foggy to wonder what that meant.

Stella and Charles walked in and greeted Larry, congratulating him on finding Baxter. When they saw Will trying to stand up, they said, "We're coming to you."

"Thanks for the assistance. Your foundation helped a lot. I think we moved up the investigation. The FBI team behaved itself."

"Behaved themselves so well you had to walk in to keep them from shooting him?"

"Well, the onsite commander made him sound unpredictable."

"Which he was."

"But he didn't kill me when he could have. I knew I could talk him down and bring him in."

Charles said, "We're happy to see you doing so well. Gave us quite a scare when Larry told us you'd gone in." He cleared his throat. "You know we've been searching for a president to lead Faith Hall. It was a harder challenge than we had imagined." He reached for Stella's hand. "To see the number of fine applicants was encouraging. Many of them very well qualified, but I, well, let's say, the board, felt we need someone who shared our vision. After days of prayer, we felt led to offer the position to one who had not applied." He felt Stella squeeze his hand. "Will Masters, would you consent to leading our college or whatever the Lord desires it to be?"

"Me?" His heart raced. He so wanted to respond with a resounding yes, but could he do it? Instantly, he knew he could with God's help. "I assume I'd need additional degrees."

"Just one, dear," Stella said, watching him carefully, "a doctorate in higher-education administration. They usually take about a year. When you find a program, send it on for my approval. By the time you have the degree, we will be ready to commission the facility."

"Yes, I accept. It would be an honor and a privilege," he said without hesitation or reservation. *The Lord will be with me. I know that.* Chris beamed. Larry congratulated him. Will sat back, exhaustion taking over, and Chris ushered him to bed.

Will found an approved doctorate program, and half of the courses could be completed online. He set his sights for a year but prayed he could finish sooner. The plans for the college had been approved, the bids were out, and Dan and Carlos were developing programs and staffing.

At the same time Jeremiah had begun plans for building-out the second floor of the office. Separate, but related, Charles purchased the front two lots and acquired a developer for student housing with some family apartments since area rents were high.

Their vision was taking shape. One day Charles stopped by Will's front office and sat in the comfortable chair. "Don't forget to set aside some of those hard, folding chairs when you need to talk with a troublemaker."

"I'll keep that in mind. What's up?"

"Well, I can't stop thinking about what I saw at Mesa Ranch—a wall of remembrance. I'd forgotten how hectic it can be when you're in expansion mode. Some plans can fall by the wayside. Like your finding the lost ones, remember?

"At Mesa Ranch I saw a tall wall as high as the full wall in the warehouse, covered with pictures of those who died in faith for their faith, not focusing on the wicked deeds, but on their willing sacrifice for our Savior. How should it look and the pictures be displayed? Where's Jeremiah's office?"

"Let's find him." Will rose, and they headed toward the back end of the building with the workbench, tools and supplies. They stepped into his sparse corner office. "He must be on site, but the drawings are here."

They leaned closer to check the layout of the structure's righthand wall. "The stairs will block it. They can't be supported by that wall."

"Could we shorten the upper level to pull it away from the outer wall? That would create a raised balcony, an overlook on the second level."

Will released the drawing and headed over to the warehouse. Jeremiah and his assistant were taking more measurements.

Charles explained his vision. Jeremiah nodded. "Do you have an example in mind?"

"I'll find some, and we'll discuss the possibilities. Jeremiah, can you hold off on final drawings for a bit?"

"Yes, we just realized we hadn't allowed enough space for the elevator shaft and some other dimensions were off." He rubbed his chin. "The contractor will have to add supports, work out the ventilation issues, but it's not too late to make the change."

"We'll submit the ideas once we've talked through them. We'll be back."

On the way to his office, the Lord reminded him again, *Find My lost ones.*

———— ⚬⚬⚬ ————

Later in the week Will contacted Atkins' assistant to check on Clyde Baxter.

"He's cleared and joined the team to find mass graves."

"That's great. May I have his contact info?"

Will sat back, waiting for the text, wondering what the Lord had meant. Perhaps he needed to keep an open heart and a ready mind to perceive God-sent opportunities.

CHAPTER 32

CHRIS NAVIGATED FROM U.S. 87 through Troy to Route 100. The reds, golds, and yellows of the leaves glistened in the failing light. Through the twists and turns of Vermont and the open, unsheltered plain beyond into New Hampshire, Will said little.

"Baxter's come a long way," Chris ventured.

He nodded. Eliza's niece had given the New Hampshire property to him. The man had not run away but had returned to raise up a fellowship from the ashes.

"Sources tell me Clyde has a good friend. He sees her quite frequently."

"Life goes on," Will stated, looking forward to hearing from Clyde himself what had helped him recover and find new life in the Lord.

He had not been so brave, having turned down the opportunity to attend the commissioning of Rosemont Memorial Park. The churches and county had risen up to mark the area with a plaque, commemorating the sacrifice of faith. Will was glad to hear they had decided not to preserve the buildings, instead erecting a small pavilion suitable for services or gatherings. His heart rejoiced to see a park with a small field, swing set and play area—a place to celebrate God-given life.

"Will, I never heard about the Oklahoma site."

"Wasn't one. Didn't need one. I wouldn't expect there to be one. Next year Chris, Lord willing, I'll take you out there. Larry turned down a promotion with the FBI in the D.C. office because he knows Texas is where he belongs. They're resourceful, effective, competent, and fiercely independent. Of all the areas, they were the most resilient. The realities of life helped them bear the sorrows. Many struggled, but it seems they never let it divide them."

"You don't need to go to Rosemont, but you do need to visit New Hampshire?"

"Honey, it's the people. I need to see Baxter and the Christians come together—not in hiding, but in the light. The ones who matter from Rosemont are with us at Purcellville or Kentucky or Colorado, or…" His eyes teared as he struggled to conclude, "Waiting for us to join them."

Will consulted the GPS navigator, looking for their next turn. "Having the Huttons lead the Foundation brings a unique perspective. Charles also understands the need for flexibility. The courses and programs will be subject to change as needed. That's why I'm coming—to see how we can help Clyde's fellowship and connect with those who might want to come to Faith Hall."

"Is that the name?"

"Consider it the working name for now. The board needs to decide soon. The window for ordering the sign is fast approaching. At least they've stopped trying to push versions of Hutton Bible College and Seminary." Will sat back, thankful for Charles' drive to bring glory to God and not himself or the family name.

Chris drove around to the front, the land sloping down and to the right with the top floor level with the road.

"He's done a lot of work." They stood by the car. Will turned to take the bags when Chris opened the rear door. "I can get that."

Clyde met them at the door. "Come in. Right this way." He headed down the short entranceway with a closet on the left and a small office on the right to the main sitting room where banks of windows overlooked hills resplendent in fall colors. "It's been just the right warmth with cool nights. They say it brings out the color."

The windows wrapped around to the left side. A small kitchen in polished wood followed the other corner and skirted open stairs to the lower level on the left.

"Quite the transformation. Everyone pitched in. Eliza's niece kicked in some funds in memory of her aunt. Seems that some time ago, once she converted. Eliza had quite an influence on her niece."

"How did she find Christ? During my college years, I had a chance to attend one of her lectures." Chris looked about. "Where are her books?"

"Downstairs. I hardly believed it myself, but she let me see a video of her talks before her conversion. She had to find a way to tone it down without exposing her secret. Lott Sarkin, her neighbor, formerly a pastor of an *official* church, as she called it, retreated to his cabin next door. Working through a crisis of faith, he established a local fellowship." Clyde tilted his head. "Truth sweetened with love and grace." He led them into the main room with restored wood floors, sturdy wooden chairs. "This is our main meeting place. We're looking for a piano, but the keyboard will do for now. The library is downstairs."

Will and Chris followed. Will paused on the stairs as he cleared the upper floor. Hardly changed, but the books were shelved, the ashes and burn marks removed. Chris and Clyde looked at him. "Smells better," he said, trying to lighten his mood. "You've kept her library."

He turned to the small desk on his left. "This is where I found your diary. The burnt books and papers. You were destroying her codes for finding the Bibles? Old English is inscrutable to us, but…"

Clyde pulled out an old slim volume. "Mary Lynch Johnson's dictionary of Old English. Her dissertation—out of print now. Eliza gifted each leader with a copy." He opened the book to a dog-eared page. "This was the code key. She hid her coded notes in her other books. As a professor and an expert in the field, she regularly reviewed many types of works. Notorious for writing copious notes in the margins, it was the perfect place to hide the locations."

Will and Chris looked at a few samples. "How the Lord works!" Chris exclaimed.

Clyde looked away. "We heard them take out Buster first. I could see vehicles up and down the main road. Eliza was six months along in her pregnancy. I told her to run to the Saab. We had go-bags there. I had caches throughout the area, but when I heard the shotgun report, I didn't have the heart to look. With minutes to spare, I burned her code keys first but didn't have the heart to burn Mary Johnson's work." He surveyed the orderly library with added volumes for doctrine, books of the Bible, children's story books. "I had to keep something."

"The shock of seeing her in the yard…" Clyde looked away. "When they led me down the hill, instinct took over. I took out the three and ran. Knowing the area well, a day later I made it to a cache and fled on a small motorbike." His eyes held a distant look.

He turned, "I had been praying for direction when you appeared. I knew you were the one I could trust when you quoted Isaiah 53."

Footsteps sounded above them, along with the clicks of a dog's claws on hardwood floors. "Nancy's here with Buster 2. In memory of the first one."

"I'll go up and help," Chris offered.

Will came to himself. "Clyde, I have a few questions. Would this be a good time?" Seeing the nod, he plunged in. "Where did you find healing? It seems you've managed to make peace, find your calling, and live for the future—not trapped in the past."

"They hired me to help find the sites. While I had not participated in any of the assaults, I knew their methods. Once we identified the target, we started with their homes and searched from there. The graves were usually shallow and close to the actual scene. They must have thought no one would hold them accountable. Chilling. To think of what I could have become. But as I saw the faces of the survivors, I realized I was far from alone. By trying to help the living see grace in the deaths, I found it as well." Clyde nodded. "Along with His Holy Spirit and the Word of God, the Lord sent many to comfort and direct." His face brightened. "Actually, Nancy was a big part of my healing.

Her husband had been a deputy sheriff in Manchester and the leader of their small group. By the grace of God, she had taken her class for the annual field trip the day of the assault. She lost her teen daughter too." He sighed, "We helped each other, and we married last month. Purchased Lott's place, and it'll be fit to live in fairly soon."

Will shared their desires for Faith Hall to help the fellowships. They talked of possibilities until Nancy's call came down the stairs.

"Buster 2 doesn't quite get it that I'm the man. He prefers Nancy, but that's okay. I can live with that." Clyde tussled with the year-old German shepherd.

Chris watched Will take in the events of the two-day meetings and fellowship time. The new Will didn't push himself forward or hint at his achievements. He seemed content to let others lead as a group commemorated those who went ahead and prayed for their children's future.

As they prepared to leave, Will said to Clyde, "Come visit us when you get a chance. Anytime, we can send a team to present the Bible course programs."

"And the Bible college?"

"In a year or so, maybe two. Still trying to settle on a name. For now, we're Faith Hall Foundation. We'll keep in touch. Thanks for inviting us."

Clyde walked them out to the car. "Oh, Will," he said, holding him back. "I know we all have to face the future, but sometimes we have to visit the past. Believe me. Sometimes, in the light of a new day, its hold is broken, and we are..."

"Set free?" Will finished his sentence.

Clyde nodded.

"Thanks, Clyde, I needed to hear that."

He joined Chris, waiting for him in the car. "Okay, you win. I'll go with Rick to the Rosemont dedication."

"I'll see if I can join you. Stella has been urging me to go."

Unrequested, unbidden, groups began to submit ideas, plans, or rough sketches for the wall of remembrance. Will collected the submissions, and working with local and distant contacts, sifted through the possibilities—a wall of plaques with picture, name, age, city, date and a verse; video clips; a brief description of their experience. Eventually, they incorporated all with a static wall of plaques with three video displays for pictures and brief testimonials.

Will shifted, seeing the proposed images from the firm heading up the development of the main building. The results were disappointing. "We can settle on a final plan later. What's the update on the balcony stairs and supports?" He glanced at Jeremiah to see if the man was satisfied with what he was hearing. The contractor was timely, he had to give him that, but he lacked imagination and seemed to settle for the easiest, cheapest solutions. A little digging and he had found stronger, more streamlined supports for the balcony. Regretting not having teamed with a top-tiered architectural firm, he recalled Charles' admonition not to sweat the small stuff.

However, this wall had to be exceptional, and exceptional wasn't what he was seeing. Will headed home after the meeting and a nod in Jeremiah's direction. He had to think, but he couldn't forget the Rosemont model. Back in the condo, he headed for the guest room closet. The small model was in the back, on top of four boxes. The brass nameplate read Wilkerson, Marsh & Terry, Architects, Orlando, Florida. He went back to his computer and opened the file for Mary-Sue's testimony. The architect's name was Daryl Sanford.

The large firm had offices throughout the United States, including Orlando. The firm now called itself WM&T⌒Architects since its international expansion. He scrolled through the Orlando staff listings but didn't find Daryl. He tried to search on Daryl's name and found him in their Dallas office. Years ago, the man had been slender, almost bookish, but with an intense focus and imagination. He was a little thicker in the jowls and with thinning hair, but he had the same impervious look of assured confidence.

Will called, working through a few layers of admins until he reached the one who could book a consult. Knowing he didn't have time to drive, he scheduled a flight to Dallas.

With the authority to put down a sizeable retainer, armed with videos, stills and concept images, Will reviewed his presentation during the flight. Not knowing how long it would take—one day or a few to work through the details, he only booked one night at a nearby hotel.

The firm occupied the fifth floor of a large building of steel and glass, located near the city center. The building was tall and rectangular with the typical modern look of sharp corners, bare concrete and polished steel. Will surmised this was one of the smaller offices—not a main location. Surprising, he thought when he recalled their extravagant Orlando building.

The receptionist led him to a small conference room with a large monitor. Will set up his laptop, bringing up the images on his desktop for presentation.

Daryl walked in, barely smiling.

Will stood, extended his hand and watched the man go from recognition to disappointment and obvious dislike. "William Masters from Faith Hall Foundation." He dropped his hand and gestured to the side chair. "Some moments of your time, please."

The architect sat stiffly, subtly shifting his body away from Will, crossing his arms, and closing him off.

"I see you remember me."

"Oh, I do—as well as the lovely London position I lost because I talked a partner into accepting the Task Force contract." He added, "They never paid us."

"I'm sorry to hear that. I submitted the invoices."

"But when they cancelled the contract, they failed to pay the fee and, well…" he sat back.

Will slid a prepared check for a retainer across the table. "You will be paid this time. I represent Faith Hall Foundation." Will described their origination and vison, segueing into the wall project. "Mr. Sanford, are you familiar with the Task Force's crimes?"

He waved his hand. "Vaguely. I have little time for either politics or religion."

"Well, many Christians were killed by this group. We wish to erect a wall of remembrance in the main building." Will worked through the images. "However, our current general contractor lacks imagination, and this is his proposal for the memorial." The image was a mediocre 3-d rendering of an industrial-looking wall with a light-blue background, stone-like bricks with a photo for the plaques, and some etched wording with three blocky pedestals in front of the wall with keyboards and square monitors. "That is what we have to work with, and for this space, we need to do much better."

Will swallowed. Mr. Sanford appeared bored, barely awake, and showed little-to-no interest. He would at least see his presentation through. The check was still on the table. He had the cash to cover this man's precious time.

"I'm not a graphic artist, but please bear with me," he continued as he grabbed his remote and stood. "We have settled on a plaque with photo and a brief inscription." Using his image editing software, he had tried to layer in the effect of a watermark of the world, with an outline of the states over it, and the plaques arranged geographically. He tried to recreate the effect of the outlines glowing faintly, but more brightly than the shimmer he'd tried to put on the earth image. Reaching up and onto the ceiling, a soft blue revealed distant stars that could be turned on.

"I'm so limited in what I can capture with this program," he added, but he drew a large arc with his arm. "Upon a shimmering, faint image of the earth, in soft color tones, would be an outline of the United States and each state in dim lights, making them easier to see than a drawn line. Within each area, we would place the plaques of those killed by the Task Force or because of them. Somewhat raised." Will directed his hand to different parts of the country. "They will be placed according to their residence—not the place where they were slain or their bodies dumped." He didn't stop to see if the man was intrigued or even interested.

Lifting his arm to point, he continued, "Above the states' outline, reaching up to the ceiling and along the upper section, the wall would be painted a soft blue with small lights embedded that can be turned on to look like stars in the sky."

"You don't want your Jesus in there?"

Will stopped. "It seems almost sacrilegious to try to attempt His face, but," Will looked at his best attempt of lit stars. "Perhaps His arms reaching down to welcome us home." He had to stop.

"Go on. Did you bring some concept images?"

Will turned back to face him, having regained a measure of composure. "I did." He sat down and worked through the images, listening to the man's questions.

"That's it? Where's the reminders of what was done? Isn't this so it will never happen again?"

"I think you misunderstand us." Will prayed for the words. "We know that all who put their faith and trust in Christ are in Heaven with Him. Many who died while their loved ones were harmed are in Heaven with them. We not only have this life, but a glorious future with the Creator God. No, this is a wall of remembrance of their willing sacrifice and of the Lord's gracious love and mercy."

Daryl lifted his hand to his face, trying to hide his impulse to laugh. He could hardly believe the nonsense of it all, but the man did come with a hefty check. "God's grace? With this result?" He shook his head.

"I used to think that way too. It took me a long time to see more clearly, but no matter what the world throws at us, God always wins. And if we have Him with us, nothing can ultimately touch us. To die physically is to be instantly in Heaven. No, true destruction is the future of all who die in their sins without Jesus to save them. Perhaps I shouldn't take any more of your time." Tempted to retrieve the check, he recalled Charles' insistence that they employ contractors for their skills, if the task was not tied to faith. *But can this man create the spirit of the wall?*

"No," Daryl reached for the check. "This should cover it. Upload your images and files to this dropbox." He slid a card over. "Send an email with the request, and I'll have my admin send the design application. Be as thorough as possible. Timeline?"

"Three months."

"Just for this wall? I think it can be done. Tell me more about the building and the balcony."

Will answered his questions as best he could, wishing Jeremiah was there. "So, can you send an initial concept to see if we're heading in the right direction?"

"Of course, the final billing will reflect the stages completed. Also, can you send links of your NFP? Faith Hall…to what does that refer?"

"Hebrews 12:1-2. *'Therefore, since we are surrounded by so great a cloud of witnesses, let us also lay aside every weight, and sin which clings so closely, and let us run with endurance the race that is set before us, looking to Jesus, the founder and perfector of our faith, who for the joy that was set before him endured the cross, despising the shame, and is seated at the right hand of the throne of God.'"* Will looked into his face, realizing to Sanford, the words were simply sound in air.

He considered trying to explain the gospel again, but Daryl asked, "And where will that be? That saying from the Bible?"

Will searched his photos for the view. "Inscribed on a large plaque to be mounted directly underneath the balcony." He found the image, showing the partially completed wall covering the second floor with the polished nickel railing.

The man nodded. "I think that will work. Has it been cut?"

"Not yet. That piece can be done later."

"You're not heading up this project?"

"Thankfully, no. I found an excellent manager who keeps tabs on all our contractors. Quite the job. I'm in charge of budgets, and we regularly review the work to make sure it's headed in the right direction."

"Good. I'll include a mock-up of this as well. A properly painted filigreed sign might be better than a bronze plaque. Not quite so heavy and easier to read in various kinds of lighting."

"Can we make the letters glow in dimmer light?" Will shrugged his shoulder, "Just a thought. I came to you because I believe you have the vision to create something that will rise above what we are able to produce with our current contractor."

"That would be the truth. Anything else?"

"No."

"Well, then, I think I have enough to get started."

Will closed his files and shut down his computer. He stood but didn't extend his hand. "I'm sorry they voided the contract. I had no idea they had broken it. They transferred me to another position, assuring me everything was on schedule when I asked. I didn't know they had a totally different agenda."

"So, why did they even sign with the firm?"

"To have a model that would help them win approval to run their own prisons. Once they had it, they violated every oath and murdered hundreds."

"Now I see. You are a Christian now."

"I am. Any more questions, Mr. Sanford?"

"No."

Will stepped forward and offered his hand.

"Send the email. Upload the documents. Return a signed contract. The sooner I receive it, the sooner I can begin. The receptionist will print a receipt for the retainer."

A year later, setting a date for the commissioning of Faith Hall and the Wall of Witnesses in early October, Will reviewed the schedule of events. Thankfully, he had a more-than-able staff to arrange transportation for those arriving at an airport, housing for those requesting accommodations, the catering, and many other details.

Taking a break to enjoy what was left of a beautiful clear fall day, he strolled over to the building, named simply Faith Hall. He shook his head, remembering the day Charles stood up and told the board, "Faith Hall. And it can be whatever God wants it to be—a Bible school, a college, or a seminary—all or none or some. *Faith*, because we believe. *Hall*, referring to the assembly of the called-out ones."

All voiced their agreement, and nothing more was said about the name.

After his meeting with Sanford, Will's idea had been to change the name of the wall to Wall of Witnesses to go along with the verses inscribed on the balcony. At the last minute, he added Sanford's name to the guest list for the commissioning ceremony. He doubted the man would come.

The day dawned, and he put on his suit that he had worn to his first board meeting. Today he knew that he had found his place and his calling. So many who came were friends, and he wished they lived closer, but they were one in the Spirit.

It was his to lead the commissioning, others would sing, Rick would deliver the final prayer, but his message would set the tone. He had prayed and written, struggling with what to say and how to convey the essence of Faith Hall until he stopped and prayed for days.

In the night, he heard the words of Hebrews 12:1-2 spoken with a firm heavenly voice and he saw, without seeing, heard without hearing the vision of an organization that discipled the body of Christ to share the depths of God's faithfulness, truth and love. Christ drew from the Scriptures on the Emmaus road the story of the greatest rescue of all times—that God saves His people—the young and old. Faith Hall would be for new believers or those with many years in the faith, for those seeking to understand the Word so they can live it, as well as for those called to search the Scriptures for buried treasure.

And that was it. Nothing further. Talking with Rick, he perceived the man would speak of the Wall of Witnesses, looking not to the sorrows, but to their overcoming faith and eternity.

Will practiced his message until he no longer had to look at his notes. He created a brief outline should his mind stumble. Relying on God's Holy Spirit to well up within him the words, whether the ones planned or others he had not been shown.

They came, they assembled. Will greeted Todd and Bruce, Larry and Merle. He looked over, watching Catherine, glowing in her maternity clothes, almost five months along, standing next to Dan. Carlos was nearby with his family. Will walked over to Jeremiah. "Your family's coming?"

He smiled. "Little ones are wiggly. We like to bring them close to the beginning. Virginia will be along soon."

Will nodded, looking at the verses scripted in gold. The podium was set, many chairs filled the open lower area that served as the foyer and main hall between expandable rooms and the left side with kitchen, dining and bathrooms.

The singers assembled. The musicians tuned their instruments. Will headed to the podium right in front of the wall. Jeremiah dimmed the lights and turned on the wall lighting. While dim with daylight, it still had an effect—as if shimmering stars and galaxies looked down on them. The soft pastels of the Savior's arms welcoming the believers seemed to glow.

Will nodded at the small orchestra, and they ran through two hymns. Will and Charles walked to the podium and welcomed the assembly. The man had resisted any accolades, but Will insisted many would want to see him. Stella sat tall and serene in the front row. Spontaneous clapping began. Charles bowed graciously, waved, and departed, hating the limelight.

The choir sang. A soloist lifted her voice with a praise song. And then it was his turn. "Today, we commission Faith Hall to the work of the Lord." Will paused. *What are we thinking? How great God is and how small are we?* "To think God would ask us to take part in His work. It's humbling. Serving Him is a gift that we do together." He looked about. *Why did it not occur to me to bring a Bible?* Noticing one in Rick's lap, he walked over to borrow it.

He held the large black book—a real Bible, complete, with no passages excised. Without opening it, he quoted from memory: "*Long ago, at many times and in many ways, God spoke to our fathers by the prophets, but in these last days he has spoken to us by his Son.*[12] These are the opening verses of the book of Hebrews. This book contains God's Word to us. It is the story of Jesus Christ, the Son of God, our creation, our fall, and how He saved us, delivered us, redeemed us from the bondage of sin. And in this Book is the truth—God's eternal truth. Truths to live by, truths we can trust and place our faith in.

"After the years where parts of this Book and what it says had been declared illegal, a group of men were led by God to raise up an institution to teach the truths found in this Book to the best of our ability. The name, Faith Hall, was selected to reflect the living faith, as portrayed in this Book. *Hall* refers to the called-out assembly of the believers who live by this book.

"Not faith in anything, or mere belief, because the veracity, power and truth of what we believe matters. We have a living God who loves us. We have a God who saved us—and this cost Jesus His life. He gave His all that we might have new life in Christ. We have a God who does not abandon us. His Holy Spirit resides in each one who has taken Christ as Savior.

"We need not be afraid. We need not pull back. We can look forward because *'neither death nor life, nor angels nor rulers, nor things present nor things to come, nor powers, nor height nor depth, nor anything else in all creation, will be able to separate us from the love of God in Christ Jesus our Lord.'*[13] Christ will build His church and the gates of hell cannot win.

"And to that end we dedicate this building and this institution to the pursuit of faithfully teaching God's truth to those in fellowships and in homes, to those seeking to teach others, whether they call themselves pastors, or by another name, and to those who wish to plumb the depths in search of buried treasure. For when God reaches down to tell us about Himself, we will find truth beyond our understanding, but His Spirit will lead us.

"These walls and halls will not contain merely academic instruction, even though that is a part of it, but practical training so we can live it for our families, our communities and those who have not yet found Christ. Truth with love. For without love we are nothing. God is love, and when we are in God, we must strive to live this love to others.

"I want to add that the love of believers drew me to God. His love, through them to me, proved beyond a shadow of a doubt that God is real. Not only that He is real, but that He is active. Some who committed acts of cruelty experienced forgiveness from those they hurt. Truly no gates, no bars, no prisons, no laws of men can hold back the work of God!

"Courage to hold true to God's Word even when the laws of man violate God's laws. Only light can chase away the darkness; only love can stop evil in its tracks; and by truth we can stand against lies. So, we commission Faith Hall to teach God's Word."

Will moved into his closing remarks before introducing the next section. The professors would briefly describe the college and seminary programs. Catherine would introduce the Bible school program.

He sat near Chris and slid his hand into hers. Rick would give the final benediction for the ceremony. Break-out sessions had been set up for those interested in learning more about the various programs. After supper, Dr. Larkin would speak on the Word of God. Other activities were planned for the next day until noon.

Too soon, Rick rose and stepped to the podium. He tried not to blush when clapping erupted. He began in his even, steady voice to describe the walk of faith he had witnessed in Rosemont. He turned toward the wall behind him. "But we do not want to look back, but to look forward. For those who have gone ahead are not lost, but have gone before. In light of eternity, the time of parting is brief. So, this wall is a reminder that we can draw courage from their example and witness. Hebrews tells us we are surrounded by a cloud of witnesses, meaning multitudes upon multitudes. Some we know, but there are others we will meet someday. And when we remember this, let us take courage and stand, doubting not. For we seek a heavenly city, and we see a Savior who will never leave us nor forsake us."

He bowed his head. "Let us pray." His prayer for wisdom, truth, light and grace reached to Heaven and back to earth. He prayed for eyes to see and ears to hear and the strength to walk in fellowship with God and the brethren. That Faith Hall would stay true to the Word of life.

Four others who had been in Rosemont joined Rick. Holding hands, they began to sing without instrument and gestured for everyone to sing with them. The voices filled the building and lifted to the heavens.

Acknowledgments

ALL PRAISE AND thanks to God the Father, the Lord Jesus Christ and His Holy Spirit who were with me every step of the way. Trials and difficulties throughout my life since I came to faith in Christ have demonstrated beyond a shadow of a doubt that God is loving, kind, gracious and merciful. As part of the body of Christ, I have been blessed, encouraged and corrected at times by other believers as we worship and serve God together. As much as the Word is central to my faith, the fellowship of believers in church is also a pillar of my faith.

The *Where the Wind Blows* series explores how we would respond if some aspects of our faith were declared illegal. Would we stand? Would we love each other and those set to stop us? Through this endeavor I am convinced God will be with us, and He will build His church. The reality of faith in Jesus Christ that exists in every nation is proof of this. Let us remember to uphold the persecuted of the world with our prayers and support.

Many, many thanks to my faithful husband who allowed the days spent writing to complete this series in the year of our Lord, 2020. Many thanks to my faithful editor who stayed the course. Many thanks to all those who prayed with me as I walked the paths of Tom, Catherine, Dan, Will, Christine, the Huttons, and the other characters.

My prayer to you is that you will seek Him, for He is near; walk with Him following the Holy Spirit; and that we will someday meet in that city on a hill.

He who testifies to these things says,
"Surely I am coming soon." Amen.
Come, Lord Jesus!

– Revelation 22:20

ENDNOTES

Unless otherwise indicated, the all Scripture quotations are taken from the Holy Bible, the English Standard Version®, copyright © 2001 by Crossway, a publishing ministry of Good News Publishers. Used by permission. All rights reserved.

[1] Psalm 19:1-2.
[2] John 7:38.
[3] Mark 13:11.
[4] 2 Peter 2:9.
[5] Psalm 91:1.
[6] John 8:31-32, 36.
[7] Philippians 3:8, 13-14.
[8] Jeremiah 29:5-7.
[9] Ephesians 5:20; Philippians 4:4, 6.
[10] Colossians 2:7; 1 Thessalonians 5:16-18.
[11] Isaiah 53:6; Romans 8:1-2 paraphrases.
[12] Hebrews 1:1-2.
[13] Romans 8:38-39.

Made in the USA
Middletown, DE
15 February 2022